The Novellas of Hortense Calisher

THE NOVELLAS OF HORTENSE CALISHER

THE MODERN LIBRARY
NEW YORK

1997 Modern Library Edition

 Published in the United States by Random House, Inc., New York, and simultaneously in Canada by Random House of Canada Limited, Toronto.

Most of the novellas in this work have been previously published: "Tale for the Mirror" was originally published in *Harper's Bazaar* in an abridged form and later appeared in *Tales for the Mirror: A Novella and Other Stories* (London: Secker & Warburg, 1963); "Extreme Magic" was originally published in *Extreme Magic: A Novella and Other Stories* (Boston: Little Brown & Company, 1964); "Saratoga, Hot" was originally published in *Saratoga, Hot* (New York: Doubleday, 1985); "The Railway Police" and "The Last Trolley Ride" were originally published in *The Railway Police and The Last Trolley Ride* (Boston: Little Brown & Company, 1966).
Grateful acknowledgment is made to *Confrontation* magazine for permission to reprint "The Man Who Spat Silver" by Hortense Calisher. Originally published in Occasional Book Series of *Confrontation* magazine, 41, Fall 1986/Winter 1987, Long Island University, Brookville, N.Y., 11548. Reprinted by permission.

LIBRARY OF CONGRESS CATALOGING-IN-PUBLICATION DATA
Calisher, Hortense.
[Novellas]
The novellas of Hortense Calisher.—Modern Library ed.
p. cm.
Contents: Tale for the mirror—Extreme magic—Saratoga, hot—
The man who spat silver—Women men don't talk about—The railway police—The last trolley ride.
ISBN 0-679-60249-6 (acid-free paper)
I. Title.
PS3553.A4A6 1997
813'.54—dc21 97-18519

Modern Library website address:
http://www.randomhouse.com/modernlibrary/

Printed in the United States of America on acid-free paper

2 4 6 8 9 7 5 3 1

Hortense Calisher

Hortense Calisher, the acclaimed short-story writer and novelist whose fiction has often been compared to the work of such masters as James and Proust, was born in New York City on December 20, 1911. Following graduation from Barnard College in 1932, she found employment as a social worker with the New York Department of Public Welfare. Afterward, she married and began raising two children before turning to writing. In addition, Calisher has taught at major universities throughout the United States and Europe. She is a past president of the American Academy and Institute of Arts and Letters and of the American P.E.N. Today she lives in Manhattan and in a farmhouse on the New York–Vermont border with her husband, the writer Curtis Harnack.

Calisher's writing career dates from 1948, when "A Box of Ginger" appeared in *The New Yorker.* Like many of her semiautobiographical Hester Elkin stories, it endures as a small gem of social history. The publication of *In the Absence of Angels* in 1951 earned Calisher instant acclamation. "With this unusually fine first book of short stories, Miss Calisher immediately takes her place among the best American short-story writers of our time," said the *Saturday Review.* "It is always gratifying to make the acquaintance of a writer of intelligence and feeling," concurred *The New York Times Book Review.* "It is these qualities which most clearly mark the work of Hortense Calisher."

Calisher spent seven years working on her first novel, *False Entry,* the chronicle of a man who gains access to people's lives by abusing information about their past. Published in 1961, the work was nominated for a National Book Award. "Calisher's telling is acidulous, incisive, intricate and fiendishly intelligent," observed *The Nation.* And *The New York Times Book Review* commented: "This brave and major book, with many of its scenes drawn to the measure of a masterpiece, fulfills and amplifies a prerogative of the novel: to throw new light on life, and provide a vicarious experience of human living, profound, enchanting and revelatory."

Thereafter Calisher alternated between novels and short stories. *Textures of Life* (1963), her second novel, tells of two New York City bohemians who discover that the very middle-class traditions they had once dismissed can sometimes enclose love. Calisher's next novel, *Journal From Ellipsia* (1965), proved a complete departure from her previous work. The book wittily incorporates elements of science fiction as it tells of an intergalactic rapprochement between a female anthropologist and an alien. *The New Yorkers* (1969), often read as a companion novel to *False Entry,* is a saga set in the city's upper and lower depths, of three households involved with a judge's twelve-year-old daughter who murders her mother on discovering her with a lover. Meanwhile Calisher turned out three volumes of short stories and novellas: *Tale for the Mirror* (1962), *Extreme Magic* (1964), and *The Railway Police and the Last Trolley Ride* (1966).

The 1970s were a rewarding and prolific period for Calisher. Two of her works were nominated for National Book Awards: *Herself* (1972), a densely layered memoir, and *The Collected Stories of Hortense Calisher* (1975). *The New York Times Book Review* considered *Herself* "primarily and at its best a long meditation on the art of writing fiction in America in the second half of the twentieth century." Calisher's collection of stories, many of which have been widely anthologized over the years, reinforced her reputation as a preeminent master of the short story. "[Her tales] are all a form of amber, sealing unforgettable moments in time," noted Anne Tyler. "And Hortense Calisher is better at this sort of sealing than any other writer I know of." The *Saturday Review* agreed: "Miss Calisher is . . . among the most literate practitioners of modern American fiction, a stylist wholly committed to the exploitation of language."

During this decade Calisher also published four more novels: *Queenie* (1971), a sparkling sexual fable; *Standard Dreaming* (1972), a powerful exploration of generational and cultural discords; *Eagle Eye* (1973), a compelling portrait of a family whose relentless upward mobility breeds only emptiness and discontinuity; and *On Keeping Women* (1977), a marvelous miscellany of all the impulses, ideas, and reflections about love and marriage that might conceivably occur to a modern woman.

In *Mysteries of Motion* (1983), Calisher's next novel, she once more departed from her characteristic contemporary urban settings to examine a diverse group of people selected to inhabit a space colony in a futuristic society. Joyce Carol Oates praised the fantasy as being "Calisher's most unexpected work of fiction . . . at once a defiantly risky species of science fiction and a thoroughly realistic psychological novel." The *Los Angeles Times Book Review* called it "a rare effort to take the human and metaphysical temperature of the day's headlines . . . a novel of ideas and prophecy."

During the 1980s Calisher also wrote *Saratoga, Hot* (1985), a book of "little novels"; *The Bobby-Soxer* (1986), a subtle and original treatment of the quintessential theme of growing up in a small town; and *Age* (1987), a love story about an elderly couple facing the last chapter of their lives together. *Kissing Cousins,* a second volume of autobiography that conjures up the rich and varied textures of her childhood and of her Southern Jewish family, came out in 1988. "In this slender yet eloquent book, Hortense Calisher plays out an extended recollection and, stepping back from her story, reflects on the nature of memory itself," wrote *The New York Times Book Review.*

Calisher's output has continued unabated throughout the 1990s. Writing as "Jack Fenno," she issued the pseudonymous scientific and metaphysical thriller *The Small Bang* (1992). In her next novel, *In the Palace of the Movie King* (1993), she recorded the adventures of an Albanian filmmaker who speaks Japanese and becomes a hero in America. *"In the Palace of the Movie King* is a kind of love song to an ever-changing America," said *The New York Times Book Review.* "It is Miss Calisher's ambitious attempt . . . to capture the mood of this last decade of the twentieth century, its glorious post-modern Babel, its wealth of new immigrants." Her most recent novel, *In the Slammer with Carol Smith,* was published in 1997. In a review, *Publishers Weekly* commented "Calisher continues to surprise with the breadth of her knowledge of how we love now and with her supple, ever-fresh writing. . . . This is a small, subtle and intensely appealing book by a writer who has been steadily productive for most of our lives."

"Hortense Calisher has never been a writer who masked her thinking self or disappeared into her subject," said *The New York Times Book Review.* "She belongs to a different tradition descending from Henry James, in which the writer's own complex intelligence—his humming eloquence, his subtle knowingness—becomes essential to his equipment as a storyteller. Far from holding the mirror up to life, this kind of writer diffracts it through the prism of his sensibility, as if to show how many-faceted it is, how much he himself has made it up."

Contents

Introduction

The novel can be anything its founder can make it be; that is its pride. It has ransacked history, elegized the future—and is always subverting the present. As soon as human beings live through a period they want to assess it, in the belief that they too have every possibility.

Novels are the counterpart of this ambition. Nations rise and fall in them, races and religions also; any human change spurs them on. A long novel can ramble the world's scenery, seductive with digression, commanding a cast of old stagers to hopscotch once again. Or in monologue, spin out a soul until it becomes a city. Certain high-colored or quiet ones immure you in a wilderness, proofing you against your own. Or so de-civilize the gracious neighborhoods you're used to that you may never again be too polite. Or realm you for hours, in a society you never want to leave. And some suffer from ideas made to walk like people. If not too fogbound, these wind-tunnels can enthral.

Every novel is a period piece. Yet in some degree has its eye on the present. Even the costume novel, trading on cardinals and kings, second-hand wit, ancient secrets and wrinkled beds, still strives to be modern by analogy. As do those pseudo-classics which have us temporarily in togas. While the war novel—which is always a glory novel no matter what peace it champions, does best when the blood-smell is freshest, as it was to Tolstoy by heritage, by army service to Stendhal. Time stops, in an eternity where only the calibre of the bullet changes, and the politics. The madness at our elbow is always the same. In the great domestic novels, or even in that modest legion of those which are not Dickens, not Tanizaki, not Turgenev, the frock coat can suddenly turn inside out, to show the frayed underclass stuff that lines it, the silly ace of romance up its sleeve.

Against these statuesque presences which in their turn become the past, the contemporary novel may bite down to the quick, but is raw with doubts. It must exist under the trembling compass-point of the now. Its strength comes from striving to see what whelms us, from hearing the near music. Perhaps it knows most intimately how all novels are skewed toward that lovely risk which makes life worth living, which even the humblest author can share. They are not just a syllabus of the facts.

The word "novel" suggests that we write in and of our own time. To me, nothing is more exciting than to try. One feels the swirl of the age, standing in its cloud.

—

The novella can take on any of the novel's roles. It has but one departure—one that can make it unique. It is not merely a shorter novel, of less wordage than commonly. It is a small one, tenaciously complete.

Embarking on one of these, the sense of enclosure at once shawls me. I see the smaller, more focused stage, the shadowy sinews of tensions to come. The sentences fly to meet one another, in a time frame that is seamless. Complexity rims the edges, but is there to be fended off. Limits are visible, maneuvers clear. I have a powerful sense that the reader is sharing this with me. As in those cat's cradles made of string, by two pairs of hands.

Tale for the Mirror and *Extreme Magic* belong to the Hudson, on whose meandering shoreline, in one place or another, I have lived. A great river educates. City and village merge; past and present converge. Voices carry, stay in the mind. The people, playing their parts almost in cameo, linger on the brink of folklore.

Saratoga, Hot celebrates luck. Spotting a world entirely foreign, yet right under the feet, its coarse magic a blindfold, through which one peeks. "In the enclosure" is an actual racing term, of a world mired in amber, manure and endless fun, exactly as Nola paints it: the people running down the fairway, the horses in the stands. Place your bets.

The Railway Police and *The Last Trolley Ride,* published together, were juxtaposed by accident. It is true that transportation enlivens. And we are a nation of vehicles. One later day a rocket ship will push my writing-machine to strike out for that absolute space in whose vacuum one might weigh what we find when in motion, against what we prize when standing still. But neither of these stories so occurred, except perhaps at the edges. *The Railway Police,* once read aloud in entirety at a university session, was taken up as woman's cry. That hadn't occurred to me either. Anybody can wear a wig. I thought it was about lying, pretense, versus coming out as you are. And about a theme that would tocsin again and again in the years to come: the yearning for vagabondage in the hearts of those who are safe.

I remember trolleys. Outmoded almost from the start, they harbor memory even as you hear the *clang.* They are pure ride, in company. *The Last Trolley Ride* is locality, at full ripeness of season, among a landlocked people, whose dramas begged for attention only long after I had left them.

There are love stories here, that end happily. In *The Man Who Spat Silver,* a person reports on the self, in both the first-person-singular and the third—sometimes switching gender as well. People do that. Here pushed to the extreme, with good reason—and why not, in a story that's a tribute to words?

In *Women Men Don't Talk About* the women talk all the time. But only to each other. Though the men are there. The lilt comes from those Irish friends who have teased me through life. Though of course not all women who live behind the important conversation are Irish. Nor confined to needle and thread.

This one could have gone on longer. So could they all. Something in a novella—a shiver of warning—says Stop. Leaving the people in camera in the double sense of that phrase: in hiding, but On View.

TALE FOR THE MIRROR

When Dr. Bhatta, the Hindu "neurologist," acquired the old Kuypers estate, which no one else would buy, and installed there his entourage of two faded, Western lady secretaries, a number of indeterminately transient guests, and a faintly rotten, saffron breeze of curry, the neighbors in the other old houses strung along the river-bank absorbed his advent with little more than mild comment. The river road, though deceptively near the city, was part boundary line of a county that brushed shadowy patroon-descended towns to the north, still sheltered, in its gentle ranges toward the west, tribal remnants with tattered Indian red in their cheeks, and had weathered many eccentrics in its time. Something about the county's topography of rear-guard hills, pooled with legend and only circularly accessible, of enormous level-land sunsets brought up short by palisades that dropped the river road below into darkness at four, had long since made it a natural pocket for queer birds, birds of privacy. Many of these were still there, appearing at yearly tax meetings as vestigially alive as the copperheads that sometimes forked before the nurserymen's neat spades in the spring. It was a landscape from which individuality still rose like smoke, in signal columns blue and separate and clear.

More than one of the houses along the river road had had a special history, of the tarnished kind that often clings longer than honest coats of arms. Houses of wood, white, with endless verandas and gabled bedrooms framed in carpenter's lace, they had been built by the dubiously theatrical or sporting rich of seventy or eighty years ago, whose habit had been to leave their trotting races on the Harlem of an afternoon, and to come, with a change of carriage, up the river, there to pursue, in champagne and blood and scandal, their uncloseted amours. And the capricious summer places they had had the native workmen build for them, though sturdy of timber, still showed, even in a new age, the shaky regality of seasonal money. From turrets made without ingress, balconies soared and died away. Iron weathervanes swung unheeded over "widow's walks" on which no rightful widow had ever paced, and at the ends of the grounds there was often a tiny pavilion, lodged like an innocent white afterthought among the romantically unpruned trees.

It was such a house that Dr. Bhatta had bought, acquiring it with some sleight of hand whereby the accompanying gunpowder pops of bill-collectors from the other places where he had lived were delayed for several weeks. When these too came, the neighbors were not surprised. Houses like the Kuypers estate had been harmonious even in decline. Descended through relatives who had not been deeded the income to keep them up, they seemed destined to be lost again by owners whose need of grandeur exceeded their incomes, often by those who needed grandeur in order to acquire income. Fakirs, healers, dealers in correspondence course faith—the river road had seen them come and go—all of them sharers in the circuitous faith that if one lived in a castle one could more easily attract devotees from whom one might then borrow money to pay for the milk. Idly the road decided that Bhatta's title of "doctor" was more than probably self-assumed, but this did not really matter. Charlatans, if one made it quickly clear that one would lend neither money nor credulity, often made very tractable neighbors. They could not afford to be like old Mrs. Patton, who had half a million but never painted her house, and let her lawn grow as high as her hedge. They painted quickly, lavishly, at least in all the spots that showed, and kept their sites trim for trade.

Not much was seen of the doctor that winter. It was an open winter, a mild one, but the doctor's tall, corpulent form only showed itself occasionally, on the broad steps underneath his porte-cochere, calling to his dog, Lili, or shuffiing in his carpet slippers as far as the greened bronzed griffins that guarded the gate, where he always turned to look critically at the house, his long maroon overcoat flapping at his ankles, the sun running like brown butter on his dark jowls and on the bald pate with its muttonchop of black hair. Occasionally he was seen, still in the coat and slippers, in front of the chain-store in the village, waiting while his two ladies made their purchases inside. Of anyone else it might have been said that he looked, at times, disconsolately cold, but to John Garner, his immediate neighbor on the road, and to others who established a greeting basis with him, the doctor's comments on the world were always showily serene. Either he was a man of inner peace, or else his trade constrained him to appear so.

Whatever his trade was—and this had not been quite established, it was of too large a dignity to allow him to help "the ladies," as he always called them, load the car. These, Miss Leeby and Miss Daria, were both blond, both small, both of uncertain age, but life had faded them in different ways. Miss Leeby's hair and accent had a New England thinness and respectability, her pale eyes and stubby, broken-nailed hands the absent look of a worker uncomfortably away from her task. It was she who was seen from dawn to dusk on the grounds, grubbing and cutting, on the roof of the barn, hammering, and once, painting away on the cupola of the house itself. When encountered, she had the stifled voice, the ducking ways, of a tweeny. Conversely, if, as rumored, the ladies were not the doctor's secretaries but his consorts, then it was Miss Daria who gave herself the airs of the boss-wife. Her streaked hair fell to her shoulders in cinematic curls, her eyes were sunk in sockets blackened with experience, or kohl, or occasionally, as gossip had it, the doctor's fist. Under her haggard fur coat she wore blouses of no illusion, through which one saw the bright satin points of her brassieres. It was she who drove the car, since the doctor did not work with his hands, and managed the finances, since the doctor never handled money—some stores had already begun to complain that they had not yet handled any of his. But, as regarded the two women, he made no other distinction that anyone could see. When the dusty old car had been loaded, and sometimes pushed into starting, he detached himself from his stance against the wall, seated himself in the front seat between the two ladies, gave a portly nod, and was driven away.

But, with the earliest March thaw, activity burst its pod at the doctor's, in advance of any place else. Armies of crocuses snapped to attention on the vast lawn, burlap was unwrapped to display dozens of rosebushes that must have been planted the fall before and were already beginning to twine properly up the chipped columns of the veranda, and all over the grounds there were peeping green evidences that Miss Leeby had indeed grubbed well. A truck came and groaned up and down the horseshoe driveway all one afternoon, depositing a sparkling white carpet of crushed stone. After it came the two women, raking it smooth, bordering it with two lines of whitewashed rocks that they lugged from the barn. When the mailman's truck stopped at the gate, Miss Daria called to him, and with his dazed help a large, ugly cement urn was eased up the cellar stairs and dragged to the center of the lawn. When he left, with her nonchalant thanks, he looked angrily over his shoulder, and slammed hard the door of his truck, before he drove away. For, all that time, with eyes squinting happily in the tawny air, with powerful arms and chest revealed by the short sleeves and Byronic collar of his shirt, the doctor had been sitting on the stoop.

It was only during the next few days, however, that John Garner, his neighbor to the north, began to take any consistent notice of what was going on next door. Garner was no gossip; in the city during the business day he was conversely rather proud of the lazy, non-suburban tolerance of the road on which he lived, but a man who owns property, or nearly, has a natural vested interest in that of his neighbor. Ten years before, he and his wife Amelia had been "that nice young university couple" whom the cautious local bank had entrusted with a surprisingly large mortgage on the big old house next to the Kuyper place. Now they were "the Garners," with four children, two in school, and during all that time both the house and the mortgage had remained a little too big for them. Garner's father had been a trial lawyer who had enjoyed to the full the strutting side of the law; Garner had passed for the bar, married, and been in practice as a modestly salaried subordinate of a small firm for some years before he had finally admitted to himself that there was no side of the law that he would ever enjoy, and that he would never be anything more at it than a respectable drone.

Each work day, carrying the briefcase that had been given him when he passed the bar, he took the seven-thirty bus to the city, a tall man with thinning sandy hair, with cheeks whose tired creases quirked pleasantly when he smiled, and each evening, at half past six, he returned, a little thinner on top, a little more creased than he had seemed the day before. His father's father had been a farmer in the magnificently tilled lands above the Finger Lakes, and when Garner, in his private shufflings of the past, thought of what might have been, he always returned to the same boyhood image of himself and the old man, his palm in the old man's fist, and the two of them standing to watch whatever might be going on at the moment on the farm. In the evenings, the old man would sit at his roll-top desk in his catalogue-lined study, poring over his accounts, and it was the image of this too that Garner had retained, even more than the memory of the plump barns, and the tractor grooving the hills. It was a feeling of not "going to work," as his father had done, but of working where you lived, where you stood, and of standing on the land. But his father had made the break to the city all too well; the son, gentled to pavements and collars, listening to the valedictorian tell him that he was standing "on the threshold of choice," would have been as incredulous as the father at the idea that the grandfather's life might have been one such choice. Only, some five years later, during that same year when he had come to terms with his private assessment of himself, he had bought the property adjoining the Kuypers estate.

Both properties fronted on the river (although the Kuypers place had a seven hundred footage to his two), and the acreages of both places ran back in a straight line up and over the hill that rose sharply behind, and were lost in the woodland at the crest. Amelia, his wife, always assumed that they had made the move for the children's sake, and because here, just barely within commuting distance of the city, their bit of money had stretched to so much more than it could have done in a newer, neater suburb. Over the years, Garner had come to believe this himself. But certain references in the deed, surveyor's jargon that granted him a portion of ground under his feet, phrases like "riparian rights," that ceded him certain calculable powers over the river, also gave him an immeasurable delight. It was, obscurely, because of this that, although he left all other civic duties to Amelia, he had allowed himself to be voted in as a member of the road's zoning board, which met three times a year to ratify building permits, to consider and defer the problem of repaving the road, and to reaffirm its one holy gesture against the cellularly creeping city to the south—that no commerce, no multiple dwelling of any kind was ever to be allowed. He had long since forgotten that his own house, stolid relic of a history too colorless to survive, had once reminded him of his grandfather's place, and that when, on fine Sundays, he walked up the back acre to his part of the hilltop and looked down over the cascaded tips of the pines that still grew here, the great blue stare of the river, deceptively motionless and foreshortened by other hills, had a look of Lake Seneca. He was an indifferent gardener; he had never learned to pull salvation, like a turnip, from the soil. But each evening, when he crawled back from the multiple of multiples, there was a moment when he rested the briefcase on the porch steps, and plowed the river with his eyes.

It was at such a moment, at dusk on a Friday evening, when, turning from the river to note that his lawn should receive its first mowing in the morning, he saw that, over at the doctor's, they had boarded up the little hexagonal summerhouse that perched halfway up the hill. The tiny peaked roof fitted like a dropped handkerchief over the columns that formed the sides; it had been a simple job to fit long wooden shutters, of which most of the houses along the road had an abandoned stock in the cellar, in the airy spaces beneath. Between two trees, in a small clearing hacked out for it, above the ground-honeysuckle that matted the entire hill, it glimmered now like a wintering carousel.

Strange, he thought, for what purpose would they have done this now, in the spring, and as he did so, a figure came from behind the pavilion and started slowly along the skinny footpath that zigzagged down the hill. It was a woman, carrying honeysuckle cuttings, two big sheaves of them that lifted her arms at right angles and trailed behind her, dragging the ground like a train. She passed him, quite close on the other side of the hedge, coarsely cut gray hair, emaciated eyes in a face he had never seen before, and trailed on through the opening in the hedge, down to the riverbank, where she let the cuttings fall into the river, and stood while they were borne away. She wheeled, and came back up the path. Even as he nodded, tentatively, into the uninflected face, he saw, with an inner, breaking "Ah!" of pity, that she must be mad. The eyes told him first—set motionless, aghast, as in those drawings where the doubled face was wrenched apart, the full eye set staring in the profiled nose. But it was the arms that told him for certain, arms still extended, cross-like, above the empty shape of the honeysuckle, as she marched back up the hill. She made three trips through the darkening air, each trip preceded by the sound of her scythe up above. When Garner finally entered his house, she had stopped coming, but he could still hear the slashing of the scythe among the vines.

He said nothing to Amelia, eating in the kitchen with her and the four chattering children, grateful for the familiar, perky pottery dishes, for the room's bright chromium sanity. But that night, as they were undressing for bed, in their room that faced the hill, he told her, and they discussed it in low, troubled voices. "It's about the *children* that I'm . . ." said Amelia. She turned out the light, as she always did before she put on her nightgown, although there was no one up the hill to see. "Look!" she said, leaning on the window sill. The shutters that had been used to board up the summerhouse, Garner remembered, had been of the kind with a small half-moon cut out of the wood, and now, in each of them that made up the blank façade, there was a weak spot of light.

The next morning, he was leaning on his new power mower (almost paid for now), and looking at his shaved lawn with a warm sense of satisfaction, when the doctor emerged for his morning tour. To date, his and Garner's over-the-hedge interchanges had consisted mostly of Garner's murmured assents to the doctor's pronunciamentos on the beauties of what lay before them—Bhatta had a way of conversationally appropriating the glories of the universe, and pointing them out to his listener (as if the latter might not have noticed them without his help) that reminded Garner of some ministers he had known. Sometimes, at his approach, Garner, out of a shyness he would have phrased as not wanting to "get too thick" with neighbors, waved and moved on to a distant task, but today he stayed where he was.

"Good morning, Misser Garner." Bhatta advanced majestically. "I see you have been up early, and worked well." He waved an expansive hand. "Now comes the beautiful time, har? No fuel bills!"

Garner nodded, paying a moment's silent tribute to the landscape, in accordance with the doctor's gesture. "See you put in a fine lot of roses there."

"Yars. In my country, the cultivation is very simple. Plenty of manure, plenty of roses. But here there is only *chicken* manure—and very expensive. A commentary, har?" Bhatta smiled broadly.

Garner smiled also—an overcompensating smile of the kind one used with people who spoke a foreign language. He could never get over a feeling, of the worst provinciality, he knew, that Bhatta was not speaking English, even at the very moment he so excellently was. "See you closed up the summerhouse."

"Yars." The doctor took another turn at the landscape.

"You, um . . . you moving your practice up here?"

"I do not have what you would call a pract-ice, Misser Garner."

"Oh . . . I see."

"Um." The doctor smiled again. "When I come to America to study medicine, I am very young, very enthusiastic. But when I finish, I find after all that I am not sufficiently—assimilated. For me, neurology is only part of a philosophy. I find I cannot sit in an office and take mo-ney for making cures. A little surgical, a little phar-maceutical housework—bang bang, one hundred dollars." He shook his head. "Unfortunately, I am not happy doing housework, Misser Garner."

"But you do take some patients?"

"For a while I do many things. I give lectures, I write books, one time I even have a restaurant. But everywhere people say, 'Bhatta, you have the secret of living, what is it?' I tell them that it is only because in India, where life is hard, we have to learn early the connection between work and love. I tell them that it is only here, where mo-ney churns butter, that people have time to suffer, because they do not have this connection. But they do not believe me. So I let them come up here and learn." He turned to look at Miss Leeby, who was standing on a ladder some yards away, clipping a hedge. "When they are grateful, they give gifts. For them it is therapy to give, and therefore it is possible for me to receive." He turned back to Garner. "You understand how this is, Misser Garner?"

Garner had no immediate answer, but he saw, from the doctor's expression, that a prompt one would have been a disappointment.

"Ah, you think it devious, perhaps," the doctor said quickly. He turned away from Garner again, looking downriver with a benignant smile. "The air is so clear in America," he said softly. "So very, very *clear*." He beckoned suddenly toward Miss Leeby, who started obediently down her ladder. "Come and see Misser Garner's beautiful new lawnmower," he called. "How that woman works!" he said, sotto voce. "How she loves flowers!"

Miss Leeby came and squatted down over the lawnmower, her work-split nails moving expertly over it, her bun and prim, altar-guild face odd over her man's shirt, dungarees, and dirty saddle-shoes.

"Is this not a beautiful machine, Leeby?" said the doctor.

"We ought to have one like it." She looked up at him devoutly. "It would give me so much more time for the roses."

"Well, perhaps Misser Garner will show you how to run it, one day."

Garner nodded, half wondering whether the doctor would not suggest the wise therapy of his giving them the mower. Meanwhile, Miss Leeby had wandered over to Garner's peony bed, and was kneeling there. "Why, you're letting these choke!" she said, horror sharpening her high voice. "If you don't thin them, the ants will be all over the buds!" She stretched a compassionate hand toward them, she had already taken a trowel out of a pocket, she was already beginning on them.

"Now Leeby," said the doctor, shaking his head indulgently. "Cultivate our own garden, please." He watched her move back to her ladder, chuckles shaking his shoulders, his considerable belly. "A happy woman, Misser Garner. When she first came to me, she was stone-deaf. Only a case of psychological deafness, as her hundred-dollar man took care to tell me."

Over on the doctor's driveway, Miss Daria had backed out the old car, and leaving the motor running sluggishly, was stuffing a battered peach basket into the luggage compartment. In the bright morning air, with her black net stockings and very short skirt, with her long curls bobbing above the withered *femme fatale* make-up and the embarrassingly evident underwear, she looked like a grotesquely debased little girl, but she moved with stolid competence. The doctor squinted at her appreciatively, but made no revelations as to the history of her cure. "Ah, they need me for the shopping," he said. He waved. "They keep me stepping, those ladies. This morning, a lobster, no less, for the curry." He caressed his belt buckle. "How they love to spend mo-ney, those silly girls!" With a salute to Garner, he started off, then paused. "You are a lawyer, eh, Misser Garner?"

Garner nodded. By a fraction, he felt, he had prevented himself from adding "Yars."

"Ah, you must take curry with us some evening. I myself have a good many legal problems from time to time."

Garner roused himself from the rhythmic sloth into which the doctor's style of address had cast him. "Guess I'm like you, Doctor," he said, with a grin. " 'Fraid I don't have my own practice either."

But it was the doctor who had the last word. "Ah, how lucky!" he said. "How wise! You too have learned, then, how destroying it is to admit the connection between mo-ney and the work one loves!"

Garner watched him cross his lawn and enter the car. The car moved stertorously down the driveway and slowly past Garner. Bland between his two ladies, the doctor saluted once more. Garner leaned on his mower for a minute, then started rolling it toward his garage. It was not until he had emerged, empty-handed, looking absently about him for the next Saturday task, that he realized that he had not learned anything more about the woman on the hill.

That afternoon he went to the village to do the weekly shopping he and Amelia usually did together, leaving her immersed in preparations for the birthday party to be held for Sukey, their oldest, the next day. Ever since they had lived up here, a treasure hunt had been a traditional part of the children's fetes; in the dime store he gathered together a collection of prizes of that familiarity imposed by the ten-cent limit—crayons, bubble pipes, harmonicas, string bags of marbles and jacks, packets of green paper play-money with which the children could play store in Sukey's new cardboard grocery, some jointed plaster snakes, some rubber balls. At the last minute, groaning with lack of inspiration, he raised the limit to a quarter, and added some water pistols, and some pink plastic babies for the smaller girls. Then to the butcher's, for the order Amelia had phoned in, and at last to the supermarket, where he scarcely needed Amelia's list. The order was always roughly the same, it seemed to him—enormous renewals on the breakfast foods, the bread and the canned tomatoes (Grade C, the canny list reminded him), boxes and boxes of frozen vegetables (these were no longer an economy except of time, Amelia had worriedly said last Saturday—now that they needed two of a kind for enough servings at a meal), the same list of staples, the two dozen eggs. Not pullets, he remembered, although this was not down on the list, for he had been a good pupil, and he knew now, among other bits of lore, that the cheaper pullets worked out to no eventual good, because of their size. Poor Amelia, he thought, it was not her fault if her prideful instructions on the arts of domestic evasion had become repetitive—it was not her fault if the evasions had always to be the same. "Butter—or oleo," the list said, leaving it up to him. Yes, perhaps it had better be an oleo week. He recalled the doctor's phrase about money churning butter. A little dig at America. Where the living is easy, he had in effect said, it was often hard on people. Garner chuckled. He was a sharp one, Dr. Bhatta, even if one could not quite tell whether his manner came from a lack of the language or a way with it. And a nervy one—to deliver that kind of sermon from a seat on the stoop.

Garner had finished his list, pushed his overflowing wire basket to the end of the long queue at the cashier's desk, and was idly betting with himself that his total would be somewhere between eighteen and nineteen dollars, when he saw, with a twinge, that he was directly behind Mr. and Mrs. Adrian Dee. The Dees were very thin, very old, and very poor—of a poverty that gentility held together like the black string tie that Mr. Dee wore to do his shopping, even in this weekend wilderness of sports shirts and dungarees. "Natives"—that is of the old Hudson Valley Dutch stock, as distinct from newcomers like Garner himself—they were, as cousins, both of a family that had given innumerable place-names to the county, but whose tenure had long since thinned with its blood. Mr. Dee had always worked hard in one of those clerkly jobs the exact nature of which no one ever remembered, other than that it had been in some outmoded business which had finally faded just as its outmoded employees needed it most. They lived now in the smallest house on the river road, a kind of baroque toolhouse, its tipsy turret supported by a wisteria vine thicker than either of the Dees, that was located on the edge of what probably had once been all Dee land. Cornered in this last briar patch of inheritance, Mr. Dee, county historian and fiercest member of the zoning board, upheld the conscience, ancient and present, of the road. For if he loved the town deeply, with the love that one gives only to the place that best knows who one is, he had an even more subterranean fright of the city, with whose approach his delicately guarded identity would no longer be known at all. And the town—and for this Garner too loved it—had been delicate with him indeed. It was aware that he had refused to register for Social Security, and no one had ever dared sound him on the subject of old age pensions. Quietly the town saw to it that he had a place on those important committees to which no suspicion of a fee could be attached; even more quietly it had made his name the sole contender for those still honorable civic duties for which he could be paid. He was a keeper of records, a taker of censuses, a watcher at polls. At one crisis in Mrs. Dee's health, the historical society had found itself in sudden need of a commissioned sesquicentennial report; at another, the library had found itself similarly helpless without a part-time custodial appointee. But still, altogether, the fees must be very small. Once before, Garner had found himself in the aisle of canned goods, behind the Dees, and had averted his eyes, his ears, from the two pairs of hands, pale as thorns, hovering past the salmon to the sardines, from the two hatted heads bent in secret consultation over the price on the bottom of a tin.

Now, above Garner's bulging basket and the Dees' sparsely tidy one, their glances met. "Mr. Garner sir, good morning!" Mr. Dee offered his handshake, ghostly version of one that must once have matched the office with the fumed oak, the black leather davenport, the wine-dark cigars. Behind him, Mrs. Dee, gloved hands clasped, nodded only; she belonged, by both personality and era, to those women who enhanced their husbands' dignity by echoing their actions but never equaling them.

"Well met, sir," said Mr. Dee. "On the part of the zoning committee, I was just about to get to you on the telephone."

Eighty, if he's a day, thought Garner. Not the man for the latter-day "Ring you," "Call you." Or, more probably, no phone of his own.

Mr. Dee leaned forward. "You know, perhaps, of your new neighbor's activities?" he whispered.

"Well . . . an unusual ménage, I gather."

"Oh, that!" Mr. Dee smiled primly, raising a milk-blue finger. "Not our concern, of course. We are not that kind of meddler here. But of late years—I have had to acquire the habit of reading the *Times'* real-estate section. Unfortunately, local transactions have grown beyond the local newspaper." He coughed, remembering gently that Garner, a former city man, must have had a history of just such a transaction, and fumbling in the watch-pocket of his vest, held out a clipping. Garner bent over it. Under the heading COUNTRY BOARD, he read: *Come to the house of the Pundit Bhatta. Great white house like castle. Crushed stone driveway. Roses everywhere you look. Build your own guest-house. Indian cookery and wisdom. Health through peaceable work. Contribution, $30 per week.*

"I thought you and I might talk to the gentleman, first," said Mr. Dee. "Explain to him that the tradition, in fact the law of the river road does not permit even two-family dwellings, much less any such communal development."

"From what I know of him, he'll do the talking," said Garner. He felt annoyed, suddenly and sharply, less by the threat to his own property—although the thought of other poor creatures like the woman in the summerhouse, all sweeping the hillside like the seven maids with seven mops, was an unnerving one—than by the humiliated feeling that in this morning's conversation with the doctor he had in some way been "sold," been "had." Some tricky sympathy in himself had responded to the kernel of what the man had said, had led him to conclude that if Bhatta sold nothing but confidence, he perhaps belonged, nevertheless, to that unique and complicated breed which believed in its own wares. He, Garner, had been "taken," like those who listened to the talented swindler purely out of admiration for the spiel but ended up with the mining shares after all.

"I doubt if we can force the boardinghouse issue, Mr. Dee," he said. "The road never has, you know. Because of the occasional hardship cases."

"But it's not that!" Mr. Dee pointed again to the ad, looking agitatedly around him, as if here, on this Rialto of screaming children, harried mothers, packhorse husbands, there were the very signs of the urban beast that waited, alert for the tip on a house that might be converted, a property that might be acquired as a wedge, a sudden amalgamation that might be made. "Build," he whispered. "You see what he says right here. *Build!*"

Back of Garner, the long line murmured, ahead of him the checker shrugged her impatience. "Oh I do beg all your pardons," said Mr. Dee. With a "No, allow me, dear," to his wife, who had once again moved a tentative glove, he emptied his basket on the counter. He took a five-dollar bill from his wallet, and paid. "Perhaps I could walk down to see you tomorrow, sir, after church?"

Garner nodded, busy emptying his own basket. Then, as the Dees filed out, he called after them. "Care to wait, I'll be glad to drop you and your things on the way."

"Oh, thank you," said Mr. Dee, "but Mrs. Borden has already been so kind." He raised his hat, including the checker in his nod, and went out, followed by a clerk carrying the small box of goods. Behind him, Mrs. Dee turned once, and smiled.

Mrs. Borden, Garner thought. That would be the old Mrs. Borden, whose vintage car and chauffeur were often to be seen parked only in front of those grocers who still sold over the counter. After he had lived in the county for a while, he had gradually become aware of some of the old, still traceable bloodlines, and although, in the course of things, he would never become acquainted with Mrs. Borden, or want to, there was somehow, because he did live here, a more than antiquarian or social interest in the knowledge that she had been a Van Schaick, that the Van Schaicks had held on to their land. No doubt she took care of the Dees quite regularly, in many little ways. For, below the stratum of couples like Amelia and himself, there was still discernible, in the bedrock of that very village which they would someday overwhelm, a faint vein of that other antique world of allegiance, still banding together against the irresistible now, still, in resentment or noblesse, taking care of its own.

That night, after the children were asleep, he and Amelia walked up the back hill, he swinging a lantern along the path, she carrying a basket of the toys for the treasure-hunt, which she had placed in the printed cotton bags they kept from year to year. Above them, the wood rose sharply, darkened even by day by an undergrowth of maple seedlings, dogwood, fern, by an ominous spreading of bush and brush whose names he did not even know. Thirty years ago, in the feudal time of gardeners and servants, the hillside had been worked and terraced, a carefully husbanded sampler of grape arbors and cold frames, of neatly curtailed dells. But now, in this suburban renaissance where people bought for the sake of the houses and the land was only extra and ignored, almost all the places along the road backed up against a dark encroachment like this one, where, here and there in the spring, an occasional old planting sparked with stunted fruit, or a sentinel iris pushed its spear through the honeysuckle, the sumac and the grass.

Just back of the house there was a large plateau where the garden officially ended, and it was here, in scuffed, already traditional places—in the hollow tree that held the swing, in the ledges behind the children's tent, in the dry channels of last year's squash vines, that he and Amelia cached the bags, not too well hidden, where the children might find them the next day. They looked lovely in the starlight, with their dim paisley scrolls and freckles—like the fey nesting of some wild and improbable bird. He swung the lantern in an arc above them—an efficient department store lantern, bought for those evening hours when he cadged a bit of time to chop wood, to fix the fan-belt on the pump. Silly or not, with its fake oil-lantern shape, it felt good to swing it in this ritual that their years here had already built for them, above these places which for the children were long since familiar and old.

Back at the kitchen door, Amelia stumbled in ahead of him, murmuring that the children had worn her to a frazzle, in and out of the house all day. He doused the lantern, and sat down on the porch steps, looking out at his acre, his back hill. At times it made him feel like an interloper, a defaulter. It came scratching at his door, not like the wilderness, but like a domestic animal, crying to be tended. This year he would have to burn back the brush, for sure.

Sometime before morning, he got up from bed to latch back a banging shutter. For a moment he thought he saw a figure move across the grass and merge behind the summerhouse. He waited, but saw nothing but the movement of the trees, stirring in the pre-dawn wind. He was about to go back to bed when he saw, down the long hall that led to the front windows, the first eastern flake of light. This was one of the privileges that went with living where he did, one dearly bought and seldom used, the privilege of watching the sun rise on the river from his own window, his own realm. He watched the yellow light shake itself into prisms on the leaves of his horse chestnut trees, waited until the red ball heaved itself out of the river at a spot where, if he remembered correctly, he had the right to seine shad. Then he went back to bed.

When Mr. Dee presented himself the next morning, Garner was alone, Amelia having gone to pick up Sukey at Sunday school, taking the others along for a ride. Neither Garner nor Amelia was a churchgoer, but Sukey's recent request to go had been acceded to at once, lest she be damaged in her natural craving "to belong." All the other city emigrés along the road were always making these little forays into the art of belonging—for this too was felt to be one of the privileges of living here. Watching as Mr. Dee picked his way toward him, carefully setting his freshly blacked shoes between the mud squelches that winter had raised on the poorly surfaced road, Garner wondered what it would feel like to be he, inhabitant of that lost steel-engraving world into which one had been born with all one's affiliations incised.

On the doctor's porch together, a few minutes later, they waited while the door chime sounded somewhere inside. It was an elaborate chime—a four- or five-tone affair.

"Dear me," said Mr. Dee, shaking his head. He stared up at the cathedral-like architraves of the front door. "My understanding is—someone *gave* him the place!" he whispered.

A second sound, of steady hammering, blended with the repeated peal of the chime. Mr. Dee blenched. He looked sideways at Garner's Sunday morning garb of T shirt, army surplus slacks, and sneakers, dropped his glance covertly to his own dark vest, carnelian seal. "I understand also, however," he whispered, "that his own credit is very infirm."

Miss Daria opened the door. Her gaze met Mr. Dee first, approximated him. "Good morning," she said, in a businesslike voice that went oddly with her waxed lashes, her dazzling blouse. "You've come to see about the rooms?"

"Indeed not!" said Mr. Dee, in a high voice. Garner, intervening, asked for the doctor.

"Come in," she said, unsmiling, and led the way like an usher, through a hallway formed by the first arc of a spiral staircase, into a vast double room, where, in a oasis of furniture set against portieres that divided the regulation sitting room and parlor of such houses, the doctor sat, drinking tea. He had, Garner thought, almost an air of being "discovered" drinking tea. Indeed there was an air of theatrical arrangement, a floridly seedy, "rented" flavor to the whole scene. Garner looked about him, reminded that Amelia would want to know. Kemtone paint, in a number of purposefully intense, but somehow failing colors—pink, orchid, acid green—had been applied to the imperially molded ceiling, the high, cracked walls, and had been wreathed, like tulle around the ravaged throatline of an old beauty, up the underpinning of the spiral stairs. On a hotel-Moorish table, set among several baronial but battered plush chairs, incense bloomed suddenly from a pot, as if it had just been set burning. There was a determined attempt at Oriental mystery, but except for two huge ivory-inlaid teakwood screens, it remained a fatally auction-room Oriental. It was, Garner decided, remembering Miss Daria's blouse, perhaps "the ladies' " idea of mystery.

"So, Misser Garner, you come to see me after all."

Garner introduced Mr. Dee, in the latter's capacity as board chairman.

"Ah, zoning," said the doctor. His nod was sage, managing to indicate that he drew upon a vast, physicianly stock of unsurprise. He shook Mr. Dee's hand, looked down at it searchingly for a moment, then gave it back to him. "Good arteries," he said. "You will probably live forever."

Mr. Dee, withdrawing slightly, bent down, not without a certain pride of spryness, to detach a bit of dried mud from his shoe.

"Very bad, yars, the road in front of my house," said Bhatta. "Perhaps now it is spring, the village plans to repair."

"On the contrary, sir." Mr. Dee straightened, squaring his frail shoulders. "Last thing we want here is the heavy, beer-truck kind of traffic. Let them go round by the state road."

"Ah?" said the doctor. "Of course, here in this house we do not smoke or drink. Alcoholism is a very character-istic symptom of Western neurosis. But I do not think it responds to superficial restraints." He moved a hand toward his cup. "Darjeeling. A very soothing type of addiction. You will join me?" He clapped his hands together, but the sound was barely audible above an increased din of hammering in the rear of the house. He looked sideways at Garner, veiling a brown gleam of amusement with one lowered eyelid. "T-t-t. Those busy ladies."

"You mistake me, sir," said Mr. Dee. "We guard only the community, nor its, er, personal habits. This is a unique preserve we have here. No coastal railway, one minor factory. On an international waterway, if you please, and *dangerously* near the city. One false step—why there are garden-apartment interests that watch us night and day. You have only to look at the other side of the river—"

Bhatta nodded, impressed not so much, Garner thought, by the phrase "the other side of the river," whose weight of local scorn he might not realize, as by Mr. Dee's competitive flow. He waved a slow hand toward the back of the house. "Well, as my unfortunate ears inform me, we are building our own Eden here. All night Miss Leeby insists on finishing the new bathroom, for the arrival of some guests. We have this evening a double celebration. First, the anniversary of Indian independence. Second, the arrival of my nephew from Allahabad, who comes to study medicine. I will get Miss Leeby to stop and bring tea."

"No, really we can't stay," said Garner. A fluttering endorsement of this came from Mr. Dee. "We came merely to—"

"To be delightful and neighborly, of course. So you must allow me. Meanwhile make yourselves at home—there is material here and there that may interest you." Bhatta motioned toward the piano, toward a pile of books in a corner, various framed papers on the walls. "Also, I must hear more of this zoning. Like this gentleman, I am also an enemy of progress." He chuckled, and rose slowly. The plush chair fell backward from him, its withered ruffle exposing its bowed legs, like the comedy sprawl of an old character actress. "Not with his admirable structure, however." He tapped the back of one of his hands sadly with two fingers of the other. "Adipose. Hypertensive. Probable final history—embolism," he said, smiling, and left the room, leaving the chair upended behind him.

Mr. Dee moved closer to Garner. "Slippery," he whispered. Chin sunk in his hard collar, he meditated, delving further, perhaps, into the penny-dreadfuls of his boyhood. The carnelian seal rotated slowly. His peaked face came up, triumphant. "Very slippery article. We'll get nowhere with him. An injunction, I fear. If we can only find out precisely what his activities are." He moved along one wall, examining. At an exclamation from him, Garner followed. He was reading a long card, in elaborate but somewhat amateurish print, held to the wall by passepartout. It was a restaurant menu. Under the title NEW INDIA RESTAURANT, a long list of curries followed, using a number of badly spaced different kinds of type. *Maharajah Curry (for two) $3.50* headed the array. Leaning closer, Garner deciphered an italicized notation to the right. *With Turban $5.00.* The list declined in rank, price, and size of print as one neared the bottom, where it rose again with a final entry added in typewritten capitals: *Mahatma Ghandi Curry—One Dollar.*

"Good God," said Mr. Dee. "Do you suppose he's running a restaurant?"

Garner, his mind full of turbans—would they be in the curry or on the customer?—was already standing in front of the next display. It was a very ordinarily framed diploma, granted in medicine to one Pandit Bhatta, from Iowa State University.

"Dear me," said Mr. Dee. He looked up at Garner, his wrinkles focusing shrewdly. "There is an Iowa State University?" On Garner's reassurance, his head sank. "Dear me."

Above an old upright piano there was a large poster drawing of a veiled woman in an attitude of prayer, seated on a pedestal formed by the block letters DESIRES. On the music rack below, a single sheet of manuscript music lay carefully open, its many migratory arpeggios blackening the page. Both poster and music were signed *Bhatta.*

They had reached the pile in the corner, fifty or more copies of the same book, a small volume, again by the Pandit, published by the Nirvana Press, with a flyleaf of other titles by the same author. Entitled *Rose Loves,* it seemed to be half poem, half paragraphs of meditation, apostrophes which had, here and there, an oddly medical turn of phrase. A description of the circulatory system swelled into diapason: *So the phagocytes swarm in my veins, stars eating stars; the ganglia make little rose-connections along the capillaries of the brain. I rise above. Swung by my dervish blood, I can return to the tree-towns of childhood, suspended above the city's begging bowls I swing like a monkey from tree to tree.*

A folded piece of paper dropped from between the leaves of the book. Garner picked it up, reinserted it, placed the book on the pile of others, and pretended to be studying the ivory inlay in the nearer of the screens, as the doctor entered, followed by the two women carrying the tea things, and a young man, who ran to pick up the fallen chair.

"Ah, Misser Garner, you admire the screens?"

"Yes, very beautiful work."

"Yars. Very valuable . . . Miss Daria here wants me to sell them. For three hundred dollars, although they are worth much more than that. Eh, extravagant miss?" Miss Daria, engaged with Miss Leeby in settling Dee and Garner in chairs and passing round the cups, kept her face bent, expressionless. The doctor shook his head at her, including his guests in his mirth. "Probably for . . . two hundred, she would sell them, that girl!"

It was remarkable how, even as the two women served out the tea, the doctor, with fluently hospitable gestures, maintained the impression that he himself dispensed it. He introduced the young man, his nephew, with a flourish that gave the effect of the latter's having been created on the spot for this purpose. The nephew, a slender brown young man in neat Western clothes, exhausted his cup in two rapid inhalations, and was quickly served again.

"He is very enthus-iastic," said the doctor, looking at him meditatively. "Very anxious to get on."

"Gate on," said the young man, nodding repeatedly, with the grinning intensity of the foreigner who wishes to make it known that he understands. He rolled his eyes in an exquisite spasm of comprehension. "Gate on!"

The doctor looked at Garner. Again his eyelid drooped. "It is a Presbyterian college—Allahabad."

Mr. Dee picked up his cup. "Indeed?" he said, with a vague, reflexive politeness perhaps engendered by the cup. "Mrs. Dee and I are of course communicants of the Dutch Reformed."

"Of course," said the doctor, with an equal flexion. At a signal of his hand, the two women departed, followed by the nephew. "Very interesting," said the doctor, turning back to Mr. Dee. His eyelid lifted suddenly. "Reformed—from what?"

Mr. Dee set down his cup, at which he had but sniffed. "It refers to the Dutch settlers, sir. This is an early settlement. Very early."

"Ah, ah," said Bhatta. "And I come to it so late."

Mr. Dee lifted his chin above his collar. Under his parochial gaze the doctor's little pleasantry vanished, incense into ozone. "You understand, therefore, the board's concern over your plans?"

"Plans?" The doctor's shoulders vibrated to his smile. "They sprout around me like roses—these plans. But I myself—"

From under Mr. Dee's carnelian seal, the newspaper clip was withdrawn, and laid on the Moorish table. "Yours, sir?" he said. He sat back. A thin pink elated his starved cheek. He coughed once, and then again, and the cough had a dry, preserved tang to it, an old flute long laid away in the musty confabulations of lost authority.

"T-t-t," said the doctor, studying the clipping. "Always in such a hurry, those terrible ladies." He chuckled. "A man's castle is not his house, har?" He leaned forward to place the paper back on Mr. Dee's side of the table, studying him. "You would like yourself to build a guest-house here, Misser Dee?"

"Garner—" said Mr. Dee. It was a measure of his feelings that he did not append "Mr.," and of his arteries perhaps, that they held.

"Dr. Bhatta—" said Garner. "Perhaps you're not yet . . . aware of the road's laws on this." He hesitated, then, squirming like a boy under the tutorial glare of Mr. Dee, he repeated them: no commercial enterprise, no subdivided renting, no double dwellings. "And no additions to existent buildings," he concluded. "Except of course for members of the same family. It's a—" He stopped. "Well—it's a hopeful attempt to keep things as they are."

"It is a real phil-osophy, this zoning," said Bhatta. "How lucky for me that Indian families are so large."

"Not large enough, sir, I think, to include all the readers of the *Times*," said Mr. Dee.

"What a peaceable world that would be," said the doctor. He sighed. "Then, perhaps the *Tribune*. But certainly, first the *Times*." He cast a sudden glance at Garner; it was the practiced side glance of the deadpan joker, that mere facial cracking by which he chooses to honor a chosen auditor. "But you need not worry, Misser Dee. Miss Leeby is very talented—you should see the new bathroom. But she is not yet capable of a gar-den apartment."

Mr. Dee stood up. He bowed, and his bow too had a stored flavor, like the cough. "As Mr. Garner would have to tell you legally, it's the principle of the thing."

"Prin-ciples," said the doctor. He studied his hands, as if he had a number of such concealed there. He sighed, looking up at Garner. "The distance from *a priori* to *a posteriori*, that is the history of the world, har, Misser Garner? That is what I keep telling the ladies. Love is infinite; therefore its services should be. Then they come running from the kitchen to tell me the curry is finite." He stood up, turning to Dee. "It is a Christian dilemma also. You have had experience of this, perhaps . . . in the Dutch Reform?"

"Do I understand sir . . . ?" Mr. Dee's voice dropped to the whisper reserved for indecency. "That you *charge* for meals at these celebrations?"

"No, no, Misser Dee. It is like the party some people ask us here at New Year's. The ladies to bring casseroles. The men to bring bottles. It is the same with us. Only without bottles." He paused. "Perhaps you will stay today. A special occasion. No casserole required." He too bowed, with a plastic gesture toward the rear of the house, and Garner became aware that the noise from that region had been replaced by a powerful, spice-scented breath of cookery.

Mr. Dee flushed, and moved stiffly toward the door. In the nacreous light from its one high pane, his nostrils quivered once, membrane-pink, and were pinched still. "I thank you, sir. But Mrs. Dee has something very specially prepared."

As the doctor opened the door for them, Garner spoke. "Matter of fact, Dr. Bhatta . . . my wife and I did want to ask you. It's, er . . . it's about the lady who seems to be living in the summerhouse. Because of the children, we were—naturally a bit concerned."

"Ah, Miss Prager. Yars." The air coming through the door was balmy, but the doctor's face seemed to Garner for a moment as it had seemed on their winter encounters in front of the stores—as if it denied any imputation that it could suffer cold. "Tell your wife there is no cause to be concerned," he said. "Miss Prager will not touch anybody." His voice lingered on the word "touch," and with this his glance returned to Garner, its customary air of inner amusement regained.

"Summerhouse!" Mr. Dee pecked past both men and angled his head outside the door. Turning from what he saw, he confronted Garner. His chin sank into his collar. "So you already knew, sir, that we had a case in point there!"

An elderly limousine rolled slowly up to the doctor's gate. It stopped, motor running. Its klaxon sounded once—not with the tut-tut of present-day horns, but with an "Ay—ooyah" Garner had not heard for years.

"Ah, how kind of them!" Mr. Dee waved a gay, an intimate acceptance toward the car. He nodded stiffly at the doctor. "If you don't mind, Garner, perhaps you'll walk me to the car?"

Going down the path, his military gait made it clear that it was not assistance he required. At the car, the chauffeur, stooping, held open the rear door. He and Mr. Dee seemed of an age.

Mr. Dee paused. "From the board's point of view, I find this unaccountable of you, Mr. Garner. Personally, I can see that man's engaged your sympathy." He put a hand on Garner's arm. "Let me give you a warning my father gave me: Beware of the man who won't admit he likes money—he'll end up with yours." He turned to get in the car, then paused again. "Darjeeling!" he whispered angrily. "If that was anything but plain pekoe, I should be very much surprised!"

Garner watched the car disappear up the road, half amused, half impatient over the way he had wasted the haven of his Sunday morning like a schoolboy dangling beneath the concerns of his elders. He had been interrupted in his soothing routine of those repetitive acts of repair for which his house, blessed incubus, had an endless appetite. Out of habit, he looked at the river, pouring along south as private and intent as the blue skeins one remembered to notice now and then in one's wrists. How far up it did one have to go, these days, before one came to the real places, short-summered and Appalachian-cool, where a broken window was vital to life, a lantern was a lantern, and the ground woke every morning to its own importance? Too far for him, staked to the city like a dog on a string. This was as far as he could go.

Turning, he faced the doctor, who had followed him down the steps.

"He has much mo-ney, this Misser Dee?"

"No. Actually . . . almost none. The car was a friend's."

"It is not his own property he defends then, this little dragon?"

"Well—no."

Bhatta burst into laughter. Silent chuckles shook his belly, tinted his jowl. "Excuse me, Misser Garner. Really I am laughing at myself—for not yet being assimilated." He mopped at his eyes with a large ocher silk handkerchief. "So—he is only a proxy dragon, har?" He swung around for his usual appraisal of his own house. His eyes flicked past the summerhouse, and he bent to probe a heavy finger into a rose. "Well . . . every man has to tell himself some little tale in the dark, har? So as not to really see himself in the mirror the next morning." The rose sprang back, released. "Even in this clear air. Even an early sett-ler."

Over at the far edge of his own property, Garner saw Amelia turning their car into their driveway. Children tumbled out of the car—his own, and several of the neighbors'—and ran into the house. He waved, but Amelia followed them in without seeing him. And perhaps because she had innocently not seen him malingering here, and because, although he rarely saw his children romantically, he had for a moment caught them aureoled against the silent witch-point of the summer-house, he spoke in sudden anger. "It's Miss Prager's story I'd like to have. And if you please—the facts. I'm not much for metaphor."

"Really?" The doctor squinted. "I would have said otherwise. But, as you say. Do not blame me if the facts are odd." He motioned to a bench, on which they seated themselves. Bhatta buttoned the top button of his shirt, shot a cuff, making, as it were, professional corrections to his appearance, and began to speak, with astonishing briskness. "Last year, a patient is very grateful; he gives me a house. Before he sails for Europe, he says to me, 'Bhatta, between us mo-ney would be an indelicacy. Take from me this house, which I have bought unseen for taxes, near the beautiful section of Brooklyn Heights.' "

Bhatta paused, shook his head mournfully, and went quickly on. "But when the ladies and I go there, I think probably he is not so grateful after all. Not a rescuable house. Even Miss Leeby shakes her head. We are sadly locking the door, so the wind will not blow it into the harbor, when Miss Leeby goes down cellar to look once more at the pipes. And there, in a room at the back, is Miss Prager. Fainted, we think. No—it is catatonic, and malnutrition. We talk with the neighbors; only one old lady is there who remembers. And what she tells us—"

The doctor spread his hands. His voice had become measurably softer. "Imagine, Misser Garner. A family has been mildewing in that house for twenty years. Years ago, there were three people, the father, the mother, the daughter. Lutherans, very strict, very distant. The father absconds from his bank—he was president—taking with him much mo-ney. Later on, gossip says that he comes secretly back, but no one is ever sure. Only the old woman we speak to remembers—the neighborhood is no longer Lutheran. Only Miss Prager, the daughter, is seen, night and morning for years now, coming from the bank, where she has always been cashier. The neighbors know of an invalid upstairs in the house, but not whether it is a man or a woman. There is never a doctor. At night, one light upstairs, one down. Then, some months before we come—a fire in the house next door. Prager's is only smoked out, but the firemen remove for safety an old person from the top floor. Hugely fat, this person, too fat to move, long hair, and a dreadful sore on the leg. From the description—maybe diabetic ulcer. Even in the smoke, the neighbors say, they can remember the smell from the leg. After that—nothing. They do not remember when Miss Prager stops going to the bank. They do not know her. The house is closed. They do not remember when they no longer see her at all. It is a busy neighborhood, Brooklyn."

Garner shivered in spite of himself, and shook himself to cover it, to shake himself free of the doctor's persuasion, which, even in briskness, had a soft insistence, as if on some central metaphor to which his listener must be privy too. The wind had become more positive than the sun—and Amelia would be wanting him in. But he had been a boy in neighborhoods not too far from such as the doctor had described, and he was remembering, with the self-induced chill of childhood, crabbed parlor recluses candled fitfully between curtain slits, dim basement monks whose legend, leaking from the areaways at dusk, scattered the children from the stoops. "Was it . . . it was the father then?" he said.

Bhatta's broad lips curved in a sudden Eastern symmetry. "A fact we do not check, Misser Garner. When we bring her home with us she is . . ." He shrugged. "She carries her cage with her, and we cannot persuade her out of it. To humor her fears, the ladies fix her the little place there." He pointed up the hill. "But I find the bank, Misser Garner. Natur-ally," he drawled, "if she has resources, we must find them for her. And what they tell me there, although they do not realize they are telling me it . . ." Bhatta paused, hands outspread. "Picture it, the same bank, but so modern, so airy now. At each desk, young ladies with hair like brass bowls. It is hard to imagine Miss Prager there. And the manager, in his cage that everyone can see is real—such a new young man, in a suit the color of chicken skin, and a bump in his throat that moves like a bobbin. He knows nothing of Miss Prager's father. Such a man does not deal by memory. Such a place cannot afford a memory. But 'Miss Prager,' he says—'until a year or so ago?—quite so. There is the Social Security index, the personnel file—and on the card there, yes, a little record of something that was not—quite so.' Two or three telephone calls, two or three moves of the bobbin, and there on the manager's desk—although of course he does not see her—lies Miss Prager and her twenty years."

Bhatta paused again. There was no defense against his pauses, Garner thought with violence—one pushed against them in vain, as one resisted a concert conductor who inexorably took his music slow.

"Banks are so jolly in your country," said Bhatta. "Like the one in the village here—a little white cottage with window boxes. And when your ladies take the children inside, the children do not hang on their mothers' skirts. They slide on the floor, and sometimes the manager gives them a little plastic penny bank—the way the baker gives them a cookie. Banks should be like the English bank in India, when I was a boy. A stern place, full of dark whispers, where the teller scoops up the mo-ney with a black trowel, and weighs it on a swinging chain-scale from Manchester. Then, at least, a child can be warned."

"You mean Miss Prager had embezzled?" said Garner.

Bhatta whisked out his handkerchief again, flirting it as if it concealed something maneuverable behind. "I forget you are a lawyer, Misser Garner. And so direct—like all Americans. Your honest men and your crooks—all so direct. It is a pity. You lose much." He touched the handkerchief to his lips. "No, I do not mean. Miss Prager was true to the bank. She herself owed them nothing. And alas, they owed her nothing. She had embezzled—only herself."

Across from them, the back door of Garner's house flew open, and eight or ten children rushed pell-mell from it and ran up Garner's hillside. Behind the high rhododendron and barberry, their creamy voices scuttled excitedly, belled by the loud, authoritative birthday voice of Sukey.

"I must go," said Garner, getting up. "My kids are having a party. They're up there now, having a treasure hunt. You see—our hill's kind of their playground. Even if you gave me your assurance that Miss Prager is not . . . dangerous . . . I'd hate to think she might frighten them in any way."

"She will not go near them, Misser Garner. She will not touch them." The doctor rose too, placing a hand on Garner's arm. "You see—*literally* she will not touch anything. She is afraid of her own hands. That is what the bank tells me. One morning they find her at the cashier's window, in a daze. Her hands will not touch the mo-ney, she says. She is resting her hands now, she tells them. Naturally, what can they do? A cashier who will not touch mo-ney! That must be why she is starving when we find her. She tells us too that she is resting her hands. But actually she is afraid of them. She does not like to touch herself with them." Bhatta smiled, releasing Garner's arm. "Pitiful, har? Actually, rather a common form . . . but developed to the extreme. We have done pretty well with her. Now she feeds herself, and she will work at clearing the brush. But you have seen how sometimes she forgets, and holds her arms?" The doctor cocked his head, listening to the children's voices. They were chattering excitedly, and syrupy wails came from the younger ones.

"Charming," said Bhatta. "What is this game they are playing?"

Garner explained.

"But how charming! And what is in the little bags?"

"There's my wife, coming after me I guess," said Garner, and indeed Amelia was advancing toward them. Through the opening in the hedge, the children trooped after her and surrounded her. "Daddy! Daddy!" shrieked Sukey.

Amelia quieted her with a gesture. She nodded briefly to the doctor, and knitted her brows meaningfully at Garner. Her face was pink with reproach. "John! The bags are gone from the hill. Every one of them. There's not one!"

"Somebody stole them! Somebody stole them!" Sukey danced up and down with excitement.

The other children took up the refrain and the dance. Garner looked at his youngest, Bobbie, who was aping the others with improvisatory glee. "You don't suppose that he—?"

"John, he's not capable of it. They've disappeared. Besides, the children have been with me every minute. We only put the bags out last night. You know what I think?" She took a step toward Bhatta, her mild face dilated. Taking their mood from her, the children clustered round her, staring at the doctor. There was no brood-hen room for them in her narrow tweed skirt, but she pressed them against her with her prematurely knuckled, detergent-worn hands. "I think it's that person you—you have up there!"

"Thought I saw someone moving around up there this morning," said Garner. "Before it was light. Forgot all about it."

"Pos-sible," said the doctor. "If so, remarkably interesting. Why do we not go and see?" He bent benevolently toward Sukey. "You are really having your hunt, har? Let us go and see."

"Indeed not!" said Amelia. "You children come back to the house with me." But led by Sukey, the children had already escaped her, and were running up to the hut. It was clear that the presence there was no news to them. Garner and the others reached them just as they drew back at the railing of the pavilion, their little ferreting noses arrested in uneasy obedience.

The doctor knocked gently at the center shutter, to which a knob of wood had been crudely affixed. Behind his bulbous, stooped form, the blind pavilion, little more than man-high, and puzzled together from old splinters of the past, had the queer coyness of a dollhouse in which something, always on the run from the giant thumb, might be living after all.

"Miss Prager?" said the doctor softly. "Miss Prager?"

There was no answer from within, nor did the doctor seem to expect one. He pushed inward the unlocked shutter, and stepped inside. For a moment they could see nothing except the small, swelling flame of a hurricane lamp. Then he opened a shutter at the back and daylight filtered in, neutering the lamp, winking it into place on a chain hung from the roofpoint. Half the rough wood hexagonal table that had once filled the place, paralleling the sides, had been cut away, leaving room for a small pallet. Behind it, on part of the window seat that encircled the room, there was a pile of underclothes, a mackinaw, a pitcher, besides some cracker boxes still in their bright paper. Next to these, a pair of black house slippers with curled silk pompoms glistened unworn, as if presented by hopeful nieces to an intractable aunt. Behind the other side of the table sat Miss Prager. In the current of air between the two shutters, compounded of the hot funk of the oil lamp and the tobaccony damp of wood-mold, she sat motionless, upright, arms spread-eagled on the table, in front of all the little gutted bags.

Sukey cried out sharply, "There it—!" and hushed. But they had all seen the dime-store money, neatly rectangled in piles, the toy snakes and babies tumbled to one side.

At Sukey's cry, Miss Prager wilted into consciousness. Her elbows contracted to her sides. She was working in a narrow space, the elbows said. Her hands moved forward, picked up a packet of the money and shuffled it expertly, counting it out. One two three four, thump. One two three four, thump, the hands went, moving of themselves. The middle right finger flicked the bills like the spoke of a wheel. At each fifth thump, the spatulate thumb came down. Miss Prager stared fixedly at the lamp, but all the while her hands moved so lucidly that one almost saw the red rubber casing on the middle finger, the morning business sun, glinting on withdrawals and deposits, behind the freshly wiped bronze bars. Beneath her fixed gaze, her hands went on transacting without her, and came to no conclusion.

This was what they saw before the doctor closed the door, and stood with his back to it. He looked over the children and picked out Sukey, who was standing well forward, one arm pressing her small brother to her stubby skirt, in angular imitation of her mother. The doctor beckoned to her, as to the natural leader of the children. And she was, she would always be, thought Garner, seeing his daughter in that quickened outline which drama penciled around the familiar. Here was no city febrile, here was none of that pavement wistfulness of tenure such as Amelia and he, even middle-class as they had been, had known as children. She was more intrepid, more secure, because they had grounded her here.

"She's got our bags," said Sukey.

"So she has," said the doctor, smiling. "She has been ill, and did not know they were yours. I tell you what—suppose you all come back after lunch, har? Meanwhile, the ladies will put all the things back in the bags, and hide them on our side of the hill. That will be exciting, har, to hunt in a new place? And in each bag, for each child—there will be a prize from India!"

And so it was arranged. Garner, following behind Amelia to herd the children inside, saw Miss Leeby enter the summerhouse, and shut the door behind her. Later, after lunch, as he carried the debris of cake and ice cream into the kitchen, while the front of the house rang with the shrieks of blindman's bluff, he saw two figures through the kitchen window, which had a view of Kuyper's hill as well as of his own.

It was the nephew and Miss Daria, stooping here and there on their part of the hillside, to hide the bags. He barely knew them, that ill-assorted pair, and it could be assumed that they scarcely knew each other, but he found himself looking at the two figures, rounded over in the blameless posture of sowing, with the enmity of a proprietor watching his boundary lines, his preserves. It was not, surely, that he resented the foreigner, the alien. He and Amelia were of the college-disciplined generation that had made a zeal of tolerance. But for the first time, watching these two figures from a ménage that had suddenly bloomed next door to him like an overnight morel, he felt a shameful, a peasant creeping of resentment, almost an abdominal stiffening against persons that different—and that near. Let them keep their difference, but at a distance, he thought. At closer range, a foreign way of life, wrong or right, posed too many questions at one's own. Questions that he was not up to answering as yet, that he was not interested in having answered. Bhatta no doubt made a career of posing questions at the uncertain, holding out the bait of answers to be rendered at a stiff fee. "Way of life" was a flabby phrase perhaps, thought Garner, but since he and Amelia were conducting themselves as thousands of well-meaning couples all over the country were, he presumed that they had one, although its outlines might be obscure. If their affiliations—he thought of Mr. Dee—were still too vague to bear perspective, he supposed that time would sculpt them clearer, doing for the contemporary what it had done for all others. Perhaps his own affiliation to his way of living was not old enough, not deep enough, for self-scrutiny. "It doesn't do to get too thick," he muttered to himself. "It won't do."

So, when Miss Daria came to the door, with the message that "the Doctor would receive them now"—there was no doubt that the doctor's ladies thought him the personage to others that he must be to them—Garner relayed the message to Amelia. She came into the kitchen, shunting the children before her, herding them with an abstracted tongue-lash here, a pat on the buttocks there, showing her own physical sense of herself as still their nursing center. All the neighborhood mothers of younger children had this; it was in the tugged hang of their daily clothes, in the tired but satiate burr of their voices, it was no doubt what grounded them.

"You're coming too, aren't you?" she asked.

"Thought I'd like to get that drain dug." He heard his own tone, the plaintive bleat of the weekend householder.

"John—it's Sukey's birthday." She went out the door without saying anything more, but he knew from her voice, her face, what she was thinking, was silently saying to him. "More contact with the children," she was saying. Fathers must have more contact with their children. All the mothers prated this to one another, and to the husbands, bravely arranging weekend excursions in which fathers had the starring role, taking the briefcases from their deadened arms at nightfall and handing them the babies sleeked from the bath, sidling the older children nearer for advices, ukases from the giant combat world of downtown. "Touch them, put your arms around them more," Amelia had once said to him. "Get down on your knees and play with them more," all the conniving mothers said, trying to give substance to these vague father figures that flitted from home at something after seven and returned at something before. And the mothers had other fears, Garner thought, fears that they shared, squirming self-consciously in the naked antiseptic light shed upon them by the magazines they all read, the books by female anthropologists who warned them of momism, of silver cords, of sons turned feminine and daughters wailing in a Sapphic wilderness.

Now that he thought of it, the remarkable thing was that in this modern world—supposedly of such complexity, such bewilderment that one could only catch ideas, precepts, on the run, and hold on to them no longer than the draining of a cocktail—people like Amelia and himself and their friends here, people who would be referred to as the educated classes in any country less self-conscious than America, were actually all the time imprisoned in a vast sameness of ideas. It's a loose theology we're in, he thought, a jelly-ooze littered with leaflets, with warnings and totems, but it holds us, in its invertebrate way, as firmly as any codex thundered from those nineteenth-century pulpits from which we have long since decamped. Even the phrase "nineteenth-century," which he had used without looking at it, as one spent a coin—was it anything more than a part of this, an old examination marker, a paper flag stuck in a bog?

Certainly his father, the lawyer, and Amelia's, the professor in a minor college, both born in roughly the late eighties, had been holdovers from that century, and he remembered, with fair accuracy, that they had been, if anything, more remote from their children than he, Garner, was from his. He could hear their voices, his father's, self-sufficient and nasal, spewing authority, and the professor's, taciturn and weighty, but with the same mantle of importance. That is what these men had had, he thought, a sense of their own importance, a sense of their own identity, solidity, in a world where the enterprise rested with them. When they had entered the dining room, heavily, of an evening, they had brought with them an illusion of a larger, a giant world of combat, but—and this was the point—it had not been an illusion either for them or their wives. And this, thought Garner, this was really what Amelia and the other mothers were after. They were trying to recast the fathers of their children in the image of *their* fathers. They wanted this authority for their husbands, they wanted them to exude this importance to the children. Poor Amelia, Garner thought, biting his lip, but laughing inwardly, for it was funny, and what could one do, when afflicted with thoughts like these, except get into perspective, or out of it, and laugh? She didn't want to let the children see, she didn't want to see for herself that father thought of himself as only a dog on a string.

He slipped out the back door. In a few minutes he'd go up the hill, where he could hear the children, already hard at their hunting. He'd roughhouse with them, get down on the ground with them, anything Amelia prescribed. Through the leaves he could see her watching the play, preserving a certain distance from the doctor's ladies, who were also watching, and the nephew, who was running and cavorting with the children—he could not be more than eighteen or twenty.

Above them, in its small clearing, the pavilion was quiet, as usual; there was no telling whether or not the doctor had removed his charge to the main house. How incredible it was, in hindsight, the calm way they all had acted, after that one fell glimpse into the private pit of that poor thing in there! For that is what it had seemed like—the tiny black core of the place, the one flame lighting the objects displayed there (he remembered the slippers—like the amphorae set beside graves), and outside it, above it somehow, the white, saved faces of the children, peering over the crater at the clockbound movements of the damned. Then the doctor had closed the door, and immediately they, the conniving adults, had all acted so very naturally—the doctor, of course, with that composure of his which was more than professional, almost artistic, and he and Amelia, acting at once in concert, on another tenet of their theology, the leaflet that said "Never show fears before children. Never communicate anxiety to the young." In time of atom, in time of death and possible transfiguration, act secure, and they will take security from you. He sighed, and without meaning to, walked around to the front of the house, the river side. The leaflets never told you what to communicate, what to show.

The river was in a quiet mood today, scarcely breathing, one of those days when its translucence gave a double depth to the air and moved like a philosophy behind the trees. He often thought of it as it must have been four hundred years before, when its shores, not yet massed with lives like pinheads on a map, had been hunting grounds for other Indians. Any gardener who went deep enough along here turned up their flints, their oyster shells. It must have moved along much as now, in the aboriginal silence, beneath an occasional arc of bird, the warning plumes of human smoke still countable above the pines. For almost two hundred of those years now, it had passed to the sea only through the piling cumulus of the city, that Babel of diversity so much feared by Mr. Dee. And now the people were returning north along its current—the diaspora of the pins—sailing northward on the frail skiffs of mortgages, wanting to take strength from the touch of the ground, from the original silence. For diversity had at last scared them, scared us, Garner thought, who were born to it. It is a busy neighborhood now, Brooklyn and all the other places, where birth and death are only a flicker of newsprint, and a life can embezzle itself, without a neighbor around to know. So we radiate, but only twenty miles or more at best—for there is still father's string. But we're all up here looking for identity, he thought, for a snatch at primeval sameness, and if we haven't got it yet, if so far we have nothing but the looseleaf, newsprint theology that we brought with us, who's to say what an emigration, what a man's century can bring? He took a deep breath, and it seemed to him that the breath contained a moral effluence from the river, a clean draught of the natural beauty and goodness of the world.

So armed, he walked up his neighbor's hill. Up at the crest, the hunt was over apparently; most of the children in view were squatted here and there, chattering and swapping over their loot. Some of them were waving the tiny silk flags and brilliant kerchiefs that must be the doctor's prizes. They had certainly started something with their innocent hunt, their bread-and-milk birthday game. Wherever there were children, of course, it was always difficult to avoid interchange, keep one's distance, but he imagined that Amelia, who managed their social life up here so efficiently, would find some firm way of maintaining the distance. Certainly she, like himself, would want to fend these people off, this extraordinary household whose difference, exhaled like the incense floating in its parlor, had invaded their calm, routine-drugged Sunday and made of it this lurid, uneasy day.

And that there was a fraudulence, too, about these people—he would bet on it, on his sense of something beyond the mere fact that incense always had a certain fraudulence to Western nostrils. If he, Garner, for instance, had seen part of his army service in India, instead of sweltering in the rum-and-Coke familiarities of Fort Bragg, he might at least have been able to judge better whether Bhatta's rope-trick style of utterance came merely from that other way of life over there, in which Bhatta himself quite naturally believed. But even if Bhatta's manner was actually only the stock-in-trade of those yogas who coined temples from California pensioners, or conned elderly occult-seekers in Fifty-seventh Street lecture halls, then, according to the storekeepers down in the village, Bhatta must be an unsuccessful specimen of that breed. "Beware of the man who won't admit he likes money!" old Dee had said, having the advantage of *his* theology there. It was no trouble to place people, if you had long since been placed yourself, and Mr. Dee was like a clean old piece of litmus paper preserved from that simple experimental era when answers were either pink or blue. Bhatta, an intelligent man, whatever else he was, had tipped to this at once about old Dee, had immediately bypassed him in favor of more impressionable material like Garner himself perhaps, member of a generation that had been schooled so tonelessly free of prejudices that it had nothing left with which to anneal its convictions.

Gaining the crest of the hill, Garner saw the doctor talking to Amelia, who was listening politely, soothed enough, evidently, to have dropped for a moment her eternal watchtower count of the children. He was just in time, too, to see the doctor dismiss the two ladies and the nephew with a lordly sweep of the hand. They came down the path toward him, the nephew skipping ahead. He had one of the little flags in his hand, and he nodded and grinned like a jack-in-the-box as he skipped by, gurgling something in what Garner supposed to be Bengali, or Hindustani, or whatever the boy's native language was—until the syllables separated themselves in his ear, and he realized that the boy had said, "Jollee good fun. Jollee good." The doctor's two secretaries followed behind. Their smallness, their washed out once-blondness suggested, if village rumors about their real status were true, that the doctor might have a certain predilection for type, but beyond this Garner noted again what scant similarity there was between them. Miss Daria's short, surprisingly heavy legs stumped down the rocky path on high heels, her hair was sleazily girlish on her shoulders, and her dirty satins had the dead-beetle-wing shine of party clothes descended to daytime use. Beside her Miss Leeby, although earth-stained, looked cleaner; she had the inaudible gentility of a librarian whom some climacteric had turned gnome of the garden, and her hands were full of plant cuttings. Both women smiled vaguely on Garner as they passed, and he fancied then that there was a similarity—of smile. These were nun-smiles that they had rendered him, tokens floated down from a shared grace, and shed upon the unsaved. It was clear that the doctor's ladies, at least, had found their messiah. What was less clear was whether the messiah believed in himself. There were these suddenly contracting glances of his, these graceful circumlocutions about money—certainly he couldn't keep away from the word, if only to decry it—these heavy sighs over the gap between practice and principle. Were they the honest man's ennui with the world—or intended to suggest such? Or if Bhatta was a swindler, was there some little subcutaneous grain of honesty that weighted him down? For at times there was certainly a suggestion that, although the doctor might climb his rope-ladder, even pull it up after him in full view of the spectators, at the last moment he could not quite make himself disappear.

"Oh there you are," said Amelia. "Dr. Bhatta has been telling me about Miss Prager." Garner picked up Bobbie, who was squatted over some private game in the middle of the path, and set him on his shoulders. Bobbie tightened his knees around Garner's neck, hooting, then squirmed to be let down. Under Amelia's quizzical look, Garner set him back on the path.

"Dr. Bhatta has given us a prize, too," said Amelia. Glancing at it, he saw that it was one of the books that he had seen at the doctor's house. He nodded his thanks to Bhatta, and slipped the book in a pocket.

"A few prin-ciples," said Bhatta. "They would interest the little man, har? This Misser Dee?"

"He was more interested in your restaurant," said Garner. "The menu on the wall."

"Restaurant?" said Amelia.

"We had, at one time," said Bhatta. "On Twenty-sixth Street. The ladies' enterprise." He smiled at Amelia, with a touch of the manner he had used to cozen Sukey. "All you American ladies have the desire to open a shop, har? The hat shop, the tea shop. You are remarkable ladies."

"I gather you served both hats and tea," said Garner.

"Har?"

"I mean, uh . . . 'Curry with Turban.' "

Bhatta chuckled. "My friend who gives me the house in Brooklyn, you remember. He is such a very smart businessman. A middleman, you call it. He tells them, 'Package it. That's what sells. The package.' So they package it. Forty-two turbans in linen and silk, forty-two glass Kohinoors from Dennison's. Special trays for the turbans. A special boy to carry, and to wind them on the customer."

"What a clever idea!" said Amelia.

Clever enough to feint her away from dark thoughts of Miss Prager and the children, Garner thought, and for a moment he too smiled down on her, though fondly, with a touch of Bhatta's condescension.

"Yars," said the doctor. "But for our own friends, who have not the tourist mon-ey—I think that we must do something for them too. So we fix for them a nonprofit item."

"Oh . . . 'The Mahatma Ghandi Curry,' " said Garner.

The doctor nodded, swaying happily in an undercurrent of the private merriment that seemed to dash him constantly between the joke on others and the joke on himself. "They are very enthusiastic. So, at the end—" He spread his hands. "We have all this Ghandi trade—and no Maharajahs!"

Garner and Amelia smiled, as they were plainly meant to do. It was really impossible not to be warmed, won, Garner thought, by the doctor's disarming habit of making game of himself.

"Curry—with Loincloth?" said Garner.

The doctor threw back his head in a gust of laughter that set him jiggling from belly to cheek, with a violence almost alarming in a man of his weight. He laughed until his eyes watered; a tear overflowed and ran, mud-tinted, down his dark face. How seldom one sees that happen these days, thought Garner, meanwhile grinning with the sheepishness of the man whose quip has received more than its due.

Bhatta poked him in the ribs. "Now you are making the metaphors, har?" He mopped at the tear, loosened his belt a notch, easing his mirth as a woman might ease her girdle, and bent toward Garner and Amelia, meanwhile gazing absently out over the river, which was spotted with a flotilla of small boats, the larger craft of the professional shad-men who came every year under some immemorial right, and here and there a solitary fisherman, one of the householders from shore, sinking his long-handled net for the first early crab of the season. "You understand, of course," said Bhatta, lowering his voice with mock secretiveness, "underneath the names and the trimmings—it was all the same curry!"

This time it was the Garners who, after an instant's gap, exploded into laughter, while the doctor's lips only curved in the slightest of smiles, his head nodding and nodding, his veiled eyes presiding above their laughter as if he had known all along that he would be able to nudge them toward friendliness. And this was the man's talent, Garner thought, whatever lay beneath it—this talent for flipping the absurd and the serious over and over like a coin, a shell-game perhaps, at which the onlooker was dazzled, confused, but so warmed and joined that here were the three of them standing together, in a circle together under the gently dropping evening light—three friends who have kindled, sighed, and lapsed into end-of-day quiet, each looking inward for a moment at the same tender picture, at the *faiblesse* of man, poor homunculus, with his absurd nets and boathooks, grappling for fish and for flashing non-fish in the salt wave-shadows of living.

It was Amelia who recovered first. "Where do you suppose Bobbie's gone off to?" She murmured, indicting herself for this moment's indulgence, in which she had forgotten to keep tabs. For as Garner knew, as she had often confessed, her servantless immersion in the children's days, her almost never being apart from them, had somehow resulted in her being unable to enjoy without guilt those personal pauses which were every human's need; it was as if she felt that her constant, tensed awareness of the children was the placenta through which they were nourished still, and at the second she truly forgot them, they would as surely die. "Doctor Bhatta—" she said. "Do you plan to . . . will you have other people like Miss Prager up here? To live?"

The doctor was looking up in the air. "Such a day!" he said. "Like a magnifying glass!" He pointed to one of the hemlocks, one of the great trees which always seemed to Garner to lift this region bodily out of the suburb into the misty realm of the uncorrupted, the undiscovered. "High as a church, har, that tree? Yet one sees the three twigs at the top." He turned to Amelia. "Other people?"

"Well, I—I mean . . ."

He knows what you mean, thought Garner. And now the evasions will come twinkling down again, from the trees, from the air, from anything handy—a rain of silver, of silver-*paper,* on us, who are so regrettably direct.

"I mean—disturbed people," said Amelia, bringing out the phrase with an unhappy flush.

"Disturbed?" said Bhatta. "Miss Prager has the importance to be mad—in an age that does not take its mad people seriously. A man splits in two? Shhh—he is only upset. He must learn better how to swallow his century. If not—a very sad case of hic-coughs." He turned to look at the summerhouse. "And all the time," he said softly, "there are these sealed-off lives, these pieces of crystal—" He turned back to the Garners. "You have seen her. You would say she is—how old?"

Garner thought of the leathered skin, the dead hair hanging like a ledge from the over-articulated skull. "Perhaps—fifty?"

"And you, Missis Garner?"

"Well . . . yes . . . about that."

"She has worked in the bank, they say, about twenty years. And according to the employment records, the Social Security, there would be almost another thirty before the retirement. She is thirty-six." He nodded at their stricken faces. "Think of it. She would be about sixteen, when placed in the bank. Maybe a couple of years older when the father absconds. The bank lets her stay on; she is innocent, she has the mother to support. An ordinary story." Bhatta clapped his hands together. "But from then on . . . imagine. The father sneaks back; the two women hide him. Sometime later, perhaps, the mother dies. Miss Prager goes back and forth to the bank, night and morning. And all those years, while she is working to keep the secret, the city is taking her secret away. The neighborhood changes; the old neighbors are blown away. Even in a bank, the city blows things away. Who is to notice, to remember, if an old man were to come out of his door, to come out on his stoop, among a hundred other stoops, and sit in the sun?"

The Garners were silent. Then Garner spoke. "You're convinced it was the father, then?"

"A lawyer could perhaps check better," said Bhatta. "But as for me, I am innerly convinced." He looked down his hillside, wider and steeper than Garner's, but as wild, although here and there old terraces had been brought into view. On the road at the bottom one of the long, red motorcoaches from the city came to a wheezing stop. "Such a pure case," he said. "Such a classic of money-injury. All for a reason that no longer exists."

"You'll . . . keep her indefinitely?" said Garner.

The doctor shrugged, threw up his hands. "Someone must. In any case, do not worry, Missis Garner. The ladies will soon build some places on the far side of the hill. Then we will put her there."

"There's a very fine state hospital. Quite near by." At the doctor's look, Amelia paused, again with a flush.

"And you say she has no resources?" asked Garner.

"None. I am sure." Bhatta's tone was almost one of pride.

"Quite the responsibility!" said Garner, and immediately regretted his own dry tone, its edge of disbelief, which the doctor was too subtle not to have caught. Ashamed, he told himself that it was a low envy which made one disparage in others the charity one had not got oneself. For after all, what did he have on the doctor, other than the mutterings of a few shopkeepers and his own carping intuition, both of which might be vulgar sides of the same thing, that fear of the stranger which was worse than vulgar, which college and International House and all that had taught him was the curse of the world? And which was against the very *laissez faire* of this place, which he had so boasted about in town.

Down at the bottom of the road, the bus moved off, with the familiar air-brake groan that was the only city noise along here, discharging a flood of exhaust gas on the passengers it had left at the stop. There were fifteen or twenty of these, and from the direction of their slow assault on the hill, it was apparent that they were the doctor's guests. Even at a distance they seemed a strangely assorted group—a periphery of nervous colors moving with brio around a more portly center of navies and browns. As they climbed nearer, Garner thought that they indeed resembled the lecture crowds he remembered from the days when he had had to squire his mother through her spiritualism period after the death of his father. In the center, there were a number of women very like his mother, vigorous elderly matrons, seemly in corsets and Footsaver shoes, wearing the flowered toques he had heard Amelia call "New Jersey hats." A few sallow young women were with them, and several elderly men. Among these latter, one wore pince-nez attached to a heavy black ribbon, and there were two or three shocks of melodramatic white hair. The color that framed the group was Asian; it came from a melange of brown skins, orange and yellow scarves, vanilla pongee suits topped here and there with a creamy turban, and the gauzy saris of three interchangeably lovely girls.

The doctor raised an arm, and saluted the people below.

"We must go, John," said Amelia. "And Dr. Bhatta—I don't want you to think that we . . . It's certainly a very fine thing of you to do."

"Har?"

"I mean, about Miss Prager."

The doctor's glance was on his guests, who had lingered below to admire the garden behind the main house. "You think?" he said, turning, and his face, softened by a question, was for once, almost open. Then it closed. "After all," he said, looking down the hill, "I receive so much. Possibly for me also—it is therapy to give." He made them both a little bow, but his smile was pointed at Garner, and one eyelid drooped again, as if he had just offered him something very special, very risible indeed.

"Yes, we must go," said Garner. "But I do want to . . . it's only fair for me to tip you off—" He was careful to make his voice friendly, surprised at how much he wanted it so. "If you do build without consulting the board . . . I'm afraid you're in for a spot of trouble."

"Ah, in that case—" Bhatta's voice was gay. He put a comforting hand on Garner's shoulder. "In that case it will be good to have a friend at court." He released Garner, waved again to the crowd below, and started off down the hill, carefully shuffling his carpet slippers along the narrow path. The grades were not easy to negotiate and the doctor's slippers must have made it harder, but with each turn that brought him nearer his guests his carriage heightened, his demeanor expanded. A ridge of shrubbery obscured the moment when he met the group, then he emerged, borne along in its chattering center, his tonsure inclining, his arms stretched in greetings papal and serene. At a point just below the little summerhouse, the doctor turned suddenly, waved up at Amelia and Garner, and then went on. The three Indian girls, who were nearest him, stood arrested too, looking inquisitively upwards—three fays, peacock, citron and lapis, fox-printed in gold. One of them said something, giggling, and the strange words, rebutted by the air and the river, traveled upward to the couple on the hill. Two answering chirps came from the girl's companions, then the three of them turned their backs, and a jingle of laughter wove between them as they ran after the doctor, who was just disappearing around the corner of the main house, his bald head shining well above the clustered others, a dark stamen in the declining sun.

It was late that night, long after the slow evening which daylight-saving time had prolonged, when Garner, drowsing over the Sunday paper, raised his head, realizing that he had been asleep and had been startled awake. What he had heard must have been the wheeze of the last bus to the city, the voices and farewells of the doctor's departing guests. Amelia had gone to bed early, as she so often did these days. "Never can understand why you insist on sitting up," she had said, kissing him good night, "just to fall asleep in a chair." He could not have said why himself, unless it was perhaps that by so doing, by this small intransigence against the wise routine for a man who had to get up at six, he was prolonging an illusion, a weak midnight illusion that time, undictated, was his own.

He got up, kneading his eyes, and went to the window. Down the way, near Petty's, the one faint roadlamp made a crooked pearl in the glass. Apparently there was a moon, from the look of the shadows on the road, but it must be high over the house already, and not large. It was the winter moons up here that were enormous, riding so close and intimate in the black air that the cornea felt itself naked against them. He remembered the first one of these they had seen their first winter up here—the great disc rising heavily from the water, as if unseen hands were having trouble pushing it upward, then the white path-shine on the water, and Amelia standing at the window, saying, "Look John . . . look! It's coming in the window . . . If I opened my mouth . . . it would float right in."

Well, they'd come a long way since then, ten years, and his moments of such lyrism were not many. Before him, in the light of the single reading lamp under which he had fallen asleep, the house stretched, doubled in the gloom, but still such a large house—the sitting room where he stood now, the parlor, the dining room, all furnished with relics of both their families, and looking almost regal in shadows that obscured the raffish touches of the children, the farm-size kitchen where they all really lived, the study off the hall. In the half-light, with the little Victorian effects with which Amelia had placated it here and there, it was true that its ancient purpose sometimes revealed itself too starkly, and it stood declared for what it was, a home that belonged with those feudal servants, that stipulated, at the very least, one of those vanished households of accessory spinsters and aunts. At these times, it was true, sometimes at the very moments when he and Amelia and their friends were congratulating each other on their living in a place where one did not have to keep up with the Joneses in the usual way, he had a sense of unease, as if the grain of their lives had too suddenly appeared, revealing them all in another silhouette—keeping up with the shadowier Joneses of the past.

Late voices came again through the night—the remaining guests of his provocative neighbor, no doubt—he could hear one of the women calling the dog. "Lili . . . Lili . . . come on in, Lili . . ." the voice said. The air of America is so clear, Bhatta had said that morning—so very, very clear. Certainly the man had a passion for clarity, or else an irony for it—it ran through his conversation like a motif. One wondered what he was like at home, when not playing to the gallery. Perhaps he was a man who could never be at home—a strain on anybody, that. Hindu, Brahmin, whatever he was, with his hybrid education there would still be a kind of Eurasian sense of values—no harm to that, perhaps good. But if so, Bhatta would be sure to make capital of it. Yes, that would be his pitch, was his pitch. "We are none of us at home in the universe, lads—lords and ladies. I can show you how to handle that better than most. Meanwhile, let us share our amusement at our dilemma. And let us also share—" No honorarium to be required, of course. But, the universe being what it was, it was probable that the secretaries would pass the plate.

Garner left the window, hesitated with his hand on the switch of the lamp, sat down again in the chair. Yes, that could be how the cult might be formed, the coterie. He found himself thinking of such, not this one, but some other suited to oneself—some warm little member-world, banded together in a decameron of talk.

Stretching in his chair, he felt the small book in his pocket, the one Bhatta had given Amelia. He took it out, idly thumbing through it. This was for the gallery for sure, the power of print for the flowered toques. It was not in these fluent pages that one would find out where, in the happy slang phrase, Bhatta "lived." He read on. *Stone in the grass,*

I must examine you very carefully. You may be a piece of the North Star, cast upon the grass. No, not here. He snapped the book shut. A folded paper fell out of it, the same he had replaced in the book at the doctor's this morning; Bhatta must have taken the same copy from the top of the pile. He hesitated; in general, though fallible, he'd managed a normal decency about such things. But probably it was only a grocery list, or perhaps the recipe for that inimitable curry. And in Bhatta's case—case was a word that might well be used; the man himself went out of his way to present himself as a brief full of tantalizing pros and cons, teasing one to make of it what one could.

Unfolding the paper, he saw that it was a letter addressed to Bhatta. *Dear Dr. Bhatta,* the letter said, *I beg of you not to say that I must stop wearing my glasses at meetings or else pay the $700 fine. What I paid last time exhausted my funds until next quarter, and the family will not consider it. They will not realize what the meetings mean to me. I know that you do not agree about the glasses, but the truth is I cannot get about without them. I ask you please to reconsider. If you will ask Miss Daria to write and say I can come to the next meeting, it will make me very happy indeed.* The letter, typed, was signed tremulously, almost indecipherably, in ink. Then there was a typed postscript: *At the very next quarter I will pay what I can.*

So, thought Garner, so. So that's where Bhatta lives. The old son-of-a-bitch. Underneath all that diversionary laughing gas, or tear gas—or rather, some formula that managed a sparkling precipitation of both—there had been only something as bare as this. If the letter had said "my crutches" for instance—well, one had heard of neurotic symbols which a doctor might reasonably be pressuring a patient to discard. One had heard also of the psychiatrists' disarming emphasis on the importance—to the client, of course—of the latter's psychic need to make payment. But eyeglasses! The letter postulated some sad fool, an old fool perhaps, with the aching, grave-humble naiveté of the old. Or one of those sclerotic old business eggs, who addle without warning. It would be a rich simpleton, or one at least with access to some money. No one knew better than Garner, a lawyer, how wistfully ingenuous the sudden simplicities of the rich could be. The worst of it was that Bhatta had at no time, in no sense given any of this the lie; if confronted he was quite capable of roguishly pointing this out. One taught the therapy of giving, quite naturally, Misser Garner, to those who could.

Garner looked at the letter again—it was a definitively good address, midtown Park, engraved, and on thick bond. The signature, three-named, was shaky—William Something Bertram, or Benthan; added to the letter, the humility of the postscript, it did suggest some old gaffer hanging to the fringe of his family, of the world, some poor old mottled pear that would not fall. A person sick with nothing more than loneliness, perhaps even persistently healthy (if Bhatta had found nothing better than the glasses to fix on) and driving his family crazy, as such people often did. Wanting nothing more than still to be involved, to be one of the member-world.

Garner stood up and pushed the book well back on a high shelf, the letter inside it. He'd been right about the fraudulence then—from the first. It was ugly to find oneself so handily corroborated. And to have been one of the simpletons, too. He had never examined the term "confidence man" for what it said, for what it shouted plain. He had merely lightly appraised Bhatta in the humorous terms of the sellers of gold bricks, of shares in the Brooklyn Bridge. Not as trafficking on the frozen-out, on people who only wanted to come in by some fire, to belong. No, this is too real, he thought. It sins somewhere, he thought, bending his head to an obscure inner heat, surprised at his own use of a word from which the leaflets had long since emancipated him.

He turned out the light, and in the darkness the moment of the three of them by the river suddenly formed again, as if he had turned on another lamp that shed the triple-enclosed, mauve light of dusk. He saw the three of them again, he, Bhatta and Amelia, in that pause so warmly joined, laughing there by the river. Wasn't that to be weighed in the scale for Bhatta? Or was it to be taken out of context as one of the good mysteries—exempted from its origin as was the true-love poem of the poet who frequented whores? "Ah, the hell with it," he said aloud. To hell with it, whatever it was—living in the country, the long Sunday—whatever had made him feel the way he did. As he went up the stairs he still tasted it—acid, greensick—the feeling of the man who had been proven right.

In bed, he could not sleep. It was that over-alert, hypertensive hour of the night when the tireless free-associational sheep ran on and on, one idea carrying another's tail in its mouth, and still another part of the mind hallooed behind, catching, concluding, with a fake brilliance from which nothing ever could be salvaged the next day. The sheets were cool; he could be grateful for that, for in another few weeks, although the thick-ledged downstairs areas of these old houses would still be damply chill, the dormered top stories filled slowly with a summer-long hot must, through which one moved weakly, cramped for breath, regretting the flesh on one's bones. Someday, when he had the cash, he would insulate. Yet, even as he lay here, flinching before the anticipated river-valley heat that would arrive, sometimes in June, inexorably in July, he felt a submerged pleasure at knowing how the summer nights would be here—the hot pall under the eaves, the languid spiders woven suddenly out of nowhere—each year. It was a satisfaction to a man not brought up to houses or the firm groove of the seasons, to be able to say, sighing with the heat, that it was this way every year. His hand was in his grandfather's; his grandfather was saying, "Tomorrow's the twenty-eighth of August. Tomorrow the locusts will be here." It cor*robo*rated something. It—

He got up, swearing under his breath, and hunted for a cigarette. If his mind hadn't circled him back to that word he could have been asleep by now, and he had, he had to get up at six. Noiselessly, he crossed past Amelia's bed and opened the window from the bottom, so that the drifting smoke would not wake her. No moon just now. One sound, the faint tweaking of the river, heard only if one knew it was there. Nobody plying the hill tonight. He crept back to bed and sat listening, smoking. No sound from Miss Prager, the small and sealed.

Curious that he did not believe that the doctor had lied about her, even in the light of the letter downstairs. He was a man who would not bother to lie. Rather, he was a man who had grasped the mordant advantages of telling the truth as he saw it—aware that he told it well, and that a peculiar vision was a prize for which people would pay. Tapping his paradoxes like a set of metaphysical tumblers, he would make a coaxing music that set his audience agape, and their pockets too. And always careful to remind them of the great paradox that was money, such a man, coming upon Miss Prager, that "classic of money-injury," might carelessly keep her to remind himself.

Creaking, the river moved against the land. Is all the evidence in, in? There was something that Bhatta had said—Ah, you think it devious, perhaps . . . from *a priori* to *a posteriori*—the history of the world . . . how wise of you, Misser Garner, not to admit the connection between money and the work one loves . . . banks should not be so jolly . . . Miss Prager has the importance to be mad.

Garner put out his cigarette and lay back, tightly closing his eyes. No, there was something else—but with a man like that, the evidence would never all be in. Lucky for himself, no doubt, that he had found that letter—not having Mr. Dee's prescience about tea. For Bhatta's tunes were catchy indeed. His phrase for Dee, for instance. "The proxy dragon," he had said, smiling—and there, for all time, was little Dee, fixing his small, gorgon face against the future, advancing like a lone stockholder waving a proxy from the past. And every now and then, in an aside as Elizabethan as the doctor's handkerchief, there was the deliberate trail of a phrase pointing the listener to Bhatta himself.

Garner sat up, straining forward. The doctor had been above him, on the steps. Behind him, the river lay like a thick darning needle; in front of him the wind had been making its shot-taffeta changes on the lawn. Once more the yellow kerchief whisked; the heavy finger probed the rose. "Well . . ." said the doctor's voice, "every man has some little tale he tells himself in the dark, har? So as not to really see himself in the mirror the next morning." Or had it been—so as to be able to *look* at himself in the mirror the next morning.

No matter, thought Garner, leaning back on the pillow; it was Hobson's choice. For, once you saw how much the man might want to be caught, you saw much indeed. "Perhaps for me also it is therapy to give." How delicately, satirically he could have been showing them the irritating little wound of honesty that held him up by the heel! For then the storekeepers would be right, in a way—as, no doubt, storekeepers, until the last trump, always would be; Bhatta was not a successful swindler. Devious man that he was, it might be that life had withheld from him only the power to be consistently so. It would be no wonder then if he talked so much of clarity—this hoist illusionist who could not quite make himself disappear. And Miss Prager could be the tale by which he hung. Suppose that, a swindler, he still set a secret table for one of the swindled, for Miss Prager, hoaxed by someone greater than he? Suppose that he kept Miss Prager, for whom no funds would come next quarter, and this was the tale that he told to himself in the dark?

Now certainly I should be able to sleep, thought Garner. But time passed and he did not. Lying there, he listened to the river moving against the land. I'm just past forty, he thought, and my own evidence is already more or less in. What would it be like for him and Amelia if they lasted to eighty, for people like them who, leaning against the leaflets, might find that they leaned against wind? Or did age always come, stripping the critical function with gentle narcosis, making of any past, because it was the past, a good backbone? He turned on the pillow. Lucky Bhatta, lucky Dee. Who each has his tale for the mirror, and therefore no doubt sleeps well. Less lucky Garner, who has so many tales to tell himself for the daytime—of Amelia, the house, the children—but for the six o'clock mirror has none.

After a while he looked over at Amelia, a dark shape of comfort sleeping, but it was the hour past love, the courtroom hour of the night, when the soul, defending, shrank to the size of a pea. So, after a while, when he had reached that black level below pride, where one need no longer pretend that one was not pretending, he began cautiously to tell himself a tale he might once have had.

He was walking along the river, according to the tale, and he was very near the place where he belonged, the real place—in fact he had only been away from it a day. It was just before dawn, and along the opposite shore there was a narrow stencil of light. He was up before it, because it was natural to be so when one worked the land, and he was wearing a thick sweater, because this was a short-summered region and the mornings were Appalachian-cool. Before him, as he walked, there was a whiteness along the grass that was sometimes hoar, sometimes the wind at the underside of the blades, but whatever the season, he always thought of it as the waking power of the ground. It ran ahead of him, leading him to the real place, and when he got there he stood for a moment, as he always did, standing on the land. This was the moment of safety, of a wholeness something like the moment after love. For although he was up a trifle earlier than the other people, he knew that they were somewhere nearby, and that they would soon be up and about with him in the simple member-world. All day long he and they would be working, in a nearness past need for arranging, and the land and the river worked with them, weaving them all the good backbone.

This was where the tale always ended, whether it failed him or brought him through until morning. But tonight, just before he came to the end, there was a sound that brought him suddenly back to the real world outside. It was the sound of something soft brush-brushing across the grass, and at first, thudding with night-terror, he thought it was the whisp of a scythe. Then he heard, blended with it, the light scampering of an animal, and breathing, he took it to be the sound of someone walking a dog—the dog scratching here and there on the gravel, and behind it, the shush-shush, soft and irresolute, of carpet slippers on the grass.

He stole to the window again, but nothing could be seen on the hill. Telling himself that the night made special fools, he crept downstairs and stepped outside his door.

The doctor was standing still, his back to the stone urn in the center of his moonlit lawn, looking up at his house. His dog stood behind him, its eyes glinting like glass, waiting as it often waited during the doctor's morning inspections—although it was always the women who walked the dog. Whining now, it tugged with its muzzle at the hem of the doctor's coat. The doctor put a hand back of him to quiet it. "Eh Lili . . . shhh Lili . . ." he said. He had moved to face the hill, and was looking up at the summerhouse. Still the dog whined, bracing its hind legs in the direction of the gate, and at last the doctor turned. "Poor Lili . . . you want to take me for a walk, har?" he whispered, and the river brought his words to Garner's ear. "Better take me, har. Better take your old man for a walk."

At the word "walk" the dog bounded, ran a few paces toward the gate, then stopped to look over its shoulder to be sure that the doctor followed, and in this way, with the dog alternately trotting and checking, the two of them came to the gate. The moonlight brought out the ungainly lines of the old bitch and the fallen-in silhouette of her master, his head prolapsed on his chest above the downcast belly, the long coat dribbling behind him like a nightshirt, making of him that poor show which any man might be at this hour, alone. I ought to get a dog again, thought Garner, hankering suddenly for the old mongrel, dead of age, whom they had not replaced last year. Nights like this, when a man can't sleep, he can walk his dog. Or the dog can walk the man.

Outside the hedge, the dog trotted north, along the road toward Garner's house. Garner leaned into the shadows of his doorway, but the dog, head to the ground, nosed him out, snuffed familiarity and dismissed him, and intent on some trail now, trotted on. The doctor raised his head, and in the thin light of the roadlamp the two men looked at one another. By day, it was always the doctor who spoke first, and Garner, taken at a loss in his shadows, awaited the florid greeting. But Bhatta said nothing. Gravely he nodded, and again, and the nod was like a touch. Then, doffing a hand against his temple in mute salute, he bent his head and moved on.

Garner listened to the sound of his shuffling, soft and hesitant and human, until it melted into the dark. It is the sound that ends the nightmare, he thought. Not the sound, necessarily, of mother or nurse or brother. Just the sound of *other*, of someone awake too, and dealing with the dark. A warmth crept up his throat. That the old man had not said anything, he thought—that was the thing. That such a man, so wedded to talk, should have signaled only, as between two who shared the freemasonry of mirrors, and have said not a lingering word.

Sleep hit him then, a dead salt-wave, and only habit brought him back up the stairs, to his bed. Sinking down, he doffed two fingers against his temple, in the general direction of north. Let the night make its fools, their gestures, that daytime might well rescind. It was a good thing. Let it. It was a good thing—to have a friend at court.

In the red-black landscape behind his lids, he sank down, down, watching the retinal images—tiny black dots circled with red—that swarmed ceaselessly upward only if he did not quite look at them, of whose origin he had wondered about since a child. They swarmed on; they were pinheads, they were people bent over the hillsides in the attitude of sowing; they were pulling salvation like turnips from the soil.

Among them was a man, not Garner, somebody else, poor homunculus, and he was bent over too, hugging his image, his foolish tale. As he bent, his string dragged behind him, but he did not see it, for his chimera was strong. He was building a world, a little antique world of allegiance, where he would be hailed by name on the main street, neighbored in sickness and until death, and there were roots for the commuter's child. The people around him pretended not to see the string, for they had them too. Even as the fences went up, same on same, and houses burst upward like sown teeth, same on same, he and the people pretended, for they were building themselves into an antique perfection, into that necklace of fires upon the brotherly dark where once life burned steadily from farm to farm to farm.

Watching them, Garner slept. His knees curled to his chin, like a child who had world without end before school, and in his dreams he smiled too, a child snailed in sleep. All around him were the unguided missiles of sleep, of dream, but he flew between them, above them, with his story. Across his still face the night moved at bay, harmless against this impermanent marble, so intact and warm. Whatever there was in the mirror, he would not have to look at it until morning, not until morning, world without end away. Until morning.

Extreme Magic

Over the rolltop desk, in the handsomely remodeled barn which Guy Callendar used for antique shop and home, he had hung, among other things, a present once given him by another dealer for obvious reason—a thinnish old almanac whose heavily scrolled frontispiece bore the title, in letters to suit: *The Resourceful Calendar*—for 1846. Printed McGuffey reader style on the good old paper of the era, its blunt, steel-engraved homiletic for weather, crops, and the general moral behavior taken for granted by its readers, had withstood the less sermonizing air of the Hudson River shoreline some miles above Garrison, New York, for almost as long as he had—seven years. He liked to see it hanging there, a tightly integrated little universe whose assumptions were only as yellowed as its paper—including that flourished motto which, despite its missing "l," seemed indeed intended for his life, for him. He had never known whether or not the giver had known his history.

At the moment he was busied in converting an old Rochester lamp, object and task both rather out of line for a shop owner who seldom bothered with the humbler Victoriana and had his own finisher, but these pretensions were his trade's and the neighborhood's, not his own. The lamp belonged to a neighbor—if one could give that name to

Sligo and his wife Marion, proprietors of an old waterfront "hotel" ten miles up the shore, really a restaurant-bar of the kind smartened up with horse brasses for the Saturday afternoon country squires. And Callendar liked any task which let him look continually up and out at any one of the weathers of his own acreage, modest in size, but vast in trees through whose ancient swirl, layer upon layer toward the river, he could see, like a natural fence that gave him the limits he still so needed, glimpses of the waterline, even of the sky—but not of the opposite shore. For this he had bought the barn on a day's decision, and the barn, in turn so neglectedly beautiful, so rescuable and then so emptily waiting, had brought him by gentle nudges to a trade that was no more out of line than any other for a man so nearly out of life.

Ten years ago, he had been an ordinary young man of thirty-one, living with wife and three children—an infant, a boy of seven and a girl of two, in a split-level cottage in one of the developments outside Hartford, Connecticut, working as a company man for the largest in the constellation of insurance underwriters in that city, and doing well enough. Born nearby, married to a town girl, he had come of that lower-middle native stock, in name often resonantly Anglo-Saxon, which the boys from the great schools studding New England called "townies"—a class that, with the will, the luck and the proper scholarships, frequently ended up years later socially alongside of those same boys. With some of the luck, two army-earned years at an obscure business college, and no will beyond that of someday having his own agency, he had been contented enough, unlikely to end up anywhere except much as he was. But that year, while he had been away at the company's convention plus special classes for men of his caliber, his house, catching fire at dead of night in a high November wind, four miles from the nearest hook and ladder and no waterpower when they got there, had burned, with all his family, to the ground. Two owners of badly scorched houses adjacent had urged him to join their suit against the contractor whose defective wiring had already been the subject of complaint. Even if he had been able to overcome his horror, there had been no need; as a model employee, he had had Ellen, little Chester, Constance, and even the baby heavily overinsured in every available form from straight life to special savings plans, college plans, mortgage, fire and endowment. He had managed to survive all the obsequies, the leaden vacation in Bermuda insisted upon by his office manager, even the return to a furnished room and restaurant meals in the best businessmen's residence club in Hartford. It was only when the indemnity money came in, thousands upon rolling thousands of it, that he had gone out of his mind.

The phone rang. "Guy? Polly Dahlgren here. How are you?"

"Hi, Poll, how are you?" An Englishwoman, widow of a Swedish ceramist, she had continued to run their gift shop at Orient Point, the farther tip of Long Island, a place he imagined to be a seashore version of Garrison, in terms of quiet estate money ever more fringed by a louder suburbia, with here and there an air pocket for people like themselves. He had been careful never to see it, though now and then she asked him down, and he liked Poll. She liked him too much for a man who could only like. "What's on your mind?" He'd said it too fast, sad for them both because he already knew.

"Those silver luster canisters you said you'd seen a set of someplace, a dealer's. Near where you fish."

"The Battenkill." It was the first place he'd gone from the hospital, in the beginning with another patient, the stockbroker who'd taught him flycasting, then, for every one of the years since, on his own. "But that was last April."

"Collector down here went wild when she heard about them. Pay anything, if they're what she wants."

"They wouldn't cost all that much," he said. "About two hundred for the four of them. If they're still there. They just might be. I could find out for you. Or she could go see."

"Invalid, can't. I do a little legwork for her now and then, expense-paid of course. Nice old gal."

"Well, why don't you?" he said. "Beautiful country in August. And five or six dealers strung out along one lovely road. Not too far for a three-day weekend. With the parkways."

"Where is it, did you say? And the name?"

"Vermont–New York border," he said, "the Battenkill." He couldn't keep the dream of holy peace out of his voice, the years of gratitude. "The most beautiful trout stream in the world." He'd never seen any other.

"I might just do that," she said. There was a pause. Then she spoke brusquely. "Like to go with me?" Into his silence, she said abruptly, "For the fish."

"Thanks, Poll, but I can't—" Get away. She knew he could, any time. He plumped for the truth, at least some of it. "It's particularly a place where I like to go alone." As he went most places.

"Right!" she said at once. "Nice of you to tell me that." She understood that he had given her an intimacy. He did like her. "And now, give on those names."

He gave her the lot, extra warmly. This was what he was good at, and where he could be generous. "Don't bother with the Graysons if you're in a hurry. Retired couple, he'll want to talk and she'll want to show her collection. Goes in for ruby hanging lamps and anything doll-size, from tea sets to iron cookstoves. Has some good glass, but none of it for sale. One of those. Then, along the road north there's a tidy little farmer's wife, barn stuff mostly, woven comforters and moss-rose china et cetera, but cheaper than most. Doing it to send the older girl through beautician's college." He stopped, at a snort of amusement from the other end. "Hmm?"

"Nothing," she said. "Just that you can't sell your specialty either. A pity. You're so good at it."

"I know." He smiled at her. "Don't hold it against me. And listen now. The lady you want is named Katrina Bogardus—and she is a lady. Gets the early stuff from the big houses when they break up. Has a couple herself. Looks like a little French marquise and is a retired superintendent of schools."

"Record of sale then, if she's sold. Or she'll remember." Poll's voice was her business one, to remind him that though not strictly in the trade she knew as well as he the range of its characters from junkyard on—as varied as its stock and as severely appraisable.

"Decidedly." He hesitated, then warmed to his specialty. "And look, Poll, if you do have time, hit there on a Thursday, when her son-in-law visits. He's a parson, I guess you'd call him, but you never saw anything like him in America, though he is one—minister, up-Hudson way. Dresses high Anglican and calls her *mater*—she must have had him refinished somewhere. Right out of a British movie, the kind they don't make any more."

"Barchester Towers," she said.

"Never saw it."

"A book." Her voice risked tenderness again.

He covered this with a rush. "And Poll, if she likes you—which I'm sure she will—she'll take you upstairs to see the drawing room. Paneled. Moved from somewhere. Lowestoft to match. Your cup of tea, as I've heard you say."

"Pennies to pounds she liked you," she said. "Well, I might do. And shall I mention your name?"

"Oh, she wouldn't know it," he said. "I was just there once. And I don't buy, you know—when I go up that way."

"I know," she said. "You just go—for the fish."

"Ah, come on now."

"The way you go almost anywhere," she said crossly. "Wonder you stay in business." At once she was contrite, but too nice to say so. "I mean—" She knew he didn't need money, and why. "Never you mind," she said quickly. "Go on and do what you like to do, why not. And *be* grandmother to the rest of us. We can use it, all right, all right. . . . Well, good-by, Guy m'love, and thanks."

"Good-by, Poll." There came the final, impossible silence in which he waited for her to hang up, and she didn't.

"Fancy," she said, very soft for her. "And you were only there once. . . . Well. See you sometime. Cheerio."

"Tell you what, Poll," he said desperately. "On your way up there, why not stop by for—lunch. I'll gather in some people. Or better still—on your way back, then we can have a gas about it."

"Right," she said promptly. "Let you know. Or if not, you drop down here. Oh, no fear, I remember what you said about weekends. For the day. I'll—gather some people." One more pause. "Good-by, you bloody old fisherman, you," she said very rapidly, and rang off.

During his two years in the first-class establishment—its rolling golflands not thirty miles from here—into which relatives and the company had been able to put him on all that money (at a yearly maintaining fee of twice his former salary, and in the company of others similarly able to be as expensively aberrant or agonized) he had been led through the gentle craft world of the sanitarium, toward its own necessary fantasy of the goodness and wholeness entirely residual in the world. In that selective company of Wall Street alcoholics, matrons at the climacteric, schizophrenic young nymphs in riding habit, and highly placed failures of the barbiturate, even the other patients had been extra gentle with him, often—as the doctors were quick to see and use—extra reachable by him.

At first he had been in no condition to notice this. Later on, under the constant encouragement from above to help one another, he hadn't questioned it. Sitting alongside one of the "Park Avenue" matrons, whose hair had been freshly hyacinthed in the on-grounds salon that morning, he and she had learned how to French-polish furniture; on leaving she had sent him—from an address that wasn't Park but at another altitude he hadn't yet been aware of—a box of the books on furniture and china which were still the best he owned. The exquisite young rider—who dressed to the nines at every hour of the day, was mortally afraid of men at less than a yard's distance, and always had an animal beside her—had been willing to dismount from her horse, leave her Doberman behind, and walk with him—he had taken it to be because as a man he was still so nullified. The flycaster had taught him golf also, and like a legendary rich uncle turned up in a poor young man's thirties, had opened to him, in the wistful after-dinner talk of a drinker on cure, a whole Barmecide's feast of bon vivant living. This man, now lapsed between bed and occasional club window, Callendar still visited, and unlike the man's own nephews, was received. He understood why now of course, long since grown used to that special kindness which in the hospital he had taken for the good manners the rich had been bred to even in their own sickness, awarded even to him who could teach them nothing, not even—as in the one try which had given him a setback—a knowledge of insurance. Only on leaving had he understood what he was to them, to anyone. Against their ills, mostly fugitive from the world, casualties from within, his case had the ghastly health of the man whose coup de grace had come from life itself, from outside. Against his accident, they still had hands to cross themselves. He was their extreme, the triple amputee at the sight of whom even the single-legged may still take heart.

The phone rang.

"Is this the *eminent,* the *resource*ful—"

"Hello, Quent." He prepared to laugh with Quentin Paterno, to join in with the preliminary conversation tic, a stutter of courage rather than larynx, with which his earliest customer-friend always had to start.

"*Spoil*sport! Now I'll have to begin all over." He could hear the little man clear his throat, see the pudge of fist kneading potbelly, the bright brown eyes straining under nobly bald brow.

"Is this the powerful *schattchen,* goodman extraordinary—?"

"I dunno, Quent. What's that?"

"Marriage broker, you Christian." Joke. So was Quentin. "Yop, you did it again, matchmaker. And I suppose you'll say without even knowing it, like always."

"Ah, come on now." Because he thought about people a lot generally, those introduced by him—anywhere from dinner guests, to the fellow who'd had a letter from him to a dealer-correspondent in the Rome where Callendar had never been himself, and had married her—almost always clicked, and sometimes paired off.

"It's just like any statistics, Quent," he said. "Nobody remembers the ones that don't come off."

"Well, this one did. The party was last night. I suppose they didn't even call you, those young ingrates."

"No. But I can't think who." He shouldn't have said that. Quent might take it to mean, who in *Quent*'s crowd? It was hard to think of them without the italic in which they thought of themselves.

"Cast your mind back, in fact *turn* back, O Callendar." No offense given then, except, in that painful laugh at his own joke, by Quent to Quent, who hurried on with the doomed rapidity of a man who had absolute pitch for the way he was sounding. "To a freezing night a nice guy, a *Guy,* is nice enough to come all the way in to hear my concert. A fall guy, in fact, for anyone his broken-down friends writes a play, paints a pitcher."

"Quent. Give." If he was a faithful, even grateful audience, always using the tickets, not just buying them, he'd learned not to dwell on the fact that he was always audience.

"Sorry." If stopped in time, Quent could tune his delicate pitch to others. Exerted, it at once eased him. "After the concert, Guy. Carnegie Taproom. Remember our kid harpist, Violet? The one the orchestra boys were teasing? 'Nobody-violates-me Violet,' they call her. And the couple you bumped into at intermission, they run a shop in an old mill down in Bucks somewhere."

"New Hope," he said. "Joe and Milly Pink." The stuff they sold was terrible.

"They had a son with them, a Princeton boy."

He barely remembered a boy who sat back, who should have been with the younger crowd. Yes, now. The Princeton boy, day boy probably, scholarship surely, who sat well back from all of them, most of all from his all-wrong parents, the mother in squaw blouse and skirt and no bridgework, the father wearing a huge free-form silver ring of his own design. "Yes, I remember now." And the shy girl, from Oberlin, Ohio. Farm girl probably, or—if they had them out there—a townie. Who sat back. He had gone over and introduced them.

"Those two," said Quent. "That boy, that girl."

"Why, that's fine!" he said. "They—they should do well together."

"Yeah, you have a fatality. Or a green thumb. And I have a headache. From the party."

"Nice of you to call me, anyway," he said. And waited.

"Matter-of-fact—" Quent said. "I'm in the slough, slow, sloo—of despond. Or how do you pronounce it."

"I dunno. If that's what you called me for." A pause.

"Tell me," said Quentin. "You heard of people named Benjamin? Must be near neighbors of yours."

"Two doors down," said Guy, grinning. "And a half a mile away. Yes, I've heard of them. They own the house between us too, but keep it empty. A sort of buffer state between them and a commercial."

"Not now they don't. They got the grandmother in it, Phoebe Jasper

Aldrich. The Aldrich Chamber Concert Mrs. Aldrich. Library of Congress, and points west. You wouldn't know."

"I read the papers."

"Then you know. They blow a horn in heaven, she hired the hall. Lucky the composer gets to feed at that trough. Trow. Troo. Give her credit, most the good ones do get."

"Oh?" he said, puzzled. Quent, rich enough by inheritance to own the house in Turtle Bay for which he kept Guy still buying, was too proud-poor in another ever to ask this kind of favor. "No—I'm afraid I don't know them."

"Don't anticipate, guileful Guy. I *been* asked. A little late in life, it's true. To make music in that celestial company. This coming weekend." When the mock accent dropped, then they were near.

He picked it up. "So?" And waited. It came as expected.

"William."

As usual.

"How?" he said, finally.

"Pills . . . Oh, he's all right. Resting quiet. We got to him."

As usual.

"I knew in my bones last night, when he wouldn't go with me. Always a sign, when he won't leave the house. But I felt I had to go. It's such a bind, you're not supposed to show worry. Y'know?"

"Mmm." He knew.

"You have to be tough with them," said poor Quentin. "Especially when you're *family.*"

For this he had no answer. "He wasn't asked up here?" he said. "To go with you."

"Oh, nothing *personal,*" Quentin said quickly. "Nobody gets to bring anybody up there. Not even *wives.* I told him. But he wouldn't believe me. You know William."

"Yes." Yes, he knew William. A swag of still true-blond hair over the high, narrow cranium of an underfed child—of which William had been one. A mouth set like a cherry pit in the slender jaw. And a nameless talent, or only the desire for one, harbored like a wound. William, barbiturate failure, still only a year away from true boy when first met.

"Yes, I know William." He had been the patient to whom Guy had tried to teach insurance. "Quent—" If I came down to stay—would he let you go? He already knew the answer, which would be given even now with pride: No. Only me. "No," he said aloud, "I don't suppose."

"Well anyway, that's really why I called you. To get a line on them. I had some wild idea, maybe she would ask him up. But I can see now how ridiculous." Quentin expelled a long, relieved sigh.

"No, I don't know a thing, I've never seen them. Except that they have cats." One was nosing the screen door now.

"Give me that high-class excuse of yours," Quent said suddenly. "The one *you* use to beg off weekends with. You know. The one you give *us.*"

He laughed, and gave it. "I say I like to be alone too much. Then they say 'Oh, we'll leave you alone!' Then I say the simple truth, that I know they will, but I never can hit the right posture for it. I don't know how to relax into being half-alone but not alone. . . . Mightn't do for you."

"Jees, no, you know *me.* No posture at all. No, it has to be something *real.*"

"Like what?" he said.

"Claustrophobia, maybe." Quent was feeling better. "Or what's that thing on heights?"

"Acrophobia." It was hard to stay angry with them—if they had to make catastrophe of some small emphatic of life, in the end they always entertained you with their elaboration of it. "But the house is on the riverbank—I know that much. And she's asking you for the weekend, not burying you." A second cat was nosing at his door. "Why not 'Ailurophobe'?" he said. "They must have half a dozen of them. Cats."

"Cats give *William* asthma," Quentin said dreamily. "Gee, whad you do, swallow the manual? I wish *I* could read. I wish I had your sense of detachment."

Burn your house down then. Burn *William.* It was the one thing for which he couldn't bear to be marveled at—why should they want his priceless capital of non-suffering? He didn't answer.

"Anyway, thanks, Guy, maybe I'll do that. Thanks a million. It's just—I don't want it to sound phony. You know? And with certain people, outside your own close circle of friends, howya going to know you not giving offense?" Quent's voice squeaked—a mouse transfixed in terror of its own moves.

"You don't give it, Quent," he said. "You never do."

"Ah, Guy . . . Anyway. Good to talk to you. Marriage broker is nothing; you could open a whole accommodation agency. But not till you help us finish on the house, hah?"

That house would never be finished—how could they afford to finish this construct that formally provided them with everyone else's troubles—and pleasures of course—from maid trouble to gourmet shopping, to spats over the discipline of the curly-headed dog-child? He didn't say this either.

"Anyway, good-by now," said Quent. "And William always asks for you. I'll give your love to William."

"Yes, do that."

"And good to talk to you. I'll be honest with you, that's why I called." Quent's repetitions were more for his own ear than for others—it was the way he knew he meant something. "Thanks again," he said. "You don't know what it means to me, to be able to talk to another normal person."

He put down the phone. Phone calls often made him think of lantern slides, the kind even the high schools probably didn't use anymore, and views of life, not Borneo. Any housewife might go through a box of them heavy enough to make her hand tremble, any morning. He took up the lamp again.

In the past seven years, he had fulfilled all the fine dreams the hospital had had for him, meanwhile never hiding from himself that these might be limited dreams. It was only now and then that the old fire lit in his head—or the dream of a new one to which he would get there on time. Life, though so much more gently, had still come to him by accident. It had been on his first fishing trip alone, driving back on the Vermont side, that his attention had been caught by a farmhouse flying two flags, British and American, and idly inquiring down the road where he'd stopped to refuel at a gas pump in front of a china-stuffed façade and further sheds receding, had been given the whole of that rum-running story. He had knelt to look at, not buy, an old lamp of a kind he hadn't seen since and now knew to be as rare as pemmican—

and had been given the history of such lamps. History, he found, could be picked like daisies all along the roadside, if one were willing to take it a little squeegee—what had fascinated him from the first was the squeegee—the narrators themselves. And in the end, just like them, he'd acquired a business, and one just like theirs, "on the side."

For not a man jack of them (or a woman in that gallery of whittled women) who hadn't been beached up on his wrack of metal and porcelain from somewhere other. Or if not, then whatever in them had settled early or late for this flotsam had done so in lieu of something else. It hadn't been until much later, of course, that he saw this clearly, and much more: how even in winter or bad times the hunt had to go on, if need be, with each other; how in the end the rooker had to be rooked. How each, drily scanning "the trade," saw this as well as anybody, but denied it for himself. And how each, like himself, had arrived at the specialty which made his game worthy and the others' silly—and which he would not exchange. Sometimes, one came upon an antiquer whose wares, invading his house, had coiled into closet and bed and pushed out the humans entirely, leaving him wedged in its clockwork like a single, bright, movable eye. In his own case, the reverse having happened, he'd been helpfully pushed out of the house altogether, where he was kept tethered like a buoy in a tide, perhaps, but still in the world's tide.

His own specialty was necessarily invisible. But if he could have stood people up in rows—like Romanies with their hands out, who were in turn his soothsayers—the shop would have been filled with them, and his best customer was always himself. He supposed they were his substitute for history—whose?—as history itself had always seemed to him in a way a substitute. In the hospital, in his last phase but one, which he had taken to be religious, he had done a great deal of such reading, only to find out that, like so many of his era, he had merely been lonely to hear about other eras, especially of that pure time when people made their own constructs of God. And in the final months of his cure, he came to understand what the dead were—at least, his dead. The dead did not own history, as he had once supposed; they only could not move forward into it, being fixed in what they had. In the worst of his sickness, he had wilfully refused to move on without them—he would stand with them. He was mad with jealousy for them and against himself—for all they would never know. He hated himself for having to grow forward into it. In the end he had been able to, to leave the hospital—and them. Sheer luck had then nudged him into a modus vivendi whose limits were so exactly modulated to his own—one exactly useful to a man able to move on, unable to forgive himself for it.

He had come to this place not long after, on a day's trip to the impeccably kind lawyer who had all that time held in trust for him his now more modest good fortune. Even the barn, a mile or so uproad, had been so forbearing with him, so high and mild, with autumn riverwind coming in at its windows just a cast too weedy—so willing to wait. Even the real estate agent might have known of his mishap, unless he spoke to all clients as if only his properties could heal. In geography, of manners as well as hills, this was still that formal countryside of the hospital he had just come from, where wealth, and perhaps goodness, too, were sometimes still ecclesiast. To the north of him, one great estate had humbled itself to Capuchin, hard by another, to be sure, that had gone more militantly, to golf course. Down below him, rectors in board-and-batten snuggeries presided over the lesser manses, alongside here and there the heart-piercing needle of a still New England church. Sports cars knitted amicably as petunias between all of them. A safe visual goodness still ringed him. Everything was in repair. And—as he had the perspective to say laughingly—the opportunities for picking up church candlesticks were endless.

He had good perspective. Down still lower in the town, in certain side streets that had once been "native," or more often now in the supermarket for new cottagers of the class just below commuter, he sometimes saw a Saturday family he recognized. They had come from the north. The young man, one infant on shoulder, was beset by two other jumpers demanding to be taken to the Mi-Dream Ice-cream. The woman, the Ellen, was still pretty in her postpartum fat and had been to Marnie's Beauty Den; she would not comb the curls out until morning. She was a girl who would name her eldest "Chester," against all lost eighteenth-century New England, because it "went with"—who would name her infant daughter Coral. She was a stranger, an utter stranger. The young man, given the privilege of naming his second child, had called it Constance, but only out of a simpler maleness, or perhaps, though he was unaware of it, because fidelity was going to be so important to him. They both were blind to him, Guy Callendar, as he was now. She was ensconced in her family, never to look at another man, never at one like him. Perhaps the young man, not necessarily smarter than she, only properly keener by way of army, business college, and business, had paid him a look, as to an example of what he himself might someday aspire to: this lean, older man who so resembled him, who still had his hair, his own long, pleasant enough Connecticut face, inside a style of dress and haircut already noted down at conventions—this older man who, in ten years and with a little of the right kind of luck, might be him. Both the couple were oblivious to his own—snobbery. The children were smartest of all; children always sense fear. For though in the book of phobia he had a clean slate, even to fire, he could not sit through any movie or story in which a child was mistreated or in peril—and this was not in the book. The children knew he preferred not to look at them at all but could not help looking. Like animals they sensed their mastery over him and often acknowledged it in some gawky mince or persistent turning back that bewildered their parents. It was in his face perhaps, what he feared for them—even the infant often gave him a patient, peach-cheeked smile.

He never saw them, that family, as any older; they stayed where they were. He was the one who had moved on. To the degree that he had, he could bear it now. Perspective was what any man carried on his back, not a cross, but an easel to which pictures were supplied slowly, always from an unknown hand. He merely knew better than most what had happened to him. The hospital had taught him not to expect that the world would continue to recall his extremity and pity it, had warned him that he must not either, and they had been right. What more had come, they couldn't have anticipated. The heart educates, and unlike the State, is no leveler. Tragedy flattens some men farther back in their grooves. Others it pushes altogether out of their sphere.

—

The lamp was finished. His hand went to the phone, then withdrew. Instead, he chose a shade of plain old white glass from his stock of them, set it upside down in a carton, placed it and the brass lamp, electrified and polished now, on the floor of his station wagon, and drove off. On Mondays, the inn's bar and restaurant, like his shop, was closed, the chef and assistant barman off; the rare guest in one of the rooms upstairs must take his chances elsewhere. Sligo and Marion always spent the day at home in retirement; any business that took them away was performed midweek. No doubt they could only feel private on the one day the place wasn't convivial. Publicans had little time or will for private friends. If they welcomed him there, as they did now and then on that day, it was more or less because it was his Monday also, and he understood the special coziness taken and given when the shopkeeper entertains others, particularly others of the same, on the day the door is closed. He went there, he supposed, because they were in the same pocket as himself. If he never thought of those two as enjoying their place in nerve and spirit, as he did his, of ever really doing more than accepting it, it was perhaps because to think of them, or of knowing them, in terms of nerve and spirit, was in itself an oddity; they were not that sort.

Good barkeeps, or "your host" as the menus said nowadays, generally kept themselves unknowable. Sligo was a good one. A big, very pale man, both tall and wide, shown ambiguously only to the waist as he stood between the dark mirrors and mahogany of a bar dating from the Spanish-American War, he might have been a mercenary seen through the spyglass of a much earlier war, or perhaps a footman of the size and impassivity then so prized. He had a blacksmith's arm girth, ending in the bartender's pouchily delicate hands. In his silence, he might have been the smith's spreading tree. From his wide gaze, customers assumed that he listened. Rumor said that he drank, or (because he accepted no offers to) once had—but this was always said of men in his profession. Some said that the horse brasses on the wall behind him came from Sligos who for centuries had been innkeepers in Britain. Others pooh-poohed this because of the name and favored the Abbey Theatre, the wives particularly. His black hair curled low and caddish—or Roman—at the neck; both were thick. Such a figure, so aristocratically pale, must have come from somewhere; the odds were that it had come down.

When the restaurant itself was full, it was Sligo's habit to leave the bar and make a circuit of the tables, inclining his head to each with a query so regally inaudible that only weeks of custom confirmed what he had said to be no more than " 'S everything all right?" Seen at a distance, above the tables, Sligo's profile was suddenly neat, set in his jowled head like one of those cameos purposely carved only half emerged from the matrix, not cut free of it. Weight was the one sign that this great trunk might indeed be hollow enough to have a once much smaller man inside it. At the moment he stepped down from the bar, wholly in the clear, one saw with surprise, beneath the white coat which hid width but no belly, that his legs, long as they were, were bowed. As for Marion, who sometimes tended bar in these interims, at first glance she was merely the good host's wife.

At a break in the hedgerow to the left of the highway, Callendar turned in—there was no sign—drove riverwards for perhaps a quarter of a mile, parked in the big courtyard behind the house, empty now except for the owners' car, and waited tactfully for one or the other to come out, as per custom, at the sound of his tires on the gravel. On Mondays, to get their quiet, they disconnected the phone. He wasn't one to drop in on a couple on their equivalent of Sunday—he remembered how it could be. Once in a great while, Marion called him the same day to ask him over; more usually the invitation was an offhand "Drop in" or "We'll expect you" that same week. Today he was expected, with the lamp. Sometimes it took her quite a while to come from some upstairs region from which Sligo would come down later—it was almost always she. And once or twice, when expected, no one had come out to greet him. He'd the sense not to knock or go in, and he'd been right. Neither of them had ever referred to it after.

Unlike his own place, this one had a straight view. The Canal Zone Inn, as it still was known, was set in the crotch of a promontory that fingered the river, really only a slice of made land just strong enough to hold a concrete pier, no trees. Behind the sandstone house, of the squat Dutch sort that never looks its size, there was backdrop enough of them. The courtyard was good for fifty cars. Nobody except the occasional tourist who bumbled here ever walked out on the little *plage* of false land, either to sit at its umbrellaed tables, or bathe from its fringe of beach. From it, it was said, one could see clear down to the Point—West Point. The inn's late owner, not from the Academy, though military enough to have seen war service in "ninety-eight," had probably acquired most of his rank and all of his legend when well out of the war, and in his last years also, a character. The legend (of cadets sneaking across river and so forth) the Sligos had kept or let stay, even to the large, gold-pronged diamond solitaire in its glass showcase on the bartop, according to its shaky Spencerian label: "Ring worn by Colonel George when he helped carry the message to Garcia." Customers who had known the old "Colonel" reported that even in his nonage he had been nimble enough in mind to have carried the news from Ghent to Aix, had he ever heard of that circumstance. Nowadays, and not merely because of time passing, there were almost no such customers. In place of the former character of the inn—speakeasy in the Twenties, dirty ladies upstairs in the Thirties, dirty old men downstairs in the Forties—the Sligos had painstakingly substituted their own. This was no longer new enough to be shadowy, or shouldn't have been—like Callendar, they too had been here seven years. Or perhaps the inn's intended character was to make them seem shadows of it.

He himself wouldn't have painted the mellow old stone with white, cleanly as it now looked, pleasingly cleft at precise intervals, even on the overhanging second story, with boxes of geranium, all of the same superior pink. The place now looked reassuringly as much as possible like others of its kind, with their same suggestion that setting was only for status, that the real shelter one got here provided the customary satisfactions—and above all, was inside. But the Sligos must know their business, for they had got plenty of it—still uncompromisingly local, if not the same. "Before we came," he'd heard Marion say, "the bar had one television, one spider hanging down in front of it—and often only one customer." If she knew that this might well have been one or another of the older residents, people like the Benjamins or their attendant cronies, who now never came here, she made no mention of it. Now, with no television or spiders, the trade came from the former trade's expensively subdivided land, from people well above cottager, often new country club, who needed to love the local tradition, and were prepared to do so in a hurry. Inside, in the games room on the lower level, darts could be played, or—as a visiting Englishman had once exclaimed at—shove ha'penny, played with half-dollars. (Drinks brought from above were likely to cost twice that, and to be martinis.) Nobody except that visitor—and Guy—was likely to wonder from which of the Sligos' backgrounds this idea had come, or whether it went with anybody else's here. Like the decor, some of it from Guy's shop, the idea was "Colonial." A specialty, like seventy kinds of ice cream, or pizza, had been provided. The rooms above were purposely empty, overnight trade discouraged. Patronage came mostly in pairs here, but not that kind. Even the hosts, shadowy as they kept themselves, were seen to be a pair.

Inside, since Marion was the talker of the two, it took time to notice how noncommittal she remained. Tending bar, when not busy she usually sat on a stool behind the glass case with the Colonel's ring in it, down at one end. The case was small and low enough for her to lean chin on hand and look down into it, if she chose. Guy, in his mild bouts of company, often sat on the last stool at that end; company at one elbow was enough. From the first, he'd seen how useful the case and its contents were. New customers always asked about it; old ones invariably made some reference to it of an evening. The big diamond, high on its gold prongs, couldn't be touched, but its gleam could always be rubbed up into a conversation. "My God, that's a convincing fake!" a man would say. "Have to look at it twice to know it isn't real." Marion would nod, not looking down on it. "Real, they couldn't leave it *here*," said another. This time she might look down on it, or smile, or raise an eyebrow—oh, there were all sorts of variants, on both sides.

"Screw the diamond!" he'd heard a woman say to her husband on one particular evening. "It's a cinch the old guy was a fake. Chrissake, when *was* the message to Garcia."

Whenever the talk turned to the Colonel's card, and thence outward from the bar to the world and history, Marion usually deserted it. She was there, however, when the woman's husband, standing behind her chair next to Guy's, introduced himself as the manager of the new jewelry store downtown, and suddenly took out an eyepiece. "Still think of musself as a practicing jeweler," he said, looking round him. "And proud of it. Want that stone appraised, do it gladly. Gladly. Looks to me from here that's no zircon." He popped in the loupe. "Can't see for sure through that glass. Lemme see now, howzis case open." For the first time, Marion's nod was more negative than—not. Her hand even stayed him. "Don't let those black spots fool you," he said genially. "Just carbon. A mine diamond that many carats could still be—" Marion was called away to the other end of the bar, and stayed there for some time. He shrugged, put the loupe back in a pocket, and said to Guy, undertone, "Be surprised how many people have an old-fashioned piece like that, don't really want to know if it has value." When Marion came back, he addressed her. "Any time your husband want to buy a modern stone for that pretty little hand, you two come down and see me personally. We merchants stand together, hmm?"

Sligo, tray in hand, was just behind them, up to fill a bar order for one of the tables. "Oh Elwood!" the jeweler's wife said quickly, smiling at Marion. Women liked Marion, who always took care of them with a kind of bar delicacy reserved for them. "I think old things are fascinating. That box doesn't look as if it's been opened since the day he put it there—no wonder she wouldn't want it opened. Why even the air in it would be the same as that day!" Marion looked down at her own hand, at her thin, pewter-colored wedding band.

"Women," said the jeweler. "She must have seen every gee dee holy relic in Italy, kissed 'em too if I'd let her, dirt and all. Yop, we just back from the tour." He appraised Sligo. "You folks . . . you . . . in the faith, aren't you?" Again he spoke in an undertone. Sligo, taking the drinks Marion handed him across the bar, bent his grandee stare on him, but left without answering. "No offense, I'm sure," said the jeweler to anybody handy.

"Cawnvert," the woman whispered to Marion. "Turned for *me*. We're both each other's second. And you know, sometimes—" Marion served them sympathetically, but never took confidences from them. She was a good bartender though. The house quickly stood everybody a drink.

There was nothing of the barmaid about Marion; in her blouse and skirt, with a sweater for nippy evenings, she might have been anybody from around here. On weekends, when the trade slid in on their way to or from dressier places, she sometimes wore one of those matched cardigan and skirt sets which the estate people had once set the fashion for but now meant nothing—even the maids here, copying their mistresses, wore cashmere. He had a theory about that, about Marion. With her short-featured face, trim bones and easily cropped hair, she probably wore clothes of any kind well, giving no sense of touting them. Not tall, because of good proportion, she looked sometimes taller than she was, or smaller. It took a second glance to see that she was middle-sized and slender, well compacted by use—she worked hard—and had looks above the average, though past their prime. In any woman's face there came a turning point after which, once passed, there was no going back, and Marion's, in its mid-thirties, had passed it. Under the eyes it had two scimitars of flesh, or in a softer light, of shadow, which put a curious mask there. One could almost see a young, unformed girlish face there, and, superimposed on it the blunter scope of the features as they were now, but never the face as it must have been in its prime. Her voice always surprised him, half because he recognized it, though no one else here seemed to notice. It was that high, rather small voice, babyish but not whiny, not lisping but almost r-less, sing-song without being really melodious, which was sometimes "finished" at certain schools but really began earlier—in the never having to speak too loud, from nanny-time on, for service. If the estate people had ever come here, surely they would have been startled by it—one of theirs. And here was his theory—that Marion had once been in service of that kind. It was in the way she tended the women, one of them but still not one of them, in the almost hungry way, as they left the place, her glance looked after them, from her distance. At first he had thought it merely the natural enough envy of the publican's wife, jealous of their freer household time. But it was in the way also in which she and Sligo were joined (rarely speaking to each other in public or private—if the Mondays he saw were private), not even in sympathy perhaps, but in some one of the wretcheder forms of closeness often to be found in marriage-cellars. For, if they shared something no one was to know and neither spoke of it, the two of them in their way would be as close as many couples who spoke. There were things that joined people far more often than love; one saw or talked to such every day—as he had not an hour ago—people in cahoots over something far less dramatic than hate or murder, some burden that together they had climbed out of, or with. Yes, he was almost sure of it. Sligo had come down in the world; Marion had come up in it. This could well have made them the pair they were.

It was even in the way he himself had gravitated to them, not knowing precisely at the invitation of which of them, but knowing that he was in some way welcome to both. For him this was relaxing in its turn. They never examined his life in the way of his other friends, and they never asked questions, having instead an air of assuming that any person with any sort of life to him had ghosts also. Or even that all three of them had the kind of life where there were no questions anymore. They included him there, he felt, though perhaps not on their scale. No questions any more—this was what the two of them had in common really, whether it was in some monstrous central arrangement, or only in the collection of bits and pieces and talismans that come from running an inn—like their glass case.

It must have been shortly after that night, almost four years ago, that he'd begun coming here now and then like today—not as a customer. That night, the jeweler's wife, after insisting on another round of drinks, had become maudlin and her husband had taken her home. Since then, the wife was sometimes seen in the Canal Zone with a woman crony, but not the husband. As the pair left that evening, Marion, watching them go, had looked speculative, as if she already knew this outcome. The hour was later than Guy usually stayed. He had never before been alone at the bar. As the door closed on the couple, Marion's chin declined on her hand. Her black hair cast a further shadow on the bowfront of the box that held the Colonel. She looked up at Guy and smiled slightly, as if her speculations had included him. "Mr. Callendar." It wasn't a question. "How come you never talk about the diamond."

Today, it seemed they weren't going to be at home to him. He started up the engine. It wasn't until he had done so that he became aware of the other sound, jumped into relief against it—a faint "plock," then an interval, then another "plock." Somebody was playing at darts on the large board that covered one wall of the downstairs games room and hadn't heard the car approach, even with the room's door ajar, as he now saw it was. Even with the large darts that Sligo had had custom-made, it was remarkable how the sound of the play carried—"plock," and yet another "plock." But anyone who lived on the great maw of the river grew used to its tricks of voices fanning or swallowed, small reports of insects an inch from the eardrum mistaken for backfire on the opposite shore. He turned off the ignition again, slammed the car door, and, smiling to himself, carried the carton with the lamp across the gravel and up the two old grinding stones that served as steps. More likely, Sligo, who had a passion for the games-of-skill he was so good at, and had stocked the room with every known apparatus for them, had found yet another one at which Guy could be trounced.

Just inside the door he set the carton down on a polished floor painted with guidelines like a gymnasium's, and stood up, a smile on his face for the player standing motionless in the afternoon shadow, on the mat at the farther end of the room. It was Sligo, poised one foot forward, silent and huge as a plaster cast met at a corridor's end in a museum, pupils as blind, one arm extended, bent at elbow, as if to shake hands with him down the length of the room. On the upturned palm there was a sliver of silver. He had time only to see that Sligo wore a kind of lederhosen whose leathern front came up high, like a scissor-grinder's apron, or was slung about him like a multiple holster, then the arm trembled, only trembled as the sliver left it—*plock*—and the hand retracted slowly, two fingers aloft, thumb across palm. His own head, following the flight, swiveled left, toward the nearer dart-board wall. At first he could not take in what he saw there. A painted bull's-eye normally there had been blanked out by a wooden target-frame just high and narrow enough to receive the shining knives that outlined a figure tensed within them.

It was Marion, flattened to silhouette but still untouched, the crown of her head held high, her eyes and mouth open, her arms raised from her sides like a prim Joan. In the wooden space between each hand and thigh a knife was imbedded. Her eyes tremored, holding him. " 'On't move," said the rigid hole of her mouth, " 'on't move. He only has two more." There were still two vacant spaces in the outline of hafts that enclosed her, one each to the left and right of her neck, between shoulder top and ear. He felt he dared not move his own head; even his eyes must hold their allegiance. *Plock.* On the left side—safe. Come again, quickly. He prayed for it. He should have lunged for her in the interval. But her eyes held him, saying *No.* Unbearable, not to know what those eyes saw coming behind him. Make it in these shoulder blades, mine, he said to it. Not in those eyes. He saw them close, slump—in the second before. *Plock.* On the right. Safe. He reached her.

When he gripped her arms, she had already raised herself and stepped away from the target, already able to stand alone. She spoke over his shoulder, in a dead voice that told him much. "Better help me with him now, will you. He's about to fall."

Sligo was standing as before, his empty right hand raised *in hoc signo,* motionless except for the sweat stealing down him everywhere. Only the sweat, patched under his armpit, banded across his forehead, held him up; the hand glistened with it. When he began to topple, his body seemed to lean from the forehead, eyes closed. His boots held him to the floor until they got to him. Once, in their gasping struggle to ease him into a chair, he several times muttered what Callendar heard as "Forty low. Forty low." Holding him around the waist, they maneuvered his hips into the heavy captain's chair. Sligo's hand, braced on the low table in front of it, slid forward on the slick maple, his head cracked upon it, and he rested there jackbent, head on arm. As they stood over him, getting their wind back, their arms hanging, they heard his deep intake, steady as a man in a coma, reassuring as the breath of the dying, calmer than their own.

"I never thought of it," said Guy. "I didn't know. Because there was never anything to— But that dead-white color. I should have known." It was a slapstick notion, that one of the veined cheek, the carbuncled nose. Those were the genial ones, the harmless ones.

"No one does. How should you?" she said. "He doesn't do it like anyone else. He never even smells of it."

They were both backing away from him with sneaking step, as from a sickbed.

"The worst ones don't." He knew them from the hospital, not the red ones, here and gone tomorrow, but the white-faced ones, with self-murder like a thirsty knifehole between the eyes.

"I never knew any but him," she said. Her voice was prim but echoing, the voice of a woman who says, "I have lived all my life in this town."

"Periodic . . . is he?" He couldn't help the phrase, like a doctor's. There were only so many to use.

"Yes." Her teeth began to chatter. "Once a week."

He got her a chair, leapt about looking for a wrap for her, expostulating with himself. "Let me get you a—" He looked down at her. They both grimaced at the absurdity of it. She nodded. "I'll get us both one," he said.

When he came downstairs from the bar with the whiskies, she had found a sweater for herself and had cowled a thick raincoat over Sligo. He lingered on the stairs for a minute, staring down with a grinding distaste. Upstairs, the late sun was buttering all that cheap brass with a commercial cheer. No, it was impossible; they couldn't leave him here.

They sat sipping the whisky. He was sure she felt the same uneasy sense of conniving. Because they had always been three, and still were, they spoke in sickroom voices.

"What was he saying there?" He glanced at Sligo, including him. "Forty something. Forty throw?" He glanced at the target-frame, and away.

She leaned on her clasped hands, her glass put aside. "His weight. He's been ashamed of it ever since—" She cleared her throat. "In recent years." The little cough made the phrase sound like an obit. "Actually—actually, he must be fifty pounds more than that by now. But when he's this way, he always says it. 'Fourteen stone.' "

He nodded, as if this was always the way men reckoned weight in America. Then there was silence. Some people's diffidence was helped by it, not hers. She was helpless against the years of her own silence. He felt that she was not to be left with it.

"Nobody else knows?" It struck him that he wouldn't be much help to her if he kept to questions to which he already had the answers.

She shook her head. After a while, she said: "Maybe both of us were—" She grimaced at him, lowering her face in the coyness of agony. "Hoping you knew."

"Audience?" he said.

Now the silence was his.

"Can you—speak for both?" he said. "Are you that much a pair?"

"Yes, why not?" she said. Then her face slipped into her hands; she must be exhausted, might want to lie down. He no longer knew anything about the energy of women. Though outside it was August, it was already autumn in this basement, in this summer-kitchen of yore. In that light, dappled from above, the polished racks and mallets and wickets, sets of balls, nets and checkerboards, hung as in an armor room, above the yellow, black, and green stripings on the modern, balsa-colored floor. Games looked ghostly when left to themselves, whether for an hour or a century. When she took her hands from her face, there were no tears on it in the place for them, only those crescents of flesh. "Why not? We suffer the same."

He saw into that tiny, stifling pit. Must he envy it?

She got up from her chair then, and strode away from him. "One gets on better without talking. Pity is fatal." At the target-frame, she knelt to a long, slender box at its base. "You won't be coming back now. Better that you stop coming." Box in hand, she stood up, her back to him, musing over it as people do who recover a memory, good or bad. "I didn't even know he had these around any more. He tricked me into standing here. After all these years with it, I'm still not very bright."

"Where did he ever get things like that, learn them? A circus?"

"Sligo?" She was staring at the wooden backboard. "By inheritance, you might say. He had a ve-ry rich . . . sporting inheritance, I'm told—at one time. Polo, fencing—though I never saw him at those. Guns." For the first time, she switched about to look at the man hunched there. Then she turned back to the target and began drawing the knives from it, one by one.

He came up and watched, over her shoulder. All haft or all blade, the knives had the elegance of any such balance. The chest she was fitting them into was lined with purple velvet. "Marion? Talk, then. Since I'm not coming back."

"What do you want to know?" She was intent on the shaft in her hand.

"I'm not sure. How can I be?"

"Ask." Her whisper went into the box, with the knife. "I don't know where to—how to. Ask!"

Another knife went into the box before either of them spoke.

"Why does he drink?"

"He always has."

"Why do you stay?"

"He has no one—no, that's not true. I left once. I even worked in—it doesn't matter. Twelve years ago. We'd been married five. Then his landlady called—he had the dt's. He had no one." She held a blade over the box. "Neither did I."

He watched the blade go in. "Is he often like this?"

"Comes and goes. Sometimes—more than a month goes by." Her voice lightened to that.

All the knives were housed now except the six that had ringed her head, a zodiac sign filled with darkness.

"He will kill you."

"Never has yet."

He was silenced.

"Sorry. I meant—he doesn't really want to. Or somewhere in between."

He shivered. "Maybe you like it."

"Maybe, once."

"Not now?"

It came slowly. "Not now."

She turned. "Once I wanted him to kill me, but that was only at first— Odd, isn't it. Ought to be the other way round." Quickly she dropped her eyes, and knelt to set the box, heavy now, on the floor, straightening its double row of hafts. "Twenty-four," she said, and closed it. "You see—" she said, before she stood up again. There was something secretive about her face again, if not sullen—the cast of a struggle that could be as much against honesty as toward it. "I—used to be fond."

He bent and lifted the box. "They're heavy. Heavy as silver. Maybe Damascene."

"Could be."

"Better let me take them along with me."

"Why?"

"Why!"

She answered him with a half-shrugged wave of the hand. He saw why, of course. The sun, now sinking outside, had reached even here, dappling on mallet and rope, on quoit and bow and all other implements for game, as outside it must be touching, one by one for tomorrow's life, the trees.

"I don't like to take away any of it. He hasn't very much of his—of those years. Before he knew me. I don't like to—seem against him."

He stared at her.

"Don't you see? He did me an injury. Long ago. And he can't forget it. Forgive."

"So you have to let him keep on—trying."

"No. It was nothing physical. Not really. Not with *those.* He—" Her hand went to her mouth. "Oh—what does it matter? He married me under a false name." She made an odd, stretching grimace with her lips, like a child released from medicine. "No worse than what I did to him."

She swayed then, and he would have shut up—but she held her hand out, for the box.

"But don't you want anything else!" he cried. He heard it echo. "You could leave. Again." All the unaskable questions—to her, to anyone, tumbled out at once. "Can't you pity your*self*!"

"I can, I do," she said. "But not without Sligo."

They exchanged a glance conjoined but unseeing, the mutual hold of two people in their separate ways looking back.

"Don't come again." Her voice was harsh. "I can't afford the perspective."

For help, he turned to the man sleeping there. It was said that sleepers remembered what was said while they slept, poison or balm in the ear. He wondered. In the hospital he had seen nurses speaking for hours on end to catatonics, who it was said registered everything, and if their lips ever broke open again, would recall. No one could lie there as Sligo was, except in stupor, the head sideways on the arm now, position otherwise unchanged. He could think of nothing to tell that ear. "Hadn't I better help you get him to bed?"

"He gets up himself. After a while."

"Will he remember?"

"Not always. Not—for a while."

"Not until Mondays?" He slapped the box.

She held out her arms, hands cupped. Quite suddenly, he laid the box along them, and strode to the door. At his name, he stopped.

"You're welcome," he said, without turning.

"Guy—"

She was holding the box clasped to her as if it were an infant, or two dozen long-stemmed American Beauty roses. "Is it sick of me? That I stay."

Hair prickled on his nape. Questions on leaving were so often for the leaver as well. He heard an answer, long ago inserted in his own ear. "Without help—" He choked on it. "Surely—? But why do you ask me?"

She bent her head.

The door behind him was stuck with dampness. He kicked it open. No sun came with it. "Without help," he said again, half to himself, hand on knob. "I'll come Mondays."

When he got home, he began rustling up his usual meal for these nights, a cold evening supper anybody might have on his day of rest. During the week he was a fair enough straight cook, though he had never been able to become one of those over-interested bachelors. There were a number of other things he hadn't been able to become, again or newly, but these did not intrude on him now. His mind was the merciful blank that warded off the black infections of others. Later on, when properly immunized, he might safely ponder those, but not now. As he banged the refrigerator door open and closed, crackled butcher's paper and clinked dishes on a tray, taking comfort in all this domestic voodoo, he kept hearing a cat mewing at the small window which gave directly from bathroom shelf to high grass bank outside. He went to open it. The cat stepped in daintily among his toilet things, then drew itself up with the wariness of all cats that are helped. It was one he'd never seen before, a Siamese with the brown and buff markings called "points," and the clenched head of its breed—like a child's fist holding up eyes. At the sight of it, he could hear his mother, all her life a yearner for more than Hartford calicoes, sigh in her grave. This one would not be fed, but circled the house, calling, and after a minute he put it out again, through the same window. He himself preferred dogs.

When he had brought his tray to the screened porch—"terrace" the builder had called it—where he had all his meals summers, he heard the cat again, nosing at the screen and retreating somewhere into the dusk outside. He got up with a sigh of his own, fetched a dish of milk and set it outside, then sat down to his meal, on a low settle he'd placed to face the grove of trees that hid the river, holding the tray on his knees. Above the grove, the sky was still full of western light. After a moment, a cat came to feed, but not the first one—a black tom he'd fed once or twice before. Shortly, a high, silvery voice, young girl or young woman, wended here and there through the grove. "*Here,* kitty-kitty, here, Max. *Ma*-ax." The tom lifted its head, then bounded off, in the opposite direction. This drama too had occurred before. The voice, still calling, after a while always blended away. He'd never decided whether or not the cat was Max.

He was still eating when a girl in a bathing suit stepped into the clearing and came toward him, head bent. Halfway, she stopped, facing the trees, put both hands to her mouth as if she were blowing on a conch and said faintly, "Max?" Circling the barn, not calling again, she came round to the screen door, hands locked behind her, head still bent, saw the dish and gave a start of surprise, saw him, and palms at her chest, gave another. He smiled tentatively at her, not sure whether she could see this through the screen at this hour, but did not rise. The heavy tray held him indolent now. The thin figure, dim in its faded robin's-egg suit, barefoot, was close to a child's. And it was his porch, his clearing, hidden without sign or path, where even in daytime he was almost never surprised.

"Excuse me," the girl said, "but you don't *have* a cat, do you."

"Well, no, I don't. But I've been feeding somebody's."

"Oh." She seemed to peer in at him. "A black one? Oh, that's ours," she said, before he had a chance to nod.

"Oh, is he. I wondered. He always seems to run the other way."

She giggled. About fourteen, he'd say, with those pointed little breasts that couldn't be counterfeited, nor the way her hands latticed at them. "Oh, he's just one I found. He's been giving the others the worst habits. But the rest are really ours."

"Are they." He couldn't help his stiffness toward those who were too casual to the young of any breed, even when they were themselves the young of another. "There did seem to be several, and there didn't seem to be anybody—"

"My p—my people are away, you see." The manner was suddenly elegant, the voice theirs from five to fifty, kin to the one he'd left only an hour ago. "Which ones have you seen?"

The tray felt heavy on his knees, too awkward somehow to rise. He judged her after all about twenty. "There was a Siamese here, just a few minutes ago."

"*Itty*-Katty!" She clutched her brow. "Oh God and criminy, that's my mother's, she'll be frantic."

"And a striped one, yesterday."

"Fatty-Kitty! I haven't seen her for *two* days. Oh dear, will I catch it. They're not allowed in the house, you see. Because we've been staying at Gran's."

More likely twelve. She was small in size, and he hadn't been around children. Possibly even ten. "We could go hunt up Itty, er, Kitty," he said. "I don't think the other one's been around today. That is, Fatty, er, *Katty.* The striped."

"Got you!" she said, clapping her hands.

"I beg your—"

"Itty-*Kat.* Fatty-*Kit.* Oh it drives everyone wild. Scat-rhythm, to coin a pun—as my father says. Makes you say it on the downbeat, you see. The other would just be Dixieland." She peered in on him, as if at another world she expected to see there. "Jazz. We all pretend to be fa*n*atic on the subject. To annoy Gran." Her voice was suddenly shy.

"Tell me something," he said. "Is any one of those creatures named Max?"

"Why, that's the one you've been feeding!" she said. "The *lost* one."

"Oh, the lost one." He looked down at the dish. "Good old Max."

She giggled. "That's what my kid cousin said. Bill, he's a senior at Stanford. He was here till today, but he had to go back early."

Good old Bill. Eighteen? He gave up. It was the gloaming hour, just before all cats became gray.

"Oh, don't get *up*," she said. "You finish your meal, fevvens sake. And don't think of helping hunt—that's my responsibility. I was going to ask you a favor, but not that one. If it wouldn't be too much of a drag. Oh gee—well, *thanks*." As she came through the door, she looked up at him. All he could be sure of was that she wasn't ten. "I guess I ought to introduce myself, hadn't I, I'm Alden Benjamin, we live just down the road." She recited this rapidly.

"Oh, how do you do, I'm G—"

"Oh I know who you are, of course." She refused a chair and sat on the floor, clasping her knees. "You're Mr. Callendar. *Gwee* Callendar." This last came very softly, as if it were being tried out for the first time. "The tenant," she said.

"Ten—? Oh." He glanced up at his own eaves, the fine old triangulated ones, deep enough for swallows to nest in, on whose rescue he had rubbed his knuckles bare.

She giggled. "Oh, I *know*. Not really, any more. But it's always been called that, kind of, ever since the land grant—it was one, you know. Some revolutionary jerk, way back. And it's marked that way on the map that went with it—'tenant's land.' " She gave a small, convulsive smile. "They still like to think . . . you know how p—" She coughed. "—people are."

"Oh." He drew out a cigarette. "Your—people."

She nodded. "Parker and Buzzie."

"Cigarette?"

She lit the filter end. He gave her another. She addressed the trembling end of it, deeply. "It's just, you know, I smoke these plain fags."

He stood up again. "Just about to get myself another beer. Would you—?"

"Oh, no *thanks*. I mean, I *do*, but no thanks."

He brought back a Coke and a plate of store cookies, the filled kind.

She ate one. "Peanut butter! God. Haven't tasted it since I was six."

"Your—people," he said. "They're—your parents?"

"Oh dear." She sat back to survey herself, unclasping her knees. Sparks flew from her, and the cigarette. She retrieved it. "I catch everything, don't I know it. There was this boy at the Proot, he used to say it."

"The—Proot?"

"Prewitt Country Day."

"Oh." He remembered the term, from Hartford. "A school."

She stared. "It's just down the road from here." She waved a hand, inland. "I used to go there."

He often had a sense of how much in this landscape was just down the road from him, from childless people living in inns and barns. This was one of the times. "Which is which?" he said.

"Hmm?"

"Your people."

"Mummy is Parker." Suddenly she took another cookie. She gulped it. "Oh, you mustn't think—Buzzie is very dignified. He can't perform an instrument or anything, but he has this very serious interest. He even wanted to go to the Newport Festival, the jazz one. But Parker dragged him off to the Casals. Spain, or somewhere. She recruits for Gran, you see." She hefted a sigh. "That's why I'm here."

"To see me?"

"Oh, no. Well, partly. But I meant here in this godforsaken end of nowhere. *Home.*"

It was almost dark now. "You must have a huge view from there."

"Oh no, our part's all overgrown, been that way since I was a child, not that I mind. And Gran won't give us the money to—" She broke off. "Anyway, the only place you can see out is up-river. From Gran's tower."

"Oh yes, I think I've seen it," he said. "An old American Gothic. Way, way on south there, there's one open spot. Through those trees. But I should think my trees would block—the tenant's, that is."

In the dark, her eyes shone. "No. You're our view."

"Oh." It had never struck him that anyone could look in on his solitude. "Dull for you."

She was silent for a time. "Summer!" she said then. "Summer around here is sure a real dark nervous green."

"Nervous?"

"Oh God," she said. "Me again. I'm an absolute *ensemble.* We had a guest last week—Hollywood. That's what they say out there. For anything awful."

He repeated it. "It does have a lilt."

"Mmm." Her voice was shrewd. "So did he."

He turned on the porch light. "You mind telling me something? Exactly how many years ago was it you tasted peanut butter. Since you were six?"

She lowered her chin, then raised it. It was a more than nice face, not quite lovely, but sympathetically planed, already shaped both to give and to receive. She tilted it higher. "Ten. Ten and a *half.*"

He was less relieved than he should have been. "I judged you older, somehow," he murmured.

Her look said that his judgment was profound.

"All I ask is to be old enough to be natural," she said gruffly. "I just pray for it."

"Other way round, I thought. When you're young is when you are, I thought."

"Not when you're me. I'm just only bits and pieces of whosever's around. *Simply* hilarious." She gave a doleful shrug. "It can last on and on too, Buzzie says, the way it has with himsel—" She coughed. "Unless you have a serious interest." She flung her head back, and her hands—flung the world off. "I don't mind Gran, though. Funny thing, when a person is themselves, no matter what, they're not so catching. To me, that is."

"She's old enough, I gather? To be nat—"

"Boy!" She giggled. "I'm supposed to be looking after *her*—and the cats, of course. And she's supposed to be taking care of me. But that's Parker for you." She rested her chin on her knees, eyes up. "Anyway . . . summer around here is sure a . . . grim. I don't see how you stand it. I should think it'd drive you absolutely nuts." Then, with a horrified glance at him, she sat up very straight, open-mouthed, arms at her sides. He had a feeling that only manners, or perhaps the delicacy which already showed so plain on her, kept her from clapping a hand to that mouth.

He was used to this of course. One couldn't expect them to be as used to his history as he was. "Tell me," he said. "The favor you wanted to ask me."

From what he could see of her cheeks they were red, but she answered in his own tone. "I was wondering. If by any chance you were going to be around next weekend. Labor Day weekend."

"Why, yes." The past afternoon rose up in him, dark pool so alien from this light refreshment its own dusk offered him. "As a matter of fact—I was planning to."

"And you don't seem to mind cats. At least, you've been feeding them."

"We-ell, that's about it, I don't mind them. I prefer dogs, of course."

"Of course," she said. "But then—you don't have a dog."

He stared at her, at their image of this clearing, minuscule in their distance, across which a toy man, toy solitary, never walked a toy dog.

"Apparently Gran isn't too old for twenty-twenty vision," he said.

Her face was still pink. She kept it lowered. "Oh—she never goes up there. It's hot as blazes, and full of dead flies. Lucky for me. You see—they're supposed to be off the place altogether. The cats. And I've been keeping them up there, or trying to." She looked up at him. "Cats need a *place*!" Her lip trembled.

"And yours is closed up?"

"Rented. So *they* could go, you know. And we couldn't ask the renter to keep *four*. And for four, there just wasn't enough—well, a kennel was just—out. So it was up to—" She cast him a faint smile. "Gran never thinks about money. Far as she knows, that's where they are."

"So it was up to you," he said.

"Oh, I'm quite dependable."

"Yes." He watched that movie. "I can see that you are."

"And it would all work out," she said. "Only dammit, just for this weekend I'm being sent away."

"Ah yes," he said. "From your tower." When his powerful garage light was on, as it often was if he worked evenings, then his clearing must hang in the trees like a fair. Still, it was cruel of him. "Like Rapunzel," he said. "Or, no. Rapunzel was *kept.*"

"Oh, I'm not *de trop,* or anything," she said. "Gran wouldn't give a hang. It was Buzzie who insisted. She's having a very sophisticated bunch up for the weekend, some of her screamers—you wouldn't know about that—and . . . and I'm not supposed to be that sophisticated. So Parker had to arrange for me. Buzzie was really very strong about it." She looked proud.

"Good for Buzzie." A sudden thought struck him. "Cats give some people asthma," he said absently.

Her face fell.

"Oh, not me," he said hastily. "I thought perhaps that was why—"

"Gran? No, far as I know she just ha-ates them. Really she's just one of those people who's mortally afraid of them. There's a name for it."

"Mmm."

"If one comes in a room where she is, she jumps up on a table. They do rather go for her extra. They *know.*" She chewed a finger. "Could be her color too, of course. She's got some vein disease that doesn't bother *her* otherwise. But she *is* blue. I expect you've heard."

"N-no, I—" He leaned back, arms folded. "Your gran. Mrs. Aldrich. She jumps on tables. And she is *bl—?*"

"Really, rather turquoise."

"N-no," he said. "I h-hadn't." Hiccups engulfed him. "Heard."

She waited until he'd finished, to stand up. "I didn't think you'd laugh. At other people's misfortunes. I didn't really think you would."

"I didn't think so either." But he felt as if he had been for a swim in laughter.

"Or you don't believe me."

"I believe you," he said.

"I guess it was me then, you were— People do."

"No, it was a coincidence," he said. "I was laughing at the smallness of the world. Or the enormity. Anyway, please believe *me.* I can't possibly explain."

"Oh, I believe you," she said. "I certainly do. And I appreciate your language."

He stood up. "Cats need a place," he said looking down at her. "But I'm afraid you'll have to do the rounding up. Or else rename them."

"Oh!" she said. "Oh-h. I could come tomorrow morning and start feeding them here. I could come here every day, so that by Friday—I don't have to go, you know, for four whole days."

She was going to be a bore, the kind that could be painful. He hadn't come near one of her for years. He already wanted to get rid of her. She was the young. "Where are they sending you?"

She made a face. "Friends of Parker's. They have a girl my age, and they keep wanting us to be. We haven't a thing in common really. Bianca O'Brian. She's French."

"She doesn't sound very French."

"Oh, she had an ancestor—some marshal. To have an Irish surname in France is the utter. And her live grandmother is a princess in Rome."

"Oh? And what color is *she*?"

She giggled. Then she stood on one leg.

He sighed. "And is Bianca at the—Country Day?"

"Oh no," she gasped, "she's already been at Le Rosey. And at Brillaumont. They couldn't do a thing with her." The other leg twined. He watched, in fascinated recall of how it had once felt, to be literally beside oneself.

She began to speak very rapidly. "She has this little face that pooches out, and she wears her hair scissored all around it, the way they do. Y'know? As if some sex-maniac had been chewing it. And all she has to do is scatter this talk of hers, like birdseed, and the boys come hop, hop. And wherever we others are wearing our belts, she isn't."

"I hope it isn't catching," he said. "It's certainly utter."

"Oh, it's very poisemaking, to have a line," she said. "If you haven't yet got—the other." And finally, the leg came down. Standing there, all of her implored him to see that she would give anything to rid them both of her company.

He would have liked to pat her, in sympathy. Instead, he looked at his watch.

"Oh, I must go!" she said at once. "Gran will be wi-ild." Her hands crossed on her bathing suit. "I hope I haven't given you a—a false impression of us. We're really a very devoted family." It gave him a glimpse of how she might be, once she had achieved what she aspired to—and a wish to give her something toward it. He hadn't been able to give anyone else anything, all the long day.

"I knew a girl once," he said. "Only a very little older than you are." It came as a shock that Ellen had been only three years older than this girl when he married her. "She wasn't any prettier than you. And probably not as—smart." His voice ground. To think blasphemy was different from speaking it. "But she had a way with her, if it's any use to you—I suppose one could call it a line. Whenever anyone paid her a compliment, or she was at a loss, she used to look at him sideways—you'll know how—and say, *Oh, you're just saying that!*" Once, at Niagara Falls, Ellen and he had donned the oilskins they gave one, and had walked through a passageway under the back of the Falls. Strange images, octahedrons of glass were at the other side of them. Ellen stood with these now. "It was very fetching," he said. "It made the boys come hop, hop."

"Thanks," she said. "Thank-*you.* I'll study it up in a mirror sometime." Then she bounded away from him. He gathered that he had somehow offended her, but at least it had made her free as a gazelle. Across the glen, he watched her bound backward over a hedge.

His own youth had been awkward. "Pleased to meetcha!" he called from it. "Pleased to meetcha, Alden."

She paused, then she came running fleetly. Halfway across the clearing, her hands clasped at her breast exactly as before. She rediscovered the barn, the screen door, him standing there. A moon had risen since, and was coldly shining. Walking as if her bathing suit were a skirt, she included the moon. It was like watching a tic of the imagination—hers—acted out on his obviously dream-forested land. "You're just the way I thought you would be," she said softly. "Good night—Gwee."

She was there the next morning, and more of each day thereafter, sharing his lunches and once, in the company of a dealer-friend up from Pennsylvania, his supper, even offering him a muted assistance in the shop—and all with a manner so altered that he could find her unimportant presence lightly welcome. The dizzy reel of her confidences had altogether stopped, like a carnival ride shared by strangers. She made no more references to her family, and in his own mind they no longer struck the monster, papier-mâché attitudes she had so carefully pointed out to him along the ride. It was probable that they were quite ordinary, in their own way. Her subdued manner now almost called upon him to notice that so was she. Even the soapbubble chain of her giggling had vanished overnight, as if somewhere quieted at the fount. Overnight—it amused him to think—she might have consulted one of those Carmencitas who squatted over such matters behind windows crayoned with the zodiac, to which the words *Readings, Advisor* also adhered. Somewhere, in the depths of herself, she was being advised. In his own, he knew he was being worshiped, and felt himself too humble to question it. It was pleasant to find himself amiably concise with her in a way he was seldom able with his sharper-tongued New York friends—in the way perhaps, if things had been otherwise, that fatherhood sharpened the tongue. As a proprietor, he was used to lingerers, hangers-on, even apprentices such as, in the late, Urbino light of those August afternoons, pottering after him in her shirt and shorts, or shorn tan head seen bent across an intervening field of objects and tasks, she increasingly appeared to be.

In that light, age was their duenna—and her hair wasn't gold; she was merely in the absolute russet of health. He recalled better now how the flesh at that age was aureoled in its own fuzz. But, as she lounged, sun-struck in the doorway, he had no visual terror of her; she wasn't Ellen, but what might have been Ellen's child. A dealer had just left them. The shop's business was always by appointment; few itinerants came here.

"I admire you," she said. "For the way you do nothing and people just come to you." For the rest of the afternoon she was silent. It occurred to him, absent in mind as he'd been all week—or elsewhere in mind—that her prayer might be being answered; she was certainly more natural.

Early Friday morning, before leaving, she came by for an uncalled-for visit to the cats, who were by now accustomed to his feeding them. He was mildly surprised at her appearance as she bent daintily over their dishes—travel suit, hat and bag, hair brushed to a burnish, from what he could see of it, and a new, sooty dimension to her unremarkable eyes. When he heard she was walking to the station, he of course drove her there, and waited with her for the dusty, division local that would take her on to Grand Central, where she would be met by a chauffeur, she said, and driven on. The station, merely a junction beneath the once Indian highland, was bare of persons on this national weekend away. Beyond the sheds and other ramshackles, deserted outbuildings of another century, that quietly rotted here and at other up-Hudson junctions, the flat valley of water took the sun. As always, the wide expanse made him uneasy; he turned his back to it. The girl beside him, taking the compliment to herself, smiled gratefully. Now that she was leaving, he was suddenly great with a four-day-repressed need to be by himself again. When he put her bag up for her in the train, he was already irritated with her for making herself out a waif to him, as she could apparently do without moving an eyelash. There were others on the train dressed exactly like her, most with friends or parents it was true, but her own were returning in a few days. Still, her hat, though so regulation, reared back from her forehead like the pure feather of flight. He felt he ought to make it up to her, for not being able to keep his mind on her, somehow to explain to her that she was simply at that interim in her life when no one was around to do it. "Good-by," he said. "And good luck on the weekend, don't you worry now. You have no idea how different you look in shoes."

He hurried home to his house, to be alone with being alone there. It was good, infinitely good to mosey and loll, a man in no way bereft of the small things of life, one whose phone was contrarily atap with friends, waifs and petitioners—merely a man who preferred dogs, but had no dog. Toward dusk, he set his meal on a tray, and once more brought it out to the porch. No one, entowered somewhere in the tree-murmurs, was there to watch him. At last he was at peace enough, if it could be called peace, to dwell on what all week he'd been powerless to keep his mind from—to let it ring its changes inside him.

On Tuesday, he had called the Canal Zone. During the day, there'd been no reason to fear she might be bereft; Tuesday, when the place reopened at four, was always a big day domestically, with cleaning to be done, suppliers' salesmen to be dealt with, and the full staff in attendance, two waitresses, Carlos the cook, and sometimes Roy, the assistant barman. He had restrained himself from calling until six, the busy hour at the bar, when Sligo was always in attendance there. Roy had answered the phone. He had asked to speak to Marion.

"The missus, she's in the kitchen," said Roy. "Talkin' to Carlos."

Everyone knew of course that Carlos did drink; his temperament, often to be heard from the kitchen, was cherished as much as his cooking by those patrons who liked to think that they haunted a bar for its colorfulness. No one would have known of it otherwise. The staff, loyal to each other and apparently to the owners, never gossiped.

"You want to talk to the mister?" said Roy. "He's awful busy, Mr. Callendar, we got a rush on that IBM Country Club crowd."

"No thanks. Just ask her—" He hesitated. "I just called to find out if the lamp I left was okay. Just ask her if everything's all right. About the lamp."

"Okay, sir."

"Maybe I'll stop by myself to check on it tomorrow," he added half to himself, as Roy hung up.

He did that. During the period when he had helped furnish the upstairs, the staff had grown used to his checking. Wednesday afternoons, as he knew well enough, Sligo and Marion were usually in town with the station wagon, doing all the weekly errands from meat inspection to talking improvement loans with the bank manager. He pretended to have forgotten this.

"Wednesday their town day," said Roy. It was the usual midweek afternoon, trade dull. Everything appeared normal. Of course, everything always had. Why was he here?

"One day gets to be like another, out where I am," he said. He knew how to talk to Roy, not that it took anything special; anyone did.

"Out where anybody is, around here!" Roy said at once. "I tell you, Mr. Callendar, we can't wait for winter." Winters, Roy did the Miami run. "We" meant his wife and mother, as devoted as he to the crowd, the tables, the money, the sun and the sea, in that order—to all the bigtime externals of life. It was hard to imagine any of the three ever suffering from one of the inner varieties of love-death, certainly not from love of death, or even perhaps from the death of love. They were happy. But knowing how to talk to Roy meant knowing that even he, they, were in their own way extreme.

"When you going?" Guy said.

"December twenty-sixth, leave here six-thirty A.M.," Roy said promptly. "I drive the buggy down, U.S. 1 all the way. Ma and Vee fly National. Next night we'll all three be in our suits at the beach, dinner at the Alcazar. And three nights after. I don't start work till the first."

"Sounds wonderful." He was having trouble keeping his mind on Roy. He stared at the diamond ring in its glass case. Roy's blunt, shaven head didn't shadow it.

"I tell you. Whyn't you pick up and go down. Even for good, you could make a living. They got antique shops galore." Roy was capable of assuring a banker that Miami had banks.

"Maybe I will."

"I tell you." Roy leaned forward. Now came the climax of this refrain. "If we could stay down there—" The preamble was always the same, the conclusion too. Only the metaphor varied. "If we could stay down there—!" Each of Roy's eyes shone as if it were the only one he had. "Nee one of us ever ask nothing more in this life. Nee one of us ask for two more tail feathers from a duck."

He almost forgot to make the drink-offer which was the ritual end of this conversation.

It was answered with the ritual headshake. "Thanks, Mr. Callendar. But I'll have a cigar."

He put his elbows on the bar, trying to recall how it felt to lean outward into life from some heavy focus, glowing or dark—instead of cordially, temperately, holding the phone. "Roy?" he'd said, as if Roy could tell him. "Roy—what's your last name?"

Roy, just nipping the cigar, looked up. He spat the tip. "Grotz. Roy *Valerian* Grotz. Must be why I became a bartender, huh, whoever asks a barkeep his full name?" He doffed the cigar. "You ever ready for info ree down there, you just write me. Care of the Alcazar."

"Thanks," he said, "I just came to wonder. Don't know why in particular." Looking round the calm, empty bar, with its faint smell of bitter from old limbos, he'd shivered his shoulders. "Certainly not waiting for winter."

"You're telling me!" said Roy.

When he came home, he found a note from Marion in his mailbox; she must have driven by to put it there. "Please don't call. And don't come. My thanks." With the proper chance, he might have met them there at the end of his driveway, she bending to thrust the note far back in the box, Sligo sitting immobile in the car as one sometimes saw him, hunched forward in the posture of men in World War I statuary groups—a member of the Battle of the Marne temporarily hacked from his stone brothers. Marion always drove.

Thursday—last night—his dealer friend, Sprague, had stayed for supper, and the girl. Though he addressed her by name, in his mind she was "the girl." He'd been grateful for both their presences. In the summer dimness after the hot glade of the day, as they sipped the wine Sprague had brought, the rise and fall of their own voices had had a pre-fall, alfresco charm. The girl had sipped too, with an over-distinguished air.

"Nice kid," Sprague had commented, in a moment when the girl had gone in for a bit.

"Lonely summer," said Guy.

Sprague nodded. "I get 'em from the summer theaters. Apprentices. Sent round to borrow." A former painter, he now dealt mostly in authentic American primitives, had a shop in the Poconos, and knew Joe and Milly Pink. "Terrible stuff they have," he said.

"Terrible." He listened to the echo. "Their boy is getting married."

"Oh, I know that boy. Different from them." Sprague, pouring himself another, had gestured with the bottle in the direction where Alden had gone. "Like her, they're luckier. Kids like her, you can see their whole background behind them, ahead of them, too. Meet a boy of the same, and with a little luck they'll live their whole lives that way. Lost in the background. The best way."

Sprague's history was unknown to him, or whether Sprague knew his—but that each had an unlikely one was one of the comforting assumptions of their trade.

"She looks a little like that print you have inside there," said Sprague. "The girl in profile—who's it by, Polliaiulo? Just a pretty girl of the day, but you can see the whole Renaissance behind her. I've got a little Federalist one at home now. A stiff little girl of the period, all her life, probably. Only the painter happened to single her out. She isn't the subject anymore. The subject is 1810." He gestured again at Alden, who had just reappeared, and was now circling the porch, fiddling with the cats' dishes. She bent there with the bursting shyness of one who knew herself the question. "Girls like that are like stencils," he said. "For what's around them. Boys too, of course. Hmm. Used to wish I could paint that way. You know? I wanted to do it for now."

Alden came in and sat again at the table.

"What's the name of this county?" Sprague asked her.

"Dutchess."

"There you are!" said Sprague. "Girl of Dutchess County, with the light behind her. American primitive, *circa* 1970, artist unknown. All I need is a hundred years."

"A hundred years and I'll be dead!" said Alden gaily. She flung it out like a garland.

"They'll be nice ones, honey," said Sprague. "Just marry some neighborhood boy."

"*This* neighborhood?" she said.

Both he and Sprague had roared, of course. "Alden's family is musical," he had said, in reparation.

"How about that!" Sprague had answered, with the trade's tone-deafness. "I took in a harpsichord once. Inlaid with Wedgwood medallions. Not the blue jasperware either. The gray."

He thought now of the girl riding to her destination, for today, somewhere on Long Island—of whether she would ride all her life jogging in the "background" expected of her, through the minor hazards to the final, profound ones—all of her happily submerged life. Right now, as Sprague had said, she was only a mild darkness at whose edges one could see the whole bright pattern of her segment of life, from costume plates of the period to chapbooks of the road-and-home-life of the times. It was in her very voice and no doubt in the fillings of her excellent teeth—all the successive decades of the woman she would almost certainly be, already counterparted by the versions of such women to be seen, in their own decades from blond hair to mauve, in the streets and shops of towns near places like Garrison. And it didn't have to be that stratum, of course. A same unconscious innocence of itself could work in any—he remembered Hartford. As Sprague had said, innocence of its own import was what was required, of the life that was the subject, as well as of the painter's hand. And even for those who knew themselves to be the extreme, there might be degrees of innocence. All that was needed was a hundred years.

As for Alden, the girl— He looked up at the trees, behind and behind whose layers there was somewhere a tower from which she had spied on him. He thought of the feather in her hat. Probably the next ten years would show. It might be touch and go—as to whether or not she would be singled out.

Toward dark, the Siamese returned to the edge of the clearing. All that week she had been away—since Monday. Her flanks were fallen in. As she drank greedily from one of the other cats' saucers, he remembered with a contraction of sadness how, last time, she had proudly refused to be fed. When she had cleaned herself, she stood off and regarded him, eyes opening and closing, head tucked in. He had no trouble identifying of whom she reminded him—that snub head, those mask-clenched eyes. Nor had he any intention of taking her return as an omen—this random, itty-kat vagrant between silk pillow and forest. Just because he was now aware of what must have been being enacted for years at the Canal Zone, didn't mean he could interpose there. Marion's note had made him see his place—he was audience. All the watching in the world couldn't force their stagelight closer to his own quiet demi-brown. After a while, as the moonless night closed in, he could no longer see for sure whether or not the eyes were still regarding him. Only a stencil remained, a head-shaped importance of darkness with the light behind it—ringed round with knives.

On Saturday, as he did the week's shopping in town, he found himself looking with a purpose, in the store queues and the parking lots, down the market streets and at crossings. He was looking for a family, never the same one of course but one always constituted the same, that over the years had now and then presented itself to him without warning. He didn't see them. But the quality of the change came home with him, like the edge slid into one at the change of seasons. He had never before looked.

On Sunday, he began the turnout of the barn, long self-promised, and never yet done. The weather was glorious, as people were no doubt saying all over the nation. Out on that highway from which he was a quarter-mile in, the smart ones were already bearing back to the city, to be safe there on the murderous third day of the holiday. There and elsewhere, cars must already be smashing and piling up, duty bound to fill in that annual Tuesday headline for which the funeral presses were waiting. Tuesday seemed to him distant as a new life, or an old one that had to be resumed. It was Monday, day of the smash, that had to be got through, here where the great stasis of land, water, and tree would uphold him in the silent conjunction of all their valleys. As he dragged object after object out on the lawn, none, however curious, lovely or valuable, seized him with that griping in the bowels of possession which afflicted others of his trade. He was neat of habit; there was really no need for this housecleaning. But he had an urge to see the barn as empty as it had been when he came. Meanwhile, there were corners of his eyrie he had forgotten. He turned up the first table he had refinished but had never sold, of itself an honest maple, but in the last rays of daylight too auburn by far. In its drawer, he found the one relic he had saved from the burned rubble, only because it predated it—a small vase of cloudy glass with a cheap scene scratched on it, from its position in his mother's window, in his childhood always called the "sunset" vase. By nightfall, the place was emptied, except for his huge rolltop desk, weighted with business, that had been the first thing in here anyway, and hanging above it, that archaic reminder to "Resource." He left those two inside, all the rest of the array turned out to the starlight. The night was as clear and soft as the inside of a grape; no rain would fall. Even if it did, all he stood to lose was some of the money which helped to keep him suspended in life, immovable to the waves of need. And he had all Monday to put everything back. He brought his bedroll to the center of the lawn, and lay for a long time looking up at the barn's dark ogives, that now seemed to breathe with him, in their earlier communion. The barn was what he loved; he had rescued it.

By late afternoon Monday, he had everything back inside and in order again except for the lamps and the pictures, touches of comfort with which he would fill out the evening. He walked down to the mailbox on the highway: though there wouldn't be any mail, there was always a chance that someone had left a note there. And it was his usual walk. Less than halfway back, having found nothing, he heard the clear bell of the telephone, brought to him by the river, a nagging rhythm of a phone that went on for a long time. It had stopped well before his desperate run brought him up short in front of it. The call had been a friend's of course, faithful Poll perhaps, homing from her three-day weekend, or Quent reporting in, or any other of his phone regulars, like him suspended in a network of friends, not relations—horses running abreast in their own National, and today, like the rest of the world, galloping home. Still he stood there, and at last he dialed the Canal Zone.

On the instant, he heard the buh-beep, buh-beep of the busy signal, a quietus he might listen to now for as long as he wanted. They had taken the receiver off, as usual. They were in the eyrie couples made for themselves. That settled it. He listened to it telling him so—just then, it stopped. On the other end, someone had replaced the receiver. He redialed, heard the ring and the connect. No one spoke, but the wire was live; he could hear heavy, animal breathing. "Sligo?" he said. "It's Guy." In the pause, he could still hear that strangely reassuring pulse of brute calm. Then the line went dead. "Sorree," said the operator, when he made his plea. "Sorree," she repeated—a flute stuck at the stop of eternal patience. "That line is out of order now." He hung there, in the queer dejection, less paralyzed than timeless, of those accustomed to lives ordered and rebuffed by the phone. When he wheeled about, the girl was standing in the archway of the barn.

"Well . . . hi!" he said. It was hard to focus on her, but he was grateful for it. "Welcome back."

She was dressed just as he had last seen her, in what must be her "best" and now showed up as rather badly worn, and perhaps not even hers to begin with. Only the angle of the hat was still freshly her own, as if just before he turned she had reached up and knocked it back like a forelock. At his blinking smile, her hands clasped at her breast. It didn't go with the hat.

"Well," he said, "and how was Bianca La Borgia?"

She shook her head ruefully. "Don't. We were horrid."

"Oh, were we?"

She took a step forward. "Why didn't you tell me?" she said deeply. "That your name wasn't Gwee."

He couldn't think of an answer.

"Bianca says you would pronounce it the English way. *Guy.* And that even if you didn't, the French don't say Gwee, but G-gee."

"They do? I don't know French."

A perfect aureole spread on her face, in time with a long intake of breath. "If that isn't just like you."

"Not to know French."

"No," she said, on another breath like a chord. "To be the way you are."

"Tell me about Bianca," he said.

She spun halfway on a heel, came inside, touched a table, intimately tap-tapped a lamp. "Oh, you've changed things around. You've tidied." She gave him a gay smile, turned away again, and spoke nonchalantly over a shoulder. "There were some boys there too. Putrid. We both agreed on that. Simply putrid. Anyway, Bianca had to wear her retainer the whole weekend."

"Her—" Impossible medievalisms came to mind.

She gave him one of her shrewd, flat looks. "Teeth. She's having them straightened. And she cheated all last year in Switzerland, and didn't wear it. Now she's getting to look all chipmunky again, so she has to." She almost giggled. "When she has it in, her mouth looks just like Penn Station. Which reminds me." The giggle was born as a shrug. She whirled again, infinitely Gallic. "Anyway, the boys had to hang around somewhere, and—I was there."

He grinned. "All in your own teeth."

She hung her head. "Of course," she said in a low voice—"I didn't let them make out, though."

"Oh?" The phrase was new to him. "Of course." He felt like a father. "Er—Penn Station, what were you going to say that it reminded you of?"

"Oh that. Bianca's dream. We sat up all night, exchanging them. She has this dream she's walking around inside something's mouth, a great big pink cave. She has it all the time."

He laughed out loud. "Common enough to all races. Jonah and the whale."

She stared meaningfully, making their eyes meet. "Don't be sil-*ly!*" Then she blushed. And suddenly she began to speak very rapidly. "Bianca says, you should never let a boy your own age make out. She says in France it's the same for girls as for men now; you have your first *aff-aire du coeur* with a much older person. Like in *Bonjour Tristesse.*"

"You forget I don't know French. He took out a cigarette but didn't offer her one. "Is that why she cheated—in Switzerland?"

She nodded, head bent.

He lit the cigarette. "Well, I can see you certainly stayed up all night."

"We talked a lot about you. Bianca thinks—" She whispered it. "Bianca thinks you're wonderful."

"Oh, she does, does she. Why, what could that little—what could she possibly—" He broke off, to look at her.

"Your . . . your *life,*" she said. She was close enough for him to see that her eyes had filled with tears but that she was holding on to them, not letting them spill. It was too lovely a sight to turn from. He could see what she was going to be.

"Aren't you going to ask me about the cats?" he said.

"Oh, the cats—they can manage." The new planes about her mouth quivered, in time with her shrug. This time, she carried it off.

"You know . . . Alden," he said. "I believe you've made it. You're natural."

"Oh? And meanwhile I've changed, I'd rather be a mystery." She said it lightly, and carried this off too.

"You are," he said. "I suppose you're both." She was near enough for him to identify her smell. He was stupid enough to touch her on the shoulder.

"Oh—" She made the most awkward of gestures, a cygnet breaking its glassy dream of itself—and yet saving it. She touched her throat, jerking her hand away from it toward him, as if, if she could, she would give him its apple. "Oh," she said. "You're just *saying* that."

The kiss tasted of all she wanted to give him. He held on to her, merged in what for her was only a whole summer's ache. Behind them, the barn waited, a bed among the trees, prepared. He well remembered that summer of himself. But even while he held her, in this silence a quarter-mile from the highway, he could hear within himself the sound of lives, regular as rockets, riding to their Monday smash. He had his perspective. He was the one who was unnatural here.

He was able to force her away from him. She was smiling, not in retrospect. He couldn't see the landscape she was looking at, but he could remember how it had felt to be there. "I'd like—"

He stopped, for honesty. That his wife had been just this age when he'd had her, that his own child would have been the same age by now, was merely one of these peculiar marvels of time from which people made almanacs, hoping to tether within reasonable, man-made bonds the life that kept escaping onward. If this girl once stayed the night, she'd want to stay on always—he knew that much about her. She was no Bianca. And a week ago—he knew himself as well. A week ago, he would have singled her out.

"But I've got to go," he said. It was true, the minute he said it. "I've got to run off this minute to somebody, somewhere." He put his hand on her cheek. "It's the only thing I can say to you worth a dime."

He could see its worth, from her face—even at her age. He was the one who was running. She was the audience.

She knelt to the line of feeding dishes and hunched there, playing hand-over-hand with them.

"It's important, where I'm going," he said. "That much you can believe."

She stood up; she nodded—both with her new grace. More than this was beyond her. "See you around."

"Oh, Alden," he said. "Luck." He said it as if he could give it to her. "Luck!"

She must have looked at him this way from her tower, small but dependable, up among the dead flies, and the dark nervous greens of summer. She was able to toss her head. "No sweat!" she said. A talisman floated down to her from somewhere, a bit of Hollywood or Stanford, or even Spain. The corners of her mouth turned down, or in. "Don't sweat the small stuff!" she said.

When she was well enough away, he reminded himself how seventeen loved promises. "And Alden—"

She turned, as if to a teacher, or a parent, without hope.

"No more binoculars. Promise me?"

Whatever her age was, it judged him. "Opera glasses," she said. "Parker's."

She was well into the trees, almost lost to view, before he called after her. "The Siamese! The Siamese came back."

—

Out on the highway in his car, it couldn't be said that he had forgotten her, an after-image still resident in his body, in his now conscious flesh—the catalyst—sunk like a performer through a trapdoor. Around him, real cars whizzed loud as imaginary ones, but with the coarser hopes of people who were on the move. He wanted to put it to them, call out to them—I'm with you again. I'm part of this violence.

The road to the Canal Zone was solitary in the dusk, but halfway there, he thought he saw lights—were there people? It was the hour on the riverland when brilliance came and went in patches of gilt, the mauve mingling with the sun. His step crunched on the gravel. The courtyard was empty. In it, the Canal Zone squatted with the prescience of an old building, at dusk aware of all its history, tawdry and benign. The lower level of the games room was black under its overhung eaves. The top story, where the bedrooms were, was dim. Light was pouring like music from all the windows of the main floor bar. He could see the chandeliers at every second-story window, at battle with the retreating sun. Who could have entered the close-coupled dream that went on here, that only the personae themselves made real? Yet there wasn't a sound, not a sound of trade.

Then in the bedroom story, a window was flung up. A figure appeared between its shutters and looked down at him. Beneath her wrists, the dim, pompom row of geraniums were a row of footlights that hadn't sprung on. "How did you know?" she said. "I rang and rang, but no answer, and then he . . . how did you know to come?"

Now that he saw she was safe, he understood better his own errand—he knew for whose rescue he was here.

"Your phone's out of order now." This was reality; he remembered it—a blow, good or bad, that slowed the mind.

"He's cut the wires. Oh, hurry. I haven't heard him for the last hour. I'm afraid . . . that he—"

"Where is he? Down there?"

"Go there first," she said. "I can wait." She saw his bewilderment. "I'm—" Her shame told him that he was still a stranger. "I'm locked in."

He ran up the service stairs, and released her. They crept down them, interlaced like skaters. "What's that you have in your hand?" he said, but she was already ahead of him, across the passage into the main barroom.

"Yes," he heard her whisper to herself. "Yes."

Sligo stood in the damage like a man in a prism, angled at from all sides. His posture, bent at the knees, head in the vise of the shoulders, arms close to his sides, was like that also, a double image of a big man superimposed on a smaller one, a man enclosed in the bottle of himself. Around him, chairs were kindling, tables crumbs of zinc, their chromium legs junked skyward. A tidal hand had swept the glasses and decanters to a thousand refractions, through which waters were still seeping. The mahogany pillars of the bar had been scored, and behind them, the dark pride of the room, the etched mirror that ran its width, was irised open from end to end.

His eyes were what was moving. By these, they too could see his hallucination. It traveled wall over wall, haunted corners, or was sometimes beneath him, a small thing that teased. He tremored to it. Sometimes he screamed to it, though no one could hear. Clearly, he himself knew he was *seeing* it. In the hospital, these had been the most desperate.

Behind him, Marion crept closer, in her hand a syringe. His eyes whitened in their sockets; he saw her. Now that he saw her, she walked steadily toward him, at a bridesmaid's pace. He trembled under her advance, but differently. He saw her, and knew she was real—this was her role. Above their heads, one saw the thousand refractions of it, of who might have forced the role on whom.

She stood beside him now, waiting. It was like a wooing. And quite suddenly, he was able to move. He moved with caution, outward through the parallelograms. He even pantomimed to her that he wasn't dangerous. See, I'm only grasping for the bar, steadying myself against it. So that I can stand, and bear what you have for me. His lips turned in. The sound that came from behind them wasn't fear, but the catholic moan of all animals, forgiving someone for the general pain. Then he held out his left arm. Cool as a lay sister, she took care of him. Then she stepped aside. But her eyes flickered a signal, at Guy.

Sligo surveyed them, amiably. Sleep was already arriving in him; he was sane with it. The shakes caressed him once, then he stood pridefully straight. He extended his right arm, palm stiff, as one did for doctors; he could have balanced a tray. Slowly he clenched the hand to a fist, drew the fist in toward his own chest and outward, shoulder high, his eye following it as if magnetized. Head in bas-relief, he stood that way, a gladiator measuring the strength in his mortal glove. He spoke to it, clearer than Guy had ever heard him, but his eye did not turn. It wasn't possible to say whom he addressed—a plaster cast perhaps addressing its own inhabitant, its small Greek soul.

"I saw you coming," he said. "All the time."

He raised the fist, triumphant. Too late, they saw, shining beneath it on the counter, the glass case, still intact with its ring. He plunged the fist in through the case and down. As the glass trap darkened with his blood, he smiled.

It was Guy who broke the box apart and got it off with his own quickly bleeding hands, his shoe, and some implement Marion brought him, that dropped back into the rubble again, unidentified. By a miracle, the artery wasn't severed; with all the glass splinters in the flesh, they couldn't have tourniqueted it in time. By some miracle so often granted to the Williams of this world, to the Sligos.

And now, Sligo's hand lay upturned in the sedated sleep that had finally overcome it, its owner, once more deserting his bystanders, stretched on the floor to which this time he had slipped so easily. It had been so lucky that the sedation was already in him; his bystanders could never have overcome him in time. By the usual luck. On the hand, the many surface cuts and slices had flooded with red on the instant, filling the box like an ewer. But the wound on the wrist, that should have been the worst, was nothing, already puckering and congealed—not a fine seam, but a seam. Beneath it, whatever directed this man still pulsed, an anatomist's secret.

And she was finished crying now, or retching—the sound, dreadful as it was, a relief to him, a sign that her life had not rendered her inhumanly able to bear anything. Still, her competence was what he had to fear. He held her, each contracted toward one another, inward and away from the blood that was sticky and dried on them both.

Finally she was able to speak. "It's the—repetition of it. The repetition. I can take each separate time. But the other finally gets to you. Like a rhythm. Like killing with drums—don't they do that somewhere?" She slid apart from him, from where they sat, on the floor too. "And now you're part of it," she said. "Of our Mondays."

He stood up at that. "Oh, no. No, Marion. *No.*"

Her eyes were the first to lower. "Of course not. How could I think—?"

"Because it's your habit, to—" To defend, he'd been going to say, but saw that it wasn't just. "Because it's gone on so long, whatever it is. A kind of double dream." He brushed himself off, plaster dust and other crumbs, wooden splinters, and here and there, a sparkle. He bent to take her hands, and didn't take them. "He's got to go to a hospital, you must know that. Not a local one. Not for local wounds. A place where he can be—for a long time."

When she spoke, it seemed she hadn't heard this. "I lied to you," she said. "Last time. When I said 'I *used* to be fond' . . . I don't know really, what I *used* to be." She looked up. "So I don't know—what I am now."

"As it happens," he said. "As it happens, I—I know of such a place. Usually it takes longer to get in, much longer. But if I ask—" He swallowed. "I think they'll come on my say-so. I think they would come, in an hour or so. Today. Now."

Her glance wandered, vague over a shoulder. "The phone's . . . *cut*." The voice might have come over just such a line.

"That stuff you gave him," he said. "Can I leave you here with him? How long does it last?"

"For hours," she said. "You can leave him. I often do."

"I'll go in the car, then."

The scar marks under her eyes stood out sharply. The resemblance bled him, but instructed.

Finally she spoke, an inch nearer. "The public phone booth, in the games room. It's separate. I forgot that."

She got up and followed him to the door, picking her way through the breakage. "While you . . . I'll—pack a bag for him. And I'll—" She looked down at her stained hands and dress, almost thoughtfully. He nodded. Both of them cast a backward glance at the room's ruin. From hers, he couldn't tell what she thought of it.

When he had phoned and had cleaned himself up in the little washroom under the stairs, he looked in again at the main bar. The figure there lay just as they had left it. There was no one with it. No answering call came from the upstairs bedrooms. He went down to the games room, in its heavy-browed way a beautiful room when bare of people and left to its armorial shadow. He had no panic at not finding her here. She would have a place of her own, where she could hide. It was intended that he find it. Through the open door, he saw a bright sweater, down on the pier.

He walked down to the little pier, past the over-cute tables and umbrellas toying against the river, the paper scurf of tourists, the beach unused, lapped and lonely, the water healing dark through its pebbles. She was there, on a last bench. He sat down beside her.

The long evening, projected by the river, was still alight. Less than an hour had passed since he had arrived here. There was still a disc of sun, the part that always sank within minutes.

"Will they come?" she said.

"In a couple of hours."

They were well out from shore here, naked to the whole expanse, whose orange magnificence would for some time hold off the arriving blue.

"Open views make me uneasy," he said after a while. "They didn't used to. Before. Or when I was a child. But maybe that's because in those days, we didn't have a view."

"I couldn't do without this place. I grew up on the river, but it's not only that. Nobody comes here much, and it's always—" She stood up, spread her arms.

Behind him, he felt her turn to look back at the house. He didn't turn with her. In front of him, the long casement of water extended, infinitely extended, on and on. In that wide, stealing amber, the little beach in front of them lay suspended, as small in that infinity as his mother's sunset vase, with its paintscratch of beach and one palmetto.

"There's not enough ruin there!" he heard her say. "There's not enough ruin to *show*."

His lips were stiff. "There never is."

When she sat down again at her end of the bench, she was as he'd always known her, the old Marion, remote, cold with an experience whose poles he was only beginning to see. He waited. This time there was no other way to help.

She spoke, an inch nearer. "Do you—want to know about it?"

He looked back at the Canal Zone, at a house which, for all its ruin, was still standing. "The original injury?"

"In comparison with what we made of it, you mean." He felt her grimace.

"I've no such secrets to tell you," he said, turning. "Everybody already knows my—" His life was on the roster for all to see, an open book. He was used to the humility of it.

Her head was lowered. "I once heard you say—you come from Hartford."

"Yes. . . . Why?"

"I went to school in a little town not far from there."

"You did? Which one? I know all the schools up there—and all the towns." He paused. "But you grew up here, you said. On the river."

She nodded. "Then you'll have heard of it, maybe. It had rather a—gardens. And a fence. Miss Trent's? In Netherton?"

Once more. Reality slowed the mind—a profound deduction, especially twice. Once more, out of his sphere. "Yes," he said, "I've heard of it."

"Mmm." She was facing away from him. The sun edged down—gone. The world was flowing; let humans never forget it. "Well, you know that old story, the girls who marry their riding masters? You ever wonder what happened to them?" The sunless air showed him every line of her face. "To her."

"I had a theory about you," he said. "But it went the other way round." On one of the hands in her lap there was still a faint smear of brown. He touched it. "This happened, then? Sligo."

"No!" she said, rubbing at the smear. "Not Sligo. Not yet. Ferenc Von Dombaretski, Captain. Son of Captain the same, of his something Majesty's umpteenth Hussars. Polish on the one side, Magyar on the other. Miss Brown, who was the Miss Trent of our day, told us how to pronounce it—Magyar. He rode like a prince, she said, too well for us really, but his mother wasn't noble. He had a bale of uniforms, swords, saddles, medals and brasses, that filled the chauffeur's cottage. Hereditary candlesticks—knives. And always the stories, stories about horses." She folded her hands. "And at the foot of his bed, a pair of black velveteen house slippers with silver crests on them, much worn."

He made the sound one made to children detailing their nightmare.

"Oh, yes, very long ago," she said. "I was seventeen."

"Ferenc Von Dombaretski," he said. "Sounds—he was a fake, then?"

"You know—" She was silent a space. "I don't know for sure. I've never been sure. And later on, of course . . . it didn't much matter."

On the river it was later on, too, but still tartar yellow and bronze. Even the world at times thought slowly.

"There's such a lot I don't know," she said. "You wouldn't believe how much. There's so much I missed."

"And a lot you know," he said. "A hard exchange. Never belittle it."

After a while he said, "Don't look back at the house. When they come, we'll hear them. Go on."

"On? Why, that's all there was, really. The rest, you know enough to imagine. In a straight line."

A straight line would be horses, men of that same bowlegged world. "Then, Sligo?" he said. "Then you married *him*?"

She looked at him for so long that he could see the *plage* darken behind her, at the pace of the seal-colored cloud traveling west like a barge. "The original injury. Have you forgotten it?"

"A false name!" he said, then. "It *was* Sligo, un0der a false name."

"Yes. Yes. There wasn't a Von Dombaretski, anymore. Oh, there had been. All his papers and medals, Miss Brown saw them—they were always very careful at Trent. And all his gear, that Sligo, traveling with him for so many years after all—had inherited." She gave a short laugh. "That's what happened to her, that girl. It was even more romantic than one had imagined. She didn't marry the riding master. She married his Irish—ostler—they once used to call it. It has its own lineage. Groom."

"I see," he said.

"Are you sure you do? Do you see that this wasn't what I minded? Do you see that after all of it, in spite of it—and in spite of the fact that I couldn't half talk to h.im, and he couldn't or wouldn't—what I minded was that I . . . *still*?" She sat back. "Oh, there were the social things too of course, my family cutting me, and my friends too, and no money—but I was young, resilient enough. That was only the part of the story you'd expect. But it was the other, that did us in. That he could never get used to what he'd done, or to me he'd done it to. And that I—" She choked on it. "That I—*still*—" She touched Guy's arm. "You know something? After all these years, I don't know him well enough to say whether it's that he can't talk to me, or he won't. After all these years."

He thought of the diamond, thankfully lost somewhere in the shards back there, and of all she must know about fakes that became real.

"And then—" Her voice was hard. "Then *I* began to do *him* injury. I was built for it, of course. Speech, taste, needs, a million discriminations people like me, girls like me, didn't even know we were born with. Oh I was primed for it." Again she put her hand on his arm. "Do you know?" she said, her voice so charged, so tender that he caught an unbearable glimpse. "He just couldn't think what else to do when Von Dombaretski died. Since he was fourteen, he'd spent his life with him."

"So you've never stopped pitying him," he said.

The cloud passed on, stately.

"When I said I didn't want or hope for anything—" she said. "I lied. The inn was my idea—an aunt died and left me money. We were on our uppers, we hadn't known anything else but uppers, and it looked like heaven. The years we worked on it—those weren't so . . ." She got up and strode away to the edge. Standing there she looked back, inland. "But now—how I hate it, how I hate it. I see all I don't know, here. Everything passes by here. All the possible. It's like perfume. All the possible passes by."

In his mind's eye, in his muscles, he got up from the bench, seized her by the shoulders and shook her, not for herself alone.

As she strolled back to him, he watched her absently pause to turn over a crushed paper cup with the toe of her shoe. She stooped to tear it up and bury the fragments. He saw how the beach—merely a prospect to the inn—was tended.

"So now you know. What we made of it—between us." Crouched over, not a foot from him, she prodded the sand again. This time, only a natural object was revealed, a worn stone. "What *I* made." Stone in palm, she looked up at him. "Too much."

He bent and drew a finger along each of those permanent shadows on the bone, her cheek marks, tracing what almost could be seen there beneath them. "No—you couldn't have helped it. You—were singled out."

At that moment, a gun reported, clearly—even with the ricochet of the river, not a gnat in the ear. She stood up. He stood up with her. The Canal Zone watched them grasp one another. All the possible passes by.

Color returned to her face slowly. "From the Point—West Point. A sunset gun, I guess. You can always hear it on hazy days here, when sound travels north."

Across her shoulder the night was arriving—volumes of blue through whose drift, down all the darkening inlets of the shoreline she must know so well, there were being lighted, one by one, the small, persistent fires of habitation. It was said of people native to this place that even if brought up from a cellar blindfolded, they could tell which way they were turned to the current of the river—by the play of the air on their faces, in the felt promise of the harbor.

"Can you see my place from here?" he said.

She took his hand and guided it. "There. Between there and there. That's your place. Between the dark stretch, and that one high light that's just gone on. There you are—in that great fan of trees, some of the biggest on the river. They hide the barn though, even when the leaves are off, in winter."

He thought of her standing here in the ice-gray winter days of people who live in inns, looking past his trees and forward, watched by whom? It was always the other people who had the view.

"I suppose . . . they'll send an ambulance?"

He nodded. Arms still around her, he understood the strain words must put upon those blind who remember or dream of another communication. The inn watched them, as if only it had sufficient history not to judge.

"Do I go along in it? With him?" She bowed her head. "I suppose."

In each window of the Canal Zone, a chandelier stood out strong against the night, beside each, its double. They had conquered the day.

He seized her by the shoulders and shook her. "Pity *yourself.* For God's sake. So you can leave here." He dropped his hands, in tribute to the brute lack of honor in the processes of life. "So we can go."

He couldn't imagine her answer. When it came, it did so on her own terms. Brutal too, she touched his cheek. "He saw you coming," she said.

Lights of cars trickled through the hedge that bordered the highway. The Canal Zone's powerful guide light, not visible from here, was there to welcome the one car that would be for them. Walking back, they had time for the swift catechism that comes when absolution is near.

"Singled out?" she said.

"It happens."

"And no one—is to blame?"

"Not—forever."

"And the ones who are left?" Even in the dark he could see her movement toward the figure lying somewhere inside there. Asleep or dead, the ones with whom one could no longer mesh nerves or spirit, were the same.

"We're the ones who've been left," he said.

"He was romantic to me once. Maybe he still is. It wasn't all bad."

"There's no need to—throw that away. One's history."

Car lights passed, not for them.

"Yours," she said. "I think Sligo knew it."

"Mine? Everyone does."

They reached the dark-browned eaves of the games room.

"But he never said. He didn't talk."

And Sligo would have been her only gossip. He recalled now how her glance had followed the women going back into the world from the world of the bar, a glance too proud to take confidences from them, across that bar.

"I thought you must have a special one, from all those Mondays—the quiet ones." She gave him the thoughtful smile of the isolated. "I thought you must have been married once, that always shows. I couldn't tell about children; unless people talk about them you can't tell how they feel about them, in a place like this. But it seemed to me—somehow . . . that you were dead to . . . family."

It moved him beyond reason, that she should have been creeping painfully, a slow but conscientious student, toward this knowledge of him that was so brashly open to the rest of the world.

"That's why I—" She flung back her head. "—ought to tell you. Children. We never tried not to. There was nothing separately wrong with either of us. I think we must have been like two acids, that could only corrode." Again her head reared. "But the things I don't know, I don't belittle them. And I'm only thirty-four."

"Mine are dead." A pale light filtered on her cheeks, those starved flanks. He traced them again, moved toward what he had thought himself never again to be moved. "But I—I can see how you would look in your prime."

"Ah, you don't know me," she said in her tough, blunt way.

It seemed to him that all the brief, successive pictures he had of her were being filled in with a tough central dark criss-crossed with broad black strokes of knowledge that might shift but never fade. "Hard to know. *We'll* be." He peered into the games room, in which a floating will-o'-the-wisp of light fancied a surface now and there to stencils of darkness, circles of knives. He turned back to her. "We'll be strange enough for each other. We're the extreme." From which the single-legged, each to each, may still take heart.

"I thought—" She put out a hand. "The quick way you got on to the hospital. You—have friends there, perhaps?"

"Yes, I have friends there," he said. "Many friends."

She took his hand at once. Standing backed against the old house, they stared into the blind current of the river, and beyond it, into a current wider than it or any harbor, into that vast multiplicity where there might be no sure order of good or evil, but surely a movement, too wide even for unease, too irrational, of which both of them knew. He knew it was there, this force that had flung him out, and drawn or flung him in again, this movement which, like some god of unbelievers, which did not bear thinking of or speaking to, both took away, took away—and gave. This was nothing to make either a religion or an unfaith of; it was merely the doctrine, not to be palmed onward, which lived somewhere in the tough, central dark of those to whom it had happened. For extreme cases there was sometimes—an extreme magic. It could be merely a falter, a pause in that vast territory which humans could never persuade themselves was not human, one of those illuminated moments when unseen kinships brushed one like lepidoptera passing, when birds flew south from a north they did not see as misery, and in a clearing, his own clearing, a man came upon rabbits, paws lifted to the quiet of evening, staring at Mecca.

"So we can go," she said. "Where?"

He pointed, to that spot on the dark where a barn which was not to be seen behind its fan of trees, not even when the leaves were down in winter, now lighted up the dark for him like the bush in the Bible. In the conflagration he'd never dared hope for, his house was burning, though no one else could see it, and because he'd got here on time, it was not consumed.

When the long car that was for them turned in and bore down upon them, it came down the lane with normal slowness, not nemesis, nor yet a miracle. Its revolving domelight bypassed the night skies, stood the trees at stage-green attention, swept white the gravel and swiveled to rest on the Canal Zone. The old inn returned the light like a stockade from another century, indifferent to either. Pointed at it, the long hood of the car seemed to him a hold in which he could see the stored lives of all those in hospitals, each life regularized round its one small hole of the possible, like those prints in which if one looked hard enough one could always see somewhere the upside down V of Fujiyama. It even crossed his mind to wonder where they might be sending Sligo, into or out of what sphere.

They walked straight into that treacherous glare.

There came back to him again how it felt to be only half-alone—in all its separate lights and darks. Once inside the double dream, one no longer tallied these, or no longer dared.

"But I don't know you," she said. "You don't need me."

"No," he said. "You don't know me."

"You're sure? You're not—you're not just—"

"No," he said. "I'm not just saying it."

Saratoga, Hot

Tot and his wife, Nola, are sitting at the kitchen table, just before dawn. The excitement of being in their own house always gets them up early here. They are waiting until it's time to go for early breakfast at the track to watch the horses work out. The August meet is already half over and they do not intend to miss a morning. They will do the same at Aqueduct, Belmont, and Lexington; as Nola says, it makes a calendar, both for the day and the year.

Tot worries sometimes whether since Nola's accident she has ever really wanted to live out any kind of calendar, though she would die rather than say. Or rather, since he was driving that day, she will live, for him.

Up here Tot is always encouraged. They are drinking champagne from the two six-sided blue flutes Nola used to tote everywhere, until they were able to afford this house, minute as it is, in which they will live one month. This is the only place in the world where he has a drink before breakfast, or where she cares to have even the one drink a day. The fizz lasts her, she says, right through coffee, and for the two and a half hours she is now able to spend drawing the regulars at the track's old wooden-buttressed clubhouse.

Drawing, she can sit in an ordinary chair and appear to be handicapping her bets for the real races later, but those in the know are aware that it is the only hour they will see her at the track. As she draws, the horses fly around the oval, but she never looks up. Even the track itself gets short shrift, though in the paintings she does at home it sometimes appears in the background, like a geranium-dotted recurrent dream. Here she has eyes only for the tables of the owners and trainers who have a stake in these tryouts, and their seasonal followers, thinned out with maybe a few of the owners' houseguests, still rubbing away sleep. The tourist tables she never notices—and she has her own inner stopwatch, rising smartly at the last half hour's edge. There will be a murmur after them, often before they fully leave—which takes some doing.

Yes, Tot has good reason to like it here. Three Augusts ago, after five years in a wheelchair, Nola got rid of the chair for a walker, which a year later, on August 31, she gave to the Salvation Army in exchange for a cane. At the time he had no idea what they had gone to the Army store for, thinking she was hunting something for the house, though with all the cast-offs from his several cousins who keep August cottages here, there was scarcely any need.

The cane she chose, dark brown with a leatherbound crook, was surprisingly one of six for sale. "End of August, we get a lot of them," the Salvation Army worker said. "Racing is an old man's sport." When they got home, using the walker which would be picked up later in the week when she thought she could dispense with it, she showed him how the cane's crook snapped open above a sturdy steel joint to form a seat. "Why, it's a shooting-stick, haven't you ever seen one?" he said. "Rootie used to order them by the dozen." Then both of them had clammed up. She because she still has her troubles over his horsey family, whose rich members give this poor one the jobs he is almost too right for. He because with a damaged spine and one leg encased in electronically activated braces, she is not likely ever to use the cane to sit on. She has little hope of discarding it.

"Canny girl," was all Tot said. He hadn't recognized the stick as such because all of Rootie's—who was known as Top Cousin in the family—had been of a yellow malacca bought in England by the lot and dispatched from the house at Epsom to the houses in Westbury and Lexington, the flat in River House, and the former long-time family seat here in Saratoga. If, instead of the cane, Nola had been holding a florist's long wicker basket of flowers marked PLATFORM—like the one she had carried up there just before he and she and that eager claque of the presidential candidate's young camp-followers had departed for the highway, she would still look like that girl. Even leaning on the walker, she had. Maybe that's why Rootie, whose son Budge had died in the crash, is so stiff with her, though somehow not with Tot. Budge should have been driving, but had wanted to be in the back seat with the girl of his choice. So Tot and Nola, met only that week, had been up front, in Budge's Porsche. How childish it all sounds now.

Especially to have been starting out from Bedford-Stuyvesant, that battered slum-end of Brooklyn where all the young friends of family friends of the candidate had been campaigning, Tot in from a Philadelphia cousin's horse farm in Wyncote, where he had been working out his incompletes at the university with a tutor his farm salary paid for, Nola not part of the in-crowd, there with a more serious bunch of do-gooders from Swarthmore—but all of them learning how to talk to black lawyers who had Phi Beta Kappa keys, the girls with their twee-twee boarding-school or Sacred Heart accents saying, shiny-eyed, "Bed-Stuy!" All of them cold sober with Christian charity—and then to end up on a tacky Long Island Expressway, like a crowd of rich collegiate drunks. It made no difference to the papers that they had been smashed into from behind. "Wealthy," the papers had said.

"Nice—" Tot says now, nodding at the still life propped on the mantel in front of a picture which hangs there regularly. For weeks she has been painting how a striped plastic dimestore tablecloth looks through blue Steuben glass. "Nice you painted both glasses."

"Harder."

To compose, she means. He knows enough of the lingo now to sell her work, if she would let him. Good for her, for both of them. But she won't; she knows who would buy. Now and then one of the racing crowd took up painting—Main Line houses in cotton snow, or other recognizable property, or portraits of friends easily spotted, though with the hands usually concealed. After which these efforts were bought in at some benefit by the gratified or obligated sitters and house-owners, never for less than a thousand bucks. Nobody ever painted a horse.

"Besides, one of the glasses may break," she says. She always gives him two answers, maybe because in the kind of life they lead there always are two. Or like to a child you don't want to lie to. Her mind is better than his, which only makes him sorrowful for her. Stop it, Tot, she said, outraged, the one time he mentioned it. My mind's no great shakes, only different. In his crowd, now hers, he watches her hide possession of it the way his Philadelphia grandmother would never mention underwear. What if one day "the horse people," as Nola calls them, prove to be more than she can bear?

He stifles an impulse to break one of the glasses and get it over with, though he likes using them. She shouldn't have to bear with having so little, and such stuff as they've grown used to having; no wonder these bits of her own home become tokens, always in the end cracked or lost. Look at this place, their first and only real home. As only half a Tottenham, the other half an actor who had happened to pass through Sewickley long enough to marry his heller of a mother, he had grown up with just such stuff, in between one or another of his mother's marriages which had now and then done better for them.

The secondhand largesse of the rich is so often insensitive. Over in the corner is an easel so huge you could only put a Veronese on it, Nola says, or else a founder's portrait before it went off to hang in the bank—which was what the easel had once accommodated. And how many bed trays, from all the houses where one is no longer served breakfast in bed or is ill at home, do his connections here think one month in Saratoga can require? Or that Nola does—who cannot eat easily lying down. The mahogany whatnot Rootie had sent when she sold the house here has, as she'd said, "a sweet dimple of a mirror for your lovely girl"—and a secret drawer to keep one's diamonds in. When Rootie is here in whatever house she and Wheatley may rent, she keeps hers in the safe-deposit at the local bank, to which the August ladies are let in by special arrangement after late parties. All Rootie's good tables and chairs had of course had to be included in the auction in New York, and the housekeeper had somehow sent all the bedding to the Salvation Army, before Rootie could say boo. Anything left in the huge cottage had been servants' stuff, his cousin said.

"Ours is a servant's house," Tot had replied. "Or a stable hand's, from the days when the stables spent the winter here. One of those shacks on one of those funny little lanes behind the houses on Union Avenue." But Rootie has always thereafter referred to it as a carriage house.

If they all wanted to save his pride, they have done so. Never send money; arrange jobs. Continue of course to send roses for any family mishap or event—a blanket of them when Nola got up here after the work on her second hip. "I believe in roses *now*," his cousin Tansie, Rootie's half sister, always said. "Why wait for the grave?" And charge them, letting the shop dun you. One season overdue being decent practice, Tansie running at least two. "Oh, the little people in Saratoga"—meaning the merchants—"they love us. They'd better."

But the family men—Wheatley, head of all its inherited operations, and the others through their special interests: Gifford at the Racing Museum, Courtwell at the Adirondack Commission, Bailey in Lexington—have all conscientiously done their best by him. Narrow and inbred just like him, if a tad prouder of it, they understand the dignities of patronage—and how for him it would have to be horses, not stocktips and a city berth.

"You know, there are still two more glasses from that set," he says now. "I was—kind of saving them."

"Where? Not here." When she sits up that straight it will always hurt her, the hospital said—can't be helped. She won't let on, but we think you ought to know.

"Uh-uh." No hiding place here except through a trapdoor to a storage space under the roof, from which he sometimes climbs out the dormer to the roof itself for a bit of air on the worst hot nights, locking his legs around the kitchen chimney. "No, at Grayport. In that closet where your mother keeps the cracked stuff. But *they're* not. In September we could pick them up."

"What a sap I am about it."

But it will be the first thing she'll do when they get to Grayport, the dilapidated fifteen-room house near Groton where her mother manages to live on, though penniless, three of her five children refusing to sustain her drunken ways with funds from their admittedly small inheritances. Nola, the youngest, named for the song Vincent Youmans had played at her grandmother's debut—and of course for her own mother, is one of the two who do help. She and Tot pretend to one another that they go to Grayport no more than once a year so her mother won't too much feel the obligation—which Tot privately thinks she never has or will. But Nola needs every illusion she can manage; he would bring her handfuls if there were a store which sold them. "You're kind not to object," she always says, making out the quarterly check when her few dividends come in. He hopes this is true; kind is her highest praise. But more likely it comes of his having been brought up to see dividends come and go. So had her siblings; she had merely been born too late for most of it.

Dawn is coming in now at the oddly high window which makes some say these houses had begun as underground-railway stations for slaves fleeing north during Civil War days. Hot as blazes already; there are beads on his lip. Never any on hers.

"I could paint, I'd paint you."

In Budge's Porsche she had been adequately pretty. Now, with a thinness like the models one glimpses undressed in Sunday shop windows—wishbone hips and an angled foot—she is bitter and beautiful. The window is part of what had charmed them into buying the place, along with the tiny, incised mantel on which he has placed the still-life, which will remain there until she has done a new painting, when it will go up the trapdoor. The walls have to be bare, or she can't work. Sometimes he thinks her whole life has to be. "Anyway, you paint better here than anywhere else in the world."

"Suppose I do. Well—"

Well—they've tried the world. Wherever the horses run, and the cousins do. This year he's working for a distant one who owns a glossy, tax-deductible publication devoted to stately homes and gardens, with racing drawn in. In a corner opposite the easel—on a small desk at which the butler at Westbury used to do his accounts, salvaged by Tot for his after-college quarters when Rootie, rather than dissolve her marriage with Wheatley had been dismantling the estate—are his clips from the local newspaper, in whose August pages the horses compete for space with their owners—usually a dead heat. Should the archangel Gabriel decide to attend the Travers Stakes, the paper will duly report whose box he was in. And staying at whose cottage, as the largest houses are called.

"See they've published the Cottage-List after all," Nola says, grinning. The year the mayor had asked the paper not to for safety's sake, there had been an uproar from a society which would rather lose its jewels than its intercom. "I think this town is actually proud of the big burglaries it has every year. Like the locals are of which of the summer people they rent to."

The locals moving out en masse to "the lake," which means up to Lake George for the doctors and bankers renting to horse owners more for the prestige than the money, or the other lake—theirs, Lake Saratoga—if both landlord and renter are small-time. It's she who has made him see what he was never before conscious of—how too, in August, at the country club, which is left to the natives in winter, locals and incomers get to mix tangentially, or continue not to. She will draw them, then, the locals fat and empurpled with winter beef, the incomers—"visitors" is not quite the word—who if they are stylishly thin seem to keep in trim by taking over towns wherever they go. Or when fat, seem to be so from all the gross goodies of their circuit.

What he can never hope to explain to her, since she isn't interested in horses, is the wonderful layering of the world based on the sporting life, to which good blood, even if animal, brings an equality where—when a stable boy or hot-walker, a trainer or jockey may at any moment talk authoritatively to a man whose horse has just been syndicated for five million—nobody is small-time.

"Waal, no, it's the thieves' union made 'em publish that list," he says in a stable hand's drawl, which he comes by honorably from softball games played with many of those elders since he was ten—and continues now as a sacred trust. "Talk is, they complained of not being able to keep track of where the parties are, so's to give people the robberies their station in life deserves. How are they going to keep an eye on Bonnie Doe for instance—that choker of egg-size ice she wore to her own vernissage?" He is proud of that last word.

"Oh, Tot."

He has got her to laugh.

"Those postcards she drew," Nola says. "For that benefit show. All the children in them with their backs conveniently turned. And practically a Winterhalter gown she wore for it. With turquoises, those were. At four in the afternoon, in a public park center. Oh, the thieves' union. You're a howl."

She will gossip with no one but him. He'll look up Winterhalter later.

But she's too quick for him.

"German. Painted royal women in hoopskirts." Then she links pinkies with him. It's going to be an all-right day. At least, another day.

And getting on for time. "I'll take the garbage out."

Next door's cat comes nuzzling, a runt like its master, a pecan-faced former jockey who also keeps his house open only for the Saratoga meet. Everybody at the meet has a cat for August, down from the thoroughbreds themselves, where it may all begin. When people leave they turn the cats loose, or, if they have a conscience, drop them in some local's backyard. Nola, brought up in a house on which a whole peninsula's cats were dumped, won't have one of her own here, but she'll feed any stray. Venezuel, the old jockey, off all day with his fly friends, maybe some of the same who years ago cost him the right to ride, cannily depends on her. Tot opens his own front door and shoos the cat in to Nola, who is already getting to her feet in her jackknife way. Hand on the fridge, she says: "Got your pad?"

He pats his hip pocket. His pencil is clipped to the breast pocket of his airiest shirt, an old one, loud in that refined Italian way. He's easy on his clothes and has a lot of what he calls his standing wardrobe, conventional clubhouse stuff, plus a supply of British turtlenecks and slacks, couple of velvet jackets and an extra dinner jacket, most of it descended over the years from Budge, who had also been a 42-long—with, after the crash, a final, sad increment. If they call him a clotheshorse here, that's unfair but he can understand it—they don't know what else to call him. Everybody at a meet has to be somebody, unless you're rich, which explains everything.

Out here he can barely stretch. The crazy little porch, only doormat wide, has one corner bayed out and encircled with a railing. When he writes on the pad he sits on the camp chair Nola had in mind for him the minute she saw the house; otherwise he bestrides the railing, one foot gangling, and scans left-right, sky and ground, as if the view will push open for him. The shaky title to his house, linked as it is with those on either side of it, gives it extra character. The lane is crooked, quaint and short, and so much in the right sector of town that Venezuel says all the realtors have their eye on it. He and his friends would like to buy the house on the other side of Tot and Nola's, but the retired police captain who comes up from the city every summer won't sell. Venezuel would probably like to offer for theirs, too. He wants the whole lane, or his newest friends do, three dark, silent men from the crowd who want to bring gambling back. But you two could always stay, he says slyly. Because she feeds the cat. Such good neighbors we need.

Neighbors my ass, Nola says, in exact replica of her mother's still dainty "My foot!" They won't want to tangle with your family, Tot. They're from that other racing association in town, not the N.Y.R.A., the unofficial one. They wouldn't gamble right here. Maybe in that strange villa just out of town, which pretends to be a restaurant, but doesn't like it when a customer comes. Or maybe there's where they consult about all their statewide business, from beer and soft-drink agencies to liquor franchises—and on to politics.

Venezuel himself collects poker chips from the casino days. His crowd is a sentimental one, old hands who knew the place when—which was always each man's own special "when," from those who had seen Man O'War himself and had ridden his issue, to those who had merely shaken the hand of Honey Fitz. Plus a few present-day jockeys, not the best ones, who now and then freewheel out here, hoping to raise a little hell.

Nobody's at Venezuel's now. He and his three current night owls will shortly drive in, the long limo with the black-glass side windows grooving in like on a fast curve from a good pitcher, almost without sound. Tot suspects those three never do anything with yahoo. This morning, like each, they'll have a fast change and shave, though he has never seen a shadow on their broad jaws and the clothes seem always the same; then they'll be off, first to early Mass, then to the track, not returning to sleep until maybe after the sixth, unless something in a later race interests them. What that would be he wouldn't care to think. All he actually knows is that jumpers are not their style.

Last year, the day Venezuel gleefully invited him and Nola in to view an entire set of poker chips he had picked up, one of the originals from the old Canfield Casino, now the museum—had been a day of jumpers' events only. "Nah, jumpers," Venezuel said, "women owners race them. They like those hurdles. Nah, this is the day these three catch up on their sleep." He's speaking for the three men shambling to their feet at the sight of Nola.

"How about the trotters?" Tot had said, meaning only to raise a laugh, which among flat-race people, a mention of the handsome harness track on the other side of town, middle class and unstylishly running almost all seasons, is sure to do. But not with those three staring chilly at him. What's he supposed to know and doesn't? Do they think insult is intended?

"Nah, that's another deal," Venezuel had said, swiftly pointing out a humidor-on-legs which had come from the old casino, too. He had spoken for the other three almost the whole time. "Shoo!" he said to the cat. "Shoo. You make Gargiola sneeze. And worse."

Nola had enchanted them.

What worse, she wants to know—do cats make Mr. Gargiola climb chairs? She had known a boy who did.

The three guffaw, the eldest—who must be Gargiola and is not that old, shaking his head No.

Venezuel seemed pleased, muttering "A boy, Gargiola. She thinks you're a boy."

Nola had persisted. It must have been sad for Mr. Gargiola's kids, not having cats.

The two other men burst out laughing; the younger, maybe thirty, is Mr. Gargiola's kid. The other man is Gargiola's brother-in-law. While Nola fired questions at them—yes, their daughters are pretty, and yes, the girls have made communion—Tot's flesh grew cold for fear they would see the drift. She was making them draw pictures of themselves to tally with the ones she already had in her head. And maybe they do see. Venezuel certainly had.

"Honey—" he says warningly, "hon-ey," when she says: "Dogs, then. Were your kids brought up with guard dogs?"

But the three, nodding ever faster, only slap their knees and burst into laughter.

When she leans forward to Gargiola himself, saying intently: "Bet you never bring the wife and girls to the track. Bet you keep them safe out of it. In some big house on the Island maybe—maybe Bay Shore?" their amusement is complete

Then their silence is, regarding her.

"She's an artist is all," the old jockey said. "She knows human people."

Gargiola shook his head. Negatively, the head moved slower. "Rich girls' questions, Vennie. You never been to those parties the N.Y.R.A.?"

Now it was Nola and Tot's turn to laugh, hearing Tot's younger cousins, and some not so young, at the New York State Racing Association's mixed public entertainments, asking the arrogantly schoolgirlish questions which their nonequals don't know they might ask of anybody.

"I'm not rich," Nola said. "We're not."

The three are nodding again; they know that. Vennie brushes his sleeve.

"Stick around," Mr. Gargiola said.

The cat, in again, nudged Nola, who bent to it. Holding the cat draped in an elbow, she thanked Venezuel, shook hands with the three men. They watched that cane of hers shift from wrist to wrist like an interpreter as she managed this, and, as she walked to the door, her narrow pelvis in its box-step rocking. People watch her the way they watch strippers. Tot had stood back to let her spill the cat and negotiate the three steps down, which at Venezuel's have a modern railing.

He is a past master at not helping her, using his own body-set to let others know they must not. It's no fault of his he has to stand back far enough to hear their remarks.

"Class—" Mr. Gargiola said. "Both of them. And perfect. Last thing we'd want on this road is people who'd have kids."

Whether Nola ever hears any of these remarks Tot wants never to know.

—

By the air wafting from the track he can tell the staff has sprayed for flies again, and incidentally for the regional mosquitoes—at which the town is grateful, as it is for so much. The city fathers have recently learned to put out flowers like crazy, and prices have graciously gone double in most shops—Nola and he never arrive in time to stock up ahead. He thinks he may know now why Gargiola darkened at mention of the harness track—a matter of property, which is the name of the game here now. Nobody uses guns anymore except maybe the Pinkerton men who guard the tracks and the bigger properties—and maybe not even them.

Property is the most sinister thing going, his cousin Wheatley says; everybody you know, or wouldn't want to know, has a finger in it, crooked or straight. The policeman next door has sold to Gargiola at a price. The town assumes everybody has one. "He can retire now from being retired," Nola said. A stable hand has found an eight-thousand-dollar watch at the Adirondack bus stop, which nobody has come forth to claim. The busy bank, which has carved on its north, south, and west walls respectively: SAVING IS A GREATER ART THAN EARNING; A PENNY SAVED IS A POUND EARNED; THE FIRST YEARS OF A MAN'S LIFE MAKE PROVISION FOR THE LAST; FRUGALITY IS THE MOTHER OF THE VIRTUES, as you enter to stash or cash, has a neat sign which says HAVE A GOOD DAY AT THE TRACK, as you exit to the new parking lot.

On Sundays, all-day baroque music brawls from the museum like an antidote. Every day, the Chasidic Jews, crossing from boardinghouse to park in their sable-bordered greatcoats, look to be the coolest people, their heat being invisible. Their boardinghouses, every year since his childhood said to dwindle, are every year still there. And here he is, ready to list his day on the much-worn leather pad bought for him by Nola in Florence, a habit engendered by the first of his scattered track jobs. Inside, Nola is setting up her paints for the afternoon. Little has changed since last year, only the cat, which this year is brindle instead of tan. And still not theirs.

After breakfast at the track, and after he has brought Nola home, his first stop will be the Reading Room, next door to the track. "Oh, a library—oh, how nice of them," Nola had said her first year here. It had been the first summer of their marriage, and she had been for some months out of the rehab unit, which had among other concerns judged her almost ready to laugh again. But when Tot explained that the broad-verandahed white clapboard house and ample rear garden, from which members could enter straight to the track's private rooms and boxes, was really a kind of summer Jockey Club in which any reading matter of note was likely to be the studbook, only her visiting older sister, Dolly, had laughed.

"Hush, Dolly," Tot said, for they were already on the club verandah. Too late; Walter Mallory, who has brought a new girl to the meet every year since his heyday of the 1950s, was leaning over their table.

"How do, Tot? Tell us the joke." He is the classic sexual playboy for each August meet and an inspiration to his contemporaries; yesteryear is a word Walter doesn't admit. Courtly, more informed on the general world than most of the horse crowd, faithful to his one protégée for a season and often keeping them as friends after, Walter is also down to the few millions and horses which his tastes have left him, and in these parts is therefore considered romantically poor. But, as all the men agree, what draws the women even more than his handsomely blunted charm is his obsessively roving eye. Women are intrigued by the naked message coming from such a gentleman—and from a rounder who must have seen everything except the woman he is gazing at. "Walter undresses a woman in public so she's even proud," they say of him. "The other reason," Nola will say when she knows him as well as she will allow herself to know people here, "is that he's lovable."

That day, Walter's eye had first sought out Nola; sometimes it still does. But when the joke was explained, and he had been introduced to both girls, he bent to Dolly, inviting her to his box. "Your time of life, don't want to keep your nose in a book. Mine neither."

Dolly, who had been Walter's bird for that summer, no longer visits here. Nola, watching them go, had opened her big new handbag, in which as she said, a girl could keep her double life.

If she has learned to laugh only with her pencil, not in her life with him, Tot is still grateful. Though she never laughs at him that way, sometimes he thinks she answers him only with that pencil—though for a couple for whom there are usually two answers, this may be natural. Anyway, he can laugh too at what comes of it, as he had at the wash-drawings of Walter in his box, Walter donating his trophies to the Racing Museum; and Walter at the polo matches in a circle of the local dowagers—in each with a naked woman at his side—and in the case of the Racing Museum, a four-legged one.

In one of the fierce impulses which overtake Nola with those she likes—and she likes such odd ones for her, including himself—she gave Walter all three, unsigned, and on a promise which so far as they know he has kept, that he hang them only in New York. "Are you surprised I did keep my promise? No? Why not?" he had asked her every year since, until one year she had told him: "Because there's no better confidant than a roué."

Tot had been embarrassed, but Walter only said quietly, "You must have a gallery by now, eh?"

"Yes, it's *my* studbook," Nola blurted, and limped away.

"She's shy about her mind," Tot said. "You know. In our crowd." And she uses her limp to cover up, something he'd never noticed until then. He rarely gets enough distance on her to. Was Walter observing that? He is very grown-up except in the one department, Nola says. Almost wise—see how even in this crowd of hootenanny nicknames nobody calls him "Walt." He's got a decent name, Tot had said. What man in his right head would want to be called by the monickers which old money with horses sticks its kids with: Oglethorpe, Peppersall—Tottenham. More often with triple-decker last names to match, which his father had at least spared him. She'd reached out to him at once, laying a hand on his cheek. He's been making her do that lately. Wondering if she noticed.

"Dolly once said—" Walter is saying.

"Yes?" They've never admitted to the fact of Dolly and him before.

"Dealer who saw Nola's paintings at your mother-in-law's house, he went for them. And some curator near Boston, too."

"The Addison, yes."

"Why won't she show? It can't be only because of—."

They had been in the garden of the house Rootie had rented that year, having drinks after Opening Day with a hundred or so, most of whom know each other well. The place had formerly been an inn. Nola goes to one of Rootie's parties a season, either at its beginning or its end. Walter spread his hands. "Because of—this?" He smiles, over his admission that anyone might not care for this hot green grass, the sail-white sky, the talk-talk between fine linen and unbecoming hats, the butlers and their familiars, the patrons—the whole horse-drawn summer, which except for his girls or any defection by death is the same as ever. The average age here must be close to sixty. Walter, whom Tot has known since his own boyhood, must be even more. Young men asked up here either rarely stay the course or are sorry specimens. Clothes are sedate at this hour, dowdy rather than sporty; Walter's own are even nondescript. Yet all the faces, many of the women's surgically kept up, many of the men's carnation with drink, are implacable in their well-being. This caravan will carry them through.

"I love it here," Tot says low. He wants at once to retract that. One should never sound hopeless at a meet.

A horned eyebrow twitches. Of course you do. But who has to say? A hand squeezes Tot's shoulder. "Shy about her mind, eh? I knew a girl like that. That why Nola won't show, eh?"

"She just—doesn't want to."

Everybody knows what Nola won't do: go the calendar, blend in—but they prefer to blame the accident, saying Look how far she has come! They themselves keep a stolid front toward physical ailment. The first lady of racing drinks martinis in the wheelchair that martinis brought her to, and from boyhood Tot has heard the elders say gently of one or the other of them still going through the paces, and held up by that as they all hope to be: "He's a little ga-ga now and then."

"She—doesn't want to live," Tot said.

—

Whatever had possessed him, to give up Nola's secret, unknown, she thinks, even to him? His year-by-year load of it, of watching the bravery dole itself out like a muscle exercise? Or Walter the trusty, who mutters Ah, now, or is it Now, Now—and lets the crowd help ooze him and Tot apart a few paces, from which distance he shrugs at Tot, deprecating this—or is it a salute? As Walter turns away, there is something infinitely sad about his haunches, maybe the practiced way the well-worn jacket skirts the rump, as if his tailor, measuring to there from the armpit, has said: Now, Mr. Mallory, this measurement we have to take seriously, we cannot be debonair. Suddenly, Tot sees Walter lift his chin; two persons under forty, or who could be taken to be, have arrived. Sisters, they are perennials here, the elder a tiny lisping woman-girl always in pointy black, the younger one angrily aloof, like a chaperone. They know Walter more than well, or had once. His coat is itself again.

—

It's light on Tot's porch now, the leaves not yet checkering the sun. The lane has a few scanty trees, many vines. Maybe it's best to have a shallow world. Maybe that's the secret of all the meets.

For lunch, for instance, he is meeting Wheatley at the Reading Room, just as he did eight years ago to inform the uncrowned head of the family that he and Nola were thinking of marrying. That day, he had just driven up from New York, where she was still at the Rusk Institute, and he was late, partly because she had agreed at least to live with him, now that she had the walker and was "half a girl again"—and partly because it was the Saturday of the Travers Stakes, and the crowd was so great that the rookie track policeman had only halfheartedly pushed ahead this battered MG with the clubhouse sticker on it, so Tot had had to park in a public lot and walk almost a quarter of a mile. Out of this combo of excuses he had kept silent, except for a "Sorry."

Wheatley was severest with those who did not insist on the privileges due them. It was understood between him and Tot that if Tot could only learn to do this, Wheatley in turn could do more for him. Tot must learn to lean harder on what his mother's side had at least done for him by bearing him. Until then Wheatley would do only so much. Lucky he hadn't heard Tot's answer to Nola at the Rusk. "Half a girl? Well, I'm only a quarterhorse myself."

Inside, the old house, smaller than many of the cottages, had been empty, except for a group of the staff, kitchen help, waiters, and housekeepers clustered at the back, all "high type" blacks, sedate elders and matrons either brought up from Kentucky or else from families which had been here since the Civil War, some with Indian profiles. One of these came forward to meet him.

"How are you this year, Jason?"

"Fine, sir. Mr. Lanphier in the lounge."

His cousin was going over the club's accounts. Some of the better-connected Kentucky breeders, he says, men who could be invited to the inside parties, use the club for sleeping quarters while they are here. Dirt cheap, and part of its function. But they ought to bring their wives now and then, though of course not here. "Do it up right once in a while, if somebody don't invite them, then at the Gideon." Sure, all the hostesses grab for any single man, but the men shouldn't lean on that kind of bacheloring. "Or at least not do it from here."

Wheatley didn't wear wing collars, but out of his presence people were given to swearing he did. Nola had later drawn him in one, in the style of Thomas Nast's cartoons, a few originals of which her father had owned and left at Grayport. It was an era Tot could see his cousin belonged to—that huge, rubicund head and body all chest, dwindling to tiny feet which in those days might have been gaitered, and in these looked their best in the dress pumps which at night he was rarely out of. Jockey bones, he said of himself—if he could have kept to the weight, and if his father had let him. His owlish hoot always made it clear that a Wheatley's father never would have, even if of less lineage than the mother, who had been a Wheatley born. Studs could sometimes be longshots, Wheatley maintained, but never the mares. At his own stables he was even stricter. Whether or not in consequence, he never did very well there; the breeding ran out; the horses ran last.

"We'll have to let in more locals as summer members," he'd said, rising from the accounts book, his eye screwed. Nola had been right to see him as political. "Kind who'll come once, then never bother us." Tot had seen those—Albany merchants, Troy bankers, Schenectady builders and local doctors, all with timidly radiant faces. Nobody precisely cold-shouldered them, but above their heads, in continual Ping-Pong, the inbred chit-chat volleyed and was returned.

"Haven't et, have you?"

"No, but I needn't. You'll miss the first race."

"Nothing in it I'm interested in."

When Wheatley was a young man his elder brother had been ambassador to the Court of St. James's. This was said to have affected Wheatley's own character, in so far as a Philadelphian one could be. Visiting his brother in a duke's house, and seated at dinner next to a prince of the realm, Wheatley had recognized some paintings of stallions on the dining-room walls: "I see our host has some very fine Munnings," receiving the reply, "I am not interested in other people's horses." He himself had much the same attitude but until then hadn't grasped the nobility of expressing it. While, when on his return, he was asked about Churchill, then still on the scene in his last stages, he was able to reply: "He's going ga-ga like a gentleman."

Wheatley and Tot were led to one of the round tables in the garden, which in spite of the crowd even inside here on Travers day, had been kept for him. He and the waiter go through their usual dance. "Yessa, chicken salad for Mr. Laynpheah. 'Longside a mahtini very dry. Not beforehand. 'Longside."

"Matthew's our oldest waiter here, aren't you? Been here almost as long as me." When Wheatley was pleased, his mouth pursed.

"Thank you, sah. And this gemmun—I remembers. Bloody Mary and a B.L.T." It was not intended that people eat particularly well here.

"Skip the Mary," Tot said. Before Bed-Stuy he would never have seen how the black help here parodied Uncle Tom. Why, the man was fairly dancing with it.

"Well?" Wheatley said, the minute the man was gone. "What about this Nola Gray?"

Tot knew what was meant. "The house at Groton's just one of those wandering old frames, on a peninsula. It's no estate. And there's no money." No need to explain where Nola's pittance went. To Wheatley, with Rootie's millions joined to his own, no money wouldn't mean that there was none.

"Mother drinks, I hear."

Tot looked around them. The drink consumed during the meet was enormous and constant, but done by convention, as a part of the general busyness which held people up. People here rarely had to be shut away for it; they so seldom appeared personally drunk. "A little."

"And the father?"

"Dead." No need to say he had decamped.

"What was he?"

"A professor. Art historian."

That had seemed to settle it.

"You're not obleeged to marry her," Wheatley said. "You've done nothing wrong."

Just then the exodus from the verandah and the tables around them begins, their tables being so centered that everyone has to troop past it. Down the steps to the private path to the track or sauntering to it from the emptying garden, his cousins are going to their boxes. There's old Gail, the only woman of them as rich as Wheatley, who when advised to sell some of a stable unprofitable for years running—and so not tax deductible—had stamped her foot: "I have spent years breeding them to this point. I will not sell off a one." Who, on being told she was winding down the family fortunes to where her grandchildren would be merely comfortable, had said: "Fine. Just so long as the horses are." The accountant informing them all of this had been shaky with admiration, and Tot proud. He and she saw eye to eye. She waves at him.

There's deadbeat Tansie, who actually rides, and as the women say, looks like a Percheron in tweeds. Here and there are the widows who take their designers and hairdressers to parties if not to bed, and the divorcées, lively or stodgy, among them Millicent, her hat so far up in back and down in front that it is a wonder she sees the two of them, but she stops and kisses. It's known that she and Wheatley have had a walk-out once—her word for it. "Hoo-oo," she whispers to Tot, "hear you're hot on someone." Wrinkles straw her mouth but she has kept her beauty pout. "Hoo-oo, hot, hot."

Longside, like Wheatley's drink, come the men, with their air of letting the women be emphatic for them, while they hold the reins. Nola says he too has a touch of it. They are known to him and to each other first by their horse commitments, after which they divide off into what they do otherwise: into committees—charity or vanity, or to offices—law or Wall Street ones, through which the trusts and the money flow toward the home and club addresses. There's Walker Watson, who claims thirty or so clubs, here and abroad.

Tot notes also the two exalted ones, in for the weekend from Wilmington and Washington, who do museums. Plus his sole contemporary and pal in circumstance, once a schoolmate at a sleazy day school where he was known as "Beaver"—whose pink-cheeked wife keeps saying to those weekend bids to Hobe Sound, Fisher's Island, Palm Beach and Cuernavaca which are a kind of underground currency here—"Leland *works*."

Once you didn't have to, it was an easily enterable society; you could even get by without a horse. If there was an abundance of women here it was because the stage dollies who had married their bankers and polo players, or the distaff fortunes married to men who had hunted well, had outlasted all of them. Heiress was a word the local paper loved, confidently first-naming them, and often allotting them their brand names.

Here comes the Mary Pickford of their set, a tiny, girlish eighty, with knuckle-duster rings, who has appeared every season of Tot's life as faithfully as a biddy on a cuckoo-clock—had she been Ralston, or Quaker Oats? Lumbering on alone is the huge, dazed woman who has had the ill luck to be the ball-bearings girl. Always good for a last-minute contribution for a charity gala's decorations, Rootie says—and always came. He spots the mouthwash heiress, a blond zinger from Chicago, and Baldwin Locomotive, ancient money now. For in time the brands fade, or mingle so with other bloods or moneys that they are lost. Or doughtiest of all, earn their honor in the right way, with the thoroughbreds. Who, watching Alydar run under the Calumet colors can care that Calumet was known best as a baking powder once?

After the horses, he really prefers those regulars who earn their characters by being here, each year becoming more genuine. He searches for the smart, unservile, elderly hat manufacturer who humorously enjoys what he sells and can couple his rise with Saratoga history. Tony, the Long Island trainer who each year used to invite Tot for lasagna and clams Positano in his cottage—five rooms and a Pullman kitchen, that he and his girl used to share with another trainer—may not be here ever again. No lucky horses, three years running. So, no more horses to train. "The owners—" Tony said last summer, discarding the clams which roasting hadn't opened, "they can shut their faces like these here clams." His girl had quit her job as assistant buyer in a big store to be a hot-walker for Tony's horses—"Jesus, I started out, I thought a hot-walker had something to do with sex and old guys." Since then they had been all over the map; Tony's horses had been highfliers then. She and Nola would get on. They had both been to Yucatán.

"Ever been to Yucatán, Wheatley?"

His cousin, busy with the extra half portion of salad brought him without his having to order it, raises his head to stare at him, as if investigating him for loose parts. "Why?" He considers. "We have Nassau."

Nola's own crowd never hit the Caribbean. They went to unstable countries only, usually by backpack; "Hoping to stabilize ourselves," she'd said with a grin, that night in the front seat of the Porsche. "Like coming here to Bed-Stuy. Not slumming. But you know." She'd had a pert way of talking then—light. But the seriousness had been there. "I was at loose ends for Easter," he'd told her. "And I knew Chop." Chop had been the candidate's son, otherwise not motivated. "Oh, I see—" she'd said, and he could see that she did, even perhaps that his only travel souvenirs were the lederhosen and Alpine skis loaned by Budge when they skied in Vermont. Swarthmore do-gooder or not, he already liked her. She spoke to him as if he were grown. When your main interest was horses, lots wouldn't. "Well, at least you're not Bryn Mawr," he'd said. To his surprise she'd kissed him—though when they were hit they were sitting quite straight. He wonders whether it would help any to tell Wheatley that.

It hurts him that she will never again be able to backpack.

Back there in the Reading Room's garden, it's a blue-chip day. Each week in the Occupational Therapy room of the hospital, where by God they have her not only painting with her arm in a splint but instructing, he tells her how much of a watching game racing really is, yet how it keeps you moving. She smiles when he tells her how painterly horses are. Ach, your pictures are so painterly, the German woman who is head therapist says, coming up to them, and can't understand why they laugh. Each day the nurses tie Nola's hair back with a ribbon. Each time he comes, she asks him to remove it. "But the people at the track—" Nola says. "You never tell me about them."

Down the path they come now, in twos because it is narrow, but not necessarily in pairs, though of course they all know one another, those silver-crested heads and blazered bellies, the unisex canes, froggy chins and swooping, shadowy hats. Of course they are not all strictly his cousins, or each other's, except as they have all become related here, working so hard at their idleness. Outside, beyond the clubhouse and above the boxes, is that grandstand they never really see, except as it frames that mile-and-a-half oval in whose center the trees rise etched in another air. When he was a kid here, some stable hand told him that running horses make a magic circle; those elms would never die. Now he is not so sure they are elms.

Nola had given him a painting of hers for his twenty-fifth birthday. He'd been twenty-two when they met. In the interim he has had a standing arrangement, not an affair really, with one of Walter's former girls. He knows about the married older man who keeps her lovelorn. And everybody here knows about all of it. Walter hadn't minded about the girl; as the notches slip by here, he'll move on, the girl will, and Tot would; it's protocol.

Except for Nola. Who stays where she is. It's no system of hers.

He had her painting upstairs there with him, in the Club bedroom he would occupy all summer, flying down to New York to see her as he could. On the first day of racing, going back to his room for his binoculars, he'd found the second housekeeper, a severe auntie-type, standing in front of it, laughing fit to kill. Hand over her mouth, she apologized. "My girl did it," he told her. "You know—the one in the hospital." The woman nodded. They too knew everything.

He had put the picture, which was unsigned, on a stand he bought for it in the art-supply store in town. Though not large, its upper half is all taken up by a grandstand seemingly dotted with onlookers. The bottom half is the Saratoga oval exactly, except that the entries are some of them still at the starting post, some already galloping down the fairway and some bearing in for the finish—which of course could never happen. A few are even scattered between, loping lone. One and all, their heads are albumed flat with the canvas. They are people. Up above, the dots are then identifiable: everybody in the grandstand is a horse.

She'd never been to a track, he'd told the housekeeper; he'd only described it. Hadn't she though, the woman said.

It's now almost one o'clock. Down the path come three stragglers. One of them is Wheatley Junior, who has been politicking inside. A blond boar of a man, he has a small version of his mother's face embedded in his flesh. The tailor who keeps all that lard in is talented. Since his elder brother Budge died, Wheatley Junior and his family have not been in tune. The family trusts, as set up by the founder, go sideways, sibling to sibling, in a kind of primogeniture which may be the one British idea of which Wheatley Senior does not approve. Rootie is not here this season. She had spent the previous August saying to all and sundry: "Going to England next, are you?" and if the answer was a Yes, crying—"So am I! For the backgammon!"—and has since not returned.

Wheatley Junior's wife is probably in their box, with their two lacy little girls pinned to her side. At Junior's side is Mary Angela McRooney, who after her marriage to a French count was annulled, changed her name to Marie-Ange. On her other side, but only because he too is late, is a character so genuine that nobody remembers his real name, which doesn't matter, since though he is spoken fondly of to strangers, nobody introduces him. He is called Liver Lips.

Father and son nod. Marie-Ange pecks at Tot. "Hah you, *cheri*? Hear things about *toi*." She leans to his farther lapel, flicking that year's job insignia, which is to get him past the guards who don't know him. "Heavvee." She and Wheatley Junior pass on. From behind, the two of them appear to be traveling in the cloud of her hair, to each tendril of which one may fancy a conquest attached. Liver Lips has already gone on to the betting windows, a clutch of greenbacks in his fist. Because of this habit, it has sometimes been falsely rumored that he makes book.

For a moment all is warm sun, with the waiters tidying in the background, from which one can hear the track's distant hurrah. After tonight, though there'll be another week to the meet, the vans will start going home. Except for a last trickle of sales in the shops, empty seats in the restaurants which have flashed open for the season, and love affairs either looking ahead to the next meet or going through the last throes—it's over. Next week, as they say here, you'll be able to shoot a cannon down Union Avenue and hit nobody but a local. Which is the soul of Saratoga, Tot thinks—them or us?

Until that day Tot had never thought of such a thing. Though Wheatley might get notices of some extra-schedule N.Y.R.A. committee meeting, or of a yearling sale at Fasig-Tipton, the auctioneers, he never comes; far as he is concerned, as with most of the others, until next August the town sleeps. He hadn't liked Rootie's selling the house, which was her inheritance, not his. Though their families never come up except for this month, they have been doing that since the turn of the century.

Back there, interviewing Tot, Wheatley doesn't yet know that in the next year's election of the Racing Association president, his own son will nose him out by a hair. Or that in compensation, he himself will take over Marie-Ange. While Rootie, living in London with a lover called Alastair, and shortly to leave for a fat-farm in Buckinghamshire, will return from there to find all her orientals and silver and other goods, including Alastair, vanished, along with her fat—and will then more or less come back to him.

While Tot, back there, doesn't yet know that he will fall pathetically ill with hepatitis, with not a soul to visit him, and that—almost as a consequence the doctors will say, Nola will propel herself free of the apparatus which tethers her to the hospital, into a wheelchair, and toward the first wedding ever in the refurbished Canfield gambling hall. Everybody will hear it was charming, with a string ensemble from Swarthmore, a band provided by Chop, the best man, the wheels of the chair strung with satin ribbon, and a makeshift pulpit made of a chest said to have once held croupiers' gloves and almost hidden by a hill of white roses—though nobody from here will come.

All Tot knows just then is that everybody here seems to him to be running, even to that New York tailor who has had to make Wheatley Junior's suit, and is yet to be paid for it.

"Eh, eh?" Wheatley says. His jaw snaps shut, recollecting what he and this uselessly good-looking young squirt, in shabby whites and loafers but thank God wearing a decent blazer and tie—are there for. If he would only use those good looks of his, the jaw says. With what the family could do for him then, a mouthwash heiress should be bearable. "I told you. I shan't tell you again. Making a three-year-long ass of yourself. You don't have to do—any of it."

The sound which Tot makes is unusual for that garden. As Nola will one day note, there are no agonies here.

"I *want* to. I want to do *something* wrong."

—

On his own porch, Tot puts down the scratch pad, gets to his feet and straddles the railing, facing west. He does this each morning, once his list is done. Today will be as uneasy as any other but these small acts smooth. Six o'clock, and a red sun coming up. Though he can see only down to the scraggle of bushes where the cars enter the lane, all Saratoga is before him, in its spruce time. Resort colors flock streets which have mustered a late-Victorian smile. The bank is Mecca. In cool niches, under the 1930s WPA murals, the Post Office is unwittingly selling more than stamps. For a month, get anything you want in this town and gamble for anything—except with chips. In the refurbished lobby of the Hotel Adelphi, the mahogany-and-gilt plastrons, epergnes of pastry and frilled young waitresses look ready for a sex farce, or else for a scene out of that movie he and his crowd loved so once—*Elvira Madigan.* A hit man was apprehended there yesterday. The man's picture did not appear in the paper. This may be an upstate town, but it knows what it is doing. The sins of a racing season are like vaudeville. They too move on.

It's time. They both like to get there early. He pokes his head in. "Ready?"

"Ready." She has on her drawing hat, a childish white cotton beach hat with a short sloppy brim that buttons on. The longish, crushy jumper and skirt hide the assymmetric hip and orthopedic shoe. It just happens—or does it?—that her pale colors and fallaway figure make her seem very much the girl of the moment, and at thirty not old for it. Only the wrong women at the track are ever stylish, but this is not that. The bag is what touches him most. In it she keeps her supplies: pencils, sticks of charcoal, paper, and a spray can of fixative, aspirin and a stronger compound for the end-of-day pain which comes of a rocking walk. But her arm alone will not support even that light a pouch—woven for her once by another patient, from cotton-string the several colors of therapy. So after all, the bag is a backpack.

Left behind is her own easel, one of normal size, on it a blank canvas he had stretched for her the night before. Once he returns her home she'll paint for hours, getting her own meals until he comes in, very late. There are as many parties and other events here as there are minutes, and the paper wants him at all of them. In the beginning this was because he has what they call the "entrée," but now, though he doesn't write well and a reporter often mocks it up for him, they like what he talks about. Two fashion magazines have asked him for articles. What he likes is to put in some old track lore, so that nobody will think that what's going on is new. He even knows who's who in those old bronzed pics called rotogravure.

All I do, he said to the young editor who asked him—is to go back in my head to the library in Old Westbury. Public library? she'd said; he could see that dampened her. No, old Elmo Wheatley's house, gone now except from a few people's heads. Oh, I know, she'd said with passion; it's only your life. She could ask him questions about it, if that would help. He'd liked her at first, so young and eager, and straight of spine. There would have to be a lot about horses, he said. Oh, put in some withers and fetlocks, she'd said. And you on a horse. You'll photograph so well.

The cat is still nuzzling and prowling. "It likes sticky buns, what do you know?" Nola says, and holds out her hand for his list, which says, after the Reading Room: "Fourth and Sixth Race. Polo Field at Five. Racing Museum—Champagne Party for Presentation of Duveney Cups. Rootie's party at Surrey Inn."

He would come back in between, sometimes twice, either to change or to check her and the house, as he always says. But also to catch a glimpse of her in her working calm. He may even be jealous of that. There's a certain hour at the stables when the horses are being ministered to and the hands fall silent, everything clues in, and all vanities stop.

"Funny—" he says. "You don't like cats that much. And I don't scarcely get near a horse. And yet—"

"And yet what?"

Neither of them knows.

Yet together they both do. They go on with what's here.

They close the door behind them. Nola's never for locking, but he always finds some excuse. Though it mortifies him, his clothes are crucial here. And the rich don't pay him any sooner than they do the shops. "Who knows but somebody might think we have diamonds, too." He locks up. Dawn is over.

"Jesus, it's hot," he says. She never feels it. But at least it's always the present, here in their lane. They won't reach the past until they get to the track.

She takes his arm this once per day. The steps are too old and uneven. Going down them, the one railing is on the wrong side for her to manage the cane as well. End of summer, when the checks come in, he'll replace the steps and put in proper railings; he already has the estimate. Twelve hundred is what he will get for his duties at the Polo Field as steward and general soother of visiting jocks and women's committees. It's not fair for her to be stuck inside all day while he eats fancy food.

Though he'll miss having her on his arm like this. Leaning on a husband is not the same for her as for other women; it's a confession, of what she will never confess. What is it he yearns for her to confess?

Watch out!—he has no chance to say it. The cat is caught in her long furling skirt; she's stumbled. But Tot has caught her.

Is that why the heavy orthopedic shoe shoves out in reflex? Hitting the cat, just as one of the sharpy cars which buzz the lane tooting at Venezuel's house, guns on through—the cat's short, snarling parabola meeting it slap under the wheel.

The car had not stopped. Cats can be surprised, then? By death only, maybe. He can't see for sure. Nola is bearing all her weight on him.

Just then the long, blacked-out limo grooves slowly in, pulling up short of the brindled spot on the road. Gargiola gets out, Venezuel after him. Gargiola peers down the end of the lane where the other car went. "Who was that." He sounds as if he knows.

"Issy and Marco," Venezuel says it reluctantly.

"They never to drive through here again, understand?"

When the old jockey nods, his dewlap wobbles like a bird's.

"Penalty, they ever forget." Gargiola's shoe tip lifts the cat, drops it back. His left thumb directs Venezuel to take it away. He looks up at Nola in his slow, heavy-browed way. "Sorry, missy."

As Venezuel bends to the cat, its hind leg moves, high and wavering, the arched body lying where it is, and the head. He cranes at Gargiola. "I don't got a gun."

"Who needs a gun? That ain't a horse." Gargiola's thumb flicks again. Under Venezuel's porch, next to the corrugated-tin trash can with his name on it, is a small neat woodpile. Venezuel squats to it. In his worn habit and boots, in outline he could be that younger track hero pictured at the time of his scandal, crouched over his mount the way men of his continent rode—but secretly ready to take a fall. When he stands up, hefting a log from the pile, the seamed phiz is a shock. He's chosen a log with a narrow end. His hands were famous.

Tot finds his voice. "Let us take it to a vet."

"A vet?" Gargiola says, almost dreamy. "Right. A vet."

"A vet?" Venezuel has false teeth. When he smiles the lowers jut. "Sure, maybe Doc McKinnon at the track? Same one who's minding on that colt they're keeping under wraps for the Triple Crown. And I come up with this job."

"There's a dog vet on Route 9." He had dosed Rootie's pug. "I'll take it." If Nola will loosen her grip on him.

"Excuse me. You are good neighbor. But it is my cat."

Its eyes are glazing. But when Venezuel advances on it the pink gums snarl.

"Take your wife inside, better," Gargiola says low.

Making a sharp noise, not a scream, she has let go Tot's arm. Brushing him aside, she grasps the railing with both hands. This means swinging the inert leg with the big shoe as a separate weight, which he has never seen her do upright. He knows better than to help. She does not drop the cane.

So she negotiates the first step. The second step creaks as she lowers herself on it, between cane and railing. That movement, with him ready, she has sometimes done. For the last step, using the cane and a balancing talked of but never dared, she brings herself to the ground. He has no more breath. Two ordinary paces with the cane bring her where she wants to be. She holds out her hand for Venezuel's log.

Venezuel stiffens. He's South American, maybe Indian and Catholic, too—what does she expect?

"Sure it's yours. But I feed it. And I kicked it."

Venezuel doesn't move.

"Tot? Bring me a log."

In the silence he wishes Issy and Marco would come back, gunning their tires over the sunlit green. Then he walks over to his own woodpile and hands her one.

"Jesus," Gargiola says.

They don't know how powerful those thin arms are, from wheelchairs and walkers, crutches and canes. She brings the log down. The cat's wavering leg stops. Then she reaches behind her to their own washline, where hang her prized kitchen towels, the old Irish linen ones the handlers used to use for rubdowns, marked with a woven-in STABLE RUBBER on a red stripe. She drops one over the caved-in head.

Tot has stepped back. The cane, that fulcrum ever between them, is on the ground. She takes two steps toward him, a third tottering one. He receives her on his chest.

"Drive me to the track."

He has to help her as usual into their old Volvo. The black limo has to be shifted in order to let them out, and it is. They do not look back.

They're late for the trials but take a table anyway. She does not draw. Most of the people have gone on anyway. She seems to want to look and look at the day itself, at the porous turf, raked to a brown crepe paper, on which the horses have been running, and at the grandstand of cloud in the very blue August sky. There's a breeze now; it's going to be one of the priceless days.

"Everything smells of patent leather."

From sister talk between her and Dolly, he knows she is thinking of the shiny strapped shoes small girls wear for best. They do not speak of what she has done.

But when he is ready to take her home, she says she will stay for the day. "For all your list."

While he drops in at the paper, he leaves her at the Reading Room, where the black staff make a nice fuss over her. When he comes back he finds he and she have been commanded to lunch by Wheatley, who had noted her. Wheatley's table today is on the porch; since his young days in England, he cannot abide this Hudson Valley heat. He is courtly to Nola in his best British style—making an effort for the ladies as it were, though in from brusquer affairs. "It's no wonder the British couldn't survive India. Don't let them tell you it was Gandhi, my dear. Sweat. Plain sweat."

"Oh, I won't," she says. "Let them tell me. But is this—the Hudson Valley?"

"River's not ten miles from here. Over at Schuylerville. Nice little stream by then. But not so unnavigable a friend of mine can't come up from New York Harbor every summer in her boat."

Which Tot has been on—a small yacht with a deeply mahogany boudoir and lemon-striped beach chairs, where the friend and Wheatley have a deliciously navigable affair, nipping off bits of the packed days—before polo, after parties, as a clubman can. While the "captain"—some young midshipman earning his summer dollar, keeps watch.

"It *is* rather like the British Raj from this porch," Nola says. "They could make a movie. Outside the hedge there, all those hawkers, and hoi-polloi. Up here all the linen and the white hats. And the tall glasses."

"Oh, you Swarthmore—" Wheatley says. "You girls never get over your colleges."

"Chickem salad for the lady?" the waiter says. "Go-ood morning, suh. And a Bloody Mary for this gemmun?"

"Champagne," Tot says. "For us all."

Wheatley's collar twitches. "Hope you can pay for it."

"Shut up, Wheatley. Just drink to the lady."

When the bottle comes, Wheatley waits to be enlightened, finally drinks. Their table is being noticed. Porches creak with gossip anywhere, but on days like this the fine tweak of it is irresistible. Such blood-unities are here; in the very air one hears the fine tinkering of the past. Underneath, what's that vascular pumping? The present, eddying at everyone's mouth.

Nola arches her chin. The day has grown beyond even her drawing board. But she is smiling; she'll catch it.

"You come into money, I could let you in on a colt," Wheatley says to her. "Some of Secretariat's haven't panned out, but there's one—"

"Oh, I'd want a mare. I mean—a filly." She holds out her glass for more. "How does a foal get its name, anyway? I've always wondered."

"Ah. So that's it. Why you so shiny-eyed." Wheatley casts her narrow waist a squire's look of disbelief. "Well, well. Never too soon to begin a family." He glances with morose pride at the table presided over by Wheatley Junior, who had never quite got through—or over—Yale. He stands up, pinching her cheek. Always royally without paraphernalia of any kind, field glasses or cigars or wallets, Wheatley's hands are always free for the pinch. "Very glad to hear it. Rootie be calling you. Well, see you at the paddock." He leaves the bill.

As she and Tot go down the steps, Nola this time rocking between the cane and his arm, the air behind them is very quiet, then murmurs again in little keyholes of talk.

"Paddock's grassy," Tot says. "Come."

They stand watching the entries stepping imperially toward the track. A jockey's outline, hip-welded to the moving horse, has a kind of cherub confidence, no matter how worldly the face above. Some horses are being circled in front of owners, others led by handlers who clomp ahead like Tin Woodsmen.

Tot has stationed himself a couple of feet from Nola, hands at his sides. He turns up his palms. "Come."

The cane hangs on her left wrist. About to fling it to the ground, she remembers its other capacity and jams its steel-tipped ferrule into the grass almost upright. It stays. One hand is on her nerveless hip, one at her breast. Her thin-skinned collarbones move with her breath. His stare says he hopes to move her toward him, with its force.

She rocks toward him, once, twice, landing each time with the heavier shoe. A third step and she is within touch of his hands. This time she does not cave toward him. She stands, and stands on her own feet, eye to eye. No one notices, or hears Tot's gulped sob. "How?" he whispers. "How do you do it?"

"I think . . . cane. I image it." She too is whispering. "And it's like it's there."

She takes his arm, but almost like any woman. "A house is so—static. Any house. Here—everything moves."

They ooze with the crowd, aiming for Walter's box. In the boxes the women sit like flowers planted for the afternoon. The men are shifting, active, as on a stock-market floor, often not talking of what's around them. Few in the boxes go downstairs to the betting windows to place even the small ceremonial bets, which would not cover a thoroughbred's weekly feed. Their gamble began a long way back. During the race itself, while the grandstand shouts and rises, these owners of strings of stallions and brood mares, who maybe last week at the sales purchased a two-hundred-thousand-dollar horse singly, or joined some syndicate for millions, will sit immobile. They look bored.

Tot has to go downstairs for the paper. He leaves her in Walter's empty box.

Downstairs is a different world. Tipsheets are being carried underarm, binoculars leased at a stall. Women wear every kind of costume, from showgirl outfits to grocery-vendor sweaters and splat shoes. Knowledgeableness runs the ranks like fever. Some are solemn with it, as if just now anointed by a hot tip from a private demon. Others holler and jostle and trample from the gambling excitability inside them; win or lose, you have had this.

He has a moment's ache to be one of the lower classes, jolly and anonymous, though he knows better than to believe that upstairs is only power, downstairs is only joy. But here, too, they are visiting deep summer, if only for a day's outing. Mornings, the longer-term old geezers—who will later fill the porches all the way from the rackety Broadway hotels to the Gideon—which sits poshly in Franklin Roosevelt's Works Progress–built park and in August will not take just anybody—will cluster all together at daffy-shaped pergolas to take the corrective waters. Now it is chance-taking time all over. Night lies ahead like a separate resort. Then toughs from Albany and Schenectady will crowd in, to broach the honeysuckle lights on upper Broadway, or to gawp at some tent left over from a last night's soirée. Under cover of those a college rapist will ply the wooded campus, though he may not make the local paper, should he succeed. That same night, four high school girls will pledge their troth while thipping thodas at McDonald's, and this the newspaper will record.

Meanwhile, in a twenty-room cottage that a genteel Catholic lady last year left to her church, which then sold it, the new owner, who has auctioned off the Tiffany votive window for enough to re-cover the entire downstairs walls, including the library's shelves, with leopard-spotted suede—is having a housewarming. There, on a sofa stacked with pillows fashionably on end like after-dinner mints, Marie-Ange will change her bed allegiance, as she does in August of every year. Men will dally with her or avoid her, all that long night. She, whose presence makes some parties, destroys others, will be dressed as Queen Mab.

What can't happen at a spa—where Midsummer's Eve is on three separate days of one week claimed by three different hostesses?

Or where on an obscure lane, a girl who in the morning will regain the power to walk alone—or to take three free steps, may lose that power—or the need—by dark. It can happen. As happened in the dining room at Grayport, to a back wall of which she had tottered once, landing with her arms spread butterfly, the cane dangling or seeming to. "Saw her father behind the swing door maybe," that coarse, tenacious woman her mother said afterward, winking. "He used to measure her growth on that wall." The breakfast table had smelled of her spirits. He had picked Nola from the wall like one did a flattened moth, before she had slid down it all the way. Had she or had she not taken a step or two to it? The use of a cane is a subtle thing. The growth marks were still on the wall.

They hadn't spoken of her mishap until a day later, lying in deck chairs on the lawn of the Block Island hotel they had fled to, which her younger sister, the one who also helped fund their mother, was that summer helping to run. In the foreground an iron dog looked out to sea.

"I just fell," she said. "I used to fall toward him. We had a game."

Maybe you still are—her mother had said, as they packed up to leave. Falling toward your father. Maybe that accident of yours only clinched it.

"She's smart when she's drunk," Nola said.

"Crap." Broken bone is broken bone. He didn't want to say that. "She's the one still falling toward him, don't you see?"

He'd surprised them both. Dr. Tot. Who would have thought him capable of it?

"Maybe if you image yourself—" he'd said. "Walking." The way the therapists had taught her to image a particular muscle move.

A rehab unit is so enclosed. In salt air its language can sound false.

"Oh, I am—" she had said. "Right now I'm imaging myself toward that dog."

—

Downstairs in the men's room he meets Gargiola, who beckons him. "Like to talk to you."

"Sure. Come along. I have to check the size of the gate."

Biggest gate of the season so far, the man in charge tells them. Tot writes the numbers down.

"You have a betting system based on how many at the gate?" Gargiola says.

"Christ, no. It's for my job."

"You have a job?"

"Of sorts. I always do."

"I didn't know."

A gray-haired woman passes, the former state governor's right hand. "Hi, Tot."

"Hi. Didn't know for sure whether you'd be back or not."

"A Guv is a Guv." She hurries on.

"She's got it right," Gargiola says. "But how does she know?" He listens to Tot's explanation with his head cocked. "Like your job, don't you."

Tot laughs. "It's here."

"Like it here, huh?"

"Yes," Tot says. "I like it here. Don't you?"

"Like the palaver behind it. And out Union Avenue, day like today, you can see clear to Vermont."

"Vermont?"

"They have horses too now. I own part a track, the Green Mountains. Not exactly thoroughbreds out there, though, ha?"

"No." As the thoroughbreds, if they could know their own exactitude, would likely agree. "But a horse is a horse."

"Not here. God should strike you dead, saying a thing like that. Say, listen. Want to ask you—."

A man eyeing them greets Tot. "Your wife admires our cannas—talked to her just now. Send her some, anytime." He passes on.

"Who he?"

"Buck Slater. Head of the track."

"Owns it? When'd he buy?"

"Lord no. Runs it. For the Racing Association."

"Ha, just an employee."

"Don't tell him that."

"He an employee, he knows."

"Yes," Tot says. "You wanted to ask me—?"

"First, I want to say sorry. About this morning."

"Couldn't be helped."

"Your wife takes things hard, don't she."

"She's had to."

"That Venezuel. He don't like women, you know."

"I didn't."

"Yah, one of those. But he likes her."

"Well. Well, I better be getting back to her." But he finds himself liking Gargiola. The man is probably a character. "She tries it every year. To go through one whole day on the job with me. And night."

"Never gives a scream, does she?" Gargiola says. "Next door, we never hear a thing."

"Well, I don't beat her," Tot says lightly.

"That's for sure." Gargiola squints up at him. "Not that thoroughbred . . . Hey. What's the grin?"

"Only, that when they say that about a woman here—and they say it a lot—the joke is, who are they complimenting—the woman or the horses?"

"Jesus," Gargiola says. "If that ain't crude." He snicks the handkerchief folded to a point in his breast pocket; it matches his tie. The suit is a beaut, but for business, a city suit. "Even men like your cousin?"

"My cousin?" It wouldn't do to ask which one.

"Wheatley Whatsis. The guy with the—." Gargiola pokes his own buttonhole. Wheatley always sports what he calls a posy, provided by Rootie when she is home, even when she is not speaking to him. Gargiola flashes a smile. "Why I'm hanging you up—I been offered membership, the Reading Room. Buzz me straight—should I join?"

His teeth aren't white but are real. His hair, cut straight up, is still dark. Some of the women will call him virile among themselves, and smell venture capital. The men will sense money maybe freshly laundered and new in the pocket, though there isn't a bulge in that suit. Such women will talk past Gargiola in the Reading Room, to such men.

The eyes are not just a character's.

"Only if you use it," Tot said.

Gargiola roars silently. Tot's hands are seized, fisted in his, then shaken loose. "Go in peace."

As Tot starts to turn away, one of the flexible hands takes him by the shoulder and turns him back again to be stared at, the way a man does when he's putting it to you. "Women had ought to scream. My girls scream at any little thing."

Upstairs, he sees a clump of people surrounding Walter's box. He rushes there, finding Nola calm in its center. The new governor, passing with his daughter, who remembers Nola from the time they both worked for the party's head candidate, has stopped there, a retinue forming behind.

The daughter is plump and plain, and gawkily relieved to find someone here to know socially. Nola meanwhile gives him that certain look. Bathrooms are a problem here, because of all the steps. She can't be whisked away, but a cripple can always leave without excuse. Only at such times does that harsh word shadow him. Under the short brim of her hat he whispers One-two-three-*Scram.* Behind them, the governor's daughter, squealing "Bye-bye!" adds tactfully, "What a cute bag."

In the patron's room at the track they have Virgin Marys and crackers after she emerges from the john, and go on. On this day, because of all the logistics, they eat fully only at home. Outside in the patron's parking lot they pick up the Volvo from between a Mercedes coupe and that coffee-colored Rolls which comes every year from Wilmington.

The polo field is a scraggly local meadow redeemed by contributions from the August people, though its marquee still looks odd. Picked locals, prodded to recall that native polo began in these parts, are pleased to serve on working committees, and as part audience to a sport so elegantly for the few. The August set supplies the players and mounts.

There's no match today, only a committee of women under the marquee, fussing over tomorrow's refreshment plans. The seats in the stands are unshaded and hard. He leaves Nola in the car, backing it up for what shade it can get under a hedge planted as encirclement. The hedge, facing the highway behind the field's farther edge, still looks tentative, but he will lay no bets against the field and its backers.

Lord Monsey is waiting for Tot with the famous polo pony, of Indian ancestry, which he hopes to have Tot ride in a match or two. Rootie's party this evening is in honor of Monsey and his lady, houseguests whom she has enticed over the water. If she cannot have England she will borrow it.

Monsey, a newspaper owner given an earldom, is long-boned, solemn and sixtyish heavy; if he ever rode competitively he is certainly past it. "Here's the nag."

The small horse standing in its makeshift loosebox is a horse in a fairy tale. Tot had once seen a royal consort emerge from a visit to a banking house in Wall Street, his silkily valeted figure and brushed hair unearthly under that frayed financial sunlight. The pony, aloof on this tough, yellowing turf it has been brought to out of its own moist midsummer, has the same pedigreed gloss.

"Won't you ride him for us? Be honored."

"Thanks." He chooses the easiest beg-off. "No kit."

"No problem."

No, of course. Some one of them here will have everything, or they will provide. His own gear lies in the vanished tack room at Westbury, along with a polo mallet and scarred ball from the last chukker of his final game, after which his teammates tossed him in the air. He can feel that rough, repeated landing, lying in those arms for a minute each time like a babe in its crib. "Thanks. Much too rusty."

"Oh, not tomorrow, m'boy. Next week's match. Brush up with the teams in between."

Even Rootie has urged it. It's not like borrowing money, Tot—which they both know she will never lend. It's done, Tot, I assure you. In England anybody might borrow a mount... Anybody who rides like you. Maybe she's forgotten how, early in his marriage, a tumble had laid him up for months. Leaving Nola to the mercies of Grayport—a practical nurse who ended up tippling with her ma. Or else Rootie, given to urging divorce as proper for the early mated and maybe mismated young, has not at all forgotten.

Tot touches the pony's flank. It stamps a hoof. Look at those hindquarters. He can feel his own astride them, as he angles down for the long scoop. A royal mount can be a worker, too. There's a twitch of the hide, a nosing, an *au-gh-h.* Tot laughs aloud with pleasure. The horse knows it's admired. "Look at that eye."

Monsey's own, as smart as his beast's and a little like them, regards him. "Why not, then?"

"Thank you, but I can't risk it. Family matter."

"Ah. Wife won't let you ride."

"Oh no, she'd rather I would. Loves to watch."

"Ha. Sporting gal, eh?"

Tot sneaks a glance at the Volvo, its blunt, faded shape iridescent with heat. He can just glimpse the white blur of hat. "Very." He turns to go. They shake hands. He takes a last look at the horse. His dead cousin Budge never played polo. That gear left at the Westbury house had been bought on its own.

"Offer stands. Anytime." The Englishman looks puzzled. He, too, has caught sight of the hat. "Two of you care to?" He gestures to the marquee. "Sun is broiling."

"She's very tired," Tot says. He cannot say she is an invalid. He has never known how to say it. Rootie must not have told the Monseys in advance. "Tonight." He's suddenly so tired he can barely get it out. "You'll meet her tonight."

In the car, asleep with her head back, she looks like tired marble, like that bust at Grayport attributed to St. Gaudens but not accredited, which her mother has never been able to sell. Marble too can grow fretful over the years. His wife's not that yet. Looking down at her, the stick, the hat, the bag, he can feel her weariness in his bones.

But over a supper heated by him from the freezer, and with her wide awake, they are themselves again. If an image hangs before both of them, they do not speak of it. Only of the party—does she still think of going to it? She does: after all, isn't this the one day? Well then, he has a surprise.

For the last few years she has had only a single evening dress, a shepherdess pink-and-green, charming, but always the same. The dress he brings out was once immured in what at Grayport is called the Goody Closet, almost empty now. "Your sister sent it back." Not the helping sister, not Dolly either, but on application the dress had been sent. "I had it washed by that old woman out the peninsula used to work for you all. She said she recognized it. Your great-grandmother's wedding dress."

"Great-great-aunt." It had belonged to the marble bust.

Rootie's evening party, like most of her crowd's, is set early. Morning horse-reasons are alleged by some, and are real enough. But the other truth about parties here, which are for the middle-aged who have no other entertainment but themselves, is that nobody can wait to get to them.

When Nola comes out of the bedroom, all antique white and lace-chokered, he is sobered, even before he turns her around to button up her back. And turns her around again. The dress, austere with lace at the top, wild with it below, nestles the long neck, pointed chin and piled hair just as he expected; the skirt hides as he had hoped. But there's no hiding what her indented mouth says to him as his brushes her hand. "Smashing," he says, and she is. No one nowadays has that small a waist, no matter the reason for it. But the dress is after all a wedding one, with that double effect—when used for other occasions, which such dresses bring. As a sometimes exacting painter of herself, she will have seen that she is aged by wearing it. Yet can she see how behind that double-edged veil the thirties casts, he can still see the girl, in flawed outline?

From behind his back he hands her his second surprise.

"Wherever did you—" she says.

"Day I drove Wheatley to Wall Street and back." In the Bentley, until then trusted only to the chauffeur, who had had a coronary. For which odd jobs Tot gets payment in kind, of the sort designed to help him keep afloat here: tickets to the Museum Ball, to which no one gets in free—value four hundred dollars, or his club memberships paid. "Saw it in a shop on Madison Avenue"—which specialized in romantic maternity clothes. The article he bought had been crooked shepherdess-style on the arm of a window model with a sensitively curved stomach. But this he does not say. Oh, she'll love it, the pregnant salesgirl said. Kind of a fun accessory. I have one myself.

A slender, cream-colored Parisian walking-stick dating from the twenties, here and there gilded just enough not to have its owner mistaken for blind, it is strong enough, too; he has tested it. Use me or not, it says to her; whatever happens, you are not to blame.

"Couldn't stand that old brown one of yours any longer."

"I knew you couldn't," she said.

—

Rootie's front lawn, ablaze with floodlights and uniformed Pinkerton guards, looks as if a small-scale revolution may be in progress, but it is merely that all the ladies have been to the bank.

"Evening, sir, madam—er, miss," the surrogate butler says, and the stutter pleases Tot; the man even tries to take the cane. This former inn which Rootie has rented is bare-walled, and furnished with nullities of which there are scarcely enough, but everybody is here, the women in the sequin-struck yardage they're used to, the men also very correct, no fey shirts or cummerbunds; a colored dinner-jacket might even get the back door.

Most correct are the two pallid sprigs who here represent male youth. They are not particularly pimpled, but afterward one tends to recall them as so, with small heads of indeterminate jaw. Being foaled has been the main thing with them, and the blood has run out, the brains too. They will have been to the small, select schools which still teach the attenuated manner, and to the less distinguished colleges. For sheer want of personality they will sometimes procure for themselves a bad name. One of them, Hardingham Biss, who is Tot's distant relative, flounders around the girls of the New York City Ballet during its season here, and is known as a brutal one-night stand with the more naïve collegers. He has better-grade siblings who never pay their devotions here, as Tot is sure he will do all his lucky life. His pal is a puffier example. A family chauffeur once summed them up: "Oh, Dingy and his pal, they just got no physique."

They scarcely nod at Tot and Nola, who do not count. They will do the same to Lord Monsey, since he does. Though right now everyone, including Monsey, is looking at Marie-Ange, who every night of this important week will break out in one of her "newies" from Paris. Tonight's is a black lace jumpsuit with slits easy to follow. She has been to the Golden Door spa to prepare for it. Everett Salls, the crowd's wit, is heard to say from his wheelchair: "The ass is the newest of all."

They eat at long trestle tables and board benches set up by the caterer from Albany, whose much decorated food is often hard to identify, what with so many yellowish sauces, noodle-cut greens, and a dessert half cardboard marquetry and flying a Union Jack. But the wine is a Mouton Rothschild; there they buy the best, though often supping it down with potato chips. In the beginning Nola asked him how it was the sporting rich got so little for their money—or was it only up here? *That* he could answer. "On the move as they generally are, it's usually the same everywhere." Do they like it all right that way—she persisted—the expensively bad food and dress? Or is it they just don't know? He isn't sure. The people she calls "they" have so recently been "us." But she has cherished his reply, now a byword between them: "They have so much else on their minds."

Down at a table's end, Rootie, signaling to rise, shaking high a wristlet of square diamonds pure enough to drink, is fending off compliments. "*Nouvelle cuisine.* At least that's what they bill me for."

As they move to other downstairs rooms which give on the entry, Bonnie Doe breezes in from a party on the opposite side of Broadway, shrugging it behind her, her white hoopskirts and scarlet sash billowing. "A tent! On a night like this. And with tomorrow's tent coming." That will be the Museum Ball's tent, already set up on the museum's grounds, whose canvas walls will tomorrow swell and depress to such a bladdery motion that cars passing by on Union Avenue will pause to watch. She flicks out her crotch-length string of pearls the size of sourballs, which are generally conceded to be real at all times, since Bonnie Doe, once a small-time singer, is not well-born enough to be comfortable with paste. "I've had it with tents. Had one last year. Only so much you can do in a tent."

Her husband, Button, who it is admitted may be the best-tended eighty-five-year-old anywhere, knows this already and has delayed at home, just now following her through the door, worshipfully. He is a mild man with only one vice. In his case the borderline between sweetness of temper and senility is close, but given his pedigreed millions, which are impressive even here, nobody is about to examine that.

"Button's been looking at movies of the Duchy," Bonnie Doe says, flinging her arms toward one and all. Button, named for that ancestor whose signature on the Declaration of Independence is the rarest, has no further ambitions, but she would like him to be an ambassador to somewhere, because she could be such a good one. To that end they have to date bought anticipatory houses in five countries, each time letting the current Administration know. Where appropriate—though Bonnie Doe complains that such countries get fewer, they build a religious chapel to match. "And whey-ah," she now says, "—are the guests of honnah?" She is not Southern, but with costume can become so.

Lady Monsey is just at her elbow, an austere, frankly middle-aged woman in what Tot's mother would have called an afternoon dress, of navy blue. Monsey himself after one quiet look at Nola being helped up from her board bench, has brought his wife across the room to meet her. To a murmur from Rootie, trailing behind them, of how democratic Lady Monsey is. "Served us tea at the castle with her own hands." And they had really bought the castle only because of its stables.

Bonnie Doe, presented, bows straight-backed enough for independence but deep enough to allow her curls to fall forward.

"Duchy?" Lady Monsey says to Button. "Yaws?"

Bonnie Doe usually speaks for him. Otherwise he may without preamble begin one of his jokes, which are vintage, but not rare. "No-oo," she silvers out. "Not all ours. But kind of a chunk of it. Being the size Liechtenstein is."

"Speaking of sizes—" Button says to Lady Monsey. "And duchesses. Know the one about 'Me compliments to the juke'?"

"She's not a duchess, Butty," Rootie says, giggling. "Doesn't want to be, do you, Leda?"

"Well, in this one she is. Visiting a military hospital. Leans over the bed a wounded soldier, and she says: 'My good man, where were you wounded?' And he says—"

"Admire your dress," Monsey is saying to Nola. "London—all my daughter's friends are wearing them. If they have the luck to have them."

Rootie, to whom the dress a minute ago was what you wear if you can't afford to buy, says: "Why, Nola. Didn't you get that from our side?"

"No," Tot says. "You gave her that big easel came out of the family bank, remember? She hasn't yet painted anything big enough for it. But she will."

"And the soldier says, 'Ma'am, all I can say is, if the juke was wounded where I be, you'd be a very un'appy duchess.' And the duchess says—"

"Ah, you paint," Monsey says. "All you busy girls. My own daughter's working as a reporter."

"See?" Rootie breathes to a bystander. "Their daughter works."

Butty is used to his words being hung on. Where they aren't, he and Bonnie Doe don't go. "And the duchess says, 'My poor man, is the bone broken?' " He puts a hand on Monsey's arm. "The bone. Heh-heh. And the soldier says—heh, 'Me compliments to the—.' Ah-hah. Heh."

"Oh you—" Bonnie Doe says fondly. "You. Isn't he devilish?" She really does think so. All their life together that has been enough for them.

"Tot's a reporter," Nola says to Monsey. Lifting her face to him, she adds low: "I saw that pony. Make him ride it."

"Oh yes, Tot," Bonnie Doe says, "but in London they wo-ork at it." Bonnie Doe is seldom mean. Where they go, people give them so little reason for it. But Nola's dress is too much what hers was meant to be. "Hear that, Butty? Lady Monsey's daughter is a writer."

"That so? That so." Button has one topic—his life—which supersedes even his jokes. "Now Bonnie Doe and I are just looking for a writer. To do our autobiography."

Monsey has had to turn away. The English, when they finally laugh, really crimson up a job. "Have they only the one?" he mutters to Tot.

"Now, Button. She wouldn't want to do us." Though on the peaks she and Butty inhabit, this is one of the things Bonnie Doe does not really believe. She lifts her pearls toward Lady Monsey. "What paper's she on?"

Lady Monsey, inspecting her own blunt nails—gardens, no doubt, is surprised, but her eyebrows are equal to it. What other paper could it be? *"Ahs."*

At that point, plumb in Lady Monsey's vision also, is Marie-Ange. She is waving her finny behind in search of a sofa, the two spriggy young men following, but no sofa seems to have been provided. And where is Wheatley Senior? Sometimes in August a host is not at his own party, but that is not Wheatley's way; he is the main cousin to too much. Perhaps that affair on the little yacht in Schuylerville hasn't yet foundered—or was that another year? Events here are crushed so close, like rose leaves all in the same bowl, that if properly attending all as ordered, one may see the progress of any affair in perfect focus; in fact, this is what most people do for reading matter here, and as the most respectable of pursuits. What's wrong with a world where people are sportsmen and -women to the end?

No, Wheatley is here, and has discovered a sofa for Marie-Ange. And who is he leading up to join her, brushing an heiress or two on the way? A good heir, like a good man, is so hard to find, yet in the nature of human account-keeping they too must exist. Why, it's Lord Monsey, his soft brown pony-eyes almost preceding him, his long-chinned complexion returned almost to norm.

At Tot's side, is his cousin Rootie about to send up a cry? Her skinny, waistless, red-lipped style, with those pointed cheek-wings of black hair, has returned twice since she first copied it from an elder sister. Didn't it come back in the 1950s? And now once again it is the very thing. The cry spins from her, imprinted upward by that flung diamond wrist: "Oh, are you going to England next month, too?" But to whom is she saying it? Walter Mallory, devotedly interested in Nola's cane? Or Bonnie Doe's back? In this crush it might be addressed to anyone, and was it a cry or a wail?

"So am I," she says in the harsh voice roughened with cigarettes or alcohol, or maybe only with the stinginess so often carried in the sporting blood like a guardian white cell. "So am I. For the backgammon."

—

Out on the Surrey Inn's doorstep, Tot and Nola are leaving early, as they do everywhere, yet he has a feeling the party has not yet done with him. He had the same feeling after last year's party.

Behind them, the door opens narrowly. A man's hand, gold links shining on the cuff, thrusts a white card into Tot's. The door closes.

Tot still seems to be standing in that brief shaft of light. He has remembered what he has forgot, though not precisely which. The gilt-bordered invitation, on the stiffest pasteboard, means that it was one of the power rituals of the month—why must his dingbat subconscious always pick those? The card will merely give him the new name or names attached to said ritual. Before he has a chance to look, the door opens again—though a host's time is valuable. "Where were you, you squirt—when they gave out the Duveney Cups?"

In the Volvo, he and Nola grimace at each other like truants, then begin to laugh. The car is facing north toward other one-month-inhabited so-called cottages on either side. Norman-style villas or American gothics or other survivals, they are only a patch of enclave now, rising perennial after a winter of solitary porchlights. Tonight they are awninged and floodlit, or red-shaded from within to set the Tiffany oriels glowing, or rearing porticoed pillars thicker and higher than any Greek Revival house ever had a right to.

Ahead, the dark cone at the end of the street called Broadway seems still to lead to what his mother used to call "the Lake Georgic silence," where her grandparents had had a rambling way station of a summerhouse, and then on to the stony, moose-hung Adirondack retreats with ten-mile-long driveways, where, sitting upright on the gnarls of rustic furniture, eating quail and deer shot on their land and splashing in icy natural tarns, the children of that generation had been tutored in vain toward the simple life. As he and Nola swing away, the festive yellow from the tent party across the way slides behind them. They face the remains of the old town now, and beyond it to the south the other highway, scabbed with fast-food huts all grimly together, lit up like the fun palaces these want to be.

Their own lane, as they turn into it, no longer depresses him. Homecoming has all his life had certain heart-sinkings before he goes in to the always positive joys of one kind or another. Today has merely been one of those days, or lists, during which you never have a full meal or drink, only the constant social sips that leave you nervously keyed up—but for what? Here what gets him is those steps. He solves this by lifting Nola in his arms, to carry her inside. Did he do that last year, too?

At the top he almost stumbles, the way you do when the known space isn't the same. Bat-sense. The air is thick, silent with objects he can't quite see. He and she never leave the porchlight on, that surest sign you're out—only the one in the bathroom at the back, and an attic bulb which shines eternally for the paintings stacked there, though who knows whether that's better for them than the damp?

"Have to put you down a sec."

"I'm no bride." She hangs onto the porch railing. He reaches across what should be a balcony-size deck with a small chair. Before he fumbles the light on he's smelling lush green and mingled scent. Flowers. But not cut stuff. His porch has been planted. Window boxes, spilling vines and pink-purple trumpet shapes, the boxes clamped to the rail. Hanging baskets of fuchsia. Urns of prim yellow-and-orange line the house wall; side blankets of fern mask Venezuel's on one side and the police captain's on the other. What makes him laugh out loud is the tall dracaena, bent solicitously over his chair, like a barber. "Look at that. My chair will never be the same."

Local taste, all right. In August the nurseries and flower shops glory, and winter in Florida on the proceeds. Bonnie Doe, leading all the rest, had once spent thirty thou lining one of the huge old drink halls at the spa with roses for Button's birthday, though gently dividing her custom among all the town's florists, and "not to look snooty," serving hamburgers with the champagne.

"She must have had a crew here," he said.

"Who?"

"Rootie. Who else?"

"She usually sends roses."

"Maybe none left."

Strange plagues of want strike the temporarily gilded town—dearths of frozen raspberries that year the hired cooks were all on the same recipe, or of bottled water, or real butter. Meanwhile, a too-obliging liquor store might be left with a load of vintages the winter town will never buy.

"Look down there," he says. "The top of the cistern. They even did that." He trains the flashlight he always brings from the car. "Are those dwarf roses?" The tight-closed buds tremble as if on trial.

She stares at them a long time. "Portulaca. We had them once, at Grayport."

As he lifts her up again, a coral fuchsia brushes his ear like a mouth and he guesses what Rootie must think she has done this for. How would Wheatley have told her? When talking of women, or sometimes to them, he likes to affect the coarse squire. "What do you know"—would he have said?—"that girl of Tot's is in foal."

No matter. Once inside the house she is clearly making the little signs women do when they are going to sleep with you—hair let onto the shoulders or the neck arching it back, a veiling of the eyes. Though she slips into the bedroom to change, he waits here; to her the actions she must go through are not seductive; she will not believe him when he says all women have certain routines they rate as ugly and often wrongly hide. Sometimes, slipping out of a T-shirt under her eyes, he feels guilty of his own body. It has not yet begun to lie to him. Maybe she is silently drawing it in all its easy articulation.

In the small bedroom, really her dressing room and just big enough for a double bed, they sleep instead, by her insistence, on separate, less than twin-width beds, since she may wake at any time for a pain pill, or to do her ever-remedial exercises. At the outset he demanded a double bed; now he no longer pretends he prefers it. The truth is he needs his sleep. Tonight, though, they are going to stay here in the room which is studio, dining room, and sitting room all in one, as their life is, and they will fall asleep on that broad couch, backed with her books and sewing kit and their tea set, on which, as she has said, they conduct their mental life. Her "they" is kind, ignoring his porch. Living in one or two rooms, as they usually must the rest of the year, and this the largest, they have reticences—nothing to do with sexuality or nudity, or even bathrooms. His comes from having grown up in other people's houses, hers from bundling with sisters who nightly told everything.

He hangs the new cane on one of several hooks near the couch. There are similar hooks near stove and fridge, table, door, and work corner. She uses them as unconsciously as any workman might trip a mechanism in everyday use, translating her cane from hand to hand to wall and back, quicker than the eye. Though he has tried to make the hooks of equal height, a rhythm remains in her progression around the room, one as hard to pin down as which two of a horse's legs are in synchrony—yet when he and she are apart this is the rhythm he visualizes her in, and would, were she to die.

"No, give it here," she says from the couch.

He brings the cane and himself, in a rhythm too.

The cane twirls in her hand, sparks light. "Too pretty to throw away. But I'll try."

He gathers her in his arms, to squeeze her until she cries out, like any normal girl. They kiss, are moving, entwining, like other people. Far back in the mind of each, only a pinpoint, is the fact that they are. When a man must lift a dead limb, must feel the sharp of a hip not all flesh against his own, when a woman cannot turn to tease with breast and buttock—then you do mark it. When a couple cannot twist, roll, jackknife, splay—and fall.

"Good?" he says, yearning into her.

"Love . . . ly."

Is that so because they don't do this too often, so many details having to be right for it?—or because of all the friendship time in between? Would it be even better if they went on more regularly, or tried? Since the beginning they have asked themselves many things. They are grateful she wasn't a virgin when they met; with her as she is, they couldn't have coped with her being a virgin as well. The physical risks, the freakish solutions for it, are seductive enough—even if you would give anything not to have it so. And the comedy—she said. Like riding a bike with one leg, isn't it, for you? The cleanest answer always goes down best with her. And for you, he'd said. "Who knows what a regular couple is? We aren't."

At times he does think of other women, healthy girls you might bat and scrap with, and rowel until they shrieked—and go pinky-linked with to the deli for sandwiches afterward. And home to do it all over again. As for her, who knows what she thinks?

He does. Wouldn't it be best for you—she'd said early on, to have some other, someone who—you know. He's not smart her way. But he knows when to slap the ones who are. "You want to deny you exist. You want to deny me—the satisfaction I get from it." Her face had stung with pleasure—that he could slap.

But that was early on. You slap a child to make it breathe, not thinking of all the pain in store for it. He couldn't do it now.

Isn't it enough that both lie there on the old paisley throw that by now has as much mend as pattern? She keeps sewing the holes together as if it's her map of the world—the one they come back to. It's enough that both their faces are wet, no matter who has wept for what.

Sometimes she falls asleep then, which completes his pleasure. He imagines her body for this one night swung in the easy hammock of the norm. Or he will go over his own accounts—mostly that attic treasure for which he wants first safety, then for it to be in sight of the world. Or, pretending that he is doing what others do when they count sheep, he sets himself to sewing a sail.

Once, when she was in the hospital at New Haven, to save money he had lived at Grayport. In order to get away from the house during the day he had apprenticed himself to three elderly brothers who still made sails in a wharfside loft halfway between. "Ever been to sea?" the senior brother asked, squinting in that airy light.

Though Tot had crewed a few times on the Sound on a friend's Star, the phrase had been of such formality that he'd felt obliged to say no, which appeared to give satisfaction, along with the second brother's verdict: He ain't no hippie. The third brother nodding, they took Tot on for the novelty of it; nobody apprenticed now unless you could rope in a son or nephew, of which they had none.

Sailmakers don't like to give up their secrets. Each of the brothers had been apprenticed by their canny father to a separate firm, and all the long day their rivalry crisscrossed the shop the way the stitching Tot was being taught zigzagged the pennant of duck he had been given to work on. Even though palm-and-needle was impractical for the small sails they now made, he had to learn it before he was allowed on the machine. Brother Dick, late of Ratsey and Lapham, City Island, had seen sail made by Ratsey of Cowes in which this stitch was inside the edge of the seam only. From Silas, once of Cousens and Pratt, Boston, he'd learned that hemp rope, when stretched, retracts fast, which is helpful in finishing off a cringle in a sail's tack. Have to shrink the thimble in, not hammer it. Ben was the one who knew all the bad stories, of amateurs who tried to sew cotton sail with linen thread, or set a new jib to dry without the sheets attached, so that the slapping of the clew punched holes in it. Ben had been trained in the murderess Lizzie Borden's town, Fall River, the two others joked, so his view of life was extra dark.

In Tot's half dream he is sitting at a bench of his own, bench hook fast to his right-hand end, where are the big pointed wooden spikes called fids. He has already done his laying out. It is his fifth sail and he has managed to get fifty square feet out of seven-and-a-half yards of yacht-grade duck. Even Ben has approved of its outer curve. "For once your roach ain't nigger-heeled."

Tot has chosen oak, faced with brass instead of aluminum—for wherever weight won't count, stainless steel wire over galvanized, and has numbered his cloths, meanwhile borrowing a needle for luck from brother Dick, the kindest. Beeswax and pricker are ready. Once he has finished that sail, his first marketable one, and takes his leave, he will learn the secret of his qualifications, and of their scorn of the modern sailor. None of the three has ever been to sea any nearer than the christening of a sloop. But right now, he is about to begin.

But he can feel her mind burning on beside him. Opening his eyes, he sees hers are wide. Outside, a car door is slammed; somebody at Venezuel's has come home. They listen for his door, which is creaky. How small-scale life here is. Does the fastest mile at the track make up for that? Water and sail—are they really another life? What is?

She sits up, using a hook, her fine hair in damp halo. Does that flower-fume from the porch cool the heat or heighten it? This is the wishbone hour of the night, when perception goes either way, and he trusts most the retinal images which have been on the inner eyelid since childhood.

"Tot. Rootie didn't do up that porch."

"Then who?" He closes his eyes for the answer. That loft, so airy. Sewing the sun to cloth so easy. Float away. Leave even her who is anchored at his side.

"Gargiola. I think he's standing outside."

"Has a right to." Maybe his left foot is a little closer to Venezuel's garbage pail than to ours.

"Outside us."

"Isn't everybody?"

His own echo wakes him. He sits up, unguarded still. What did he just say? "Flowers make me groggy." He snaps his fingers, a falsity he despises in others. "Right. The window." He pads to it.

"He there?"

"He is." Standing in the light of his hired limo. Not many of those up here. They mean New York, or Jersey, and men dressed for business, not lounging toward it, like here. Though by the glare on a white jacket he can see Gargiola must have somewhere along the line changed clothes.

"He looking up here?"

"Might be."

King of the mountain, in a white suit. Gargiola isn't smoking a cigar, but he has that air of self-appreciation a cigar gives. Yet the night makes him look small—even on this lane.

He hears her percuss across the floor, the swish of a dressing gown plucked from the wall. The tiny dice-shaped house has its own sympathetic creaks. She stands beside him at the window.

"Why would he do it?" Tot mutters.

By her sigh, so seldom escaped, he can tell he should know.

"Because of the cat."

He turns on the light.

"Oh, don't. He'll think we think he's a prowler."

"He is. He's stolen your sleep."

Out there Gargiola is looking up, dazed or hopeful. His feet are on his own land—or Venezuel's.

"Now we'll have to ask him in," Nola said.

At their signal Gargiola throws up his hands gaily. He had expected it.

As he enters their door he bends deep, a man not too tall for it but acknowledging he brings in the night, and a life other than theirs.

No, he wants no drink but he'll have a seat. The heat has not blurred him but has maybe softened his voice. Choosing an iron garden seat, cracked, he sits, looking around him. "Nice. Venezuel said. I like a crowded house."

"And porch?"

"Hah?" He catches her smile. "Oh. Oh yeah." He can't pretend not to know her meaning. He doesn't. But he dismisses it.

"But—thanks. Really, thanks."

"You're welcome," Gargiola says broadly. Clearly it was one of the things one does for women, and a gesture gone with the day. "But—listen." He lightly touches Tot's knee. "You have wine, I'll take a glass. I don't whiskey." When the wine comes, he sips, his eyes creasing.

"White wine. Very *in,* Pa, my girls say. Oh, Pa, don't drink no more that Dago red."

Those tawny eye-creases hoard shadow. Maybe these two on the couch can sense the held-in resource of a man whose knowledge is wider than grammar. He clinks his glass with both of theirs, "Lissen." His idle hand grasps the chair arm, knuckles high. There are no rings on it. "Lissen, I joined." He leans back, twirling the glass. It is one of the blue ones. Tot, watching that grasp, is not worried. "Phoned my three girls all down Long Island. 'Your pa's joined up.' Gloria, that's my youngest—'What, Pa—the Army?' 'No,' I say, 'I joined a Reading Club.' "

For a second that gets past them. Gargiola has meant it to. The crinkled eyelids expect it, the hand on the chair as well. Then—who knows who starts it?—they all three begin to laugh—and they all know why, though it would take a month of Sundays to say.

When it dies away, Nola says: "You dog."

He and Nola smile at each other like cronies.

"You girls—Gloria said 'You devil.' " Gargiola clicks his tongue for his girls' manners. "Only the boys grew up their mother. So those girls think they're all mine or I'm all theirs, know how it is?"

Of course they do. Tot the fatherless has maybe learned such things best, from those most consistent educators, the long line of house-and-stable underlings—vaqueros from the Argentine, nannies from the Midlands, trainers from Palermo, and Indian-profiled blacks from Saratoga itself—to whose spiritual care he had been left since he was born. The nannies were never his own nor the stables either, and the only help he could lay claim to personally were "the couple"—a terrifying Finnish pair his mother had briefly been able to afford, and the Scottish gardener at the one school where Tot had not been a day boy—and that man only because Tot had picked up from some other servitor what the game of curling was, and would listen to talk of it. Such people like you to be lorn or out of place; it makes them feel safer. Nola, too, had had them, in the people on the peninsula who had cleaned and repaired the old house, sold it eggs, and remembered its ancestral dresses.

Meanwhile you learn from them what your own family will not

supply. Generally they adhered to strict churchgoing but did not always go—these nurses who at home had played the pools but here might gamble on something more foolish, these chauffeurs who disapproved of your mother's divorces but lost their jobs because of drink, or light-fingeredness. A low-grade criminality affected them—or their relatives—like an expected disease. Sex might come in any variation but was never described in words. Mothers died early, and the girls did or did not take care of their pa's, or ran off with the boys who had run off early.

It was a code of conduct like any other, leading to the strengths a code can lead to, when like Gargiola, whose nose now lofts proudly, one has done well by it. "So from now on I stay at the Club, I tell them. Now the boys gone home, don't look good your pa bunk with Vennie." He chuckles, easing back in the iron chair. "People might talk." But his smile, finding a horizon even in this tiny room, is not for that.

"Why?" At times Nola has the cripple's naïveté. It's the constant removal from so much.

"He's gay, Nola."

"Nah, nah," Gargiola's hand fans stiffly, meaning that's not the way to say it. "The girls know him since kids. He was barred from the track that time, he cooked house for us."

"Oh, of course; why didn't I—" She gazes into space with the cartoonist's squint. "He's always munching those liqueur chocolates. And those goons in that orange car, are they that way too?"

Gargiola gives a blurt. "Don't never offer them no chocolates. Anyway, they don't come this way again."

"Yes, I heard," Nola says. "Penalty. What's a penalty, Mr. Gargiola?"

He leans forward to pat. Men on the knee, women on the hand. "Nothing you'll ever have to pay." He stands up. "Thanks. Lose my only horse, get a bid to join the bigs. Been a day."

"You lost a horse?" Tot says.

"You weren't there for the seventh? She broke a leg, had to be put down."

"My God—Straightaway?" Syndicated for three million—and the two-year-old hope of the year. "Straightaway was your horse?"

"Me and two Japs not here. So the trainer gets me down from the stands. And when it's over, who should come by but your uncle Wheatley?"

"Cousin."

"Cousin. Extends me his sympathy, the horse. Insists me back to his box. And by the way, why ain't I a member that Club? So I say, 'Funny, I been tipped off this very day I should be'—and slip him a check then and there, ten times the hunner-dollar membership—Jesus, you guys keep it piker. And then I say, 'And you won't find me no no-show, Mr. Wheatley. You kindly tip the steward I'm a member, I'll stay there this very night.' " Gargiola's eyes, slitted almost closed, opened wide. "He goes that dark shade pork—he do that regular? He better watch his pressure. Hold the breath like that, you could pop a vein."

"Oh, he would never say anything," Tot says. "Anything wrong."

"Not him. Only that Wheatley ain't his last name, he says. And would I kindly not call the place the Club."

"But what were you doing in the stands?" Nola cries. "Owning a horse like that."

"I come from there." Gargiola's voice is colorless; it has given this explanation before. "My old man's dad worked a track. Goshen. You know Goshen, huh? But he always bet our money here."

"Why don't your girls come here, take care of you?"

At times Nola has a certain Grayport arrogance herself, which abashes Tot, but only because he wants people to see through it to the purity.

Gargiola is not bothered. "They say, 'Pa, build us a showcase house, buy us a box.' I say"—his head moves side to side; he has the habit of audience—" 'You're us, you're smarter you don't buy no box. You do something you get offered it.' " The head seeks Tot. "What do you say?"

Tot hesitates. "Will you buy more horses?"

"If you say to."

Tot knows that this is so. He shivers. But will you love them?

"Just say the word."

It could happen. From this small house, spiraling out of its one-flue chimney, a new syndicate. Meanwhile, the pliant old framework of this city gives a little, as it always has, like the plushy sofas of its heyday.

That savvy August calendar, never too discriminating where there's dash and funds to nudge it, unrolls for Gargiola's girls. Some circles they'll never get to, of course, never even know about. Except for those, aren't there invitations enough for everybody?

But not enough for this man. Not far enough.

"There's a couple here," Tot says. "Big politico from New York State. Member of the Commission, natch, a box. Stay at the Gideon, though, don't own a house. No horses of their own. After ten years, last year they build one. Right in the district, next door to all the parties. Finish it last June–July, just in time. Give a housewarming. For the hundred fifty people they thought they knew."

"Yeah?" Gargiola says, his face alight. "Yeah, what?"

"Twenty-five came."

"Jesus. A closed shop, huh."

"Not at all." To the end of her life that woman would consider herself done in by the merciless calendar and its hostesses. Or blame it on her being Italian or Jewish or even Democrat, or whatever they happen to be. But the prejudice goes deeper. Or the religion does.

"So, what's the answer?"

Can't the man see? What do the owners talk about in those early-morning trials—will talk about with anybody in their same fix-mix of hard cash and sentiment? A syndicate is one thing, a stable another—and horseflesh a stricter calendar.

"Somebody here run that end, too, huh?" Gargiola whispers.

Tot can only nod.

"Name of?"

Man O'War, Citation, Seattle Slew, Alydar, Affirmed, Secretariat. But not only them, and their kind—with here the white blaze held high as a tiara on some noble head on canvas in the Museum, there the red dapple that was Secretariat even on the day he lost to Onion—each shining without need of studbook, in the eyes of somebody who has an operation of his own going. After them, why, all the possibles, the no-names or nearly, slogging the Exactas, the Electas—and always that twenty-to-one dark creature, who might end up a Triple Crown.

Some owners are more devotional than others. Some are monstrous people, or ridiculous. A horse doesn't necessarily dignify. Nor do you need to love them at the start, or even later. Some owners never come to it, only loving the gamble or what it can get you—a guest list, girls. Whatever—have to fly your own colors, if you want the full, multicolored return. Gargiola won't have figured that out yet. Some of the smartest never do, especially those who will gamble on anything.

"Pay you twenty thousand for that answer."

Tot stands very still.

"Oh dear"—Nola says—"now he can't answer you, you stupid man."

Gargiola whitens. "I'm good for it."

"Oh dear, oh dear." She plucks a cane from the wall and rocks toward him. "I'll give it you for free. Or almost." She places her hand, the drawing one, on his lapel. She's liking him but watching him, too—he's a good subject. Drawing them is understanding them. She always likes them during it, and sometimes after. "You tell Gloria—" she says, and Gargiola at once smiles, relaxes. "Tell her—here you build the barn before you build the house."

Gargiola freezes, head cocked—a man who is learning something. He is not stupid. "You're—a doll." Quickly, he kisses her. Poking a mischievous glance at Tot, he steps back. Behind him, the rickety end table from Rootie's servants' wing falls over. The crash is blue.

Gargiola stares down at the iridescence on the floor. " 'S late, isn't it? And I've done it. And I'm sorry. Too late." He gathers up the shards in his handkerchief. "Where can I replace?" He sees in their faces that he cannot.

"It's all right," Nola says carefully, "I have more." Involuntarily she and Tot glance at the still life on the mantel. All three look at it.

"I heard," Gargiola says huskily, "I heard she paints art."

Tot silently brings him a wastebasket. He drops in the handkerchief, still gazing at the painting. "So you have them. What a girl." He turns to Tot. "And you—you work." It's their turn to stand dumb. He sighs. "I wouldn't offer you no job of mine. All on the level, don't worry. But you wouldn't take it. And she—she'll want that picture. But Venezuel says she does them all day long. So tomorrow, I come around, eh, look at the stock. Pick a couple or more. Any price. Preferred high." He bows. "So, *buono notte.* Good night."

"No," Nola says, turning away. "But thanks."

Again that alarming clench at the man's nostrils. What has that other white-clapboard side of summer here, of Main Liners and Marylanders and Kentuckians, taken to its iron-railinged, one-month-a-year heart? "My girls have lovely dining rooms."

"She doesn't do that," Tot says. "Sell to anyone."

"Never? You swear?"

"Not so far." Tot notes his own feet are in running shoes; when did he do that? "Galleries have asked. And worry not. The price would be high."

The man is surveying the room again. "You two could sure use it."

Tot begins to laugh. "We sure could."

Nola swivels at this betrayal. Lovemaking has made her face supple, though. It could pass again for a bride's.

Gargiola takes no notice of that. He may be one of those men who love regularly, without much regard for the personal. Or equally one of those who love once. He towers over her as if she's a kid. "Why the hell not? You keep them all? Where are they then? ... Up there? ... You making an estate your fourteen children, no? Huh." His anger is more than financial. He's assessing her the way an oculist does, with the speculum between his eye and yours, right-left, left-right.

Nola, studying him too, is already drawing him in her mind's eye, maybe paying him for his flowers, or making him pay for them. He won't know which until it's done.

But he knows something—after all, three daughters. He smiles at her, one end of his mouth up. Yes, the women will go for him, the younger ones even, doomed to their pallid or fat-boy specimens. "What's the crap?"

She's studying her stick. The old trusty that takes her between stove and fridge. "Because I can just barely"—it comes out a whisper. "Afford to give."

Or did she say—to live. No, that's his own nightmare, true as it might be.

It's finally cool. Gargiola looks at his watch—almost time for Venezuel to drive in. The air's bestirring itself, getting ready for the push toward razors, and other penalties of the morning. Gargiola looks tired; maybe his own three are not all paragons. "So you keep your foot on your husband's neck, huh? Better you scream."

She is already coming toward him. Dropping the stick to the floor, she has lifted the stoutly framed still life from the mantel and clasped it in front of her, like those men who walk the streets with signs hung on them fore and aft by straps over their shoulders. Tot himself sometimes forgets how strong her forearms are. There are no straps. And there is no cane. He holds his breath. Maybe he will die of it. Leaning on the picture as if it is not in midair and held by herself, she is walking toward that man—not to Tot. Does that make it easier?

Gargiola, across the room from her, doesn't move. He has caught the image.

Hayfoot, strawfoot, she reaches him. "Here."

If the man takes it, will she fall?

He takes it.

Now she will fall forward on him.

She stands.

Tot stands alone, under the shadow of the big easel. It's a peculiar thrill, naked and cool along the backs of the hands, this feeling of separateness. All these years the easel's high triangle has kept this waiting for him. He thinks now of its front side, of jumping up, light as a cat, to poise there, a foot on each of its oaken joints, his head at the peak, hands at his sides. Man on Easel, Alone.

"You knew I wouldn't catch you, missy, didn't you? They always knew when, my kids." Gargiola crosses the room in two strides, picks up her cane. Straightening up, his head bumps the mantel. Rubbing his crown, he sees the picture concealed until now by the other. "What's this one?"

"She gave it to me. One birthday."

People need a minute to decipher it. But only a minute. That's what's wrong with it, she says of the picture now. Cruelty, to be worth anyone's time and study, ought to take longer than that. But when you painted that, you'd never seen the place—he always answers, hoping to let the matter rest. She never will see it, that lovely, shallow spa which for a month hovers never-never, as real as you and me and the postman, over the locals' church suppers and death notices. She wants the deeps.

"Haw. Haw. Haw haw haw." Gargiola laughs with no mouth-stretch, a rumble like a command. "Blow that up a photo-mural, I got just the wall for it. Out Lake Desolation, that old-style nightclub, dates from the early days. We renovating. Got no plans to open yet. See what comes." He says this last with dreamy authority. "We got a new governor." He shrugs. About to hand her the cane, he says: "Or maybe you want that other one on the hook there."

She accepts the old trusty. "Notice everything, don't you."

He regards her, a muscle in one cheek winking. "I was a kid, we had a large family. Healthy but also invalids all ages. Trusses, walkers, crutches. Field-pickers from the old country, have to walk looking their knees. One granddaddy with a stroke, sits all day on a seat with a hole. Two my cousins, TB-ers, headed for the coffin early but meanwhile pretty spry. Nobody in a home. People wear out, you keep them with you. My own mother wore a breast."

At the door he says: "She could paint that wall herself, out Desolation. Any subject she wants, so long it's Saratoga. Fix her a chair with a hoist, no problem. Don't mind offering *her* a job."

He peers back to where Tot is. "Or she could paint my dead horse got shot, to fit on that thing. Human size."

He pats the still life under his arm. "Thanks, I appreciate. But I got two more dining rooms to supply. Nobody takes care me, see? Without I take care them. So I come back tomorrow, after the seventh. And this time—I buy."

He points a finger at Nola. "She don't offer people no leeway. That ain't safe."

—

Tot is in his favorite summer-night place, on his own roof, his back against his brick chimney, never pointed up since built and not yet needing it, an arm negligently around the much newer turn-of-the century housing for the bathroom vent. Porches, no matter how amiable, are for display. If he falls, it will be onto the mock-orange, and soft turf. It is long before dawn; even the birds have not begun. Nola took a pill, then another one. She sleeps. He can smell the alien note of the gift flowers. The porch is no longer his only, and he is glad. He will nurture that new setup like a father.

After the first pill didn't put her under, Nola said from the other bed: "My father was a gambler, too. Sure he was. Didn't we live for years after he left, on the art he'd collected? He used to send us instructions on what and where to sell next, and for how much. He never lost." Then no more letters came, and they surmised he finally had.

"What'll you sell?"

He has actually said it.

"What did he mean," she says, "that it isn't safe."

"He doesn't like to owe."

"I can understand that. But I go on doing it."

"He"—he lets the long breath ride—"doesn't have to."

After a while she says: "What can he do to us?"

"Squeeze us out."

"He wouldn't!"

"No. Some lawyer."

At this hour the small nesting house is at its best. A lane, a porch—even a swamped one, a door, a couch. And a roof. Even if the title to all this has never been properly searched.

"He has a—kind of dignity," she says. "What he said when he broke those glasses. Like a verdict. I admired that."

"It won't do—to like him. Yet that's part of why one does." Tot feels a certain kinship. That may be just what the cousins say of him.

"Tot—." She is rolling the pill bottle on her bedspread. "I don't give you much leeway. Do I."

When he is unable to deny this, she takes the second pill. Quickly it makes her dreamy, even giggly, as a release from pain can. The pill is not just for sleep.

"I'll invite him for tea," she says. "With the governor's daughter."

"Wrong governor."

"So he is." Her profile is calm but looks its marble age again. He supposes that this alternation will go on recurring. And he will go on noticing.

"Lake Desolation," she says. "What a name for a gambling joint."

"Some priest was martyred there. Indians."

"Tomahawks—" she says. "If you make too much moola off the house." They should laugh at that but don't. "You think he and his crowd could bring gambling back?"

"If he has a crowd. Or—" He won't say it.

She does. "Or if Wheatley's crowd becomes part of it." Her lids droop. "He's so old-fashioned," she says, slurred.

"Who?" His cousin?

"Gargiola."

"So's Saratoga—or that's its pitch. And he comes from Goshen."

"Wha-ts—that mean?"

"Trotters. Famous once. But he wants to make his stand here."

"With the thoroughbreds. And Gloria meeting them . . . Like to . . . meet Gloria." She is almost asleep. "Hope she likes . . . picture." Her eyes open, wide.

Now they're coming to it. In their routine, always year by year the hardest for her to ask and him to answer. Did she—really get out of the wheelchair, yesterday? Leave that walker at the Salvation Army? Let the cane drop?

This time he cannot bear it. Because they are coming to the end of it. "Go back to sleep."

She sits up, hair wild, eyes too. He never saw her at the time of the accident. Knocked cold, he had been taken to the hospital before they got her out, only seeing her after they had knitted her together, months later. Since then he cherishes her calm, connives for it. If he had seen her at the worst, would this have been different?

"I don't want to hear," he hears himself say. "I don't want—"

"I walked, didn't I. I walked, holding the picture. Not an image. A real canvas, and just carrying. I walked. And then I stood. Because I had to. What he said was right. Because I could see he wasn't going to catch me, if I fell."

And you always would. She doesn't say it. It's merely a fact—the last of them. They have connived as they can.

"August." He says it like a confession.

She gathers up his hands and holds them to her mouth, pressing deep. "Leeway. I want to. What?"

He might be the one with the pills in him, the answer floats out so easy, past the palisade of jobs he will never get or be dowered with, and the ones he will have to take, if he can get them. Passing it all by. "I want to stay here." Waiting for the horses he wouldn't want to be without, but not following them. Here when his cousins come, but not because of them. "In my own house."

He's never seen her crying. She cries like anybody, blotting at the nose. It occurs to him that with time, passing through the small leeways others allow themselves, he and she may end up like everybody else.

"I'll paint him," she's saying. "I'll paint him three times over. One for each daughter. On that easel. He can buy and buy."

He pats her cheek. "He'll still owe you. But maybe he won't know."

"And the attic—" she says.

"What about the attic?"

Shining like a child giving a present, she snaps her fingers.

She is asleep. "And then I'll paint you—" she says in her sleep. "Over and over. Oh, what a relief it will be. To paint life-size."

—

On his roof, the warm brick is a poultice at the small of his back. If he could ride again, that ache would disappear. No matter, he's locating himself, and Saratoga too.

It lies between his cousins' big cottages—which should be beleaguered by the times but aren't yet, and all those small, steady merchants of family life television-style, who take over in winter. Northward of it, those Adirondacks lumber away from this shallow-set valley to the Canadian grandeur. On his right hand, a vagueish Vermont, on the best days a cleanly modest mountain line, heavily settled now with what Nola's mother, still sharp-tongued before dinner, calls the young old-timers. College-bred peasants from the decade just before he and Nola were young, some are now selling off the dusty acreage where they grew herbs and handcrafts to the newer dilettante horse farms, which are half tax deductible. Vermont, for all its icicle high-mindedness, is ever a summer state.

Again on his right hand, but back in his own state, are the two river-remains in the vicinity—the Mohawk, with its memories of Jesuits and knitting mills, and the Hudson, a mere stream at Schuylerville. In his Saratoga, these two rivers scarcely bisect the consciousness. No matter, this is his map.

We—are August. To the east and south of him the racetrack spreads satisfactorily, coiling its tentacles around Albany and the ship-of-state, bypassing a big city jeweled only with its sister-tracks, from each of which some pure-numbered U.S. highway will lead to Lexington and the Derby, and on to England, Japan, and to all that lesser world which returns here as the yearlings do, every year.

We are in truth our own state. Wars and famines do not enter it, not even for the poor. Childhoods are always big if horses were in them; second childhood flows gently. Chance is a better pursuit than happiness. Where there's only one month to a calendar, all life is in it. Tinsel can pierce with the hurt of steel. And a horse, or a girl, can break a leg at the right time.

Maybe he can get a horse now. No more steps, thousands of them, down and up from porches and long verandahs, struggling across rooms. Down payment might cost no more than a railing. Or he will borrow—a horse only—the kind only Gargiola can afford. He'll pace and canter it, even feed and curry it, until he himself is a character. He will be the cousin who rides.

The heat is still sparkless above the small town he's never had time for. By day two church spires, just yards from each other, dominate. The taller one, in need of repair, deserted by its white congregation for a motel-style sanctuary and rented out now to blacks, may soon go; even the rector of the more prosperous church opposite, hit by a stray shard from that tower, hasn't found himself Christian enough to help. Tot will miss the dawns the two towers make. But Satan can always tempt Saratoga with a new silhouette.

Stretching his arms, he begins to sing from a ditty heard each year in the town's piano bars, ever since he was allowed in. Verses endless, names too. The names come from the old horse nation—Vanderbilt, Phipps, Whitney, or from those late of Hollywood, like "Admiral" Gene Markey, who married three movie stars, and then an heiress, blithely introduced as "Meet forty million dollars," whom he eventually loved the most—or often out of the smellier corners of finance, now grown respectable.

You knock the table, at every owner's name:

> "Oh—
> At the races
> Is still my fav'rite places—
> Though swapping quips with a ——— can be a bore
> And ——— pays up as slow
> As the jitneys she is famous fo-or—"

This year there's even a Watanabe—rhymes with hobby, and the Frenchman Weill, pronounced with gusto as *Veal.* But in order to last, both story and name have to have a certain chime. Meanwhile, with all the tipsters around, no stranger should find it hard to join in.

> "So—
> At the races
> Would surely be God's spot—
> If horses could only talk
> And Wheatleys could trot."

It may take some doing to find Gargiola a rhyme.

Still, who knows? Squint far enough and the whole sky is a grandstand, spotted with geranium. Stretching wide, he slides down and off, onto the mock-orange bush. He always wanted to.

Pulling himself up, tallying his scratches, he sees Venezuel, just getting out of his Le Car. His jacket glitters with some brand of official epaulet not known to Tot. The track has relented. Or been sweetened.

"Where'd you come from?" he asks Tot.

"Fell off the roof."

"Heh. That's what the women say, when they—you know. Get preg." Venezuel is drunk. His dentures have a foul smell.

"No," Tot says. "When they don't."

"Heh. Been drinking, you, anyway?"

"Some." He thinks of Wheatley and that champagne. "Been up since dawn."

"Heh. Dawn is not yet."

"Yesterday's."

"You seen Gargiola anywhere?"

"Earlier. You working the stables now?"

"Not me. Management."

"Ah good." Low-downs like this poor old boy are everywhere at a track, along with the flies. But in the stables, in that air of liniment and gold dust, the horses are soon to be ministered to. Everything clues in.

"Leaves me a note he's sleeping in town," Venezuel says, "where you suppose?" Hawking up a bit of phlegm, he spits. "That man don't sleep around."

So he's begun his adventure. Long race, Mr. Gargiola, even from where you sleep now. Maybe for luck Venezuel will lend you his antique poker chips.

"Hope he loves horses."

"What the hell does that mean?" Venezuel said.

The Man Who Spat Silver

After work is a special feeling in my case. I translate good books I myself don't have to write, slowly pulling forth the soul of the writer, along with the tongue. When I am finished for the day the floor of my little study on the park is covered with broken words from which rises the mild incense of my craft. Once I tried to bring back a supply of the long joss-sticks sold by the monks at many pagodas in the Orient. When I opened their slim envelope here it was full of brown half-inch bits in straight lines, as in a kind of telegraphy. The bits were still burnable. In the same way, I will use some of the words on the floor tomorrow.

As I close my desk I smell my own sharp lather, of a horse that has not raced but has been exercised. The last thing I do before my bath is to close the shutters on my non-view. The study, which once looked north across two low-built blocks all the way to the Tavern on the Green, is no long "on the park." Two high, flattish buildings now intervene, their tawny planes slid one over the other and pocked with the same size windows, as if some architectural prodigy had been playing with monstrous cardboards. Yet, I always close my own high window's lower shutters as if the view were still there. By the time I return from my daily walk it will seem to be, merely behind those by now experienced chestnut slats which might generate anything. At night, late enough for all the facades to be dark, I will reopen—for the morning stint. I work with reality. Only one not always mine.

The Fifth Avenue corner I walk towards is one of the hubs of the planet. Not to be compared to Lenin's square, or the great political campos of Rome. Or that square made by Mao Tsetung and said to be the largest in the world, Tienamen Square in Beijing—once Peking. Perhaps this part of the Avenue is closest in spirit, if not symmetry, to the Etoile. The air of course is more naive, less cynical than French air, the taxis are dirty yellow carryalls, not Mercedes. Yet limousines are channeling alongside each other like mausoleums on the move in their separate oxygen—this hub is fashionable.

The wind here comes from Central Park south, two blocks north. Pale and raw in cold, pale and dusty in summer, it has a lyric twist to it, like a hundred dollar bill cockaded for one's mistress' stocking, or for a grandchild's birthday-plate. While up there on Fifty-ninth Street the sad horse cabs clock one century into another; on what farm do they still find those saintly nags? Human drivers seem always available for indenture: college dropouts who want to wear top hats, hawk-nosed anonymous artists, missionary youths, and girls who see themselves as the city's classic Greek messengers.

History competes here. Some anciently regal buildings still flare, a few of the low height now so precious. The Bunny Club, once across the avenue, is long gone; sex is nothing like the joke it was. The Plaza Hotel is still hanging on. Around the fountain, so are the people. Next spring those wrong-colored tulips will still spatter the eye. And half the women walking past me or along with me are in conscious costume. As am I.

Some days I slouch west in jeans and jacket to buy food, but if I walk east I dress for it. Not for the friends I meet embarrassedly, who stare at me anew. I dress for strangers, in the smartest clothes I have. Most of these my confreres in the trade—editors, publishers, distinguished colleagues—will never see me in. I am dressed like a woman who may just have lunched at Grenouille, Plaza Athenee, or any other of those interchangeable spots always arriving or forever there—although I never lunch.

Perhaps I dress for my past, never quite so solid as represented? Because of the books always to be done, my future is as solid as anybody's at forty-five and in health. I make it a habit not to speak the language I am at the moment translating from, saving that only for my desk and my eye. For those border tongues or street dialects which are my sideline specialty I would find few interlocutors anyway. But the books to be done stretch before me, angel rescuers every one.

Whenever no new ones to my standard come along I do fresh editions of old classics, into English of course—the language by which I live, and in which—with one exception, I perhaps dream without knowing so. To recover which dreams—if I could first write them down in my own way, I would gladly die. They say Russian grips those born to it like that. And Mandarin Chinese. Although I am said not to respect others of my trade as much as I do writers, I honor any who work with those.

"Oh—she's a writers' groupie," they say of me. "She doesn't deign to hang about with us." Actually I avoid meeting writers in the flesh. I'm a groupie of the book. The ones that seem to lower slowly from the heavens on their own umbilical cords. Or are spat up from the depths, pure as the devil's catarrh.

Translating a book like that is like training a dog to be your own. The breeder has vanished, is only a name. The obedience trials of such a book and its final submission are as much a matter of whips and leather—and wrenching kindness, as any rigmarole from De Sade. When I must give up such a book as finished, then ends also the full torture cycle of a translator. There would be only one way to keep such a work for one's own—to retranslate it from English back into its own language. In my own version.

What keeps me from that wild course? Money—the gritty salt that often keeps us from the madness skid? I do like a good living. But reason too, and maybe love. So, I let the pup go. And as the next work pushes toward me, I am not sorry. What comes in the mail may be merely a slim volume of poems, but the syllables dripping like nacre from a spoon. I won't be paid much. But the publisher can depend on me—and I'll manage. Redemption is at hand.

Today's a sunny November day, my favorite, as long as I can walk wrapped in fur. The coat has a hood of the same clotted amber fur as the rest of it, and the hemline flips my ankles as I walk. One acquires such mantles in northern climes that need them, old-line countries with no scruples on the fur score—Denmark, Canada. That way one escapes guilt for the slain fox. Since I'm tall, with good eyes and skin, I carry the huge wrap well enough. My goal, beyond either warmth or style, is to be comfortably anonymous. On this street, where women of similar aims pass constantly, this is easily done. If I were to push through that purposefully heavy glass door at Bendel's which in turn admits one to looking-glass territory, I'd be merely one more approved customer, worth scarcely a glance from the clerks pretending to be disco debutantes behind the cosmetic counter's rainbow barricades.

But I continue my walk. I am not here for the stores but for this whole combo of sky and square, people, wind and cold, and myself hidden among them, loping along in the youthful stride that sensuous ease surprises one with, in my head these rippling insights I've had so often before—and return here for. For this hour or two, prying on through the traffic hoots and sirens that have replaced the church bells once a part of city dusk, I am in absolute balance between vanity and intellect.

I need this. Women like me often have. Eighteenth century women, say, educated to the philosophical riposte—and to the lace-encrusted stomacher. As for me, born into a time too explicitly right for women, of late it has seemed to me that I myself am being translated willy-nilly, often by dirty-fingered public scriveners who would push my malleable self into such slots as suit the day's by-lines. Can we exist these days, men and women both, except in versions of ourselves too popularly phrased? Where does translation stop?

Well—here's the hub so much mine and yet everybody's—Fifth and Fifty-seventh, southwest corner, and all packaged as usual. Across Fifty-seventh, Bergdorf's windows are a weekly lesson on the kind of vulgate used by manikins in order to teach human beings style. Across the avenue Tiffany's doll-size cases are intent on being jewels themselves. Whether or not they show timepieces, each is like the innards of a stopped clock. Or of the worldly world in miniature process, there for anyone to see. Money, say, frozen into a blue stone that in a twinkle could be money again. Or Paloma Picasso's daughterly designs—art for customers, but with the master's multi-dimensional profiles kept in mind.

Yet as I wait I am enclosed by the bumbly warmth of others. The standees of a corner are always its rightful tenants. Here for the day only maybe, that round matron with a shopping bag—picked from a pile in the hall closet—of the same mauve as her down coat. Here every day the gaunt, frothy-haired office worker in her thirties, slinkily dressed to catch a boss. On my right—one of those spastic boy-men who carry manila envelopes on foot, testimony that some benevolent firm hires the handicapped. Ahead, just in front of me, is a well barbered man in a navy blue topcoat, a man the doorman of any good hotel would recognize. And here am I. We're an assorted mixture, as the sweetshops say, but destined never to reach any home intact. A clutch of mathematical probability whose randomness no computer would bother to solve, we wait for the light to change.

I am warmed by you, though. For the moment—until we have crossed the street in the usual ragged unwinding, you are my true friends. All the way east to Sutton Place—if I choose to go that far—and at any pace I choose—I can acquire a clutch of you, as well as this same pause repeated as I will it, caught in its centrifuge like a canoe in white water, before the drop. Stories I want daily—but not to finish. Riches of probability—and doubt.

Lights change. We at the curb were a movie still; now we reactivate. The dumpy shopper is already out ahead—and must backtrack. A police car shoots alarums at us, boring through the gridlocked traffic—and we are going to lose the light. In front of me the man in dark blue waits obediently, like the rest of us. I notice his haircut, one of those international ones, Italian or French or fifty-dollar American, the brown outline of nape superbly natural, no overt sideburns, headcurls discreetly cropped close enough not to be Romeo, but not military flat. A good head, too.

I don't see the face and don't strain to. Such heads, such coats on easy-postured shoulders are legion here. On men who counterpart the right women—married to them, or their lovers or friends. Men of that Magritte poster which shows the same man silk-screened over and over, men who commute by the hundreds between the top offices and the VIP airline lounges—anonymous men of style. Swiss underwear and a watch with a hyphenated name. Brainy or shrewd, nice or scoundrel—not too many fools. Not an artist, except from South America. If French, possibly a chic scientist. If from here, perhaps a composite who has long since assembled himself, maybe even around an origin hidden like an Achilles heel? But in every case men of that similarity which comes from coldly fixed habits and purchases, and the assumptions born of being always in pocket, with a smile fresh from dentifrice. Men suited up for these shallows, this hub. I don't notice this man individually; he is merely one of my insights. Maybe my reactions were a little slowed because of that.

For as the light went green, the man in front of me bent sideways—to his right—and spat.

I am taken aback; indeed I recoil. In a winter wind, spittle blows. Just then a cyclist wheels a contemptuous figure-eight between me and the others on the curb, who move on home free—the man among them. I am left behind, the red Don't Walk already blinking.

Over on Ninth and Tenth Avenues the pavements are scabbed with spittle, but rarely so around here—it's a matter of class. Men of that dark blue persuasion, or their gray-striped or sportively khaki kin, seldom spit on the street; it was odd of him. On a cold day in a poor district the blobs of spittle freeze to opals. As the green light shines and I step off the curb I glance down.

No, all's clear; probably the feet of the others trampled what he spat. This is the city. These layers, from the eyes, elbows and breathing either side of you down to whatever intimate detritus lies at your feet—are part of living here. Nothing is on the road beside my boot but what you often see half-trodden into the surface tar, or other compound—a cheap-jack glint which may be a smashed earring, or a few links of tawdry chain.

This is such a glint, of no worth but clearer imprint than most. Silver chain it seems to be, in the form of a bowknot, or once that, but now almost part of the road's surface. Once, in the jewelry district in the Forties, I passed a shine on the pavement and turned back, but was forestalled by a man who came from behind, scooped up whatever lay there and hurried off—but that had been a louder gleam, an anagram of gold in his hand. Now I am sophisticate—and move on.

Corner of Fifth to Madison, south side. Mainly a causeway for behemoth suburban buses and frowning shoppers, with now and than an imperial young couple, six foot each, identical hair streaming, and clearly flesh of one another's flesh. I love matched couples, even when the matchmaker is only youth. These momentarily blessed pairings make one feel there is a balance to the world.

As the traffic bombs on I see I am this corner's solitary standee. That can happen. The city can make one doubly alone. But I can always take refuge in language. I have time to reflect on why I sometimes address the world as a "one," other times as "You"—the truth being that language for me is an immortal stammering.

Then shanksmare tugs—and "we" all press on. The next block, so frivolous, will be a relief.

The block from Madison to Park reminds me of a British friend's description of his country's class system: "Oh yes, the levels remain the same. But new people are always rising to fill them." Nostalgia Ltd. used to be the tone here. Countess Mara cravats for the rococo chins of would-be royalty. Antique dealers with engaging monikers like Sack, or Shrubsole. Or that decorator whose window, always a complete sitting room covered wall to wall to the last ottoman in one hugely floral fabric, hinted of the patterned people lost or lurking there, safe under that ruthless signature. Now I see that the terrible rents have excised the last holdout, a shop all spotted with color like a precocious child's daybook—Chelsea figurines, eighteenth century table settings, curly paste-china lambs.

But hey nonny nonny, as long as private greed and public progress leave the buildings,; if "the authorities" keep these facades for my strolling, I won't carp. Deep fur, shallow ruminations, and shops whose truck I don't crave—that caramel colored boulle chest for instance, prissy as a Pekingese. But for a walk out and away from your own part in the once and future holocausts of things—a boss combo. That's a phrase, useful for Celine maybe, if working from the French. "Truck," used that way, has the same letter count as Dreck—the German for trash—when you mean shit. Meaning pushes languages toward each other. The words move as limbs do, part of the whole.

Pity about Park Avenue coming up here—all gone to banks. In the window of the Bankers Trust I see myself muraled: a long column of fur, face still angled, not yet fallen, Toulouse-Lautrec boots. Ah vanity, prickling the nose like champagne; after work is no time for the thorns of intellect. And I have passed the corner without marking it.

"F,M,P,L,T"—we Manhattan girls used to advise the girls from other boroughs as we rode the freshman bus to our joint high school—public but on upper Park in the old Hunter College building—"Fifth, Madison, Park, Lexington, Third. To remember them just say to yourself, Foolish Mothers Praise Little Twerps. After that it's just numbers: Second, First, and after that—just York." "—And then what?"—one of the girls we'd been patronizing said. "—Oh, just the river." —At which her sidekick, a tough strawberry blonde whose father ran a gym where boxers worked out, spoke up. "—Why not just say Fuck Me Proper, Like My Tits—" and after a silence in which the rumble of the bus nicked our ears like a scolding, one of us said softly "—No fair the second M—." Yet in that school, where we picked at Latin the way you pry walnuts out of a shell, and mewled French that would get us nowhere in the twentieth century, and were warned off glottal New Yorkese—was where I came to my profession, and in time to what I am known best for. Those who write short—in thwacks. That's what the publishers send me, more and more. Rough Trade.

"Never dreamed you might be a woman," the Master of Caius said to me in his bed at Cambridge. "Such versions, m'girl, of the Latin vulgate"—and he made that palatal sound, British as bangers, which copy editors who have eyes but no ears have conveyed as Harrumph. Those lipless sounds made by the Anglo throat are closer to the ng ng of Asia. And have rhythm, but do not exclaim. I kept that pedantry to myself, this being bed, if one as narrow as any colleger's. "Ah—had you all been hoping I might be a boy?" With him still wattled with our pleasure I knew he was safe—and his neigh of a laugh reassured me. "Not all."

Encounters in travel are the easiest; their end is in their beginning.

Transiency is the spur, rising to reluctance at parting, but not to pain. Not so here at home, where the smart men I go for, and who go for me—men who wear their own professions like crowns—or helmets?—can scout me out. Also, I am closer to the study here, and more careless of what I say. "You are truly not marriage-minded, are you?" my most recent lover said to me—Has it been over a year? "Never met a woman that wedded to her work. That masculinely. Without fuss, I mean. And yet—" He searched for and lifted one of my legs, which are good, if not great. I like negligees that though not ruffled, abound.

I waited. —And yet—what? I wanted it said. By him. *And yet—feminine?*—Or not?—what? Like the Cambridge scholar, he was a great, fleshy man, with an important nose quite equal to his career. I like to nestle in such arms, my little finger tickling the wrist that commands, that feels itself born to do so. His vanity is as much tied to his gender as mine is, but on the male presence it doesn't show so much—and he is never shamed by it. Women, being less certain of themselves, or else more certain than we should be, are either more random about style, or more scavenging. If his clothes occasionally ran to cashmere and ties from Charvet, these seemed to have been quietly in his wardrobe for some time, and probably gifts.

His vanity—alternately as vulnerable and as flaunting as mine, was in his choice of women, always those known to the photographer, and to print. Or had been, until he chose me. Compared to his previous lover—that Italian star we all love, or her predecessor, that minister who may some day be her country's premier, I was a more than modest substitute—how was it he wanted to settle me in his house? I liked the house, and its visiting cast of grown children of a long dead wife.

But those women who have a study on the park like mine cannot always domesticate. Blinded as the study now is, the transposed books still parade from it, some say even more energetically than before. Or with a power—in the translation itself, that they never before had. And maybe shouldn't? As for me, although I must monitor my solitude and be sure to walk like this daily, there is something to be said for being walled up. As the moments thicken, one has words in the blood instead of corpuscles. In the hilarity of one's own company they howl free.

"When I think of you in my house," he said, "I see our conversations in bed. Not you in any of the usual roles—food, household stuff, decor. Even if you chose to play them."

He really did honor my head, that man. When we lay on the chaise in his library, if a book on his shelves chanced to spark an idea from me, he joined with it at once—never meanwhile letting his hand play between my legs. And perhaps so warmed, my own words trilled to him from that deep interspace where the single persona is at rest.

"But those were afternoons," I said crankily. "And not in bed."

"Nightime, once. Deep night. You told me your favorite dream. You and I talked until dawn. And slept until afternoon."

"I must have been very drunk." After work I don't mind getting a little muzzy. Or with lovers. "It's a very short dream. The bookshop?" He nods.

A junkshop really—one of those run by a mind that can no longer disassociate. Quiche pans hobnobbing with corsets. A blown out umbrella in a bedpan. Each a pearl to the owner in the rear, whose haunches have grown to his chair. "Books mostly," he says in his floating voice, and pointing. "Other stuff creeps in. But you just want paperbacks, go try Stan, down the line."

Where he points, a row of hardcover books is moleskinned with dust. Boys' serials: Tom Swift, Stover at Yale, county maps and state surveys, and nineteenth-century editions of poets and novelists, in stiffly stamped bindings of maroon, gamboge or leaf green, the author's name encircled on the spine in gilt. I reach into the space above as directed and pull out the thin volume that the dream says will be there. Poe's Tamerlane, the ultimate rarity—or extinct. "Give it here," the owner says, "I'm reading it. It defies translation"—and floating toward him like a voice, I leave it in his hand.

I never try Stan.

"Give me a night like that now and then," my friend is saying, flipping on his muffler for the last plane to Washington, D.C. "Or a day like this has been. The rest of your life is yours to say." But a life doesn't divide like that, and he knows it.

"Like to give you a present," he said, meaning me to know that he was leaving for good. "Shall it be the New York Edition?" His library far exceeds mine. "Or a trifle from Cartier?"

"The Henry James?" It's a mint edition, bought from old Dauber & Pines, in their heyday. But too extended for my shelves, and the text in no need of help. Nor does one take jewels from a man because he goes. "Thanks. From my heart. But I don't—collect."

"No, you only dispense. To your books. All transient ones."

He really was smart.

"The lady was a tramp," I say with a smile. "You knew that. You were told." Not to depend on her. By herself, and others. If not why.

His scarf is finally tied. "I know you wrote a book of your own. That sent you to hospital. Because you couldn't ever finish it." He could be cruel too. "But your work—which I believe to be truly your life—is also your excuse against it. Want me to tell you why?"

At my nod he took me in his arms. I nestled there. The chest of a man like that is a barrel on which one might be saved from one's own depths—why can't I cling to it?

"Women are doing strange things to themselves." I had never heard him whisper before. "Out of vengeance for what has been done to them. Grudging out first babies at forty. Or holding up their intelligences like grails—there's one of those in my lab. Hair smells of anchovies—last night's pizza. She must wipe her hands on her sacred cranium. Dresses in those woollies they must weave in the Orkneys during a bad blow."

In his arms I laugh out loud. He squeezes me. He wooed me first with his lively tongue. "And underneath all that, a rosebud mouth and legs like a chorine's."

"Sounds as if you should go after her."

I feel his shudder. "You don't collect. I don't clean up women."

I know that. If I come to inhabit his house he will harbor me, not reform.

He nods as if he has somehow heard this. "But you won't marry me. Or even live with me. And I know why." He drops his arms, leaving me to stand alone. "I also have a friend whose wife thinks she left him for her computer. For another scientist, you might say, like herself. But the real reason is that women like her are afraid of testing themselves with anyone except themselves. But—she's still young."

And I am not.

"But aren't we all confused biologically these days? And electronically?" Biophysics is more or less his field. "We're confusing what your lab can do now—with anything we think about time and space."

He hugs me again, growling "Come talk to my lab."

"Why won't I? Marry you. You say you know."

At my admission he groans, not for himself. Backing up, he encounters my fur coat, hung near the door to the outside because of the cool. He leans against the coat as if it were me, yet stares across at me, pulling his nose. "Partly—it's because I'm your equal."

Note how he didn't phrase it as most men would—that I was his. Nice of him. Smart.

We both smile. How was it that I could bear to let him go out that door?

He draws my coat around him, even the hood. In it, his face jutting, he looks like that explorer of the northern latitudes whom one could most trust. "The day you took me on your walk—your special one. I knew then it was no go. If not altogether why. I still don't. But you took me. On that odd—demonstration. I felt at times—as if I was with two persons." We held each other's gaze. He has a fine upstanding throat. I saw it swallow. "Both of whom I know."

I feel cold. I feel farther and farther away, sinking back, although the hallway is so small, and my feet are standing firm. Yet it had to be done; how could I do otherwise? Think of his library. Could I ever work among those primal books, even if I brought mine in? And nothing sad. —*We of the books have to be sad for the world, at least in surrogate.* —A book I worked on said that; I appear to have translated it well. Could I maintain that in this man's bear hug? In his haven of a house?

Suddenly he breaks for the bathroom. Toilet. But when he comes out his eyes are red. At the door, in his own mackinaw and gloves, he says: "Your loneliness. It's majestic. Your books are your empire. But empires crack. If that ever happens—call on me." He blew his nose.

He sent me a ring, a crystal oblong with a carved face in it. I thought he must have had it made by a modern holographer, but where I have my mother's pearls cleaned the man told me it was old. Sometimes you see the face, sometimes you don't. I don't always wear it. The note that came with it said, "You want a man who's your alter ego? I'm not that. Or else a man who has one? I don't."

I wear the ring on these walks. Perversely, it cheers me up, this sign that I have effected myself somewhere outside my usual world—and harbor. I may walk all the way east to Sutton Place and back, and on the way home stop at what used to be Harry Cipriani's Bar on Fifth. It's still a place where some of the staff know me, all the way from the real Harry's in Venice, dating from the time when I was working on a book in their own dialect. Where even in New York they sit me at a good table suitable to the way I look, and to a woman who after two drinks will call for the check with a sober smile. Where they would never commit the New York crudity of hiding or even edging out the woman who is alone.

Basta. Here's Lexington corner, that plebeian hub. The group waiting here, lined up irregularly like notes on a stave, has a modernist rhythm. It trembles with the need to sprint. Stark still, poised at the curb—is that the man in blue? The same?

The same. As I stop short, keeping him in my line of sight, I observe the whole tic—for that must be what it is. The arm snaps up. The right arm. I glimpse his watch. The arm slides down his side, sneakily. In that same second, as if the one move would conceal the other—and at the exact moment the light changed—he spat. Jackknifed upright again. And hurried across.

I have time to follow, but I stay on the curb. I saw nothing arc from his mouth. Are people with tics sly—or oblivious of them? Passing such a person, as the smile twists or the torso goes marionette, does one also see a beaten down, hideous knowledge in the eyes? I can never decide, but am always affected. When I was a child I had an aunt and an uncle, unrelated to each other, whose mouths twitched regularly, while they seemed not to know. Such tics must have gone out of fashion; I haven't seen one recently. Our era's repressions no longer center at the mouth.

That's not an insight. That's conversation. With someone, my girl, to whom you no longer talk. Whom you'll no longer see, to tell that to.

And will you once more risk looking down? "If you're going to walk the cracked pavements, the swollen crossways"—I hear him say—"you can't always expect to hold the head high."

Yet it is unwise—I tell myself—to become the scavenger.

I look down.

Again the bowknot—much less blurred. As if this time heels have missed it. Otherwise the same. I will not touch it, but I believe that it is there. And am half reluctant to leave that insignia. So sure of itself, of its shape. Like a word.

The blessing of the daily walk is that willy-nilly it carries you on. Lexington-to-Third is all welcome bustle; here the shops tug at your sleeve. I search for the man, who must be far ahead. No shop will snare him, not he. How do I know? Only that this comes to me without question. He's out for a walk. How far? Maybe into the sunset, like in a movie dissolve? I smile a correction to myself. The sunset would be the other way—west. Besides—even in this world of teasing holographs and other special effects, one learns how to believe what one sees.

A translator has to be a kind of detective. The clues abound. The mystery is in the writer, and by God can they be sloppy about that, or arrogant. The kindly ones carry you on their hip, or in their pouch, comfortably kangaroo. The great ones offer you the immortal cup, like Ganymede.

Once in a while, before I found my specialty, I would hire myself out to do a Simenon. He offers you—among luscious menus composed by his hero Maigret's wife, Madame—a method. He paints logic like a Van Gogh, in straight lines irrefutably crazed. Let the crime's solution come from below the line, beneath what you see. Damnation, in a mended sock.

His heel! That could be it. A simple shoe repair. Which might leave an imprint from the Lord knows where. Hobnailed in, or a traveler's touch-up, now wearing off. Simple practices from other countries often appear odd. Or are merely sleazy. Like those token sewing kits the chambermaids in some hotels in Asia leave you, not hoping for tips but proud of their amenities: a single needle, bent, and one spare button, its hole perhaps broken. But one day you may need its laughable four inches of thread. Just so, a heel might come off in say Kuala Lumpur. And must be sent for repair. On perhaps—an orthopedic shoe?

By now I am loping. I want to catch up with him. I don't doubt that he and I are in a rhythm of sorts. As I gain the center of the block I see him, loping also. As I slow, he slows, head swiveled just enough to the side to have seen me. Often in the city there are these brief for-a-block-or-two companionships.

We are almost to the curb. I lag a foot behind him, like some compliant wife. A dressy couple. Both his shoes are normal—slim buckled black.

I step abreast of him, to the curb. I have that citizen right.

As I do, the arm comes up, to the left of me, then sidles down. In profile his lips are parted, like on those statues, all over Italy, that spew water. A blob of silver arcs from them, but I am not quick enough to see it connect with the ground. The setting sun, burnished from a skyscraper's top windows, is in both our eyes. When I drop my glance to the roadbed, the silver imprint is already there. Freshly gleaming, iridescent in sun. I start to bend, but he shakes his head. The mouth is closed. As we straighten together, the pattern on the road has already sunk in.

"You've spotted it. Not many do." His voice is pleasant, educated, faintly New York. My own kind. "Would you care to—could you possibly walk on to Second or even to First? Behind me—to check? Then stop for a drink with me somewhere?" His glance is steady but does not plead. "To confirm."

When I draw my coat closer my ring glistens. He stares at that icy oblong. It says I'm single, but complicated. I check the road, where whatever came from this man's mouth is already dulling into the ground. Everyone's detritus does that, all of us paring the nail, clipping the hair, as if nothing is lost. Savages know better. This man is not savage. Rather—over-educated in a way I recognize?

Yet most people hawk in their throats all their lives without bringing up such evidence. There's still a faint sparkle to it, still in that same shape. A knot known from childhood, ever since one tied one's first shoelace.

"I dislike silver on myself—" I hear myself say. It sallows a skin I like to think of as matte. "But on others it can be the more subtle metal." Though one always seems to speak of it in that mincing way. A sentimental substance, suitable for graduation pins and Victorian photograph frames? Whereas gold is gold. One syllable, indivisible.

He sees I'm wavering. "Look—this is not a pick-up. You've spotted me. You can't know how important that is to me. And I've spotted you. At first I only sensed you. Tracking me. Now that I see you—don't I know your picture from somewhere? Maybe—from books? Should I know your name?"

"My picture is never on books." How hoarsely that came out.

"Ah, but you work with them, eh? I buy a lot of books. But airport to airport, it's hard to hang on to them."

So he thinks those are books. Yet face to face he does seem familiar, though I haven't a clue. Yet I'm not afraid of him. Or not personally. Only of his somehow—drawing me in.

"Sun's going down. Time we'd get to Sutton it'll be dark. Would you settle for a turnaround? Look at that sunset! Then maybe a drink at Harry's Bar? They know me there." He says this last jauntily.

"Oh—do they." If I turn west, the orange light will draw me safely home. I can't see the sun direct either way from my north window, but the sky above is often generous. And the orientation of a room long occupied contains much that one can no longer see.

I turn. All the way west the buildings are ejaculating light, some soaring, some low ones leaning toward each other like the frontispiece of a fairytale. "What makes you think I was aiming for Sutton?"

"Oh, were you?" His nonchalance seems real. "It's simply my walk. I've had a little office near here forever. In the former F.A.O. Schwarz building. Tiny, but just right for my business. But that building's done away with small tenancies. I'm temporarily at the Hotel Elysee."

I don't know the Elysee, though from his gesture it must be near. But any mention of Schwarz's, the old toy store, is disarming. "Are you in toys too?"

His eyes flicker. Hadn't I got the phrase right? It's useful for me to know the way certain trades speak of their own gear-and-tackle. If you sell silks and velvets you're in the "rag" business. Armaments cartels have been known to be "in pig metal."

"Not quite," he says.

"Pity."

"Why?"

"You could have been—just testing some gadget for your catalogue."

"Oh?"

"Don't laugh." He hasn't really. But I am almost cross with him. "Commerce can get away with being lots freakier than the rest of us."

He's staring. "It's not to be believed."

"What isn't?"

"How gentle you turn out to be. With the bizarre."

I don't know how to answer that. What is more bizarre than our daily selves?

Just then an editor acquaintance stops me, eyeing what I have on. "God Lord. Had to look twice." She wears tweed and loafers the year round, her trauma being that she grew up with nannies on Park, and now must be seen to empathize with any rag-and-bobtail who might write for a serious review. "You moved in with that marvelous Israeli with the nose?"

They never expect me to marry. "Britisher. No, I didn't."

The man in blue has faded back. Her arms crammed high with packages, she pays him no mind. Or does not connect him with me. "Well, you must have had three at once, by the look of you. Gents. Or books?" She tinkles. "On you it looks good. Never'd think you had a decent sentence in you. Though the books you do don't run much to those, do they? Well, cheers, I'm doing the gifts early. Stop by for a wee, on the Eve." She has never before invited me to that notable Christmas party. But now—I too am a mystery.

As soon as she's off he's back at my side. He does have manners. What I can't understand is why there's nothing eerie about him. Or not to me.

So I nod, and he nods back. We speak at the same moment. "Harry's Bar."

Except for once, I've never been there with anyone. For me it's where words are suspended, eased off into the silent latitudes of the self. Gianni, the waiter who serves me, saw that early, and is always discreet.

Turning in unison, we walk westward. Since he and I are of a height, our stride is about the same; we even strike a kind of pace. But as we near the first corner in our path I am troubled. "Should I—?"

He has my thought before I phrase it. "Walk behind?" Head bent, he doesn't answer right away. "It's okay when I'm accompanied. Doesn't happen. Only appears when I'm alone." His voice is an ordinary one. More his than my word-battered one is mine. Mine was ordinary, once.

"You did see? It does appear?" he says, and when I nod—"well, thank the gods for that. Or so I tell myself. Better at least if someone else sees it too."

Would it be, for me—if I were he? Why think of it? I am not.

"So—if you want to check again?" He's glum. Yet eager?

"But when you're with someone—it's okay."

No answer. He's leaving it to me.

I take a step. Close to his side. Once more we are abreast.

At the curb I am trembling and dare not look at him. We cross without event. His arms swing normally at his sides. And so we negotiate each curb. By the time we reach Fifth Avenue, when he raises a gloved hand to retrieve his muffler, one end of which the wind from the Square has blown free, I am not alarmed—and cannot even recall whether or not the hand involved in the tic was gloved.

"I love that park wind," I say. "It's always so—"

"Impudent."

"So it is. That's a better word than—." Than "saucy," which was never quite right.

He doesn't ask me to finish my sentence. Not sure whether I like that—almost an intrusion. Yet when he extends his arm to me for the few yards to Harry's I take it. His left arm, since he is on the gentleman's side of the pavement. I can't now recall whether or not that was the arm in the tic.

We make a nice couple as we pass in. Gianni, always there at this hour, greets me as usual, showing no surprise at my companion, and shows me to my usual table, seating us on the wall side.

On a chair at the other side of our table is a not quite life-size teddy bear in striped cap and shorts.

"A joke," Gianni murmurs. "Belongs a very old customer, who has just arrived from Milan. And between you and me, Signora, is a little—"

"Ubriaco?" I love their word for "drunk." It staggers.

"Altro che!" No, that they would not allow. "Only a little—" He searches for the word and finds it, beaming.

"Instabile."

"Ah."

"You are supposed to order a drink for the animal. Then its master will come speak to you. Our apologies. Un signor nobile—and a good customer. But have no fear. The drink is on the house." He grins. I grin back. What I like about his nation is their acceptance of the bizarre as a part of human nature.

"Molto bene," I say. "Bring the bear the same as me."

My companion must have gone to the men's room. I go to the ladies'.

When I return he is seated to my left on the banquette. I explain the teddy. On the table there are now two glasses of my usual aperitif, one in front of the animal, one in front of me. Just then an old man who must be the bear's owner bends over us. He is tall, thin, white moustached and in the narrowest of black silk suits. "How kind of you to help celebrate our name day," he says in Italian. "Umberto Torlonia—who is eighty today. And he—what are you, little master? Perhaps one. My great grandchild gave him to me at the plane. I promise him to have a festa in New York for us both."

I wish them both happy returns of the day.

"Oh—you're part Italian?"

"Part." That's what they always say—part—when I respond in whatever language, my accents being seldom as good as my idiom. Actually I was born here, like most of my Scotch Irish, Huguenot Dutch, and London Cypriot forebears a generation before me, so am one nationality—American, all through. Though surely by now I have translated myself impartially, a pound of flesh here, a pound there.

Borne off on the old gentleman's shoulder, his name day animal looks at me with a long lashed brown glass stare.

"How did they ever make him look so Italian?" I murmur to myself. I've almost forgotten my companion. I apologize for ordering ahead.

"No need. I too like Cynar."

That's reassuring. Few know that mild aperitif. While he sips I watch narrowly. But he swallows like anyone.

He sees me watching. "Let me explain."

"Please. And I should tell you—I never have more than two drinks here." Bad enough that I've already gone this far with him. Unnerving even. That I feel this comfortable. As if he at any moment might say what I think. As if I half expect him to.

"I've an appointment at seven to see a new office," he says. "Just down the street, west corner of Fifty-seventh and Fifth. The tenant's just vacating. So I won't keep you long."

"Oh—the tower they light up." Although I don't care for all that gilt crackerjack, in time that tower will have a persona for me, as anything seen daily does.

"Won't exactly be in the tower. My business, I need only a cubbyhole." As he screws up his eyes at me I see how charming he would be to some, maybe less so to others, not unattractive or dull, but simply not for them. Just as at times one sees that in a mirror, screwing up one's eyes at oneself.

Nor, despite his good looks do I feel interested in him sexually. Nor am I prepared to be sisterly. I feel a violent interest in what I saw—and how he will explain it. Then I wish never to see him again, or run into him. I want that as violently.

"Oh—I do well enough," he says hastily, mistaking my stare. "A million and a half last year—gross of course, not net—if you don't mind my saying. Normally I never do say. All perfectly legal. But my business, we tend to keep it dark."

"What is your business?" What's it to me? My lips are dry. I take a sip of Cynar.

"Manufacturer's agent. Know what that is?"

"Sort of. You market other people's goods."

"That's why I don't need space. Secretary, part-time. Only an answering service, if I travel. Carry most of my business in my head." He waits. As if he expects me to nod understandingly.

Of course I do.

"I work from other people's warehouses, you see. Arranging for space in each country—there to here. In other words, I don't stock. It's all liaison. And thinking up what products will go."

"That's fun. I mean—it should be." I'm embarrassed—at my empathy. After all: Gross. Net. What would he care what it is to find a book?

"That's how I started. We were in Rome for two weeks, our whole family—for my father's fiftieth. I was eighteen. And I saw those net shopping bags you can get all over Europe. In some version. Theirs were nylon string, two bright plastic bracelet handles—cost ten lira at the outside. Women used to knot them, at home, or while they peddled. And we in the U.S. didn't even have the shopping bag idea yet—can you believe it? I cornered the market." He smiled to himself. "Or thought I had. Went all over the campagna around Rome. In my little Fiat. And all the stalls in the city. My father helped—he had a warehouse at home. And when the stuff arrived over here—bales and bales, and I'd waited eight weeks for it—I had done the U.S. customs declaration all wrong. But we got it all to Jersey—my God, truckers—and to Dad's warehouse." He stopped short—as if to measure my interest.

Men will do that, when talking trade to a stranger. Half ashamed of its minutiae in their lifeblood.

"Go on," I say. "I'm in trade."

When he does go on, his voice strangles. If each of us has a particular stress area of the body, then is this man's fixation in his throat? "Dad was a pioneer. He was using modules for storage before they coined the word. Up against those forty foot high stackings my stuff looked like the stuff on tables at a church sale. Then one of Dad's clerks said, 'Try Woolworth's. They might take them.' Turned out they wouldn't. They had standards, their buyer said. I hadn't known what a buyer was, much less standards. But Kresge bought them. They were the rival dimestore on the opposite side of the avenue, then. And sold them out by five o'clock that same day. Wanted more—but I didn't have it. That's the story, many a time."

He seems in need of breath. "Or somebody else corners ahead of you. Or the stuff doesn't go. But the next year, college vacation, I went back. The Romans were making ballerina slippers out of old Army innertubes. I bought thousands. Every girl who saw them here wanted a pair." He sighed. "Standards. Rubber doesn't let the feet breathe. But by then I was hooked. Quit school, and never went back. Never looked back." He is staring at the chair the bear had vacated. "The objects you find. The wonderful, simple objects you find."

"I had a pair of those," I said, enchanted. "All one summer. Burned the feet, yes, but the cure was easy. You poked a few pinholes."

Has he heard me? Have I spoken aloud?

I push the bear's drink at him, but it's as if he's on the other side of a windowpane, although I have heard his every word. Those slippers mean nothing to him now; they are from an inventory years back—I could understand that. I thought of the girl who had worn them, that summer twenty years ago. Sometimes I think of her—myself—as she; she is so far back in the inventory.

The first time she did a book she was still in college. A townie friend's mother had a Ukrainian fortune-telling book from which she read them marvelous destinies while they ate home-stewed dark plums. The girl herself was studying Russian, not at Middlebury, the college, which hadn't offered it that year, but at night, after her other three languages. At the time she thought—or knew—that language was a substance. You could make curlers out of it and snake yourself into being Medusa. You could cook up poultices of it and cure your best friend of acne, if both of you could believe. The two friends translated the fortune book together, and the girl learned the mother's brand of Russian, primer-style—that is, with live tongues and warm hearts at your side. To learn those border languages she would specialize in later—Basque, Catalan, the dialects of Brittany, Platt-Deutsch, Quebec-ese, Magyar as spoken by gypsies—that is still the best way.

"My first trade," I said, "—we found a tramp printer, ran off one thousand copies of a fortune book—on credit, and working meals provided, and sold them like hotcakes in the Ukrainian section of the Lower East Side. Which didn't yet know it was the East Village by then—and our bright province to be."

Where we will leave her, that girl. The present is always a translation of the past. Some resist that; some bend too deep into reflection. It can be dangerous, yes, to see oneself in the second person for too long. But what if, by an act of creation—and without derangement—one could manage to see oneself—in the third?

I knew such a lot of grammar back then, I thought. For instance, the three classes of pronouns. First Person—the one speaking. Second Person—the one spoken to. Third—the one spoken of.

One learns that the problems of narration are the same as the problems of persona. One has only to be sure who is in charge.

Did she bend to take a sip of the bear's Cynar, that girl, before she left again? If she has gone.

"I specialize in small exchanges," the man next to me said. "Selling one civilization's minor objects to another. For years I thought it a wonderful trade to be in. Bringing—maybe a whistle that yodels—to American cows."

"Oh yes? Maybe that's why—" we're allies. "Why I saw—what I saw. I mean you."

What is said over drinks descends into the glass, and doesn't have to be answered on the double. Everybody knows that. It is allowable to muse. But he remains so separate, in profile, his lips closed. He'd said that when someone was with him he was safe from what overtakes him, but could one trust that? What if he has such a spell here? Or what if I am the eerie one?

At the door, the white haired man is exiting, his birthday gift still on his shoulder. Two of the staff are shaking hands with it. They look harried; even such a mild affair is a strain on the sophistication here. And on mine.

As Gianni passes our table I lean up at him, smiling sympathetically. "So they've left. I did see all that—them, for real, didn't I?"

He laughed, leaning over confidentially. "Eh, old Torlonia? Si. We all saw."

"And everybody here had a drink on the house, eh? Did he pay?"

"His uncle was a prince in the old days, Signora. What can one say?" He swept a practiced eye over the two glasses on the table and left them there, ignoring my companion. Funny, how waiters can express preference—maybe especially to their women customers. —"I liked your friend"—Gianni said meaningfully, after I had that once broken my rule of solitude here. —"We have noses like his in Venice."

"Stuffed animals don't always export well, though," the man at my side said. "I brought home a marvelous tiger from China. A foot long, narrow as a breadstick, and with a snarl on it like from a tapestry. Until I had it tested. Its skin was cat."

Suddenly I have a swelling revulsion for what I have brought here, and sneak a look at my watch.

But my wrist is bare. When this body wears the ring, it doesn't wear the watch.

"Use mine," the man at her side said, thrusting out his wrist. His right wrist. Didn't most people wear their watches on the left? . . . Why should the sight of that wrist, next to her own bare left one, scare her—blue? Why shouldn't it. . . . Except for a black strap instead of tan, his watch, a plain, white-faced round one like many from the nineteen forties, was a ringer for her own—which had been her father's.

"I like a watch I can wind," he said. "This one has a modest case, for its capabilities."

"Stop-watch," she said, in spite of herself.

"Mmm. My dad's." His eyes neither see hers nor avoid them. Rather, their brown depths seem as familiar as her own.

She wanted to cover hers with her hands—until I remembered where I was, and instead picked up my glass. The level in each of the two glasses on the table stood at half. Had I been drinking from both?

"Take it easy," he says. "Plenty of time. For you to have your two drinks. And for me to acquire my cubbyhole. Or not to. About half an hour, between us."

"There's nothing between us!"

"You spotted me. Isn't that as close as one can get?"

"Anyone could have."

"And I spotted you," he says, his tongue caressing that. "With my back turned."

"I'm not responsible for that."

He smiles. "In that coat?"

Then I can show my teeth at him. Sometimes one gains strength from being a divided person. Like that tiger of his, hardened now with glue, with lengthened fangs and inked-in nose, but nevermore just a cat. For I too have seen those over there—though I did not buy.

He's onto my vanity, I think. Now let him try for the intellect.

"I started at the beginning of my story," he says quietly. "Now let me begin at the end."

What's there about that statement to bring tears to the eyes? Except that this sometimes happens to me over the ending of a book in perfect tune with its own beginning. While I am tossed and twitching with the cost of my own livelihood. The books I dread the most are the ones—did I say dread? I did.

The books looking in at the hospitals of themselves. They come in any dialect.

"After that I'll go quietly." He's tucking his cuff over his watch. "I find I can guess time now. Even more so when I'm—walking. It's those curbs."

"Or Time's chariot. Drawing nearer."

His eyelids flicker. "That's a quote, isn't it?"

I estimate his age as about mine; we have inherited the same watch. Yet in a fluctuating way he will sometimes be older than I, then again younger. Like those siblings of almost the same age who all of their childhood—or throughout their lives, vie to be one or the other.

"My business is all quotations," he says. "I cite prices morning to night—and across the international dateline. Which can be tricky if thirty day discounts are involved. I enjoy all that—it's not that I don't enjoy."

I listen to that double negative as if it is my own.

Then we are silent.

"I don't think you want to tell me," I say at last.

"I don't think you want to hear."

We look around us—together.

Is this our first act in unison?

The equivocal light of a place to which people go in order to be elsewhere is making a teagarden of every table. Good as the food may be, there is that other hankering. The waiters know it well, and in between courses stand musing, napkins in hand. Next morning a food critic may have to decide whether to censure them for daring to stargaze, or praise them for exquisite nonchalance. Nobody in a bar leads an unexamined life.

"Forgive me." My almost vis-a-vis turns to face me as squarely as a couple seated side-by-side can. "It's hard to give an explanation only. These weeks since I got back—and lost the office—have been like a darkroom. Black. But brilliant too. As what you've been waiting for appears." He took a sip from the glass in front of me—his first? "I get along in the Orient. Not that I'm a guru buff. But they understand the philosophy of toys out there—that they should be disposable. Empresses' necklaces of gold and red, that cost thirteen cents and wilt in a day. Paper flutes, on which you can blow an unforgettable tune—only once. To recover which you would pay the earth. And I know how to sell such stuff—not always to Woolworth."

So close to him, I feel he can sell anything.

"First you have to sell yourself on an item. And sell a piece of yourself with it, something the business schools don't tell you. My buyers appreciate that. We get along fine. All of us sharp customers. And I like their women. In case you're wondering, I have a woman friend in Hong Kong. Only girlfriends, over here."

I had wondered. And the distinction is clear.

"I agent in Europe too when I have to, but it's not the same. Except for Germany—I won't deal there. They make things to last and last—so if you lose or destroy them you know what you have gone and done. It's a country where you always understand your punishment. And are taught early to anticipate it."

I won't ask how he learned that. Or how it is that a man who deals in the fugitive, and buys his reading matter only in airports, should be the one to bring home to me why I've never been able to translate the modern Germans, those majordomos who wheel out their atonements like bowls of the best wax fruit.

But isn't that—just what a toy salesman might know?

Gianni is hovering.

We both raise our heads to say No Thanks.

Now is it up to me, to delay?

"You understand a lot about countries," I said. Although my lover-friend says—said—that such knowledge too often comes from the art of avoiding people one by one. The great travelers, he said, often suffered from that. —Ah, at least there you won't find me, I'd answered. Among the great.— When I said things like that, why did he always take me in his arms and hold me, even rock me? —You travel at home—he said.

"Oh I have my peep-holes," the man with me is saying. He has raised a forearm, but only to gesture toward the bar near the front entrance, whose patrons are not visible to us. "How to order in a bar in Czechoslovakia—and what to be careful not to say . . . Where to get a late night marmite in Paris—and find an open supper club in London, not too pricey." His head is bent. "Or to know that to a Thai of the old school, crossing your legs with the foot pointed is beyond rude."

He's not boasting. When somebody compliments me on my knowledge of languages I reply in his same glossy tone. Modesty is not always false pride. It may have terror behind it.

"My mistake—" his head came up, the eyebrows winged back, "—was to try to—do something permanent, out there. Or as near to it as I could get. The people I did business with were bewildered; you go into any showroom of what we deal in, it's either all year round tinsel—or one-shot ideas. But my friend—she was all for me branching out. She saw. That—"

He turned a choking red.

My own throat was taut with empathy. "That—?"

"That I wanted my own warehouse. That I'd wanted it for twenty-five years."

And he was eighteen when he began? He must be exactly my age.

"Is she a scientist?" That burst out of me. But I must have been in better control than I thought. None of the nearby tables appeared to have heard.

"Head dietitian. In a large hospital."

I could visualize her to a tee. Dietitians have labs of a sort, don't they, where they measure out the biophysics of digestion? Or of nutrition. Being Chinese, she likely wouldn't have a high-bridged nose, nor, being female, a large one. But she would be in some way larger nonphysically than this man and with the broad-chested confidence that comes of not being sunk in self-estimation. She can be her lover's friend.

A woman can achieve that state on her own; I've seen it. Others require help. But the men who can help us to that state are rare. The ones who require us to be ourselves.

Sometimes I'm sent a book, from either sex, so scabbed with self-esteem—which is the other side of self-doubt, that it shivers in my hand like a pustule about to break. But now and then a book torn out of its wrappers at mail-time opens in my cupped fingers like a green herb, breathing a holy medicament.

"It all depends on what one translates—" I said to my lover, the day I admitted him to my walk. We were staring into a shop window that lent a portrait-brown to our images. The lustral shop windows of my city lend me my second self. He spoke to my image. "No. You depend upon it."

All down the next block I felt him watching how I swung my arms. He has a theory women do that less, and with less scope—though there's no physical reason for it. And when we came to the crossing he grabbed my arm fiercely, my right arm, since we were on the southwest corner, and he was walking on the gentleman's side. "Break out!" he said. "Not necessarily toward me. But . . . break . . . out."

It was then I invited him to join me at this bar. To show him how serene I am, or can be, when on my own. I knew what he meant of course. In his library in Washington there's a shelf of the books I have translated, visible from the chaise where we sometimes loved. Fifty or so—fifty-three to be exact, two a year usually, not counting the anonymous ones I used to do at night. Once upon a time I did porn originals for a French press of some note in that line, which briefly made it to bona fide publishing with a couple of those. And once I created a fake primitive, a memoir done in the dialect of one of the Channel Islands, which except for the introduction—the work of a well-meaning and innocent British novelist—was entirely written by me.

My friend hadn't known about those, though in time I would tell him. But when I first saw that shelf—and felt I should exclaim, in the lightly pleased tone people expect when they wish me to observe that they own a book translated by me—"Oh, my books—" he did not reply.

In the following months I usually managed to turn my back to them. But the occasions of love can't always be pushed to comply in that effort—and shouldn't be. So once, dallying there, I found myself facing that shelf. He too was staring at it. "They're your Maginot line, aren't they? And so beautifully done." He had read them all—all. After a while I was able to say: "No one else must ever have done that"—and he gathered me in. Never again alluding to that hour, or saying more.

I knew what he wanted of me. Or rather, hoped I could admit to wanting of myself. Who but I had told him that in translation you can go from refinement to refinement, as with a drug? How, led down such byways, you can desert the major works you were once so proud to be tapped for. Or which now, fenced in as you are by your own freak specialties, you are no longer awarded.

It can happen even in a lab, he said. That girl who wiped her hands on her hair, for instance—"She's of a caliber to branch out on her own. But she prefers to be a dogsbody to the rest of us." What did that mean? I asked, too eagerly. He served in the navy when younger, and I'd learned valuable nautical slang from him.

He has the poker face that must come from staring hard at the basic universe—a face that pulls you to stare there too, but won't ask you to. "Junior officer. Who runs errands for the brass."

You can so often tell by the clothes women adopt, I was meanwhile thinking. Not the ones who honestly don't care, or have other priorities. The exaggerates. Who hang their depression right out on the line, like that poor slob. Or those who go for the vanity cure—like yours truly.

At his door, when I was leaving, I said: "I was a slob once, when I was a young girl. When it's natural. Maybe someday I'll go back to being a natural one again. When this coat is worn out, maybe. Or when my vanity is."

He has the kind of ramrod house in which on every floor you can see straight from front to back, in that lemony light which comes from openness, even at night. Not an ascetic cell; the rugs are good, the chairs deep, and there's that chaise. Comfortable as the place is, it's a factory of ideas and has a maker's tautness to it. Even now, here in Harry's Bar, I can see clear back to the library, and that shelf. There's a small space, scarcely more than an inch or so, between my most recent translation and the leather bookend. Not a space left by a housekeeper; he's a precise man. I know what that niche is waiting for—a book with my own name on it, though from the pretty speech he made to me last thing, you might never suspect so. "Yours is not vanity, but gallantry."

And yet—I let him go. His remark has faded some. But not that inch of shelf space.

"You've forgotten me." My companion sounds amused. "Perhaps you too were thinking of a friend?"

When our glances met again, almost as lovers' do after an interruption, was when I noticed. They take your coat at Harry's when you come in, and carry it off to some garderobe—at least so when they are as crowded as they were tonight, every table taken and a constant bustle at the door. But he is still wearing his dark blue. As if they haven't seen him enter? But the entry is small, and keenly guarded.

His coat is no mackinaw. Made of that thin, fine stuff which never obtrudes itself as the best, it had obviously been tailored to him, on the principle to which such clothes adhere: I am this man's second skin. But not all men who can afford such clothing wear it to remain invisible; perhaps he too has vanity?

"I thought it wise," he said. "To stay as you first conceived me. So I left it on."

"I—conceived you? All I did was to go for my walk."

"The same walk. As mine."

What begins to frighten me is our rapport. We are like two quarreling friends, afraid to stop because that might be the end of it.

As if in answer he shifts into the chair opposite me. He is now truly my vis-à-vis. What will happen if I lean forward ever so slightly—while preserving all decorum—and smile?

I do so.

So does he.

"Like two worms in the same apple," I say softly. "My grandmother used to call that out to any of us kids when she heard us infighting on her porch."

It made no difference to her that I had no siblings, and that the actual kinds might be unknown to her. To her, we all partook of the same fruit—childhood. Sometimes, looking deep into my eyes when I was being what my parents called "obstreperous"—or when I couldn't make up my mind what to be—she'd say it to me alone. Which didn't solve my inner wars but calmed them. It's always a help when somebody knows you have them. Later on, when I couldn't bring myself to marry some of the nicest men whom she knew had asked me—she would say it again. She'd have said it to me when I was in the hospital, if she'd been alive. "Brown-eyes—" she always called me that—"two worms!"

"That an adage?" he says.

And my heart melts, as it half did when he asked—That a quote?

As it does toward any who will pause in their own maybe far-flung destinations—to ask about a word.

"Only from my grandmother. She was an original."

How had she spawned my mother, who was too seemly to marry anyone but a cousin? My parents never quarreled. If you asked the time of day in their presence, they brought it out on the instant, in perfect chime. Her watch, which swung on a chain, was not saved.

I look for mine, and again find my wrist bare.

He holds out his, on it that so familiar circle of what was called white gold, with its black forty-year-old lettering still forthcoming. My parents expired, as they would have preferred to say, on the same day. On the railway cars, which they favored over planes—by appropriate accident.

I was more than appropriately fond of them. They tried for travel but could not really accomplish it. My grandmother now, she gardened in one spot all her life, but with seeds from around the world.

When I was in hospital the doctors of course reminded me of all this. Playing chess with my life—and always winning the game. Psychologists place great trust in symbols, and they pointed my life healthily toward those. When all I wanted was to get down to brass tacks.

"We've spent an hour." I rarely spend more. And never order a third drink. Gianni would not approve. Perhaps even now he doesn't quite. I see him, tray upheld, just now serving a party of four. But he's very fast, imposing a kind of rhythm on his customers.

"And now I can tell you," the man says. "Now that I've lost my cubbyhole."

"Lost it?"

"If I didn't keep my appointment, there was another bidder." Smiling, he's a changed personality, even the curls on his head appear to be unflattening.

"You—delayed on purpose?"

"Delay is a kind of decision, don't you find?"

"I never went—came—that far."

"Not to China?" The corners of his mouth turn up now. Not in the grimace of the Roman fountainheads. More like the Venetian ones, relaxed and spewing their rosy argot instead of the Tiber's gray Latin. "Not to the Gate of Heaven? Where the Emperor went once a year, to pray for crops?"

"I must go," I say at once, half rising.

"You have an appointment too?"

"Only with myself. But a firm one."

"Oh, those are the best. But can't you keep it here?"

"There's no desk." Even if I only sit there of a night, and write nothing.

He glances down at our hands, inches from each other on the tablecloth. His nails are flat and tidily clipped. Mine are split and worn; there's no hiding them.

"Books, yes. I can see you write them."

"Translate."

His eyes are clear, shallow, not inhuman, but like mirrors with no backs to them. "D'ya warehouse?"

"Not those." Across the restaurant I see Gianni is free now. I give him the nod.

"Which?"

"The ones I don't write. Or haven't yet."

I can feel them at the backs of my eyes, I can persuade myself that they still lend the eyes depth.

He's smiling like a child who has caught a ball. "Like my bicycles."

"Bikes?" The last thing one could connect with him. With those who walk.

He leans forward in what I recognize as the businessman's huddle. You see it anywhere they lunch. The intimacy is in the contract, not in them. In the old days they wrote right on the tablecloth. Maybe in places where cloth is still cheaper than paper they do so still.

I saw my uncle do that in the townhall commissary when he was mayor of our town in Jersey, and the salesmen for fire trucks and Burroughs calculators—and tees for the civic golf course—came to sell. While my father, the stationmaster, looked on.

"Bicycles," he whispers. "There are five hundred thousand of them in Beijing alone at this moment, my dear. And more ever coming. Like the people. If I swing it right, half of the new ones bought in the next two years will be mine. And in every city. And in every model. In the People's Republic many have three wheels, with maybe a baby buggy in front of the rider. Or a platform or bin to carry to market, in back." He straightens up. "So my invoices will use the full and total world. I mean—word."

It's when he straightens that I see his watch hasn't moved on. Or else I had read it wrong. It still says five-thirty, which is about when we came in. But that's all right; it's a stopwatch. Maybe it totals only the past. Or keeps an eternal present.

Gianni comes over. Will he put the check down on the gentleman's side or on mine—or center table, as they do in the cheaper joints when there's a question who is the host? But Gianni is a first-class waiter and a European one. The check appears, male guest or no, as it always has, settling like a feather, no nudge to it, convenient to my hand. Gianni himself is already some tables away; good waiters maybe levitate, a foot from the floor.

The bill lists two drinks, as it must for the bar's record, but charges only for one. I set down a twenty, the change to be for the service, and cheap at the price.

"You did well," the other half of my table says. "A woman should not be shy of scrutinizing the check the way men do. And should tip well, but not overdo." He seems not to mind that he himself was passed by. Perhaps he's used to it.

Of course he is. I am beginning to realize our relationship. He is never going to give me his story on his own. In either across-the-table or under-the-table negotiation. I must dig for it, clue by clue. That is the contract. Yet I must leave him some ego. I see I can't live without his self-respect.

So we get together at last. This sub rosa agent for manufacturers, and I. Neither of us wanting to.

"You have your warehouse then?"

How he shrinks back. Even the coat fades. His throat dilates like the pulses in the throats of certain lizards when you speak to them. As if they know their ancient beauty is hard on us.

"My father's was sold. For the land. There's now a motel. But Jersey's the place to look. Jersey will be the place."

Ah, I know these sought-for places, travels, encounters. And that building a warehouse does not depend on any of them.

"And will you sell only bicycles?"

He leans toward me to whisper again. On our fringe I catch sight of Gianni. A good waiter's eyes are like glass jewels; they reflect but do not hoard. Perhaps he thinks I am an international spy? And haven't I been so all these years, in a way. Though not a good one. A good agent doesn't yearn for a country of his own.

"Not to be at random anymore," the whisper comes. "To have one product that goes from me to them—ping pong—and is understood by everybody. Without a word."

"Cycles—." Luckily a new wave of customers at the door covers my cry. "What could be more random than those?"

Why do I want to put him down this way? Because I can't? Or because the corners of that mouth turn obstinately up?

He leans forward, smiling again. "Yet more single-minded at the core."

Does optimism lean forward? And the negative in us lean back? I never can decide.

"Why can't one do both?" he cries—though the other tables pay us no mind. "Live at random—ride at random—or provide for others to. And sell single."

I know someone who does that. Yes, that's what he does essentially, in that clean, sunny house.

"I live single," I say, smiling through my teeth like all such tigers. "And think random. Won't that suffice?"

"Why not? There's no law. Long as there's some mix to it. But we're not there yet."

He was verging toward me, and yet quietly upright in his chair. While I, as quiet, yet leaning forward, felt myself pass through him and out his other side. Though flesh is not our pass-through.

That is—I could no longer challenge his saying "We." This dark kinship which I have invited in, but refuse to name. Or don't need to name?

I gave him his character, didn't I—deduced so insightfully, even from his haircut. Hair so cannily shorn to resemble mine that we might have had the same barber—and of the same brown that crisps under my comb. Even his suit might be one of my striped pantsuits—the kind the women's shops are calling "power suits," this year. The genders are huddling closer these days, not knowing what is to become of them. Now that the Super-ego, the self and the soul all sit in one ess-shaped saddle. Specifics for which turn up regularly in the Sunday supplements.

He is staring at me as well. What character has he given me?

"You want a third drink, don't you?" he says softly. "But you're only a workaholic—so you won't."

I bow my head. He knows my habits. Or else, even from his freakish afar he has to keep up with the Sunday explanations.

"Besides—" he's whispering again, "—you have to help me with my getaway. We can't leave without each other. And I must go."

So must I. But not still in his thrall.

Now I lean forward—as he leans back. "So be it. But not without—" How shall I say it?—"the silver."

His mouth closed. Like a statue's sometimes will, at a second look. Had it ever been open? How can a mouth appear both open and closed? "Call it spit—and we're in business."

I should have known things would end this way. My own taste is for the short word—I'd always maintained. But my parents taught me to say "expectorate."

"You haven't the courage of your vanity," the mouth says. "You deem yourself too ladylike for your real job."

How can a mouth that isn't stone speak so immovably?

"Because I derive from art," the mouth says. "From your own thoughts of it."

That's a word never to be spoken, according to the books I translate. Since it changes its meaning with each person who would speak, it is only an embarrassment.

Then the mouth itself is gone—or my image of it. There's only the man as I made him, vain as I. "Very tiring to hear your fancy thoughts," he says. "Worst part of my job. So let's be quick. No, don't lean forward. To talk about spit we have to sit up straight."

So we do.

"The Gate of Heaven—" he says. "That's where it was laid on me. The palace where the emperor went one day out of the year. To pray for crops."

He makes me climb with him, through winter air like a blade against the cheek. We are walking on circular designs set out in what over there is only reasonable antiquity; from their worn omnipresence they might as well be inherited patterns in the blood. Each flight of stairs has a broad carved stone plane at an angle to its either side. Carved waves whorl and rise there. Stone cranes—the bird—fly above. Pavilions succeed one another, their roof-lines all to the same simple curve, their gilded borders in obvious crenellations—like a good teacher's brain. At the very top, he says, there will be only one circle, set in a vast pavement of stones radiating toward it. There is where the emperor stood.

As we climb, all China climbs with us. Tall men with bold hatchet features, black hair coarse as a cow's, and wives in mountain clothing, sallow pudge-faces from the cities, dragging small boys in miniature army uniform. Old men in scholarly tailoring and with noses delicately mandarin, pimpled youths dressed like drugstore cowboys of the nineteen-twenties, and sauntering like brigands, their sharks-teeth showing. Shy honeymooners, the girl two giggly steps behind her groom. Doll-like tots of either sex in candypaper clothes and red shoes with turned-up tips. And here and there, led by solicitous family, a tiny tottering granny with bound feet. Loosed by the new economy and their newest masters, they are all touring their heritage, with a passion that crams the halls.

"They tour with more acceptance than awe," he says. "Chinese eat symbols with their soy. Like anti-toxin. When your country is that old, you have to. In order to stay real."

Oh yes—I remember. How, underneath the gewgaws and cinnabar, and gorgon images, no nation is more down to earth than they. Particularly the women. Balancing the nightsoil down the fields, in two pots swung on a pole carried on the shoulders. Or squatting in the open latrines, their backsides bare to the wind, and finishing their duty with a characteristic little shake.

"And you were alone," I say. "Although nobody is really alone in China."

"Yes, I gave up my friend," he said. "We didn't quarrel. We simply gave each other up. After which I took myself on tour."

"Yes I know."

He gives me an admonishing stare. Are we never to admit our relationship? Perhaps not.

"I mean I know how it is," I quaver. "Go on. Please. Aren't you going to tell about—the arrest?"

Then he truly freezes. Beads of rime, on that coat. Clammy to the touch, if I dared?—which I won't. "Perhaps you better go on from here. If you consider this account to be as much yours as mine."

"Not yet. Not quite. But perhaps I should."

In my waking dreams I see that arrest still. Forcing its stiff apparatus on me, who am not at all political.

Strange, how a country whose history is both ancient and revolutionary is where you really see the regime most clearly. Not at all as with us new democrats, where the government is a fence we squirm through, most of us.

"The crowd turned around once, when the two guards grabbed him—didn't they. Then they all turned away. That's what I can't forget. That they wheeled away." While the two policemen, in their greatcoats of olive-drab cloth the color of a frog's slime, bore off one of their millions of most ordinary citizens: neat gray cloth, round head, thin taut face, a peasant maybe, with the rural custom still slack and easy in his mouth.

"Against the law there now, you know," my opposite says. "To—" I see he is struggling to say it, his right arm slightly raised.

The balance has shifted again. I must be quick.

"To spit. Yes, I know."

He shudders. "I was all for it over there. The law. It was only when I got home that reaction set in."

And I never again thought of the incident, so far as I knew. Until five nights ago, when I sat down at my desk, under the mute glare of the dictionaries' shelf—I who meant never to sit there again at night in anyone's service except my own.

"When we were kids—" I speak softly. Or perhaps only in my head. Where he's under my control now, though tables could again turn. "They used to tease us that people in China walked the planet upside down. But maybe it's us who do."

"You mean—us?" He dares it again. "Us?" He speaks as softly as I do—lest the tables turn. He shakes his head. "Better for me to go back to the Gate of Heaven in that case. And stand in the exact center circle where the emperor did. And spit. And when I do—it will be spittle. Not some sentimental metal that people like you turn into—"

Bowknots.

He's right, he's always half right. I shrug.

"And if I'm caught—let them arrest me. I'll be free."

Of me? I wonder.

As for me—I would like to smell again that honorable nightsoil smell, on those subtle gardens. And be free—of him.

Touch me, he says, is saying.

If I do, will he disappear?

Gianni's at my side. "Anything more, madame?"

"No, no. Have to make my getaway."

Gianni smiles. "Like that bear."

So the bear was real for sure. I know I've already checked on that. But in a bar one has to be sure of such incidents, even on only two drinks. Or when you have walked alone perhaps once too often. Carrying your little bundle of insights. Those homemade knives that since yesterday seem to have sharpened themselves in the dark.

Gianni is teetering from ankle to ankle in a movement very unsuitable. A waiter's legs should always carry him somewhere, or be inching on the way there. "Old Torlonia. I should not have let him bother people. But I have a soft spot for them. Not for the family. For their land. The land they once owned. I come from it."

Waiters can muse—like statuary on call from any Pygmalion. Gianni stands rooted there. He is dreaming the short dream.

"Land you once owned," I say. "If you come from it."

He snaps to attention then, but only to dust the table with a napkin, something not done in a New York restaurant like Harry's. Though a waiter might do that, flicking the serviette miraculously from nowhere, in a village once owned.

The bear's chair is now as empty as the bear had long since left it. Nowhere is there any sign of the man in blue. He's made his getaway, in the way only such as he can. The way he got in. If I want to make doubly sure, Gianni is the one to ask, all the more so because of his brief lapse. A good waiter knows he is half apparition to most people—adjunct to a menu, a service-cart, a tip. No bona fide customer escapes him.

"I drank the bear's drink also, you see. Thank you."

"But of course, Signora. Everybody did." He is bland now, bored. As a waiter should be. He goes to fetch my coat.

I stand near the entry, waiting. At the moment absolutely no one is passing out or in. Even the best restaurants have this stasis, where what has transpired is waiting for what will. Even the best people.

My coat appears, my long symbol, draped high in a waiter's hands.

I bought it with money earned from my nightwork. Not from the porn, which was long ago, although now and then I see reference to those two books from quite respectable scholars. I bought the cloak with the fat sum paid me to keep my mouth shut on the source of the "primitive" reminiscences presumably found in an eccentric ninety-year old Channel Islander's effects—a volume that made it to best-seller without me, as it might never had done if admitted to. Writing it on the Metroliner each time I returned from Washington, although it was in a dialect probably unknown to my lover, I could still test it against that just relinquished British cadence—and it seemed to me that I wrote each chapter while encircled in the safety of arms that upheld me like barrel staves. Yet I couldn't send him the finished product—for that is what it was. A fine jape, but nothing for that shelf space of his. Only one more deft emplacement in my Maginot line. Though he would never twit me with that, his talent was to make me think it, his remembered eyes pleading "One step more" above his handkerchief, while he pretended to blow that nose.

So, my coat, though made of the original fox, was bought by an anonymous me. Still, it has no tincture of translation. It is an I, not a she.

Gianni is still holding it patiently. Turning my back to him obediently, yet with that lofty curve of the neck with which women who are used to this service accept it, I hunch my shoulders in the approved way, intending to slip my arms into the sleeveholes—but find I can't. Sometimes it's awkward to do so because the man holding the coat is too short, but Gianni, one of those lean Italians who seem never to feel the need to uncoil to their full height, is as tall as I.

My right arm is rigid, that's it, fixed at an angle I recognize. But not as if the arm is mine. The wrist has a watch on it, a stop-watch. I am in one of those terrifying moments when we realize the body from a point outside it.

If we are ever immortal, that is the time. As mortals, the moment is not bearable. But for that pure instant I am immobilized, seeing myself to the full in the scene that harbors me. Then my arms slip easily into the armholes.

"A beautiful coat, Signora."

"Yes, it is."

It is my cloak. In it I can feel my separate she-ness, as women do. Our variation (as even my lover must have his macho he-ness)—on that genderless other who walks in each and every being, from time to time.

Nothing to go to a hospital for—and perhaps it never was.

"When I came in, Gianni, the man who came in behind me—was he somebody you knew? A man in a blue overcoat—navy blue?"

"Ah Signora, you came in the busy hour. So many people at the door. I see only that you are alone. And that your table is free." He frowns, puzzled. "I check the overcoats myself tonight. No navy blue."

"Perhaps he kept it on."

"Ho ho, that I can tell you. Nobody do that here. We have the rule."

"Guess I was mistaken."

"Somebody you know, Signora?"

"Not really. Not by name."

Nor needed. For that other who can come upon us in any guise or gender, full of our own shadows. Who walked me to Harry's Bar.

Even down in Washington, in that house filled with clear, lemony light, where the phones chirr proudly with good fact and all the corners trust one another, doesn't the master there now and then find himself so visited—by the unalterable of himself? Although he said not?

"Ciao, Gianni."

"Arrivaderci, Signora."

Two versions of See You Again.

But I will not come again to Harry's Bar.

In which, by the way, there are no banquettes.

Outside, the evening is ringing all its changes, magical or humdrum, pick your style.

The building with the tower shines with gold paint and wattage, showing its teeth to the heavens like a totem pole, but the evening rejects it, every time. Cloud and that brash stagecraft do not mix.

It's the ordinary pavement here that rises in gentle illusion, like smoke from behind the footlights of old classical plays, when the actor on signal stamps his foot. Gray and well swept, as befits these few blocks, this pavement takes no imprint from the passerby. Insights dropped here skitter away like lost jewelry and are borne away by the park wind. But if stepped on steadily, stubbornly by someone on a mortal errand, this plain, dun surface will spread its squares before the eye like home truths, and carry that someone home on a cloud.

The woman standing outside Harry's Bar knows this, and in a minute will take advantage of that familiar path, hup hup and shanks-mare. But for the moment she is choosing her style. How to be tough enough to offend the genteel, as has been her aim most of her professional life. Yet how to spew the magic at last freed in her, so that even the poets will pay mind.

And so that he who runs may read? She has never understood that proverb. She'll write for walkers. An account of a walk—how a walk connects with a life, both drawing on it and avoiding it. Prose already blushes in her veins, a long-buried love song. Buzzes in her forehead, clicks with her bones. Tic tic. Let me out. Let us out.

Language will out—like a park breeze. And change its season, but be like an inner weather, always there. Mine. Her raised arm is a branch. Her mouth is silver.

Bending low, but slowly, so that anyone running by may see she is not impelled but in control—ah now she understands that adage—she spits. So as to be sure of the gap between vision and tale. Between self—and a story that either half of a self might tell.

On the pavement there is now only a spot of damp. A kind of night-soil of the tongue. Not collectible—which is why they rule against it. And because there are so many of them? But most of all because to spit is to express the secret language of oneself. Now even the damp has faded, as either on Fifth Avenue or Ninth such spots may. As she straightens up and walks away her coat blows wide. At the first curb she stops short. Remember the bowknot. How awkward it must be to spit silver in the sight of all. Yet it had a shape. Remember it.

So she walks home, over the squares of meditation that come to meet her. This pavement is modern and not sacred enough to be visited only yearly; she doesn't wish otherwise. But at each curbstone she stops, to remember, her coat streaming quietly behind her. She has been in China too.

—

So—I have finished. Have I finished? Now there is only the call to Washington to make. If he has a woman installed there by now will I hang up? Or go through with it.

Three nights, three days I've sat here, all the time walking—and still in the pajamas in which I began. Superstitious of changing them, like those actors who have to incorporate the lucky scarf in every costume. Acting is what I've been doing, isn't it? In that bare theatre whose sole audience is your own pop-eyes. Even my own stink was enjoyable, telling me what I was up to. Desk-sweat oils the muscles, lightens the head to a godlike ease. I ate as I wrote. The downstairs grocery is expensive enough to cater to eccentrics, and quite prompt—and talking to the grocer doesn't count. The phone, otherwise, on a ration of five rings before the machine takes over, can only ping.

When I was done, or thought I was, I fetched a wine glass, a good one, as I always do when I finally put to bed a translation, sipping my congratulations to myself from its thin balloon. This manuscript is so thin—to contain what it does for me. There is no litter of words on the floor. Any discards, if not crosshatched on the page, have receded into my brain.

Does one use them again? I'm such a neophyte here. Meaning—a beginner. Plainness please; I pray for it. I choose the words here. I cannot get over that. I feel the way I did in my first grown-up bathing suit. My own words are beginning to show—like breasts. First breasts. And since, when you are translating yourself, a word could at any moment become a piece of brain or organ, or arise from the serum that floats you as body and being—there are no discards on my floor.

The study floor itself is a counsel—and endlessly instructive—the way the ground is to a toddler. I'm learning to walk—here.

The word "narrative" lies there in a corner, a long, dangerous toy left there by others, many others, with no instructions for its use. One learns that as one learns the uses of a knife, from table manners to the kill. And abandons the manners, in time?

What I want most is the view from behind those blind shutters. For three days and nights I opened and closed them, alternately darkening the room and flooding it with light. Yet did not stir from my chair except to fall on the couch, in a sleep moving with armies readying for dawn. Or to hunch on the toilet seat, mulling did I defecate or shit. I ate like fury, fueling the keyboard. Where a phoenix must rise, or a corpse burn?

Until the shutters melted, the buildings beyond dissolved, and I saw above that keyboard—whose pods will rise and fall as long as I am able to press them—my jigsaw life. Which won't burn except as I live it.

I'll learn. How not to translate. What punctuation is necessary, when it is your own. How the present and past tenses may be mixed, so as to rush beyond grammar. Whether or not one must name the characters. And finally—what is a just ending? Does the page lie there, like a certified check? Or like a charred but open hand? I always despised a book that dangled a L'Envoi. Lamely twisting its sail toward the finish line, when all its carrying wind should come from behind. One ought to be able to say good-bye without saying it.

What is technique? Is it to shop for Christmas at the first sign of the autumn equinox? And give a party on the Eve, at which everyone may exchange? Ah look at her—the other guests will say. She wants to brew only honesty on the page. She'll learn. That you can only fly from technique when you have it.

But blind shutters tell one a lot. They hint of heresies that leap beyond art—only to find it again. Where it stands in a basement corner, a caryatid the curators have forgot. Meanwhile the naked floor consoles me that I can leave a story without deserting it. One can, my naked floor answers. That is life's guarantee.

Dawn's coming through. Nights are chancier. A night can rustle up anything. But if you've been around enough daybreaks you know that they always seem appropriate to what's happening. In reverse, if necessary. Gray as good manners, when the mildest parents in the world are passing over a railroad trestle for the last time. Yellow-bright with sun, the morning a grandmother dies. Or lacy pretty as a greeting card, the coolish five a.m. you curtsy to a hospital's receiving desk.

This is the hour the crisis breaks, in the old medical books. Or the good soldier lies on the field. Or the student cramming for finals snaps shut the books that should never in a lifetime be put down—in order to graduate.

What if you say good-bye—as if it is hello?

I see my view.

At this hour, down in Washington, that empty inch of bookshelf is about to be barred by the sun. Or if the day is rainy down there, stays a clear, waiting gray. Upstairs, its owner is sleeping, the hairs stirring in his nose. In sleep he has his own biscuity smell. He doesn't wear cologne because of the lab. What would a scent confuse there, I once asked, and he replied—"Me." And what results was he after? "Human chlorophyll." He and I shared a keener than average sense of smell—and a kindred hatred of banana ice cream. Quite enough congeniality for a marriage, he once said. And what did I smell like, without perfume? "A bundle," he said instantly. "The one I always wanted. I can't otherwise identify. But I swear it. As a boy, I used to smell the bundles in the hall."

If there's a woman with him she will be sleeping in the crook of his arm. He'd do no less for any of us. And I don't begrudge. Or scarcely. I still believe him about our conversations. So I've sent him what used to be called a night letter. Seems appropriate.

EMPIRES CRACK Stop IM WELL Stop AND WITH WORDS OF MY OWN Stop IF CONVENIENT CALL

It looks good in caps.

—

And now, while I wait, isn't it fitting that "she" continue on what "I" began? I don't plan—or need—to desert her entirely. All depths should be heard from, though at best not inadvertently. From now on—I call the tune. But the tune should be sung.

I took out my old stopwatch and put it on. Normally, according to the cranky habits we all acquire in the daily process of bowing to ourselves, the hand should then be bare, the ring go into its box. We bow to ourselves daily in order to acknowledge we exist, no? Recognizing the articles on the dressing table, the hand that brushes the hair and which way, the clothes that slip toward the body, willing it there. A mirror merely seals the contract. Today I need all the equipment I can muster. All my armorial signs. Even the coat, hanging there on its hook like a doffed uniform, is a help. Most of all my bookshelf—stares back at me.

All those books without my picture on them, with only my earned name on the title page—they count in their own way. What these pages here are, their value, who can say? I can. These words are my own.

Do I believe in the special duality of women—man-made or not? Life-made, or not? Or only that there are house diseases we are subject to—as men are heirs to the martial art of the streets?

How can I tell you, except in the desk-walk?

How powerful it is—to be alone. How necessary—not to be.

This is what my shutters say, as they swing.

What is it that both those old nineteenth-century romances which specialized in assignations missed by a hair, and that line of fauve books on my shelf, whose confessional sentences never quite finish—know equally about their heroines?

What is it in us that lobbies against birth?

I didn't want to write that down. For doesn't anything we record—anything—betray that trust in life which should antedate it? Is this what people have against artists?

And—oh say it in the smallest type available to print—is this what artists have against themselves?

That's enough of that voice. Little amaze should seize us that it's the "I" in us who yearns for dialogue. While the "She" sits stubbornly by a window or a door, or a table of her own contents, and waits. Gambling that the "He" in some man has been doing the same.

When that nose came round the door I saw by his smooth, talc'ed look that he must have shaved on the Washington plane—though he never uses talc. He has merely had the trig year one expects of him. In Stockholm, where he teaches for a portion of every alternate year, the Swedish girls let a man slip in and out without snag. Of Paris, where he fills out that year in a lab whose goals are as intense as his own, I had heard him say that women of such pug measurements between pelvis and rib cage, clavicle and earlobe, as the French, have therefore little space for the impractical—but that their chatter, made up of many tiny "tilts and tolerances," was perfect for a night. It was the English and the Americans, who could twist his mother-tongue between him and them, he'd said—who racked up the dawns with him. His dead wife had been a Londoner.

From his face, coldly unashamed of its yearning, I think that he has brought none of them home with him. It's the rakes who can be trusted to be true to the imagination. I see he is thinking the same of me.

My hair is dribbled in knots. Sweat is orange in my armpits. My fingertips are stubbed lead. Catchall bathrobe, coffee spotted. Face steamy with revelation. One shoulder higher than the other, in relief. Is he thinking that this is the costume of the artist, a modern version of the old plush collars and ringlets, and put on just for him?

No, he's staring at my desk, at the manuscript there, a thin pile, but shuffled square, as if it is all but done. I could say—"I've been walking,"—but better to say it on the page. I could add—"And this particular walk is finished"—but I see he knows that.

He could say he sent a telegram ahead, to say he was coming. But he could tell I wasn't surprised to see him, even though it hadn't got here yet. Even from a plane you can send a nineteenth-century message of the blighted kind that arrives too late, or never at all. We wouldn't need it. "It's convenient," the yellow form with his answer will say when delivered, but his nose, blown until the eyes pinken, has already betrayed him.

My raised arm is a branch. So is the other.

"Here's your slob," I said.

From all the hidden places in the room the words rise, forming pillars at the corners, scurrying like ants across the floorboards, inching the shutters wide—in this narration which is our life.

Women Men Don't Talk About

Some girls like to marry drunks," Ailsa says, shifting the new dress she's made for a customer to the back of the rack, in case that copycat dressmaker up to Newport Beach who calls herself a designer has the nerve to drop in. What Ailsa wonders, not for the first time, is whether her own father was a drunk.

"Hope you won't be one of those."

Her mother sounds as if she's biting off a thread, although these days she merely manages their small in-house shop in her own fierce style. At the moment she's stuffing two days' receipts, all cash, into the hem of her skirt. Ailsa's married brother Eamon, who runs a tow-truck service, will drop by later to pick them up. Next morning, her mother, looking in at his place, will retrieve the bundle and deposit it at the bank. Once you give in to credit cards, her mother feels, you have to deal with anybody.

"I'm not the marrying kind," Ailsa says. "But I'll make the tea."

Black Irish, the tea is, like them, and just right for end-of-day confidences in a tight little island of a shop. With each spoonful put in the pot she considers the males she's thinking of, all in patterns that seem to repeat, although a drunk may be in any of them.

Pattern one: Poets with flyaway tongues, met at the college receptions up the hill, where her mother and she are hired to serve.

Two: Handsomes, with noses like John Barrymore in *Hamlet,* a precious print of which the church parish fund shows every year. Some of the local boys she's grown up with qualify.

Three: Sweet Gentlemen—middle-aged, with money. Habitat: Offices, political clubs, the bars at benefit galas.

Category one has no money. Two's noses are always that much pinker for the ladies. Three—waiting for rescue, but fighting it, like drowners at the beach.

There. Tea is steeped.

The girls who go for the drunks are much the same type. Big eyes, passable figures, no chins. Hard workers. Not all of them churchgoers, but holding firm against being any man's live-in. Where they and their men do it, if they do—is up for grabs. All of the girls are the marrying kind. Some have. Those are the ones who go to church. There. Tea's done.

"Uff, uff" her mother's groaning as Ailsa carries in the tray. She's closing the zipper on the pocket in her hem. "Gets harder every time."

"Looks like you have water on the knee."

"Never you mind." Her mother glances at the brass plate prominent on the mantel: DEIRDRE MCCOY, DRESSMAKER, once tacked to the right of the house door, until word-of-mouth got to be all they could handle. "We were only seamstresses once." She smooths her skirt. "You can drop my hems. And Irish women are supposed to be thick-legged. We have a dispensation from the Pope, it's said. To wear the thigh end of our leg downward."

Both giggle. They have this exchange, or one like it, most teatimes.

"We could take checks, Mam." She already knows the answer; that's what makes this hour as comfy as a fire in the grate when the sun goes in.

"With cash you never have to get too close."

Astonishingly, that is her mother's real reason. Receipts are reported to the tax man to the last penny. Over at the garage, the brother does the same.

"Mmmm, black and smoky" her mother says. "I'll die happy with this smell in the nostrils. Pour."

On the telephone table a fancy gift-box nestles a cardboard pie-plate covered in aluminum foil. Clients' donations strew that table most weeks. Her mother nods at the box. "Chocolates. That dean's wife who just got back from France. Said nobody there was more 'swan yay' than she was. That's French for 'chick.' "

Ailsa knows how to say "chic" properly, and how the other word is spelled, but this is not the place to be better educated than the Mam, who when the Dad had vanished, Ailsa not born yet, and the brother just three, had waitressed her kids across the continent from Boston, her portable Singer sewing-machine, with every possible attachment, trundling alongside.

"I'll have one of the scones." Made by the grandmother at the Garfields', next door, and sent cannily at this hour, their buttery innards still warm. Ailsa's mother keeps Mrs. Garfield in house-dresses, size fifty-two, that make her so tidy a package her husband still goes to bed with her, and supplies the grandmother, size six, with wrappers in which she can "receive" at home.

"Already had one" her mother says. "Past ninety, and her touch gets better every year."

They're settled in. She may sit back now, waiting for Mam to ask the question hoarded since Ailsa went to put the water to boil. And mulling her own questions. All this is respected. Suppers together are seldom; each has her own pursuits. What the neighbors might think of a house where the mother lives on the ground floor and the daughter has what in all other houses on the Row is the second-floor "income apartment" was ignored by her mother two years ago, and has been since.

"Your sister deserves it," her mother had said to Eamon, who had indeed been troubled, standing there at Ailsa's graduation from the community college, the huge, shy, thickbrowed creature that he is, alongside two handsome women in first-class pink tailor-mades and Ailsa in her three-cornered hat and academic gown from which the pink showed now that she had the diploma and could fling the gown back. Her mother had outfitted Ailsa, Eamon's Rosalie and herself like for a wedding, formal but smart. "All right, so she didn't finish the nursing degree I pushed for as being a port in any storm. What she'd do with the fine arts degree did give me the willies. Pottery classes and museums, and 'modulars,' whatever they are. Thanks be, here she is, coming in with me. But with even my customers warning me, that these days a girl has to have living-space. And Eamon—this isn't Roxbury, Mass. Which by now I hear is all black people anyways."

The red had rushed to Eamon's ears. Twice he'd driven the three thousand miles and more to his mother's birth town to ferret out what he could about her and the Dad, but until that moment their mother had never given a sign that she knew of it. Had she known that his search would come to nothing?

Rosalie, a chartered accountant, but with dimples, had intervened. "It's that mortarboard Ailsa's wearing. Eamon likes to see around corners, before he guns off." Rosalie had had a time getting him to have kids.

"That what they call the thing?" her mother said, pinching her nostrils at the sight of the lid on Ailsa's head. "What in the Lord's name made them put a tassel on it?"

College had been a long pull, though only a "junior" one, nothing like the great university up the line, where she'd worked in the commissary alongside her mother all her high school years. Seeing and hearing a lot though—and swallowing it. At the college, her deft fingers, and what the profs called her "eye," had got her through the art classes, almost as if her mother were at her elbow. For the written-down courses, the sneers at them as "Substandard!"—overheard as she served the university profs their macaroni-and-cheese or diet salad, had actually emboldened her. Perhaps the Dad's side of her, whoever he'd really been, had helped.

A father who had deserted is not simple to talk about. Early on, Eamon and she had known that they might never find out more about the Dad than what Mam had told them from the time they were able to ask—at first only his name, "Cathal McCoy," his profession, "Teacher," although because of his politics he couldn't practice it, older than Deirdre, and second-generation Irish here, to their mother's first. "From Chicago"—the three syllables always said dreamily, as if the speaker was evolving it from the Midwestern mists. "From the exact center of the country, you kids. Boston has no wit of it." Nor, at eighteen, when Mam met him, had she.

As for living-space, Ailsa muses, wherever the dean's wife and the fancy students who are falling over each other to buy from her and Mam may get the ideas they bleat to each other here, she recognizes their tone. But the prospect worries her. "You're my right arm—and aren't we cozy at it?" her mother has said to her since she was fourteen, and through the long trail of evenings such as tonight. So what is she really giving her the space for?

Munching a scone to keep the sadness from oozing in, Ailsa gloms at the doorway of the back bedroom, on which there's a small sign: FITTING ROOM, for which the room serves as well. When they'd been only renters of the house she and her mother had slept and dressed there in a muddle of boxes surrounding their cots, the front room, where they are now, having been shut off for trade. Eamon, called "the brother" from the time he was seven, had been given a small back room overlooking the air-shaft; he was the man. Her mother excusing what Ailsa took for favoritism, by "He's to defend us if robbers come down the shaft."

As for the rape fear overtaking Ailsa's twelve-year-old schoolmates—her mother refused to join in. "Just walk a wee hunchback, as if nobody wanted you. And maybe mumble some, like to the rosary." —"We have none—": —a sore point with a daughter whose chums at the public school were mostly communicants. "Your great-aunt's is somewhere. Better still, sew yourself the beads." There were some glass-pearl ones about, that would do. And a bit of the chain used to weigh jacket-hems with. "Where there's a will there's a way. But it helps—oh, how it helps—to have needle and thread."

The minute they became their own landlord, they'd acquired the six-piece bedroom suite she can see through the door, purchasing it at one of the clean, sky-lit outlets, an accepted part of the California economy, where anything from plaid livingroom suites and brass bedsteads to the lowliest kitchenware could be rented and later returned by the temporary resident. "Just came in—" the salesman had said. "Took it in a swap. And a bargain, if you care to buy. Dresser, twin beds, boudoir chair, vanity and stool. Somebody's family once. No call for that here."

Now ruffled in rose taffeta, it looks to any customer like it could be Mam's own wedding suite. "You Easterners—" one had even said "—you never let go."

On the glass-topped/skirted vanity, centered so that the three-sided mirror triples it, is what her mother has hung on to and Ailsa can see without looking—a framed photo, same size as many a movie star's, of the Dad. On how the imprint of the man who had been her father happened to be what the fan clubs called a 5 × 9 glossie her mother had been as vague as always. "I suppose, wedding photos, you take what they make. And on a Saturday. And they think everybody wants to be a star." Whenever her mother speaks of the past she says "I suppose"—as if it still might be happening. Why a mention of Saturday makes her eyes wet, or why she chortles when she wakes to one, is easy to explain. All Mam's working life—except for "the motel year" that had journeyed them here, Saturday has been her day off. "There I hold with the Jews" she always says. "Sundays are a flop."

In Roxbury, Eamon had found Mam's birth record right enough: born in Eire to the widow of a man killed as a bystander in the Belfast riots, Mam had long ago told them. "He was a bystander, my father, from the start. I never knew him." Their young grandmother had emigrated that next year with baby Deirdre in her arms. "They'd had the application to leave since the day they were wed. Blooming, my mother was when she came here, like TBers sometimes are. The immigration wouldn't have let us in had they known. Neither had she." The mother's older sister, already long here, had brought up the little Deirdre. "Worked in a hospital commissary all her life, your great-aunt Nora; got a service medal for it in the end. Buried with it. Hospital for loonies, name of McClean's. Thanks to the name, until I was grown I thought all loonies was micks. Except those there was rich."

Eamon had found nothing on the Dad.

"Illegal immigrant—I suppose," Mam had long ago said, "I was head-over-heels; I didn't ask. And he was an older man. We met at Harvard, if you please. Me serving at a reception, which I did often. He there in what capacity I never knew. When I left he was waiting, bottom of the back steps. Thought I was a working student, being as I was carrying the Harvard book-bag. 'I carry one because they're green,' I said. When he latched on to me I took it that he was Sinn Fein; among my aunt's kind there were still some had a lock-in with those. I wasn't to hear until later what he'd really been. And not from him." What, what was he?—Ailsa and Eamon had said, munching some goody from the special Sunday breakfast that was Mam's excuse for not going to church.

"He was—an Orangeman."

She hadn't said further, her voice had been special enough. To them Ireland was already a country blessed or plagued with colors, the green that jumped from its leafage to its flags, the Black-and-Tans, guerrillas that speckled its countryside. Eamon had taken to studying the photo for that tint in its skin, claiming for its depths a kind of tawn. Ailsa, taking her cue from the foodstuffs their Mam told them of but back then they never got to eat, saw the Dad at once—a great orange, in the shape of a man. She imagines him that way even yet—an orb of a certain color, hovering above the voting booth that is every Irish mind.

Mr. Garfield, their neighbor, a Socialist, says her mother has no politics. "Only prejudices." To which Mam laughs: "That's what you get working the food services. Not the smoked salmon, nor the Brie." Her mother won't have either in the house, even now that she might afford. "We'll have the smoked cod's roe" she said, for after the graduation, when the neighbors on the Row would drop in. "Or will if I can get it. And the soda bread."

Eamon, cocking an ear to Mam's talk after a spell away from it in Massachusetts, had confided "Mam's so Irish I'd wonder if she really is, weren't it for the birth certificate." His and Ailsa's read properly: Eamon Maloney McCoy, the middle name being Mam's maiden, the Eamon for the man slain in Belfast. Born in a Boston hospital ward—"I hadn't the insurance, see." Ailsa Maloney McCoy, born in Chillicothe, Ohio, during the "motel" year.

"In a house I rented for the occasion." The Ailsa being for a girlfriend of Mam's youth, "And a made-up name maybe, never met it since. But I wasn't to lay on you my mother's TB." Son and daughter respectively of Deirdre and Cathal McCoy. "The Cathal was real, I suppose. I can't speak for the McCoy. But I hung on to it. Seemed best. And I liked the snap of it. 'Maloney-baloney' was what I was always getting from the other kids at the nuns."

"Parochial schools keep fine records" Eamon had reported. But no banns had been posted at any church he'd checked. Some civil records had been lost to various fires. On the marriage, Deirdre herself is squat honest. "Illegal. Even if God was there. I was taken in." But she has never said where.

At Ailsa's graduation party most everybody on the Row,—this odd street of eight houses with a back-East air, had crowded in. Flushed with that, Mam had taken her and Eamon to a front window. This house has no water view. The Row, for factory workers once, had been built by a Hudson Valley textile manufacturer who had craved a western paradise. A brick factory, now shorn of all but two of its many smoke-stacks by an outraged suburbia, survives as a storage warehouse for a Sonoma vintner's wines. Mam had pointed out the window.

"'In California, brick is an illusion,' Mr. Garfield says. That's why I walk past there every day. I came out here to vanish, see? California was where you could. And be in your own movie. All new for you kids. But you, Eamon, you won't allow me. But I'm the deserter now, see. So leave off, eh. That's what I want to be." Then she swept her ring hand across the sky, saying "Ample."

Ailsa's throat had tightened, for Eamon and Mam both. "Ample" was the dressmaker's way of saying there's sufficient cloth for the cut. Wasn't she saying that the sky out here was yardage enough?

Not that Eamon would see it that way—and he hasn't. "We lived in a boarding-house" he'd whispered. "She had to keep me quiet; I remember that. But I don't recall any steady man." Poor Eamon, she thinks now. Mam's my inspiration, even if food and money seem to be her only sex urge—unless I've not caught her at it. But to Eamon she's like a truck he can't get to the garage. Along with the Dad.

The photo, once in plastic, is now framed in gilt-stamped leather. The man in it, in three-quarter view—square jaw, fine profile, well-cut mouth, deep brow, hair smartly clipped but a shock of it, on a head altogether aware of how handsome it is—is recognizable at once. Pattern Two. Whether the nose was on its way to reddening can't be known, nor if the glance full-face was quite straight. The man is the taste that her perhaps misguided mother would have had then.

Nowadays, disdaining the "lunks" her friends in the parish keep pushing at her, mostly widowers and pensioners, she gets along like a house afire, conversationally speaking, with neighbor Garfield, who is sixtyish to her forty-plus, and a Jew, one of the big ones with a football physique. Eamon, with black hair like his mother, and thick brows to match a nose more commanding than he is, could be the man's relation sooner than his own father's. It's Ailsa herself who has to admit a resemblance to the photo. Not near as beautiful as the man is handsome, but could pass for his child. Hair blond when a baby, but now gone to the same chestnut as his appears to be. And yes, probably Irish, one would say, both me and him. She won't say "the Dad."

Need one have a taste in men, all formed and waiting? Not if one keeps cool. What she can't manage is to bring her own doings—much the same as any girl of spirit these days, into this house. Even though it has a back staircase, having the apartment above serves only to hem her in. An open little fling? Her mother would hoist it into a philosophy. Mooch toward something serious—as she had once, with a medical student now in Edinburgh, and Mam, at last allowed full sight of the prospect, had jumped the gun on the decision that Ailsa had already made on her own—that Hal was no stayer. Saying, once he was out the door, "Hmmm. No, I don't suppose."

Tea's over. At eight-thirty Ailsa's due at an engagement shower for the girl who's marrying the drunk. The gift she's bringing is a dress of her own dream-design, not one of which is suitable for the kind of crowd that gives these showers. This model will only confuse the recipient—is that mischief?

Mam will be wheeling their neighbor, Loretta O'Day, former movie extra and still pretty as a worn picture, to her film-of-the-week. "That wheelchair—its very joints are stuck together with studio gossip" she'll say on return. "Loretta's never off the phone. I'd tell you who in Hollywood's splitting from who over the weekend, only I can't recall all the names."

"And which is the good deed, which the bad?"—her mother always concludes, putting away the leather gloves she wears to handle the chair. "Loretta always hates the film." Yet her mother would have no social life at all, stand-offish as she is, if she didn't live in a row house.

Now comes the pause when an animal in the room would be useful, not just the two of them and their known characters.

"So you're not the marrying kind, Miss" her mother says. "May one ask what kind you're planning to be?"

"I have been giving it some thought."

As her mother is well aware. Up at the university, Ailsa still helps out at the fancy receptions, on the excuse that she'll pick up a client now and then. Sometimes Deirdre will join her at it, saying she misses the entertainment. But it's really to keep watch.

"So I saw" she says.

But who else is there to tell? Her mother has spoiled her for other friends, either the raw girls, or the ones who have been there and back.

"That last convocation." Ailsa says the syllables solemnly. "Where that woman and that man read from their books." She and her mother had sat in the back.

"Where the cheese was sent out straight from the freezer, and the cake was carrot?—sure and I remember it. And them." Her mother sits up straight. "A woman who fancies women, and a man who don't—you're not—Ailsa McCoy."

"Not them, silly. But in the audience. Those others."

Women, neither teachers nor faculty wives. And not always name-people but connected with them, if only formerly. Often they do a little something in the artistic line. While the glamor of the fame they'd married or slept with still clings to them. They drive their own cars, bring escorts totally out of the picture, if at all, and were always invited for free. In the Sunbelt, where the face-people keep you young, and climate makes finding a crowd easier, they are like a chorus line at the events she services. "Doubt if you'll ever be dressing any in that circle" the dean's wife had whispered in passing, as Ailsa served white wine to three women who might have been sisters and were talking so, the famous first names that even she knew and the long fancy words she didn't spilling alternately out of their pale lip-glow mouths. Whenever she hears that talk she tries to get close to it. Mrs. Emory, a prof herself once, had been wearing a leftover from those days, a cobalt ethnic with a fine swoop. "Saving yours for the big time" she'd added. "But those brainies on the loose are sure having their day; you know what I mean." And she'd whispered that label for them. Which sticks in Ailsa's craw, but with a lovely taste.

"Take a deep breath" her mother says. "Spit it out."

All right then. "I'd like to be—one of those 'blond literati,' that's what."

The silence. You can hear it tearing, like a piece of silk.

Deirdre gets up, goes to the sideboard where they keep the customers' own yardage and digs out a pack of cigarettes from the top drawer. The trade is always leaving them. Or asking for a cig—those who won't carry them—when a fateful decision is near.

To Ailsa, Mam, who doesn't smoke, is being Deirdre now, as she is intermittently. "White silk blouses, those birds wear" she says through the puffs. "With the real French cuffs. Gold links. Never a skirt that isn't black. And the hose and shoes as well. The real tailor-made appeal. And their hair out straight, like doll-floss. Women who look like they've been kept in the fridge until party-time. Husbands,—more than one. Under the sod. Or else never appear. Saw that university kind in Boston, in the days when I had to leave through the back." She stubs out the cigarette. "And you, my lovely, curly, pink-and-white mess with the tippy nose, some man's armful, leggy though you are—wanting to be like one of those longnecked know-it-alls with naught but ice in their veins and their tongues black with printer's ink—." She breaks off, trundling to the clothes' rack on ankles swollen with the day's standing about.

The models hang there, severe ensembles in the darks that people take East with them, and made for tall skinnies, but everybody wants one, and with some wild adjustment, buys it.

On another rack are Ailsa's bridals, all ivories or pastels, for she won't do pure white, and all as soft as morning light, and yardaged to a fare-thee-well. The live-ins who are making it legal are flocking in for these. At first no hard-edge jazzies ever came, but now they sneak in. Yet none of these dresses looks like a bridal. Each comes on more like a single's dream. For you will want to wear the dress afterwards, and looking as you did before—still allowed to dream. The question is will the dream change from before?

Between the two racks is a space. Her mother is looking there. She doesn't have her glasses on but doesn't need them. "Your bridals—they bring in the cash and I'm grateful. But they break my heart."

—

The poet on the podium is no flyaway. A big man, light on his feet, he has a fan of pepper-and-salt hair above a face that doesn't fit any of Ailsa's patterns but is hard not to hold on to, appearing to fix everyone in the audience with its bold, heavily circled eyes.

"I am going to open this reading by opening my shirt" he says—and does. The shirt is white with a washed-out stripe. On the broad, naked chest is a jagged scar so bright-pink that even people in the rear, where Ailsa is poised ready to sneak out for the serving trays, can well see.

"My latest poem—" he says. "I show it everywhere. Even on the street, should I meet a friend. That's why my friends got me shipped West for a while. For they did, you know. Broadway is a long street, but they and I live within say twenty blocks of one another, and the magazine offices where we take our coffee-breaks. And we all walk, as long as we are able. And talk, then and afterwards, the phones constantly ringing. On the walk, they can see the scar. On the phone, not yet; our phones are all old style. But they can say 'Did he show you? . . . What's he trying to do—make the rest of us look like nothings?' So. And one says 'You know what?—I was even walking with my wife along. And he opens that damn shirt of his like he's exposing himself.' So the sentiment is: 'Let's get Leonard off Broadway. And in fact, off-off Broadway. He's a playwright also, remember? So let him be the road company of himself.' "

By this time he's smiling, a key to that his hearers can, and Ailsa finds she too is smiling, crookedly.

"Ah, there you go" he says. You're going to be a good audience." He drinks from the glass in front of him. "So—they know where the lectures grow; they wire hints. 'So, send that poem to the Sunbelt,' they say 'Where it can get a tan.' "

By then everybody is laughing. He nods a thank-you. And closes the shirt.

Just then her mother sneaks in. She'll have been to the bank and shut the shop. Fumbling for her glasses she whispers "Ah a comic, is it? Good" and sits back.

"Technically the title of this poem is 'Triple Bypass' " the man says, and waits until the sighed murmur comes. "Yop. That's how I got the scar. But 'a triple,' that's baseball lingo too. And 'bypass'—that's for the roads and bridges as well. And for lucky or unlucky drivers. And I think to myself—everybody will have some kind of scar." His voice isn't much, not like some of the baritones that speak here, but it reaches you. He knows who he is for sure. Whatever that is, she has no slot for it. She'd like to stay. But it's time to check the food set out to be served in the reception hall next door. For a minute longer, she does stay.

He smooths that fan of hair, extends his right arm high, palm forward, folds his hands to a stop in front of him, bends as if reading from them. "When I was a boy, I thought all boys were Jews like me. When I became a poet, I thought 'Nobody's like me.' But when I went under the knife for my ticker, I thought 'Everybody has a heart.' "

He leans over the lectern. "So I'll read to you about my scar—" he says, and now his voice swells to fill the hall and echo there. "But not only mine."

She taps her mother's knee. Time to go for their duty. With so many here, she can use the help. But her mother doesn't move.

Deirdre has her clear glasses on, not her shades. Her hands have half risen from her lap; she's breathing hard. "Oh you will now, will you?" she whispers. Looking nowhere else but at the podium.

She must know him, Ailsa thinks, as Mam edges backwards and through the high double door. But from where? Where else but that other life—East, that Deirdre, Mam, will never speak about.

In the reception room there's quite a spread. Not up to what was provided for the Senator, but more than for the usual. This man's right about himself; he's a somebody. At the interval her mother may tell her who. Though maybe she merely once served him, the guest of honor somewhere, never catching his name. That'd have been the case, as in her own experience.

There's even a tea-urn here. Those haven't been used for a dog's age; it'll have been brought out for him. But what do you know, only tea bags have been provided. As her hands begin tearing the bags apart to let the tea loose as is proper, they tremble. What a balls-up, her mother would say, if here helping her, and then, quickly—Never let me hear you say that; don't know where I learned it—It's not Irish, for sure. —And then the two of them would laugh.

She tries to. Instead, one of those all-over shudders that come from nowhere vibrates her so that her teeth click. —Oh, you will now, will you?—her mother'd said, exactly as she does to family. With her hands raised, like when her kids had given her a silly present she must pretend to like. But even with the specs on, and in the black dowdy she wears to serve in, has her mother ever in years looked so—? Say it, Ailsa. So young.

Outside there's a tremendous clapping. That means the crowd will stay on, and eat everything in sight. She'll have to have help. But when the doors open and the people surge in, with that man riding the center like he's on a parade float, her mother's not among them. Nor has the guard seen her go. "Musta snuck out the back stairs."

She snares a student she knows, then another. As she's marshaling them at the trays, one of her own customers pauses at her elbow. A nice one, who never talks down. "Hear the poem, Ailsa?" and when Ailsa shakes her head: "Well, rather like that gray model of yours I don't have the figure for. Great. But you couldn't tell where it started and where it stopped. He's a charmer though. We got our money's worth."

When there's a lull she rousts out the smoked salmon hors d'oeuvres she always saves some of—for too often the honored guest, busy with being pestered and adored, doesn't get to grab—and sallies toward the big man with her tray. He's surrounded, by—guess who?

Three of them, in their cream-cheese and black-olive outfits, topped by the gilded heads. All three mouths moving, or waiting to. The envy gathering in her own throat is brunette.

"Salmon, sir?"

"Oh, thanks very much." He takes two, pops them in, then a third, and bows to the ladies at his elbow. "Now if you three had had trays—wouldn't have been able to *choose.* As with your kind comments. But here's a healthy student, with a heavy tray—and I'm starving. So—*excuse.*" He turns his back on them. She bursts out laughing.

"You laugh. Why?"

"Was that the poem?"

"Ah. You are a student."

"I was that. Not here. But I'm finished." Her voice is more lightsome when there's a chance to say that.

"Are you now. In my trade, we never admit to that." He leans back, like she's an object to be studied. "You ever a student of mine? Across the landscape somewhere?"

"No sir. Never been across."

"Never? Pity." He's caught her lilt. People do.

"Except in me mother's belly." It's popped out. In answer to the lilt.

"Ah, so." He's not fazed. Amused, rather. "And is that—your scar?"

She's still holding up the tray. These trays never lighten, what with the frail bits served from them. And the company one keeps.

"If so, sir, I'm not about to open my shirt for it."

Wheeling off, she works her way through the thinning crowd. Two of these women are still there, the third maybe picked off by another guest or by the message that a car is waiting; she's seen that happen time and again. One of the pair stays Ailsa with a hand—"And what did he say to *you,* dear?"

"Oh—we had a tilt." How many people like herself blab the truth because they don't know how not to?

"Do tell."

"At least preserve it for posterity."

"He's not th-at famous." The first one sulks.

"Oh, just for kicks."

Neither of the two has ever as much as nodded to her in recognition at these functions. They're talking at each other.

She lifts her chin. "It's what I said that counts."

She sees by their faces that he's behind her. Has been, all the time. She runs off.

In the commissary again she can set the tray down. The two students have ticked off. Still shaking, she reads the note they've left for her. "We put away the food. Swiped two sandwiches." That last has been crossed out. "On second thought. Four. We have dates."

She's cheered. They're posterity. Should have told them the staff always gets to take home the party's perishables, the flowers too. Next time she will see to it. Her thoughts skirting the night's events, she puts up a packet for her mother.

Sign over the door says Last Person Out Lock Up. When she pulls back the door, he is standing there.

"Like to know your name."

"Ailsa. Ailsa McCoy." She's trembling again. "Why? I remind you of someone?"

"Uh-uh. Only as all the Irish remind one—of all the Irish. No, Ailsa. Because of what we've already been to one another. And so fast." He touches his shirt. "No one young speaks to me like that anymore. They all pussyfoot." He sees the packet. "Hah. Caught you with the goods."

"We're allowed. Next party's not for a week."

"Week, huh. I'll be gone. Speak again tomorrow. Be gone by Thursday noon." He touches the packet. A signet ring on his fifth finger, no marriage ring. "What's in there?"

"Cheese. Guacamole. Macaroni salad. Some ham. No more salmon." She has to grin. He grins back. "But kiwis" she says. "And a chocolate pear."

"A what?"

"Specialty of the caterer. But from last week."

"At least they don't grow those out here."

"Oh sure and we're trying. Back East they'll buy any we can send." Her tongue's flying away with her, customer style. The young ones, she's watched them here.

"Back East." He's all of a sudden somber. "It's no longer just a phrase. You born and raised here?"

"Raised. Born in Chillicothe, Ohio." That one meaty fact is always good in her mouth. "We were there beforehand for a month, in a motel."

"Born in a motel. Mother and child doing well." He taps the packet of food, rat-a-tat-tat, ratta-tatta-tat-tat, along with his half song. "Let's not keep me standing here, eh? If I invite myself to your place for supper, Ailsa, will you accept?"

She has to smile. "Not in a poem, I can't."

"Just nervous tics. Come on me in hospital. To keep the nurses at bay." He winks, to show he doesn't mean that. "Okay is all you have to say."

"Okay—" she says. And with a gulp—"Is that how you talk on Broadway?"

"See—you've caught it. So did they." He clears his throat. "But it'll come to an end."

It does. "I'll have to phone home."

The phone is a wall-box, two feet from where they stand. How much will she say?

"Mam. . . . Yes, I'm late. But why'd you leave?"

A pause. "It felt like . . . like my period coming on."

That hasn't happened to Mam for months. Some women around here say they welcome the menopause. What Deirdre welcomes in that line she keeps dark.

"I'm bringing somebody home. We can eat upstairs if you like. You needn't wait." They have been through this before. "Somebody" means a man.

"Can't stop you." This meant for a joke. "Anybody I know?" This always said too. Later she'll ask after those who don't turn up again. Crooning comfortably—"Ailsa, you're a hard one to please."—Meanwhile always opening the downstairs door to them, to let the neighbors see she's there, whatever might be going on upstairs.

"It's that poet, Mam. I'm bringing him. The man who spoke. He'd like to share the party food I'm bringing." And with her hand over the mouthpiece—"I don't know his name."

The reply is so long in coming the man behind her says "Skip it, maybe. I'll take a raincheck."

Her mother answers like from way back in the phone. "His name is Leonard." Pause. "If there's any funny business I'll be at Loretta's."

"No, Mam. Stay."

Walking him to her car she feels she still could stop this. "We live a far drive on. My Mam, she won't live in anything but a row house." Which are in short supply this far down the coast.

"Won't she now." He laughs a lot for a man with what he has on his chest. "Most people can't wait to get out of them. . . . But don't worry, I'll take a cab back. The university gave me a number to call."

In the car he says "So you have a Mam. Well, that's better than a Mom. Though I was hoping for a family."

A strange thing to say. But it's clear he's a person who says things. "You a family man?"

"Other people's. Draw the line at godchildren. But I'm the best Christmas uncle you ever saw. Or Hannukah. And Easter bunny . . . Go ahead, laugh, why don't you. You'd not be the first."

A person who says things is the kind you can say things to. "We never had uncles, my brother Eamon and me. Or family. The Dad moved out on us. So it was the Mam who moved on."

He takes his time answering. The road down the coast is not for the careless but she sneaks a look at him. He hulks in her little runabout the same as her brother, the one time Eamon'd had to cadge a ride with her—to answer a volunteer fireman's call, his truck being needed at the garage. "Feel as if I'm riding Smoky Bear," she'd teased Eamon as he leveraged himself into the bucket seat, though she was proud of him for taking on every township call offered. This man has the same outline, except for the hair.

"I've known Eamons . . . , And Seans, and Malachys, too . . . They like my songs in Ireland . . . Even though I'm a Jew. . . . Hey, watch that wheel."

"Do you know when you do that? When a poem's coming on?"

"That's just rhyme . . . and a bad habit. But on the real songs . . . maybe half I do, half I don't. Same for the ticker, the doc says. 'You neither smoke nor drink' they say 'And the muscle's been a good one. So whyd'ya give it such a hard time?' . . . So why do I? . . . Your Dad was Irish, eh?"

"Name of Cathal."

"Aha, was he now. Know more than one of those." He's caught the lilt again. "I can tell you why the men move out, Ailsa. Irish or not."

She waits until she rounds a curve. The night is like almost all of them here, made for love, and for wondering if you're not going to. Or haven't yet had what you could call that. "My brother says 'We're soakin' in being Irish because we've got nothing else.' That if we found the Dad we could get on with our own life." She manages the next curve and rushes on, the car and her both. "But he has three kids and him not twenty-eight. So he has got on with it, hasn't he?" She crouches over the wheel, knitting herself to it. "Of course he's a tow-trucker is all, and a lot on the road."

"So maybe he's found a solution to monogamy there. . . . Hey, slow down, if you're going to ask me anything more."

"Sorry." She drops back to sixty-five. "I can't slow too much. There are people behind me." She's gripping the wheel even tighter; it won't let her go. "So then, were you ever the one to move out?"

Is it a wild guess only? Or is she knitting herself to him in the way blood is said to tell?

He answers calmly. "I did that, yes. More than once. You don't write songs to the women you live with. But it's the same for any man, streetsweeper, or bank clerk. Or the man with money smarts. Even to all those tails wagging the corporate dog . . . Moving on is moving out."

She's never let herself be angry at the Dad before. Whether or not this unlikely man is him. She finds her English-class voice. "I come from women who seem to have done just that. My great-aunt,—our first to come here—they say she kicked the husband out. Though he wasn't even a no-good. My grandmother, she left the husband, wounded in gunplay she wanted no more of, to come here. And died of it. And my Mam? She says she was left." She glances at him sideways. "But maybe she wanted to pioneer? We keep a shop." Her voice breaks. She can feel him looking at her

"Ah, that urge—," the voice at her side says "—Or was it California beckoned?"

Maybe all his women left this man? She guns the gas. But for sure he knows all the answers. If you get paid to speak you must have to. "My Mam's not run-of-the-mill. She won't let the shop be called a boutique. And she keeps proud of being from around Boston."

There's her turnoff, and free and clear. She wheels left and into it.

"Around 'n' around—" he cries, as they grind up to the McCoy curbside and stop short. "Whew. Boston's terra firma. It certainly is that. When I was a young instructor there it was damn near the whole globe." He steps carefully out of the car. He's wearing Western boots, the leather deeply stamped. "You sure drive third-generation, Ailsa. And so this is the row house."

There are no driveways. But every owner's car is in its slot of curbside. Second cars go on the streetside, opposite, which is a fire-fenced empty lot. Eight peaked houses this end, with just a few feet between, buff brick at the base, brown siding at the dormer tops. Cheap even in their time, with a respectability that nobody out here now wants.

"You all must be full of pride here," he says. "There's no place to hide." And makes her a face.

All the downstairs lights in the place are on; the neighbors will be wanting to know why. Mam doesn't do that even for customers. As he and she go up the brick path he mutters "Eight steps, Leonard. Take it slow."

She has a qualm for not having at least warned him, of what might be in store. But what could she have said?

"My mother knows your name" Ailsa cries, when they reach the top step. Breathing heavily, he acknowledges this with an absent nod. People will know it already. He must never have to introduce himself, even. What a boon.

Mam opens the door. She has on the round lenses, dark as molasses, that she wears to the beach. And has changed from the dowdy, to the gray model that shows she has the figure for it. More usually she plays that down, saying a dressmaker had ought to be dumpy; comes with the trade.

The man Leonard has relieved Ailsa of her packages. "Good evening, Ailsa's Mam" he says. "We bring the feast."

"Please to come in."

Eamon looms behind her. He'll have the money bundle somewhere on his burly person, in the many-pocketed overall. He'll not be staying for any of the other concerns of this house. To him the men encountered here are on sissy errands: husbands picking up a wife's dress, men paying for a girlfriend's. As for what a sister does on her own these days, a brother is better off not knowing. Nor if offered will he share what's in Ailsa's packages; he doesn't approve of her and Mam hanging about the university, and not just for the pay. What you get that way is dangerous.

As he stands aside, then passes with a nod, his sister sees the two men in silhouette. About the same height they are, Eamon's hair the silkier, and of course not grayed, the two heads fairly similar in outline; Eamon's nose even juts. She sees how he could be a half Jew; she can't say more. He's gone.

"A customer?" the poet says, smiling.

"Our son. He sees us nightly." Deirdre is brisk. "Please to come to the nook."

She sets out the food on the round table, always cloth-covered, where they have tea or any meal. There is no nook really. Her mother has created one, via what she calls "the powers that be." The room is full of those now, playing like searchlights, crossing and recrossing this oblivious man.

"Make a good tea" her mother says as they sit, her voice a mite steely for cordiality, maybe only from disuse.

"You are kind," he says, tucking in. "But thanks, no tea." He pats his chest. "Off the list."

Ailsa is starved, and eats with them. "I never eat at the plant."

"Ah, that what you call the university?"

She considers. "The plant" is what Mr. Garfield calls the nearby warehouse he still serves as accountant, part-time. So do others on the Row. Whether or not they work there, it's the one that's near. "That's what it's been to Mam and me. Until—this." She waves a hand at the room in general.

He's been staring around, between large if gentlemanly bites. "I love being in—environments."

Does he mean slumming?

"Pleased to provide," Deirdre says.

She'd opposed the stained-glass-design wallpaper. The high-looped wire basket holding their rag-bag snippets in a column of color also offends, as both waste and hinting of labor that should be concealed. But she was touched by the black iron cat now to one side of the stairs, found by Ailsa at a flea-market, and a ringer for the long-lost one once at the great-aunt's mantel side. And now admits the worth of it all.

As for the customers, they hug their elbows and stare, charmed on entering. And stay to spend.

"All those misty garments." He's on to Ailsa's bridal corner. "This must be the dressing-room in every woman's mind." Another scone goes down him. Feeding men is different. Delicacies get swallowed whole. "No TV?"

"Mam gave me hers."

"People on screen, forever confessing, like it's the priest." Mam grunts. "People glued to it—not sure they're alive 'til they hear the news."

Her mother has only so much rigorous conversation: Samples of what she says in private. In company, Ailsa tries to sweeten it. "Granma Siegel, next door—she likes to have any war news to bake along with. Says it makes her own kitchen smell sweet as a church." Her cheeks flush for all the environment she could spill to this man.

He has seen the sign on the mantel. "Deirdre, eh. Come across Noras and Bridgets over there by the dozen. And Mary Margarets. But never one of those. Always think of it as a name to be sounded across a lake."

"Never?" Ailsa quavers. She can feel her scenario going down the drain.

He doesn't answer. Why should he? So much nonsense these platform people have to respond to. Like with those blonds.

"Aunt that raised me called me Deir," Mam says. "I thought it was *dee ee ay are* she was saying. 'Til I went to the nuns, didn't think I had a name; kids teased me I didn't. Told them I had a secret one. When I said what, they howled me down."

"What was it?"

Is he being kind to this dead old story, which he must know is that? Or is he after Mam's scar?

Her mother takes off the sunglasses. The ceiling light is cruel to eyes pinched by years of sewing, under the mannish nest of clipped gray curls Loretta can't persuade her mother from. Yet with the baby nose and the broad lips Mam calls her flannel-mouth, it had once added up to a winsome enough girl. The naked-pink ears, not aged at all, are as tender as Ailsa's own. Which the medical student used to put his tongue in, lifting the long hair that covers them.

"Annie," she says. Is this why the lights are on? For there she is—young again, even if only Ailsa can see.

Is he going to laugh? He has the grace not to. "Ah—I've known those." Pats his belly. "Lovely tea." He burps like the Arabs are said to do, in thanks. He bows low. "In London, where I had my op—cheaper there,—ladies ask for 'the loo.' Gents say 'May I see the house?' . . . May I, then?"

It's Ailsa who has to motion him into the bedroom they call the 'best,' it being the only one, barring the box Eamon grew up in. She can feel her mother's heaviness behind her; had she expected to be recognized? When Ailsa turns to see, she is not sure.

There's a moment when women no older than her mother, in the forties somewhere, suddenly turn middle-aged. Ailsa's crowd is used to watching that, mostly in church. Sometimes it's said to be when the grown-up children leave. Or when the wife finds out the marriage is not worth leaving. One Sunday, there she'll be, in a saint's alcove fumbling a candle, not yet with the elders but halfway, in sensible shoes with cut-outs for bunions, and a crock hat. Maybe it's not for what Ailsa and the other girls have thought, though. Maybe it's not only when you have no future that you become middle-aged. Might be when you no longer can believe in your past.

At the door of the bedroom, he's sucking his teeth. "Unbelievable. Do women never get over *couleur de rose*? And what's the slithery stuff, that makes a sound when you lie down on it?"

"Taffeta" Ailsa says.

"Right. Had me a rosy bedroom once." He smirks. "Moved out of it."

"Bathroom's in there."

He's a big man, slower than he should be. The spool bedpost creaks when he grasps it. As he lumbers past the vanity, the tail of his jacket catches the photo, which falls flat. "Ah, sorry." He rights it, peers at it. "What d'ya know. Never knew old stage stars this vintage came anywhere near Hollywood."

"He didn't. He wasn't. He's the—" Her mother's face stops her.

"Don't tell me." He waggles a finger, plucking at memory. "Old matinee idol, the nineteen twenties . . . Boarding-house where we teaching assistants could buy a Sunday dinner had pics of the actors of that era all over the walls. Old girl who ran it, retired actress, she collected them. Hung all the women stars in the—um—house she had a half-interest in, next door." He smiles. "Residence for single young ladies it was supposed to be. Run by some of the town bankers for their convenience. Girls were nothing much. . . . But the wall collection—Ada Rehan, Margaret Anglin, all the way to the Floradora girls, she had them all." He bends to the photo again. "Where'd you get him? He come with the suite?" He snaps his fingers. "Ro-bert Warwick, that's who you are. . . . My youth salutes you. Dusty rose enshrines you, old star." He bows himself into the toilet. The door grates. He has to slam it shut.

Opposite it, the door of the wardrobe, where customers trying on may hang their own clothes, pops open in the air current from the slam. It always does that. Ailsa begins to laugh and laugh, chokes.

Deirdre slaps her cheek hard, then grabs her, holding her tight. "Baby, baby" she croons. "Hysterics. You have to. Sorry."

Ailsa has caught her breath. Heaving, she draws a deeper one. "And where'd you learn that?" Hauling off, she slaps, knocking her mother to the floor. Slowly, her mother gets up. They help each other to the nook. They sit.

"Is he in there the Dad," She's not going to cry. "Spit it out."

Deirdre's feeling her own jaw. "It's not broken" she says, on a sigh. She stretches across the table. "Hold my hands first. Like when we—you know." They'd attended a séance once, a poor session the medium said. Nobody came through. "Close your eyes. I'll close mine."

They hang on, hands tight. There's no sound from the bathroom.

"No, but he was the one I said that to, about the book-bag." Her mother's voice is a little like the medium's—far. "He walked me home—to the boarding-house where I went as a live-in maid after the aunt died. . . . Leaving nothing but her burial costs and her gift to the St. Vincent de Paul Society. He began eating Sunday dinners at the boarding-house. But he wasn't after me. Nor I for him. I was for nobody." She stops, begins again. "Then he one day brought a friend when I was waitressing. 'She's the one carries the book-bag because it's green' he says, introducing me. 'But I doubt she's ever met an Ulsterman, only Sinn Feiners around here.'

"And that was true. But when the friend opened his mouth he had a brogue on him broad as any of us. 'Call me an Orangeman' he says, standing tall,—though he wasn't that. 'There's too many from Ulster who are not.' "

Ailsa can see him almost. Coming through.

"He was the McCoy. I liked him. This Leonard kept talking for both of them. Then once, the McCoy came on his own. By that time, I was in love with him ... I went up the stairs with him ... I'd never been with anyone before ... He was from Chicago ... He never came back ... So when the Leonard came again, maybe I'd have gone with him, just to talk of the other one. But we never did. He had a woman somewhere. All he was after was what he said today. The environment." Her hands let go. They both open their eyes. "But that's shit, isn't it? I'm the one who remembered."

They both listen for the toilet to flush. It hasn't yet.

"And what about my brother? He's from the Chicago man, then?"

"No. It was months later I got in the family way." Mam's face is bent away. "I went to one of those retreats to have it; that was the worst. Bitter broth around the clock. But the old girl who ran the boarding-house wasn't bad, she let me come back. And the boy with me. For almost three years."

Her mother looks up. Most of the time she's Mam. Then again she'll be Deirdre. That's always been—and nowadays expected—They can't always be mothers, her sister-in-law Rosalie says. Nor will Ailsa want to be. It just happens Rosalie's own mother is a stick.

But now there's the Annie too. Green and yet not green. Who got in the family way.

"Mam?"

"Yes?"

"The old girl. Which side of her houses did you work?"

"Both."

And they hear the toilet flush.

"So, who?" Ailsa whispers it. "Who was the Eamon's Dad?"

"Don't know who" her mother whispers back.

"So why did you have the baby?"

"Wanted it."

"But this man—and Eamon. They even look alike."

"We had their custom. The 'Israelites,' the old girl called herself and them. It would have been one of those. That's why she let the little Eamon stay."

The little Eamon. He's still that to her. "Then who—? Then—who am I?"

"Ah, you" her mother says. "I never dared tell you. Because of what I didn't know for Eamon, poor lamb, how could I say what I did know, about you? The father—it had to be for both of you, that photo. But for you—yes, I do know who. Not that it'll be much good to you. But for you—I planned."

There's a slither, a heavy creak. The bed in there is being sat upon.

"If that man is resting his boots on my counterpane—" her mother mutters. "Ah then—" she calls out, in the put-on voice Ailsa will never again want to tease is for her customers, "shall we be phoning you a cab?"

No answer.

When they go in he's on the bed right enough. Splayed there, tugging at his open collar.

"What's that john up to?" Deirdre says, advancing. "Eh there, get them sham boots off my spread." She crouches over him. "Eh dear God, what's the matter with him?"

"He's had a bypass." Never did Ailsa think she would be opening that shirt, massaging that scar. "See his eyes are rolling up."

She and the Mam look at one another. Both have had mouth-to-mouth resuscitation training; rescue is big on the Row.

"I'll do it" her mother says. "You get onto Eamon." When he's in town he's head of the emergency ambulance squad. From the phone Ailsa sees her mother squat over the man on the bed and put her mouth to his.

—

The grace of an emergency squad is that you don't have to explain. You have no time to brood on connection. Here's the body or bodies, fellas—what's the bind?

"My scheduled mate couldn't make it" Eamon says at the door. "Ailsa, you come along to cope." He has a driver though, from the Row, big Keezie Zigler. She helps them get "the pick-up" onto the stretcher and into the ambulance.

"Vital signs?" Keezie asks, once Ailsa and Eamon have the body stowed in. A bookkeeper turned computerist, mother of six snotnoses, husband a racing-car tester who ran against her for president of the parents' association and lost, her explanation of her treadmill agenda is "Have to keep my energies out of control."

"Still there." Eamon already has apparatus out and attached. "Ailsa, get the boots off this man."

"Keep it up!" Keezie yells as they lurch off. Squad members claim that's what she yells to hubby when she can find him time.

The boots rear at Ailsa, their uppers handsomely scrolled. This what it means to turn up your toes? And die with your McCreedy's on? "Can't. He's swelled up in them."

"Who is this guy?" Eamon has to know if he can, for the intake nurse receiving them. And this pick-up is also from his house. Bent low over the body, ticking off what pumps and tubes he can from his arsenal, his head isn't far from the body's. From his baffled crooning the body may not be going to make it much longer as a man. Eamon is white-faced with effort; the face beneath it might be its reflection, drowning in a pond.

Israelite. She can see that pearly-voweled word hanging on an old woman like a brooch. Or handwritten—with too much flourish?—on a man's birth certificate. Eamon's partner Lou is one, a laid-back Californian; hipped on anything with wheels and into Buddhist cookery with his Chinese girl from Toronto, he may not even know the word. Would Eamon himself mind that other half of him? Far worse if he were ever to find himself in that other whirlpool. What would it be like to find one's father only in an eddy of men?

Meanwhile, she herself is still unidentified.

All the lying her mother must have done floats her on. To give Eamon the present of his life.

"Hold fast to what you're at, Eamon."

"I'm doing that, woman. What's it to you that I wouldn't."

"If I tell you who he is—promise you'll never say a word of it to Mam?"

"You been in the sack with him?"

No, but could be our lying mother has. She's still seeing Deirdre mouth-to-mouth with this man. And with how many?

"Promise, I say. On whatever's holy to you."

"All right then. On the kids. And be quick. I think he's going."

The rasp, like a sewing-machine, fills the vehicle. And the eerie white silence within. "He's—the Dad."

"You're—off the wall."

"Mam won't admit it, not to her dying day. But she as much as did. She took off from the lecture hall we were serving at—when she saw him. And before that—, at something he said from the platform, she answered right back, only to herself. Like she knew him from when. So I brought him home. And turned out he was at a Boston boarding-house where you and she were when you were small. Before me." Her voice fails her. Where is she herself now?

"Ah, it's a woman's story." He's doing something with a clamp. "You've cooked it up between the two of you. Because I—." He curses, but not at her, holding a tubing high.

"So it is—" she says half amazed. Half in glee. "A woman's story—who the father is. As it has to be. As it mostly is." And now she can cry. For Mam, who had to find that out.

"So why tell me? And just now."

He knows why. Because. As for now—look at them. The son tending the father. I could half believe it myself.

"When I saw the two of you in the hall I was sure of it. Look at him. You're the image."

The man with the life supports looks down at the man who may have given him life.

"He's the one in that Harvard story of hers, Eamon, about the book-bag."

"So there wouldn't have been a marriage to find," he says slowly.

Ah, he's taking it. "Fancy not."

The man between them is breathing steadier, as if to help.

"That Orangeman. I never believed in him," she says, biting her lip. Because she does. In him most of all.

"But the photo—what about him? All the years we lived with it."

The rasp begins again. "It's a photo of a long-ago stage actor. He recognized it. That's what nailed it for me. He'd seen it before. In the boarding-house. She must have hooked it from there. To show."

"She must have wanted no part of him," he says slow.

She has to admire. His hands are rock-steady. While between the two of them—and the man beneath him of course, he is being conceived. And in the end?—She stares at her brother. In the end, he'll blame Mam.

They are driving up to the hospital.

"Maybe they can massage the heart," she says.

"With what he's had? But there's a spark."

They stop with the same lurch the ride began with. Out pop the stretcher bearers from the emergency ward's door.

"Go along with him, Eamon. I'll take over for Keezie." Who has been known to heist the empty ambulance anywhere her own agenda takes her.

"You're a sister to have." Enmeshed in his procedures he hasn't once looked at her. Only at the patient. Eye to glazing eye.

"Just keep up your promise. Not to say I told you. Mam would deny. And never let me hear the end of it."

The team of orderlies is at the door. The stretcher slides out and Eamon after. Under the white blankets that shroud the body the boots point up. Eamon has his hand on them.

When they're gone an orderly sticks his head in. "Name of pick-up?"

"Leonard" she says.

"Last name or first?"

"Do you know—I don't know."

"So." He shrugs, salutes.

"Stay. He's a bit famous. Speaker at the college. They'll know who he is."

With a nod he's gone.

Once an ambulance has delivered it's as quiet as a vault. Keezie passes her coffee from a thermos. "How'd we do?"

"There's a spark. Eamon's following it."

The cup trembles in her hand—what if the man himself lives to deny? Though if she knows Eamon, he will never ask, only hoard his secret; he's not in it for show. Safest if the man dies. She can't bring herself to wish that. But if so, then her brother would have a father to follow like most do, from death's safe distance. With all the lies resting in peace.

"Come up front with me for the drive home" Keezie says.

Against the rules, but she does. "Eamon thought I must spell you."

Keezie snorts. "He doesn't trust me to put the old boat away. Okay, I do have to check on the kids. You can drop me. Girl next door is going to sit for the day. Nice family. Moved in the Row last week."

"Matt off at a race?"

"No, for once. Well, yes and no. Gone off to the harness races somewhere in New York State. Those horses that pull jitneys, can you believe it? For a man who test-drives cars, which is worse than racing them? Says he wants to slow down. Says he might consider breeding those trotters. Less dangerous."

"Breeding can be dangerous."

"Right you are. Look at me. Six boys in nine years. When I'd give my ass for a girl. Maybe for once I should try not just giving it to Matt." She laughs, gives Ailsa a sidelong glance. "Ailsa—you still a Catholic—?" Not waiting for an answer she pilots the ambulance into a garage that also serves the Knights of Pythias Hall. "Old boat is going." They nod at each other. The squad will soon have to take up a collection. But the life equipment is the newest of its kind. "Don't worry, I'll hitch," Keezie says.

She's already out and on the highway, waving her flash. Locals know her habits. Anyone else who stops soon will.

Ailsa walks home. As she approaches the Row the morning lights are popping on. She knows the program of each house. Which man will soon be on the corner for his car-pool, which works late shift and can sleep in. Dark window at the end house, where the breadwinner has been laid off. That new girl sitter,—her family doesn't know yet how they'll all be co-opted into the ways here. Or maybe that's why they moved in. Not everybody is the one religion here. But families are drawn to this stretch of workers' houses: all the same, built by the textile factory—old for California, the nineteen forties, that could no longer make a go. "Like some people are drawn to antiques" Mr. Garfield says.

Only one light in her house, in the kitchen at the back. Terror lights up in her chest. Mam is going to tell her how she was planned.

Right now neighbors may be there, having seen the ambulance. She can name those who would come for gossip, loners who crave a hotpot to gather at, and one stronger than tea. The cars at the curb tell her who's still at home, who has left.

On the clothes-tree in the back yard the rose bedspread is hanging. Water stains taffeta, shrivels it. Deirdre would have washed it only because she had to. What substance had the man left on it—urine, or only the sweaty shape of him? It hangs on the mild morning like a ruined flag.

Mr. Garfield and her mother are sitting at the kitchen table. As a semi-retired accountant, he also works some at home. At a party at their house is where Eamon met Garfield's private student, Rosalie. "Mr. G.," as he is called, sees himself as a bridge between this female house and the world of men. He waggles a finger at her. "What kind of people you bring home, darling? We were worried sick."

"The kind that die on you," her mother says. Nobody is going to build a bridge to her. "Eamon just phoned."

Ailsa is relieved she's not glad. She makes the sign of the cross.

Her mother does not. "Eamon was upset."

"We got him there alive. It won't reflect on the squad."

"Death reflects on nobody" Mr. Garfield says.

"Anyway thanks, Gabe. I'm okay." Two cups are on the table. "Another cup?"

"No thanks, I have a customer coming."

"So have we" her mother says. "But please God, not until noon."

When he's out the door Ailsa says, "What else did Eamon say?"

" 'He's dead, Mam' he said. 'Tell Ailsa.' Then he rang off."

"So you've told me." She feels the teapot. It's cold.

"Off in that hearse with your brother—you get a chance to talk to him?"

She takes a deep breath. "I did, yes. I told him we were driving the Dad."

"You . . . what?"

"Only that he was the book-bag man. And the boarding-house one. Some of the details."

"What details?"

"How you knew the man's name. And ran from him. And hid behind the sunglasses when I brought him home. How I saw the man recognize you. For he did, you know. When you said 'Annie.' But was too cute to say. And how the photo was cock-and-bull . . . and that was all. Nothing more."

"Nothing. You call that nothing?"

"I made Eamon promise not to tell you he knows. I said if he asked you, you would only deny. . . . But that if you did, you would lie."

"And he believed you?"

"Mam. He's been wanting to believe something all his life."

Her mother's lips are white. "And do you believe that I've lied to you? When I've admitted—far more."

"I did it for Eamon. So that he would have somebody for God's sake."

"God?" Her mother says. As if asking who he is.

"Keezie asked me just now. If we were still Catholic. I put her off."

"My religion was to do best for the two of you. As I could. Still is." Her mother stands up with half a laugh. "Maybe I'll do what you say about Eamon; maybe you have the good eye. I have little enough of that for the men. Either to love or to hate. There was never a man in the house before I was born, nor after; how could I? You at least have had Eamon. And the college. You girls—maybe you see how to do for them." She marches into the bedroom, about to pick up the photo.

"No—" Ailsa cries, "—leave it. It's been the man in the house. I've grown fond of it." But now that it has a name? Only gray-and-tan paper, looking as if it's been bled?

"I took it when I left the old girl's. Never knew who it was. That's how I could fancy on it. If you fancy on what's not real, you can forget what is." She puts a hand to her cheek. "Ailsa?"

"Mam?"

"You slapped me harder than you thought. Inside. Come sit over here. I have to tell you the rest."

They are in the nook. Under the powers that be. But at least not holding hands.

Mam's are fisted together. "The child put me to rights. The old girl took me back to the boarding side of the house, and him with me, claiming it lent the Sunday dinners a good touch. My days off, I sewed, earning extra. Then the old girl fell ill, and the new owner wanted none of me. But this time, I planned. It was then I hooked the picture, for Eamon's sake. Bought a jalopy, and we're off, the three of us. Counting the sewing-machine."

"Wasn't I on the way?"

"No. I was clean as clean. Had to be, if I wanted to keep Eamon. Not to go back again to that hostel where I'd stayed until I had him. Where when you left the place, with only your belongings—if you'd given up the babe that is, there was always a scruff of men hanging outside the office, watching if you had no place to go."

—"Hope you don't have a Sunday mind"—the medical student had said to Ailsa,—their first time. "Fallen women—all that unhealthy guff the nuns fed us. Hope you're not still in that corner."—

And no, she hadn't been—nor since. But now she feels like she's there. Fingers prying at the curtains. Voices hissing through the keyhole.

"Times I was tempted" her mother says. "To go back to the second house. Oh—not toward the men. Not that we hated them. It's a business. But we in that house were lucky. We needed no pimps. The men brought themselves. Courtly ones. And it was the only place I had women friends. During the day, we'd have such fun. Tea-parties every four o'clock, just before the trade started coming in. And the tea black, I'll tell you. For we were all of us Irish girls, every one of us. The Jews don't like bringing down their own kind."

Deirdre's still in that corner, Ailsa thinks. Even cozy there. But where am I?

"I'm getting to you, duck" her mother says, as if Ailsa has spoken aloud. "Night I left, I crept over there. All the johns were gone, except for one regular. The girls gave me and Eamon early breakfast—'a hunt breakfast,' one said, and how we laughed. The regular packed the car for me, suitcases in the back, Eamon up front with me. Food and drink in the trunk. One girl who'd waitressed herself up from the West Virginia Cumberlands gave me a list of motels all the way to Pittsburgh. I was going roundabout, to earn. 'The mom-and-pop ones are the best for you' she said. 'Won't ask you to do more than clean, especially if you pitch your price low. Watch out for the chain motels though, where the big-timers stay.' The girls all accepted what my bent was to be, from then on. But it was the regular who gave me the hint that stayed with me. Good little guy, he ran a department-store, and for once the sick-wife-at-home story was real. He knew what I wanted the photo for; the girls only thought I'd a crush on it. 'Might as well claim that actor E. H. Southern for the daddy bit' he said to me. '—This man here was near as well known. Some grandaddy's sure to see the light.' But the road I was to travel, nobody ever did. Out in the car, he pats Eamon. 'This little fella'll keep you straight, Annie' he says. 'So you don't know who his Pa is. Don't make him pay for it. Have another young one, why don't you, whose Pa you do know. And make it an Irisher.' He's not joking. 'And by the way—' he says 'Heard by the grapevine my Lily's about to tell me she's lost her ruby ring. She offers, you take it. I always wanted to give her an emerald' . . . And I'm warming up the engine, for it's ten above and not dawn yet, and she comes out, says 'Shake, kiddo,' and I find the ruby ring on my fourth finger—they'd all seen I'd bought a wedding one. 'Telling him I lost it' she says. 'Don't worry on it.' "

The ring on her hand, a modest stone, much worn, commanding no special respect. "That why you never let me borrow it, like for the prom? Because of where it came from?"

Is Deirdre going to slap her again? "You—college girls." Her voice is grimy. "I've heard them up there. Crapping about sisterhood. Seen the posters too. Let me tell you, anywhere there's females there's some scratchpaw. But I never found better friends than I found in that house. And you're here because of it." She reaches out to smooth Ailsa's hair, then her palms press her own lips. "No, I wear it to remind me. That whores have to lie."

There's a faint knock at the back door, no more than a fumble. When Ailsa opens up the plate is on the back steps.

"At this hour—" her mother says, uncovering the scones. On top is an envelope. "Mrs. Deirdre McCoy" written underneath, above a flourish "Addressed." Inside, a scrap of paper in the granma's shaky print. SORRY FOR YOUR LOSS.

"What's the Addressed mean? She knows where we live."

"That's what it means. And that it was delivered by hand. We had a patient at the loonies did that. Very elegant she was. Wrote notes to herself with a feathered pen . . . I've no stomach for these, have you?"

"Mam. Are we on the road with you, or aren't we?"

"We are," her mother whispers. "But you're not yet with us. Please to bear with me."

And then she does the odd thing. She picks up the iron animal, lifts it to her lap and cradles it, not looking at Ailsa, talking to its black head. "We're at Pittsburgh. It's taken me near two months, working my way. I'm doing it for Eamon, I tell everybody. For him to meet my folks. Only one place propositions me, to be the in-house girl for trade. Wouldn't have to make the beds even, only be in them. For big tips. But I turn it down. Meantime, well along the way, I catch on I'm being followed—a trucker who stops every place I do. It's Eamon who falls for him first. And him for Eamon. He has the Philly-to-Chicago run. He takes me for a legal woman, and who am I to say? A good man, even shy. Plain. Not one for the easy path. But by Cleveland—him on his way back and me forward, we settle it, and team up. I'm in that one place for some months, he back and forth, until the motel manager catches on. Then it's me they boot out—after he's gone." Mam pauses. She's half smiling. "But on my way west again he tracks me down; he's gone off his route to do it. It's winter and the motels open are fewer. I'm his wife, he tells folks, and we're looking for a house somewhere on his run. It's understood between us he won't leave his real wife, not that I ever asked. He and she have no kids, but they once had a dead boy. Since then she's a mite—not off, but downbeat. 'I won't leave her any more than I will ever leave you' he says. And I believe him. He's just caught. So we find a house. Start to fix it up."

Her mother stops for breath. Ailsa breathes with her.

"Still, it don't quite agree with me. I'm still thinking on the West. And when he's off again the other way, to Philadelphia—I think about the East I left. And which is the beckoning . . . Is that the phone?"

Deirdre has such a sad, sly face on her. Like the high-school shoplifter who crammed one of the bridals down her front to meet her months-along belly, half wanting to be caught in the act.

"No Mam, it's not. So serve it up."

"One night, when he's off on his route, I find out for sure that you're on the way. Eamon's sleeping on the new youth-bed we've bought him, me on the double with the two pillows, one of them over at the edge, and for the last two nights smooth as cream. It's not a bad town we're in. There's chestnut trees all down the main street. And I have the right child, by the Irisher, though he's from Quebec and his mother still lives there. And the machine looking at me from its corner. He'd already phoned, which he did each night from his last stop, telling me where. He didn't phone the wife while he was on the road, he'd said; it upset her to hang up again; she only wanted him to appear. I believed him. And do to this day. He was fit to be the father of the child I was going to have. But you know what decided me not? Can you imagine it?"

"I'm imagining it," Ailsa says. "Just don't riddle me."

"It was the sewing-machine. Squatting there in its corner like a witness. Showing me how I was going to be there, there, every telephone night."

I can see it, Ailsa thinks, Like those two machines over there, hers and Mam's. They sulk.

"—'Well, I'll show you' I said to it. 'And leave you here in the bargain.' For of course I couldn't take it along, not on the double, and on the train, which is what I would have to do. To Cincinnati. Nice town too, but I couldn't linger there either. Wasn't on his beat—but you never know. Had to lose myself."

"You were afraid he'd find you?" Ailsa has never met a man she could be afraid of. Is that a lack?

"No." Her mother is stroking the iron beast in her lap. "I was afraid I wanted him to."

Her mother stares down at the thing. Ailsa reaches out to stroke it also.

"So we'll wrap it up, shall we?" her mother says, harsh. A quote from Eamon, when he wants out of here, which he mostly does. "How did I get to the town where I would stay for the rest of that year? I no longer had the machine but I'd managed to pack along the attachments: the needle, the bobbins, those that did gathers, hemstitch, punchwork, a lot they don't have today. Laid them on the night-table like fortune-cards. And they spoke right back:—Go to the Singer people, the company that made us.—"

"Ah, you didn't" Ailsa says with a chuckle.

"But I did. And they had openings. Towns where a qualified seamstress might get to own a machine by serving as its demonstrator. So I was set up after all." Her mother squints forward, like into the future of the young woman she was. "Not by a man. By my machine."

The older of the two in the corner is the one she earned. She nods to it. "Before I go, I demonstrate to them. Right there in the shop. And I choose the town I'll have by the lilt of it. Chillicothe."

Ailsa repeats it, with a loving twirl of the tongue.

"But there's a snag—almost. They say 'Of course, you have a following?' And I think—by God I do. And I say 'Of course. And in addition, my husband, a trucker for the Allied, scatters my cards all along his route.' " Her mother takes a scone, but only crumbles it. "Some lies are scabs that itch on and on. But not that one. It was saying goodbye to him." She slides the load from her lap. "So—you and me—we were born."

"That's the way it feels?"

"It did to me."

The two machines sit like an audience. Naked. There's never time to cover them. Unlike Eamon's first truck: The Heap, and his partner's spanking-new Class Act, these two aids have no names. Their presence is too small. The aunt's machine had had a treadle, Mam had said. You worked it with your feet.

"Did he never track you down?" . . . Us. Though he wouldn't have known that.

"Who can say? You remember those chain-letters that used to come every now and then, year after year? I didn't send them on. But I saved them, thinking each time: one day I would. So as to escape the bad luck of breaking the chain."

"I do." And how Eamon, then in his teens, coming upon the pile under his mother's desk had lined up the envelopes on the floor to examine the postmarks, whispering "So many. Like signals. What if they came from the Dad?" But had found nothing. Except one of those pressed-in box numbers with a line saying for five dollars sent there you too could have your custom-composed chain-letter. "Just a scam" Eamon had said. A bike pal had rung the doorbell and he had left.

"You came along, Mam, saying 'Will the two of you never tidy for yourselves, I've two fittings on the way,' and I said 'Eamon's thinking these might lead us to the Dad.' And you gave me an awful look and scooped them up."

"After you two were asleep, I laid them out on the kitchen dresser and studied them. And do you know, every postmark but one was from a place on Rick's route, and that last one—from Canada. It could be a coincidence. Or I could dream his life since then had set him to find me and reach after me in this backhand way. But you were ten years old by then. So what could he be telling me that I'd want to hear." She's looking to the far end of the room as if there's a figure there, waiting to come forward. "And maybe it would be only a scam."

"His name was—Rick?"

"It was." Her mother is seeing a face out there for sure. "Francis Patrick christened, but called Rick. At least on the road. . . . Will you be wanting to know the rest of it?"

"No!" Ailsa shouts. "I mean not yet."

"Ah. You don't want to be like Eamon. On the hunt."

. . . How shrewd. Do you only get that way if you lie? . . .

"Maybe anyway it wasn't the real name. That crossed my mind. A truckers' motel was where he found me. Could he know for sure I was being straight? And he had a wife at home to consider."

"You think Eamon has women on the side?"

"Whatever makes you—think that?"

"That man Leonard. When I said my brother was a trucker. He hinted it."

Her mother's lips squirrel inward. "All men are men on the road, one time or another.... And that Leonard, he was at the end of his."

The phone rings. Her mother answers, a string of exasperated okays and yesses. She hangs up. "That was Loretta. We won't go out today; she and her wheelchair might have a job. In which case they'll send a car.... And she's seen the bedspread hanging, and didn't I know that water's death on taffeta?... Of course I knew, what does she think me? But what else did you do when the person who's done you the most ill in the world leaves his mark on it?"

"But he wasn't the Dad."

"Not on your life."

"Then why lay it on him?"

"The last Sunday dinner he came. He was alone at table. I'd served the greedy gut extra dessert so he'd stay on. And then I charged him. With talking the other one into not coming again. He didn't deny. 'He's only a teacher now, Annie' he says. 'But if he's to earn a place for the Terror's forces in Chicago he'll have his work cut out for him. McCoy can talk the birds from the trees when he has a blast ready in his pocket. But he can't afford to be soft.' 'He was once,' I said. And he says 'So I hear. But he and I, we had a chin-wag. So don't build on anything, there's a good girl.... And thanks for the pie.' "

It's always the food she and Mam end up with, that's true.

"That Leonard, and the Irish Terror" Mam says. "Like it was one more environment. He's never done more than listen to himself."

"And to his scar."

"Eh? All I know is I never despised a man more."

"So the Orangeman was real?"

"No man ever more so." And the voice still soft for him.

"So the one man does you the injury. And you hate the other one for it?"

"Fob off. What do you know about it."

"And the real man comes along maybe, and you can't even stick with that."

For answer her mother stalks past her and out the kitchen door. Only to come back. —" 'Tisn't dry yet. But there's a terrible big stain."—and bursts into tears.

"I'd join you," Ailsa says. "But I couldn't be sure what I was bawling about."

A knock at the door.

It's Eamon. He and the mother stare. She says, "You never knocked before."

He drags in a basket of flowers, the tall kind, its handles looped high. "The hospital. Passed it on. College sent it. He was already dead. I was there when he went." Hauling the basket in with him he slumps into a chair and puts his head into his hands. But when he rises up his face is alight.

"They were working on him. Right out of my arms, they took him. And he come back, for a minute and more. 'I'm the son—' I said. And they let me kneel by him." He wiped his face. "'I'm Eamon, Dad' I said. 'Son of Deirdre McCoy, the woman you left.' And he says, not opening his eyes 'Annie the chambermaid. Minute she opened that mouth I knew who she was. Kept mine shut on account of the girl.' —And I said to him 'My sister. She was born later.' . . . They have the oxygen to him by then and he opens his eyes. 'Watch out for the scar' he says, but they already seen it, the intern and nurse shaking their heads. And he says 'A son, eh. That would be Cathal' and I say 'Eamon. I drove you here.' There's like a red moss on his lips He says 'Good man' and in a minute he's gone. And they push me out of there."

He stands up. "But they're waiting on whether to send the body back East, for burial. If so, I'm going along with it. Plane or train."

Their mother is inching toward the stairs, a humped creature. "I'll be upstairs in your bed, Ailsa. Give me the key. Can't stomach the bed here. Can't bear more of this." But when Eamon opens his arms she comes into them. They don't note that Ailsa is left out.

When he's gone Mam says "Plane or train? Rosalie will head him off." She goes up the stairs.

Twelve noon. Time to open the shop.

Now Ailsa's alone she enters the Fitting Room. Its sign now seems to her absurd. The photo is on the floor again. The three of them must have pushed it there when they carried out the body. Her arm muscles still ache from that.

Face-down is the way that glossie belongs. She turns it over anyway. Her middle finger, which she is forever forgetting to thimble when she handfinishes, is pricked rough. She draws it down the photo like an emery, like it might make that semi-profile come full-face.

It won't ever do that. Maybe that's its worth. Sure and I'll keep you, Robert Warwick, I'm used to you. But where? She pushes it to the back of the wardrobe, behind some garments that have never been called for. Now she'll sleep, no matter the bed.

Too tired to shower she slips into one of the long undergarments she makes for the bridals. China silk, that dressmakers line good dresses with, and as soft on unmarried skin as on the wedded.

The house-and-shop on the Row is quiet, if at an odd hour. One member upstairs, one down, and with different dreams surely. Or too alike, in the style that all women are blamed for? "Our dressmakers" the Row says of her and Mam. "Gone a bit classy, but they still take care of us." She dozes.

In the front room, is that the phone? No, it's the doorbell. The client, no doubt, come for her finished "afternoon dress," as are once more in vogue. A bouncy mother of three, young Mrs. Mason's confided she's through with childbearing. Hair to the waist and that tennis look to her, but the bust and waist are spread enough to need custom-made. "Imagine—" she said hungrily at the final fitting "—me having afternoons."

Ailsa opens the door, to a man. His white teeth flash a name; that's the effect. "Mrs. McCoy? My wife, Liz, had to be off with the chickadees. You have a dress for her." Between those teeth and a crest of dark hair is a face without category, except that it is surely among the best the male sex can offer. "Oh—excuse me." She's decent enough in the filmy white slip but an experienced eye has already approved what's underneath. "Is Mrs. McCoy in?"

"My mother, yes. Please to come in."

She and Mam are used to mismatches: old to young, hairy trolls to silvery girls. As well as the norm of potbelly married to double chin. Then why does this man dazzle her? Speech as casual as his shirt, no obvious nationality, and, in the spectrum of Sunbelt tans, even no certain skin color. A father to those chickadees, yet he must have other exploits, should he choose. He's that ordinary wonder, the other-world male she sees from a distance, whom the Liz types meet "along the landscape," or already have at home.

He has stepped inside. "Lord—" he says. "How charming. So this is where my wife and her friends spend their time. And patrimony." He smiles at her. "Pat Greenberg? Connie Baehr. Trisha What's-her-name?"

She nods; she knows them all.

"Liz says you don't charge the earth yet, but you could. And with justice, I'd say, for the place alone."

She knows what he means. Like the antique soda parlors that have popped up all along the coast. "Oh, you mean, like for an environment?"

Those eyebrows do twitch. Quick study, Ailsa; she's pleased with herself.

A voice from the top of the stairs. "Who's ever there, tell him to come tomorrow."

"Oh, it's only the Mason dress, Mam; he's come for it." They always refer to the clothes that way. A dress acquired during a marriage belongs to both members.

Mam appears at the top of the stairs in an old bathrobe of Ailsa's. "Please to come tomorrow, sir. There's been a death in the family."

"Oh no matter, I'll—" Ailsa begins, but the man says at once, "So sorry." He takes note of the basket. "I didn't see. Mrs. McCoy, is it?" He turns to Ailsa "And—?"

"Ailsa." She hesitates. "McCoy."

"Thank you—" Mam says with dignity, coming down the stairs. "Didn't have time to notify."

"Tomorrow then? Something after five?" He's turned to Ailsa.

"Or Mrs. Mason will call herself perhaps?" Mam says. "The work is ready. But we do like to see it on."

"Thank you, Mrs. McCoy. Perhaps she will." He smiles at Ailsa. "You're the designer. I remember now. They do talk. I'll watch out for the dress," and he's gone, the door softly shut. He won't likely be back. But he's raised the standard of what's possible.

"Humbug. What humbug are you up to?" Ailsa says, flailing round. "And will you be hanging the basket on the front door?"

"Any death deserves a mention." Mam picks up the basket. "I'll take this back upstairs." At the top of the steps she turns, laboriously, as if she aches. "And I've been thinking. Time for me to be up there, and you down. Meet your friends as you please then, at the door. And you must have your own bell."

"And my name above it, Mam. Like: 'Sillery,' maybe?"

The basket rolls back down the stair, dripping water. The flowers are wired tight. "He couldn't have got to you. Not after all these years."

"Those envelopes you tore up. I patched them. Like a puzzle. That was the name with the box number. Why would anyone put a last name on a chain-letter? But all the same I always kept it in my head, sort of. Not to do anything. We had broken the chain. And I didn't want to spare the five dollars. But it was a nice name."

"Ah, you poor love. Poor, poor love." But Mam doesn't come down the stairs. "To think that you got that far. Sure and it was from him; I knew that. He was a shy man, and maybe never could make up his mind. I'd done that for him. By running out. So why get in touch? I figured the wife must be gone; why else would he move back to Canada. And what would he want of me? To say nothing of you? All he'd done was to put you in me, that's all. And that's all he might think of you. I couldn't risk that." She moved down a step, then another. "I spent a long night at it. And then I figured it out. All he wanted—all people do mostly want, is to get in touch. And to that one has a right to say 'yes' or 'no.' "

She comes close enough to Ailsa to breathe on her, but no more. The way a tranced bird will do, or a loving animal. "So I did nothing. . . . Which was 'no.' "

For a minute Ailsa, who is taller, sees Mam's lifted face as those men once riding her might have: the squashed-heart lips its owner calls "flannel-mouth," a nose of no importance, blue-chip eyes under the arched black brows even she knows are her beauty, now and again saying in her bogus Irish what she said to Ailsa and Eamon when as kids they traced the brows with a finger: "Ah yiss, you like my wings?"

The old bathrobe has slipped on her. Ailsa smooths the work-rounded shoulder blade.

"Sillery's a suburb of Quebec. He hadn't the nerve to be himself, that was it, poor Francis Patrick Corrigan. So will you go hunt for him?"

"I was ten then. I'm twenty-four. What would I do with a father?"

What will Eamon do? He's of different blood from her; did she always feel so? Or is it only brother-sister, like anywhere?

Mam goes for the pail.

They mop up. Mam seems closer to the ground already, as scrub-women do, rooted in soap-and-water ideas.

When they're finished they straighten. Stuck with each other, like all scrubbers. Mam has a hand to the small of her back. "So I couldn't give you your rightful father, you see that. Because of Eamon. Who hadn't one."

"No wonder you talked so on and on, about working with the loonies. That must have been the better half of it. Compared with the bordel."

She can't believe she's said this. After thinking herself so calm.

"So you know the word" her mother says.

"You've never faced what I do know."

"Neither have you. Nor girls like you. Motels, is it? Or at the beach. Everybody at it for the weekend, like Loretta's movie stars? Or it's the other sort, with the engagement showers, all sticky good. With the men still having the ball in their pocket, either way. And the mix no different from when I was a girl. Not in the way it turns out. Who chooses a child's father at the beach?"

"The Orangeman? Him. Would you have? Chosen him? On that once?"

No answer.

"Maybe he was soft on his own, Mam? That Leonard only gave him the push."

Silence. She wishes she was out on the road like last night, with what's coming at you rushing back under the wheels. A road is an answer. "Or that Leonard himself? When I told him it was just you and me here, he said he'd been hoping it was a family. And now he's got it, Jesus." The mop wrings from the handle. She twists it dry. "And all the time I'm thinking, I swear, it's the women who threw this man out."

The other mop is wrung. "I'd have done that. Scar or no scar... He'd never have thought of me as having one."

On Ailsa's way to slap the mop on its kitchen wallhook she stops short. "How did you know about that?"

"From outside the door, I didn't leave the hall right away. I heard him go on about it."

The phone rings.

"Don't answer it, Ailsa."

No—they are the bereaved.

Of a sudden she dashes to the shop's wastebasket, a wire one bought at a crafts fair, tall as a column and filled with remnants of all weaves and colors. She up-ends it, scattering the torn silkies, velvet clots, dotted cottons, gray wools and peachy gauzes. Only no blacks; she won't have blacks in the pile, added to in the little ceremony when the week's scraps go in. Fill it up in a month, the black scraps would.

She turns on the fans, one on either side of the room, seldom needed. The rare fat customer will sometimes sweat; the ultra-thin, often the rudest, may feel faint.

"What you doing? It'll take hours to gather those up again."

Strips of every shape and weight, the sheer ones whipping like scarves, the nuggety ones bouncing, they pass each other, cling, drop, rise. Whirl. Fall.

She stops the fans. The scraps waver, settle, are still. Yes, it'll take hours. And with each bit returned to the basket she'll tell herself: That's how people are made. On the whirl. With the fans blowing from anywhere.

Her mother, sitting on the stair four steps from the bottom, hitches herself up a couple more. Not as certain now where her place is to be?

Yesterday a pair of women were resident here, related for sure by the flesh that can make itself again. Today the house is full of men. The Orangeman floats the room, a helium-filled balloon. The dead man rests on the bed. Truckers grind in and out of the ear, each a capped man whizzing by in his high cab, and never quite identified. Even the man who came by for his wife's dress is here, within a second giving her the eye—and she giving it back. Even Eamon, once a teenage brother charged to save her from rape, later custodian of his mother's cash. And now tailing off to his supposed father's fatherland, like those savages the telly shows you, carrying their ancestors in a canoe.

"Ailsa."

"I'm here." Whosever I am.

"What did I do wronger than I could have?"

"Way on back? That's for you to say."

As Mam stalls, sputters, talks a blue streak, she can see her. Annie Baloney as was, hired to help out with the loonies, under the aunt's thumb. A rabbit of a girl, not pretty yet, and ignorant of her own steel. A step up would be to serve dinners to real persons. Bankers even, bachelor university men, plus a sprinkling of widows and spinsters living cheap enough to ignore being a front for the house next door. And happy indeed to have a serving-girl.

"One of them wanted to get me a cap to wear, to serve in." But was laughed down. A giddy table it sometimes was, with jokes passing like money under the table.

When did Annie find out about the bevy of young ladies next door?

"A residence club it was supposed to be, for young women in the theater. Copied after a famous one in New York City."

If it was ever legal, it had soon eased over. Uncles and fathers to visit in the evening. Or a brother. Tea served. No drink except what a "relation" might bring, for upstairs. No dinners, but visitors welcome for the Sunday lunch across the yard.

"Learned the truth about it over the garbage"—from the maid and laundress to the girls next door. Two women chattering, teasing each other that they too could work between the sheets instead of just doing the linen. "If only we wasn't black." And one saying "I know one who still has a taste for it, Waleeta. Only at sixty-seven, you'd be a mite past it, for pay." And the other—"Still, ain't a sporting-house in Boston puts out the linen starched like here."

It's suddenly quiet, like a stage can be after a long speech.

"I can hear them, Mam. Never heard you do—like accents. Like it's an old-time skit. Like on the radio."

"Some of the girls did get part-time, in the dramatics. Backroom joints that crop up in blue-law towns. And there was a famous burlesque downtown. The old girl had a pass. 'You'll like the comedians' she said. And so I did. But it was the costumes that grabbed me. Colors I'd never seen on a human. Cuts there ought to be a dispensation for. I was mad to sew some of that, and for a few piece-jobs I did. Until she grabbed me to sew for the house next door. Lingerie you could chart your anatomy by: Told myself I was learning the trade. Spare asking me which one."

"I think—Mam, I think neither of us should be spared."

She doesn't yet know what she means by this, but she already likes the sound of it. It's herself, catching up with her education.

"True, I already knew about such women," her mother says in a diminished voice. "The loonies had been free with their tongues, 'specially the younger ones coming in from the colleges. They liked to have me about, being their age. Winsome, some of them. My practice tea-party." Her voice trails off.

There's a knock at the front door.

"Rosalie—" her mother whispers. "That's her knock . . . So to answer you quick—yes, I crossed over." Her hands are on her hips, a posture she's prone to and has tried to school herself away from, as not suitable for the shop. "From the honest trick to the hoor's."

An aged priest in Ailsa's childhood used to pronounce it that way. Now, among the tee-shirts making the rounds on campus, one is printed: Whore's Luck.

"Mam?" Her mother is bent to a scrap of blue gauze, twisting it. "Annie Baloney?" Half a smile in response.

"You asked the question," Ailsa says. "Not me. About what you did wrong." A hug hovers, which is all hugs have ever done, between them. "I'll beat you to the door."

Rosalie is in what she calls her "Sundays," though she wears these tee-shirts with hula-girls on them, over ruffled shorts and white leather boots with dangles, whenever she wants to get her personality away from the accountancy. Her round pretty face looks just as competent as when she's poring over numbers. Sometimes too much of an arranger, she's also the best stand-by friend a sister-in-law could have.

"Take a gander, ladies. Went to the hairdresser minute I got the news." She spins. The back of her head is shaved; the top is a ruff jutting forward nearly to the tip of her nose. She stops. "What's these rags all over? New-style decoration? Too-oo much."

"I had a temper fit" Ailsa says, giving her the wasted hug. "But I'm enjoying it."

"I slept some" Mam says. "But I didn't enjoy it. . . . What news?"

"Yours, of course. Oh, have I been yearning for one of our sit downs, just the three of us, all the while Eamon and me were sweating it out." Rosalie slings a bakery sack on the table. "Had it with old lady Siegel's lumps, good as they are. Whatever they are. Admit it now, how would an old lady from Rumania be making scones?" She draws down plates from a shelf and sets out an array of jelly doughnuts, crullers, Danish pastry. "And a chocolate layer, in that box. Peace offering. In case you been having a fight?"

"Not a fight exactly" Ailsa says. "Maybe a heart-to-heart."

"With some spar-ring. At intermission." Mam's accent is suddenly heavier.

"And could we have coffee?" Circles under Rosalie's eyes. She's not as sprightly as pretending. The even voice has a plaint. "Tea gives me the runners, God's truth. Or that tea."

"Yee'r in the mood for revelation, that's for sure." Mam exits to the kitchen. They hear the grinding. Ailsa and Rosalie wiggle their brows at each other, but don't say anything; that wouldn't be fair. But there's a lovely feeling between them that spans more than being sisters-in-law. Any reaction they have to topics-of-the-day, is likely to be the same. Often, undergoing a third person's conversation, they need only exchange the odd browlift, or faint shrug.

Mam's back with the coffee. They sit.

"Hrrrrrrr," Rosalie purrs at the pastry. Nobody's taking a single bun. "Well okay, here it is, folks. Eamon's not going off with that body. Instead, tomorrow he's treating me to that new nightclub in the Beach, sent us cards. If we like it, week from Tuesday is my birthday, you and the Row are invited to a party. Time we celebrated—and more than a birthday." She takes a jellyroll. "Mmmm, my favorite. Love that squishy." She signals they'll have to wait until she finishes for her to say more, so Mam and Ailsa each take something from the platter. "Danish is good at any hour" Mam says politely. "I've always taken to the Danes."

"Actually—we must have been starving, both of us" Ailsa says.

Napkins are kept in a wire basket Mam has slung on a notch under the table's wing.

"Love that basket" Rosalie says, wiping.

"For a nook, nothing does like a dropleaf table with a wing." Mam makes a face. "Said that a hundred times, I guess."

The two younger women blink at one another.

Then it's hands folded, all round.

"Before I say anything else," Rosalie says "—I want to say what I feel at this table, this house. Warmth. War-rrrmth. Even without Mam's br-rogue." She flips Deirdre a glance from under the eyelashes; they're a bit short for that. Rosalie is short all over, neck to stubby fingers to stout legs, but still a package few would mind having. "Like you know, my mom and pop, both taught math in the junior high. Good folks, but no cozy-wozy. And I was an only; it's okay for Protestants. White bunny-coat and muff when I was four. One peck at bedtime, and then the night-lamp. Ah, skip it . . . And here I am, Miss Twinklefingers on the Macintosh. Computer, in case you haven't heard. Fine. But gives off no heat . . . And the other thing I get here is—" She waves a hand at the drizzle of color wafted over the room. "Design? Nah, not only that. No matter what that rival of Ailsa's puts on her ad. Nah. What I get, every time here—dunno how to say it. What's not in the multiplication table. What's irregular. Like in fractions." She hoots out a laugh. Do they get it? Maybe not. Has she insulted? Not yet. "And I'm telling you—nowhere else in my daily dozen do I get what I get here. It don't surprise me the kids nag to come. Not just because of the candy apples. Though those count." She broods.

Mam says "Rosalie. Make with the story. Or I'll stick an apple up yours. And not your ass."

The sisters-in-law sneak a look at each other.

"To put it short—" Rosalie says, and even she laughs. "I told Eamon he could have that body—or have me. If he leaves with it, I'm leaving too. And not with the children. I said 'If that corpse was really your dad, then we should all go, huh? But you don't believe.' And he yells maybe he doesn't but at least it will stop him from not knowing. 'From ever having to go East again' he says. After this he'll take things for granted and not investigate, he says. And all the time I know what else he's up to."

She pours herself more coffee and swigs it, though it must be cold. "All I say back is 'Oh.' " She flips those small, able hands. "Not 'Oh?' mind you, like I'm inquiring. Just—'Oh,' . . . So we'll never have to say one word between us about that woman he sees when he's on the long route. Who I've a hunch he wants to stop seeing. So for that body to come along, what an out for both of us. Like I'm saying 'No, buddy, you don't go cross-country. Not one more time.' And he knows I know. But he can't say. That body takes the blame." Is she hunched over just from confessing? She's not used to it.

"Spilling their seed in motels" Deirdre says. "When Eamon took up the long-distance route I didn't think of it. Still it was a blessing, when you insisted on the kids."

"Not in a motel" Rosalie says. "To cover the kids' expenses, he takes an extra cross-country once a month. A phone call comes always just before. Please to check in at a certain garage. Maybe she owns it. Or works there. Anyway, sure sounds like she has a place of her own. Area code 812—."

"Indiana—" Mam says. "The part near Southern Illinois."

"I know. Wouldn't I look it up? But how come you?"

"Didn't have area codes, my day; you had to get the operator. But I look up Chillicothe once in a while. Just to see how it's doing."

"Where I was born, remember?" Ailsa says. She covers Mam's hand with hers. "We."

Rosalie nods. "Close, the two of you. Like I said. Like it should be. Like I don't always feel toward the kids. When the girl came I thought—that'll fix it. But not so far."

"Eamon with the kids?" her mother-in-law says.

"It's a work-day. Him and the new partner, Sid, they have a job at the college. I know that for a fact." She tosses a grin at them. "So after him and me had it out I parked the kids at Keezie's. On the sitter, we'll go shares. Keezie's working that new neighbor's girl around the clock. The girl knows I'm here. Let Eamon worry where I am. And where the kids are."

"Nine kids to watch, little and big"—Ailsa says. "I know sitters cost. But ain't that pushing it?"

"Got to get on her list. Me working at home, and always there when Eamon's on night-call, I'm not on any regular one. But I will be now. I been neglecting my needs."

"Nights in Chillicothe, I sometimes had a sitter for myself. Fifty cents for the evening, it was, if you can believe. Girls had to be driven home early of course, that town; I took you with me always, Ailsa, when I did. All I went out for was the fish-and-chips dinner. That was fifty cents too. But it felt like a million, to get out and see folks."

"So it does" Rosalie says, with such meaning that the other two look at each other.

"For yourself, you did it," Rosalie says softly. "Ah, Mam."

"That woman—" Mam says "—she call him at home?"

"Either she's a fool, or she wants me to know. Maybe to have it out on the table." Rosalie's lovely nails do a smart rat-a-tat, signifying how that will be handled.

"Oh girl. Don't you be the one to start that." Mam leans forward. "Could be—say she's even, well, a nice person. Like—Eamon is after all no fool. He's not for jumping over the traces. It just happened. Maybe to her too. And waiting there lonely—lonely as you those nights Eamon's away, what she wants is to hear how you sound, just your voice, the one that's keeping him off from her. The wife."

"What movie did you see?" Rosalie breaks a cruller in half, crumbles it. "Or she could be gunning for me. Eh? So, what's my strategy?"

Rosalie has been popping that "strategy" line to Ailsa ever since taking a session in her field at the business college, one of those courses guaranteed to hype you up on what you already do. "Let me check it out with you two, huh?"

Ailsa envies being able to take a refresher course, to pick one that fits your personality even before you go. "Us?"

"Eamon himself gives me the tip-off. He says 'Leave? Where the hell will *you* go?'" Rosalie gets up, coffee in hand, sees it's only dregs and is about to fling it in a sink. There is no sink in the front room. Ailsa scrambles to take the cup from her hand. Rosalie's forgotten she's not in the kitchen. "Not 'Where will you *go*?'"—she says, glaring. "But 'Where will *you* go.' That's it, isn't it? They always know where we are. For a fact. And where would we? Excepting you, Deirdre McCoy."

"Me? I been here since the millennium."

"Here, yes. Sounding your r's like crazy. To let us know you are. Am I the only one hip to what's bugging Eamon? He told me once, when we were mellow. All the time he grew up in that boxroom he thought it. That you'd been the one to leave the Dad."

Rosalie bends to flick a scrap off the chair leg. "Or that maybe there hadn't been a Dad to leave. He can't remember one, and he was almost three when you left. . . . And that's what he goes East to find out."

"That what you come to tell me? That your news?"

"Nope." When Rosalie stretches, the arms don't waver; the fists shoot straight up, and hold. "He says you're always fair. Fairer than you give yourself credit for. Or maybe should be. Like you told him he had to be the man of the house. But you never really leaned on him." The arms come down. "And that's how I mean to be. You never lean on anyone."

"Oh no, Rosalie. Don't," Ailsa says. "Besides, she does lean. On me."

"You? Huh. We won't get into that."

"Ah, this is your day, Rosy" Mam says. "We see that, see? So get on with it."

"Yes indeedy. Right. We-ell . . . I'd had the hair done for confidence. And I'm wearing this here blouse he hasn't seen. 'Where'll I go?' I say. 'I'll tell you where. Just three words—my favorite film title. "The Lady Vanishes." That don't say she's totally invisible. You'll know exactly where I am. For a fact. *Half* of the time.'" She struts around the table, whips out her chair as if a man they can't see has done it for her and grandly sits down.

"Shenanigans" Deirdre says, but with a gleam in her eye. "And how'll you manage it?"

"Fold hands" Rosalie barks. "All together now."

Six hands slap center table, one over the other. They've done this before, at crucial times. Or what seemed so, though not to be compared with this.

"Right—" Rosalie whispers. "I'm having my cake, and eating it too, see. Keezie and me—we've been spelling each other. Because I am-uh, al-uh, ready—uh—*gone.* Exactly half of the time."

"You aren't." Ailsa.

"You are." Mam.

That means both of them believe her.

She smiles with a cocky shake of the head, losing their hands. "For a fact."

"That Keezie" Mam breathes.

"She's different from me" Rosalie says. "She likes having kids. In times like these, she says, it's our responsibility. Her middle and last are her best; they aren't Matt's. She aims to have one father from every one of her agendas. But Keezie, her responsibility ends with having them. She'll let the older kids mind the younger, in a pinch. But I'm like you, Mam: I put 'em in the world, I'll cope." She winks. "So I have simply got to be on that new girl's list."

Which of them giggles first is lost in the family resemblance. Meaning the female one. They had giggled through their teens. Not with each other, and not on this subject. For years they had dropped the habit. Each in her own way had been a wee solemn for the practice. They savor it the more now.

"Pa—ter—nity—" Ailsa burbles.

Rosalie, taking it up, screeches it.

Mam moves her head side to side, majestic. Is she saying Maternity—in the gargle from her wide mouth?

The gush from the three of them sounds like underwater animals. Or the far plash of overhand swimmers. It stops. But they've had it.

Into the shared quiet, Rosalie says "Don't you want to hear who I'm gone on?"

"If it's the university president, sure" Mam says. "Who happens to be a hunk as well. And a free, widowed man this past year. Or if it's that avocado king serves those to his guests with loose diamonds hiding in them like sand—glad to join you there any time, won't we, Ailsa? But if it's that accountant in your extension course who you said is 'into diversity'—then no. . . . Who do you think don't know, on the Row? Keezie talks. Our Mr. Garfield knows the man, he buys the granma's Tiger Balm in the store the fella runs. Where he'll roll a chippy or a lady her personal vitamins, in his rooms at the rear. As for Keezie, her Matt is so glad to be off her agenda he don't mind an extra foal. The only person on the Row who don't know your big news is Loretta, because you ain't a movie star."

She gets up, pushing down her chair with a bang. Whatever Mam thinks goes into her muscles. Ailsa takes this for granted as a kind of sign language; she's always had it too, subordinately. It's how you signify your presence in the household—if you're a girl. She'd known this by instinct even before a man had told her so. "Your Mam, she queens it that way by necessity." But in households where there were men, he'd said, women might "signify" so much or continuously that they became naggers. Or else—pitiable.

Rosalie here has no less of that language because of her job keeping her on the mental side. Her signals are merely more mixed. Those blond literati, they've muted their muscle manners in public, but back in the household who wouldn't bet that they too revert? Even the gran next door; watch how when because of being in a mood she gives the old hand egg-beater a bad time—and maybe prefers it to the electric mixer for that reason. Or twitches her shawl—and God help Mr. and Mrs. Garfield if she has had to ask them to hand her it.

—"And a woman's largest muscle is her voice" the man had added. "And nothing they teach us in anatomy has convinced me otherwise."—

Not that she, Ailsa, wasn't physically what a man wanted. On the contrary, he'd said. Actually he'd been courteous to her at all times, and the more so when in bed. "I'm what?" she'd said. He'd written it out for her: *Callipygian*—and explained what it meant. "Oh, a big butt, huh?" she said. "Well, that wouldn't be so good, would it, if I was to wear one of my own bridals." He'd given her that glance of his whenever she was smarter than he liked to admit. Answering from deep in his chest—"No."

—"I'll never forgive that guy for what he said to you at the end,"—Rosalie'd said once he was gone, though she'd never met him. . . . Yet what good does that do—what women confide to each other, and wish they hadn't—about their men? Correction: About the men who aren't theirs.

Still it's Rosalie who at the moment is silently holding her hand, in nervous solace for both of them.

Mam, moving oddly slow, is at the wall-phone brooding, but also tossing them a look that means she's shortly to communicate.

"Eamon'll know I'm here" Rosalie says dolefully. "Just not where I might go later." But she's not downed. "So—everybody knows where, you say?"

"Not me" Ailsa says.

"Oh you, Ailsa angel, you're not expected" Rosalie says. "You're our—look at those dreamy dresses."

"Is that why you didn't tell me?" Ailsa says, breaking their hand-clasp.

At the phone, Mam, waiting for the garage to answer the phone, says "My own guardian angel; he's a mite retarded. When I'm born God must have said to him, 'Go down there. There's room for all of us. Try her.' . . . So I do everything late." Her foot dawdles, alerts.

"Sid? . . . Mam. . . . Eamon about? . . . Put him on."

The girls wait. Late or not, there's no telling. Will she give him hell? But about what? There's such a choice. Or will she console?

"Eamon?" Mam barks it. "Where's the body? . . . Still here? . . . They hear from New York? . . . Well go find out. I know hospitals. No room for the dead. . . . Because you are right, Eamon. A member of the family should escort. . . . And the college will be darn glad to get off the hook. . . . Eh?" She pries the receiver from her ear in order to look down at the two on the floor. "Yes, she's here. Passing through, you might say. . . . All I know is you two had a fight. . . ."

On the floor Ailsa and Rosalie have clapped their hands to their faces, their feet in the air. *"Clowns!"* she hisses at them, and to the phone, "No, she don't want to talk."

When she grasps the phone to her again it's with both hands. "But Eamon, I do. I agree you should go. And listen Eamon . . . I'm going with you. Plane or train . . . Oh yes, I am. It's an obligation. . . . Oh not to him, son, though I've made my peace with him. . . . Alive—I had to hate him. But now let the bugger rest. . . . No, my obligation is to you. . . . And I take my cue from what he himself said here, not twenty-four hours ago."

There is a long pause, while Mam listens. The two girls, sitting up, regard her. Whatever one says to Mam, christened Deirdre and self-styled Annie, she is never not listening. Any talk going, she keeps faith with it. And save your spittle; she'll recall every word. And replay at will.

Now she nods to the phone. "What he said to you is sure to be sacred to you, yiss. A man's own breath, not counting the oxygen . . . What he said here—not knowing he was to have a heart attack on my very bed, was maybe just by-the-bye. But he said it. . . . He said—'I love environments.' . . . And you and me will be that to him. All the way home."

Letting the phone dangle a bit she's still a perfect curve of devotion; you might think she was in a pew, at high Mass. "There's a good man. And the Row won't forget that we've paid due honor to a deceased. You want to go into the automotive parts business, you can write your own ticket with Mr. Butler at the bank. . . ."

And now she's really warming to it, like as if her number's come through on the lottery. "I'll pack me a bag. And meet you at the garage. Then I can leave my car there, for the while we're gone. . . . Stay the night with you. Pop a kiss to the kiddies, like granma should . . . Soon's you know how and when, I'll get us a motel in New York. . . . Of course. That's where you and me bow out. The Leonard's friends, let them handle the burial. . . . And Eamon—hah! It's just come to me,—where the hospitals send the dead. To the funeral parlors, of course. Try the Jews."

But when she hangs up it's a crumple. "My head's doing a jig."

"Better than your feet doing it." Ailsa wants to be hard, but the smile won't pull off her face. "What'll you wear to the funeral? The gray?"

"Give off. Let Eamon go if he wants." She claps a hand to her mouth, looking over it like a child. "Though that could be complicated. . . . Nemmind . . . But yes I'll take a model or so, if it's all right with you. And the suit I made for your ceremony—they're wearing light shades in the East. . . . And the brown skirt-and-blouse that was never called for; I can handfinish it on the way. Borrow your suitcase if I may; mine are—" She's seeing into a distance. "Gone." Glee quirks her face. "Buy me a New York handbag; won't miss that chance . . . Shoes thank God I don't stint on: I have. The red coat. I'm not a mourner. . . . But a hat— There's only that straw for the back yard. Whatever will I do for a hat?"

Is that how we are?—Ailsa thinks. Always putting on what we can't slough off? Was Hal right?

"Settle for a New York haircut" Rosalie says, sharp. "They go bare no matter the cold. . . . And that's where I'm left, eh?" She springs to her feet, stamping them. "The kiddies. Bet he didn't even ask about them . . . Oh, gee." She stops short. "I can't remember whether Ashley has her sweater along. . . . That driver for the schoolbus, he used to be a butcher, he ups the air conditioner like the kids are meat . . . and didn't Eamon even ask where I was going from here? Maybe I should've gone to the phone, I wouldn't have told him nothing. Just to sound him out . . . Do you think he knows?"

"You mean whether Ashley has her sweater?" Ailsa says, smart-aleck.

Rosalie sticks out her tongue.

"Rosalie," Mam says. "Have a double life if you have to. But don't expect folks to keep up with the schedule. . . . And now, anybody want the toilet? Before I shut myself in the other room and try to remember how to pack?"

All accept that Rosalie has a weak bladder, from having the last child. Which will keep her handily from having another.

"Go ahead—" she says haughtily. "I'll use Ailsa's." Once she's up there Mam whispers "Nobody knows about her and that creep. I was just—pushing that. For her own good."

"Like you think you should make the judgment?"

Her mother stares. She always has. With the help of the powers that be.

"Forget it. Mam—what was the Leonard's last name?" Receptions come and go. Even when the college puts a poster up Ailsa rarely notices. What counts is the audience.

"Search me, Leonard was all I knew him by."

Rosalie emerges. "Why are there flowers in the upstairs toilet?"

"Because Ailsa has no vase up there. Not being the marrying kind. With the kind of followers that send you flowers . . . Though that medical boy did write from Scotland, asking whether she wanted him to bring back a pullover. Far as I know she hasn't answered him."

"Wasn't clear whether or not I was to pay for it. Or how."

Both her listeners lower their eyes, and chins.

"And there's the phone" her mother cries, in relief. "If it's Son, tell him I'll be as quick as I can."

There's no one on the line. They are clearing the table when that happens again. On the third *pip-pip* Ailsa hears Keezie yell "Stop throwing things, you little bastards, you hit me." And then, roaring in her ear "The stinking sitter didn't show."

"I heard that," Rosalie says from across the room. She's proud of her hearing, which she says her numbers games and long computer hours have enhanced. "Poor Keezie. She shouldn't call them bastards though."

"Not all of them, no" Ailsa says absently. She rallies. "And certainly not yours. . . . Listen. She's been putting the kids in the slots they were due for and picking them up again all over town. But now she's due at the women's reformatory, to coach them on martial arts. She'd take the kids with her she says, only they might keep them."

"Hers, maybe," Rosalie says. "He-ey. You know of any woman's reformatory within miles of here?"

"No-o."

They smile at one another.

"You should hear what Eamon says about poor Matt" Rosalie whispers. "All the men do. She and her agendas." Then suddenly, she shivers.

"Take it easy" Ailsa whispers. "Mam was laying it on about the Row knowing. Nobody does."

"I know—" Rosalie whispers back. "I *heard* the two of you."

"But not too easy. Keezie's dumping them all here."

"Here?" Rosy's head snaps left-right, like pulled by a string. "But I—" Her voice tolls. It's the small things that are tragic to Rosy. Like when the numbers don't add up right.

"All nine of them?" Mam says, popping up at the top of the steps, tripping down a few. At Ailsa's nod she flumps her hands wide, clasps them together. "Good. Just in time. Set them to picking up those scraps." She beams at them, a ringer for all the magic housewives on TV. Then she's gone up again, not like a deer, but pretty good.

Rosalie bursts into tears.

Ailsa doesn't comfort her. It's tough when you're re-estimating your only confidant. And your only married one. "Perk up" she says finally. "And don't blow your nose in that; it's Thai silk. Here's a piece of handkerchief linen."

"Screw you," Rosalie says. "Don't think you don't divide your life."

"What do you mean?"

"Like when you make a velvet dress for somebody, you allow yourself a velvet day. And cotton for ordinary? Like you're walking in your sleep except for what your cloth and scissors tell you? But when a guy offers you cashmere, you're afraid to accept. Whyn't you start designing your own life?"

"Whyn't you stop counting up yours?"

They glare. Then they're in each other's arms. Whatever's holding back us two from being ourselves, Ailsa tells herself, burrowing deeper, it's the same.

When they break apart Rosalie says "I told you why. My folks."

"So you had your kids only because it says so on the graph? Huh. Your folks are your excuse."

When Rosalie answers it's like she's been hit in the teeth. Which have clamped tight. "What's yours?"

Then it's like they're even. Rosy says it aloud. "What's with us?"

And here is Mam. Pink-suited, in high heels the ankles aren't too thick for, coat of the wrong red on her arm, and weighing on a shoulder not trained to strap-bags, Ailsa's heaviest. But the spotty shawl slung overall is a triumph. It does what each of the three—and the customers too—asks of life's design. Mam pats it. "Pulls it all together, doesn't it?"

Whatever happens to her, this the meanest daughter would not deny. Mam is Deirdre now.

The front door sounds its ladylike chime.

"That'll be Keezie," Mam says. "And your nine. There's apples enough in the refrigerator. I'll go out the back. Me bag's already in the trunk." When they move toward her she laughs "No, don't kiss me. I'm put together with pins." But she pauses. "Rosalie?"

Rosy lifts her chin, shrugs a ruffle defiantly.

"Train or plane—" Mam says "whatever Eamon does about that eight-hundred phone number, I'm likely to catch on. But I'm not sticking my nose in, understand? Not for either of you."

Had Rosy hoped she would? Looks like it.

"Ailsa?"

"Yes?" It comes out almost a yiss.

"Ah but you're too bound to me, darling. Time to go. Took a dead body to wise me up. I must be slow."

Ailsa quirks a smile, through tears. "Not so slow but what your hem's dragging."

"Sure and I took the week's receipts; you won't begrudge? And there'll be a whack off the bank account. But this lady won't vanish, I promise. Only for a while."

"Where'll you go?"

"Nosy around Canada. Never been to Chi." She tightens the shawl. "Walk through my history. But not like I did here." She struggles with that, shrugs. "What you already know—you wander with. What you don't know is what lasts."

"Mam. Oh, Mam."

Her mother's eyes crinkle at that. Half out the door she digs in the shoulder bag. Puts on a crock hat.

—

The children's army is picking up the scraps. Bright spots of sweater-wool, and tee-shirts, curlyheads and braids. Keezie's two older boys shaven to the bone, alongside Rosalie's floss-haired toddler, they look to Ailsa as if they're harvesting for her all the work of the year. As the younger ones hand their plump, multicolored fistfuls up to those tall enough to dump these in the bin, she can recall each model dress from its scrap.

The blowy bridal stuff is the hardest to capture; the kids laugh and pursue. Yet she can recall each bride—which wore the tiara, or the trendy pearl choker, or the all-concealing veil. And the band singer who requested a silver bikini and shorts, but with a four-yard train. Whoever holds that weddings are out hasn't seen the McCoy appointments book.

"Good kids," she says to Keezie Zigler's husband Matt. Having delivered this onslaught of sneakersmell and gaptoothed charm, he lingers. A pale breadstick of a man whose wife talks for him except on racing-car matters, he is reported to wear his goggles in the house, maybe to ignore Keezie's agenda, in case she's targeting him. Today he's wearing a sombrero.

"You got tanned in the East, Matt; that's a switch." Rosalie is meanwhile tallying her three, aged seven down.

"You liked the horses, huh?" Ailsa says.

Neither expects more than a nod.

"Horses are just as responsive as cars" Matt says. "Maybe more. It's the jitneys are the challenge. Ought to be in museums. If I open a track, hope to persuade Keezie to take up the whip."

At their stare he flushes, knocks back his hat. "If you could keep the kids for the night she and I would discuss" he says.

At their tranced nod he blurts "She got all their gear packed in the car."

He brings in a suitcase of pajamas and underwear, teddy bears, a batch of toys and a small television. "Kids divide on the programs. And we know you got only one set."

"How many televisions you have?" Rosalie says, snide.

"Can it, Rosy," Ailsa says. Keezie's latest agenda recently gave her a third, plus a video-camera to take pics of her youngest, whom he and she share.

Matt says "Could I have the kids outside for a minute?"

They trundle after him. "Poor guy" Rosalie says. "He going to make them say a prayer?"

They trickle back in, each child dragging a sleeping bag according to age and ability. Matt lines them up. "All new bags. And three extra for Rosalie's kids."

"All singles?" Ailsa says, thinking of where to put them. "No doubles?"

"Not these days. Not with what they can see for themselves on the box."

"But you only got eight bags" Rosalie says, squinting at the line-up, which shifts guiltily. "Your six, Matt, my three, aren't there nine kids?"

"Middle kid's off with his godfather. Count again." Matt cracks a smile. "Anyway, thanks, Ailsa. Keezie or me'll pick 'em up in the morning, before school."

As he shuts the door Ailsa sees the large Erector Set on top of the pile. "Oh no you don't—" she says to it. "Not on my shop floor."

Toting it, she catches him at the car. "They build something great, there'll be a ruckus if I have to tear it down. Sorry."

"You sure look ahead" he says. "Like your ma. What's with her, by the way? Whizzed by me like a rocket, never even waved."

"She and Eamon going to New York, to a funeral."

"Must be somebody important."

Deep breath. Start the facts. "The Dad."

"He turned up dead, huh. What d'ya know. Where was he?"

"Long story."

"Well, now. Maybe now she'll take herself a guy. Though according to Keezie's old man, my father-in-law—women your ma's attitude, they've had enough of us."

"What's he know about it?"

"Assistant football coach, way back when, up to the university. Your ma first come to town, he made a pass at her. Says she knee'd him, like only a professional."

She's seen the guy when he visits, on Keezie's steps. Sunday stubble, hair still cut G.I. Stomach like his shoulderpads have slipped. If anybody was to dog her mother's history why did it have to be him?

"She should have used her foot."

When she gets back inside Rosalie is grouping the kids in a circle on the floor, each on a sleeping bag. In the center, on a carton, are the candy apples, a thermos and paper cups. "And here's a mug where you can put the empty sticks. No fights on who's to the toilet; little ones go first—and you older kids help. Spencer here can leave on his battery radio, real soft. And no locking the toilet. Anybody need anything real serious, your Aunt Ailsa and me are next door. *Now.* Everybody throw each other goodnight kisses before they eat. And once again before they lay down their head . . . Okay. Go."

Inside the Fitting Room she and Ailsa collapse on the bed. Through the half-closed door they can see the kids, munching solemnly through their program. "You have a talent for motherhood, Rosy. You just been hiding from it."

"You think? I can organize. Like I can't expose my own feelings. But maybe to be a mom is more than smooch."

"Like Deirdre."

"You calling her that now?"

"She deserves."

"What did she mean, all that you-know and you-don't-know stuff?"

Above them is the ceiling fixture where Mam once put pink light bulbs, and was hurt when Ailsa scoffed they were weird. "That dead guy set her off, about her own history. Maybe she wants me to take a look at mine."

"You? You don't got a history yet. Opportunities, you're always turning them down."

"Not every guy is an opportunity."

"They think every one of us is. Only they got more range."

In the next room Spencer Zigler's radio begins playing. He is Matt and Keezie's oldest, and definitely theirs; he's the one who caretakes the others and doesn't seem to mind.

"Except poor Matt." Rosy sniggers. "You figured why we're here, din't you? Keezie don't want to move East to those horses. So Matt is her agenda for tonight, poor slob."

"So she'll have another kid? She always says she's not on the pill."

"Not if it's to be Matt's, I bet. Maybe there's one already in the oven."

"Well that's an opportunity."

This sends them into gales of laughter.

"More range" Rosalie howls, then in a whisper "Ouf, we blew it."

Pushed in by Spencer, her youngest child toddles in. Gerda, the girl. No, she doesn't want the toilet but Rosalie takes her there anyway, sighing when they return "She's always wanting in bed with us. But after age three you're not supposed to allow."

"Go ahead."

"Rubber pants don't always hold."

"We're not keeping the bed." Nor the suite. She finds she has just decided this.

"Hah—We? So you're in the mood for cashmere after all. No? Ah, you." She is sliding the little girl under the covers. "Come on in, Ailsa. Snuggle a minute with us."

When they are all three tucked in, with the kid warm between them Ailsa says "Yo, Rosy, what are you going to do?"

"About Latouche? Daniel? That's him. The guy. I dunno. The half-and-half route is not really for me." She rubs her nose on Gerda's cheek. "Anyway, tonight I stood him up. And that's progress."

"You like giving them the brush-off? Like they're the enemy?"

"What messed me and Eamon—we were saving. For the future. No nightspots, restaurants, like before I got the ring. No fun. You should never let a guy save on you. He'll spend it on somebody else."

"Some of our tailor-made trade, the young ones with jobs? They don't want the ring."

"They will. All over town I meet those kids already, on my accounts. One of them even says to me 'How did I know it helps against cancer if you have a bay-bee before age twenty-four?' " She blows disgust into Gerda's curls.

"I'm twenty-four."

"So loosen up. Maybe not with him. A guy who says 'No deal' right at the start. Or practically. Like: 'Be my lay. But nix on the friendship society.' "

Just then the music stops. Rosalie puts a finger to her lips, mouthing "What can those little devils—?" There is indeed an acute silence in the next room, if you consider how many children are there. From Ailsa's side of the bed she can reach over to push wide the bedroom door.

In the next room all lights are off except a small time-set lamp at a front window, once meant to illuminate Deirdre's sign. The children are sitting up in their circle. The hair prickles in Ailsa's neck. For a second each child, erect from the waist, legs in the sleeping bag, appears to be rising from its coffin, or grave. They are blowing kisses to each other like soap bubbles. Behind them, the silhouetted wire basket is once more filled to the brim.

"Look at them"—Rosalie breathes into Ailsa's ear. —"Aren't they the dolls?"

Ailsa breaks into tears.

"So write the lover-guy off." Rosalie lies back. "You already got friends."

Next door is normal again, faintly murmurous.

Ailsa lies back on her pillow. Under the joint sheet her and Rosalie's toes poke up at them. "He told the truth is all. As he saw it. He was my friend, Rosy. He just didn't know."

From Gerda between them, satisfied angel asleep now, there seeps a warm wet.

—

Upstairs in her own bedroom, sent there by Rosalie who leapt up hissing "Git to your own room, I'll take care of this!" Ailsa is writing a chain-letter. That being the kind you have to write but might never send. Or if you dare to, you do it because by now chances are the address is a dead one, from which mail might or might not be forwarded,—and at best to who knows where?

Dear Hal—

That was typed hours ago. Outside, it's almost light. The way it used to be when he stole down the stairs—the front ones, since she never had the nerve to tell him otherwise, into the fresh dawn, and she lay on in the sharp odor of herself and him. Though she never showed herself at the upstairs front window to watch him go she could somehow see him descending the porch steps, a tall, pale young man with a mouth that lifted at one end when he was being his most cynical, a spot she tried to kiss when she could. On the freeway he'd be standing illegally, as he had the day she first picked him up, his cowlick straight up in the traffic breeze, his intern's white jacket glinting reassuringly under the old tennis sweater, his beaky nose already pointed toward

Scotland, the one place to which he wouldn't be sure of catching a hitch.

Trust him. Six months from then, almost a year ago now, he would get there as a courier for a freight airline no one's ever heard of, at a nothing price. —"Surgery"—he says, their last time, he fresh from on the ward, where he'd assisted at scooping "a node the size of a nut" from a brain—"Surgery is half seeing the road to take."

She hadn't asked the size of the node. Afraid he might answer "Peanut," which might be hinting at the size of her own brain. Not that he'd ever talked down to her that personally. It was just that she was to understand the situation. His.

But first—how am I to measure the distance between now and back then?

. . . After he left she'd had the one letter. Full of Edinburgh it was, and quite poetic, and as she could well see, not really written for her. "The city is a citadel. The people seem to think the whole country is." A fortress, the dictionary said, the big one she went to buy. She'd chosen the Oxford over the Webster, as nearer to Hal. "Some of the stone is as dark red as the blood in a vein." She'd tried to recall was it arteries ran from the heart and veins toward, and whether the blood in them differed, but could bring to mind only the habit he had, while telling her these things, of smoothing her breast with his hand. She would be close in the cuddle of his arm, face against the bone of his shoulder. It would be his left hand, on her left breast. The bone protruded, but she would not move.

He had a landlady's address, not a hospital's. "I can describe the landlady without rancor." She'd no trouble with that, the phrase being from a favorite sports reporter. While he was here she'd read the boxing accounts faithfully, although that since had dropped off. "Though unlike most Scotswomen she suffers from obesity." He'd been daunted to find that the natives resented being called Scotch.

So he too could be found wanting. Reading that, she had linked hands with his absent one. Which they hadn't much when he was here. It had been all brisk walks on the beach, for him to get rid of his hospital emotions. Tall as he, she could look him in the eye, and the rhythm of their steps had matched, like good partners dancing. Leading them to bed without a word said. She still took the pill. Though there'd been no one since, it was a link. Sometimes, chiding herself, she walks the beach. Avoiding sunsets.

They had never gone anywhere together. This had made his niche in her mind only holier. An affair apart from other people, and for a good reason that both took for granted—his terrible grind, and the pittance he got for it. But according to Rosalie, who hadn't become her confidant until after he'd gone, "Fatal. It was always you who had the time." At the bottom of what he'd written, which some would call only a note, there'd been a scrawl, just above his name. Four letters, she was almost sure. But not whether it said Love.

The dictionary weighs on her rickety schoolgirl desk, waiting unused. After that one letter there had been only cards, if oddly alternating.

"Dublin had beautiful doors"—on a picture of one such entryway.

The cliffs of Dover—on which, could it be?—he had penciled two stick figures at the cliff's edge.

At Christmas, a glossy Yuletide message, quite large and requiring extra stamps, but addressed to her mother as well.

Then suddenly, a seascape from a museum: sunlit ship, murky sky, below which he had scrawled what she yearned to confirm but hadn't shown her mother.

"Ye-es," Mr. Garfield had said, deciphering. "That's what it says."

On the border, just under the shoreline, an inked "If you were here—we would be here."

She had caught on, finally. The cards alternate just like he had, when he had been seeing her. At one meeting he would be educating her, swinging her up to his level with energy and a smile—like a father pushing his girl on the swings, though he was only twenty-nine. Other times he would be silent, holding her close. Even the sex would be different.

Sometimes running toward the heart, might you say? Sometimes running away from it.

Dear Hal:

No, see I'm stuck again. So I'll just hash it out with myself, but like you and me are talking. I never had the nerve to. Not like I wanted to. But if you're bringing the pullover, not just mailing it, I swear to God I will. I have got a history now.

Only this is a chain-letter. It don't only come from me.

There was a man here, he knew Mam when she was even younger than me. First time I could credit she ever was. He almost died on us right here, downstairs that is, not on the bed up here. We gave him mouth-to-mouth—she did, then the emergency ambulance. He made it to the hospital, then no more. If you'd been here, could you have done something? I thought of it. Like I could have said "Just happens a doctor friend's upstairs" and you'd jump into your shorts and run down.

I know better, Hal. He had a bypass scar on him, almost collarbone to bellybutton, like they had lifted a two-pound icebag out of his chest and sewed it back in again.

And you weren't here. Only one real letter. And some cards.

But for me that man's still breathing. Because he talked to me. We had a conversation like educated people do—flip flip. I participated just fine. Takes practice of course. I don't need the college for that anymore. I hear enough in the shop. But both have their limits. I'll need to branch out.

(I'm not hinting, am I? Hal and me, I could never talk to him. But I am now.)

I hear that "out" business all the time in the shop. Or on the porch. A young married, leaning out of her Jag, if they're rich, or out of a Ford Taurus, to take the dress package from me, in the broad sun, her hair blowing. Saying "I got to get out more." Not to me but to the air. Or in the shop, to each other. That Mrs. Mason, that man's wife, saying to her sidekick who's never bought yet but always tags along "I have to get out." And the sidekick saying "You should gripe; you're the one has the au pair.—" Those foreign girls they advertise for . . . The Mason answering low "No, I had to get rid of her."

I am as far from those two as from the moon. Yet I feel for them. What is "out"? . . . They mustn't know any better than me.

Mam, who heard them at it, laughs. "Maybe for them two it's divorces." Later, when I ask her more serious, she says "We don't expect to act on our own. We don't expect to be single in action. Men do. A man's single that way all his life. Whether or not he cheats. In his mind, he's always on his own." Then her eyes get misty. "Out?" she says. "I dunno. I once thought it was here."

I know what she meant. When she got to California and this place, she threw all the tatty valises and carryalls she'd accumulated into our attic, which is really only a letdown ladder and a space above the rafters. When she bought the house she cleared all that stuff away.

So when she left here, she had to borrow her luggage from me. That's all right. What I had was only for weekends, though none the kind that would interest Loretta O'Day. Remember? You saw her once being walked in her chair, Hal. And you said "Nothing withered about those ankles, those legs. Stretches like a cat. And look how she's holding that telephone. What's she in a chair for?" And when I said nobody knew, but that's the way she earned her money you said: "Well maybe it's worth it to her. To be a star." And walking on, you said—"Don't ever be the kind of woman who wants to be that kind of star."

I wanted to say, flip—"No chance with you at my elbow."—Instead I said—"I'll hold on to that."—

So I'm still here, yes. But seeing everything with my eyes peeled.

I'm seeing that my brother Eamon should get out of the trucking, maybe take courses in the engineering he never got to, they married so quick. Maybe half-and-half is their best answer. Whether it's an agenda or a strategy.

I'm tiring of the clothes. Even if clothes can't be compared to surgery, you have your work cut out for you. You pay for being responsible to bodies. Yet I don't want to be responsible for just mine.

There's a husband I'm pretty sure I could soon be having an affair with. It would feel a little like being a whore. Somebody I know was once a whore. Somebody I knew well.

I see that a girl can't have too many fathers. I've had a photo, faded now, but for the first years not so bad. Also an Orangeman, the sound of him being good for dreams. That Canadian trucker is maybe the least of them.

Downstairs I'll soon hear stirrings. Little demons for sure. Maybe some leftover kisses though, floating in the air. I'm twenty-four. I'm seeing relationships. Maybe that is my scar?

She'll have to go out for milk. Is that getting out? Mr. Garfield will likely be up and in his garden. He walks the floor with the granny for her asthma every morning, minute she wakes, around four. He loves answering questions, making statements. I already know what his answer to my question about "out" would be. His statement on the solidarity of his shut-in household is ever the same. "We three got out from under together—the mother, the wife, and me." From the country where their name began with a *G*, just like now, but had ended with *escu*. "They told us we wanted to leave. We didn't. But here we are." The three sons were all born in the house, and according to the oldies on the Row, grew up marching in and out of it like automatons. No surprise they are gone.

"None of that lot ever in hospital, Hal," Mam said to you, Hal, the one time you and she met. "And the boys never ate perdaders until they were grown. The old lady can't stomach them." We were watching the Garfields take her for the Sunday drive.

"She pretends like it's against her will," Mam says. "That's why they never fail to comply." Mr. G. is carrying her. Mrs. G. behind. The stretch of path from front door to curb, is Mrs. G.'s weekly walk. The car sags when she gets in. She smiles at Mam, who is making a vast coat for her. The old lady, light as a feather, sits in front. "That's a solid relationship if I ever saw one" Mam says as they drive off. "Of course, it's a triple one."

When you say goodbye, Hal, you are far politer to Mam than to me. "Your Irish accent is exceptionally pure, Mrs. McCoy. None of the nurses I work with can come up to it. Though I understand you were born here."

True, "horspital" and "perdaders" are Mam's favorite Irish put-ons—but how could I say? And you were saying goodbye. I'd thought you were on the edge of asking me to save up for a package deal to Scotland, midyear. But you did not.

But I still see you over there. In the citadel I shan't be seeing. A red city under a white sky.

Dear Hal,

She had fallen asleep, with her head on the dictionary. When, half awake, she sleepwalks downstairs, they have all flown. A Little League tee-shirt is puddled in a corner. The room smells of wee-wee, children slumbering with their mouths open and vinyl sleeping bags. What a scurrying there must have been. What a helter-skelter there must be, morning after morning, for the mothers she's seen screeching to a stop at the schoolyard, nodding to each other with the thank-God smile. "Oh for the days when I could sleep in—" she's heard Rosalie say "—yet driving them does give me a breath of outside air."

Under the table in the nook there is a sock. Ought to be a round table there, or none. Not this kitchen relic, once covered with oilcloth. That wastebasket; she can get rid of it and its scraps; they'll never make a quilt. In the Fitting Room, the bed has been stripped. Gone are the powers that be. It comes to her that she need not open the shop ever again. She can hold a sale.

Through the wide window she can indeed see Garfield, nose lifted to the day that is always too mild for him. If she shows her face she'll get one of his statements. Like "For the best view there should be some dust in the air." Or "Nature is always telling the truth. I have just as much garden as I can take."

"He's talking about death," Mam said. "That's all that kind are interested in. The politics is only a sham." What Mam was interested in most she never said. But it comes to Ailsa now how sharp she could be, on other people's sham.

Upstairs again, those salutations of hers stare at her. At the nuns' she'd been taught that all letters of thanks must be penned by hand. Though this family has needed few.

She is hunting out a felt pen when she hears a car draw up outside and goes to the window. A silver Jag. The Masons have two. But this gray one is not hers. Hers is red.

He stands at the bottom of the steps but doesn't mount them to ring. The sun shines on a head of hair cropped just short of the longer way many men are wearing it, and on a vest that must have cost. He looks up. She shrinks back. Has he seen her? She isn't sure.

Neither is he. Indecisive, he still looks good. But not as firm as a man who walks on foot.

She watches him drive away. He'll have been on his way to work. "To the office," rather, as the wives say it. Where he does the money, and the law.

At the desk she writes, this time without salutation:

I have your note, from after you left. Also the cards. And your offer. All appreciated.

Mam is gone. Back East, where she'll likely stay. I'm closing the shop. Going back to school to be a nurse. Bodies are great, as you made me see. But that profession is more responsible. And now she's gone I'll have more voice. Though nothing that would offend.

I'll be selling the shop off, including the bridals, since I'm not the marrying kind. Also the house, which should bring me a sum. And leave me free to wander.

What I don't know is which school. Could you recommend? I'll wait until we meet. I take it back—that you were too medical.

Or if you just want to mail the pullover, that's okay. I don't own a black one. But black lasts.

You were my friend. But you didn't want to know.

Thanks.

Yours sincerely,

Ailsa

The Thanks is scrawled some. But not so he could mistake it for Love.

Even so, she has a struggle to make herself mail the letter. For to be sincere, she will have to make it all come true, even to the not marrying. Finally she adds a postscript that helps.

P.S. It could be a lambswool pullover. It doesn't have to be cashmere.

But when he arrives, after two months unheard from, the long soft streak of black is as promised, though he has had to buy it in the U.S. She hears the full extent of her gamble. Her letter, covered with addresses, had been received the day before he left. All the landladies having been honorable. Hal has mellowed. She has waited. There is still a difference.

His arrival had been brooded upon to be exactly as she last saw him, only in reverse: he would be walking toward her in his freeway style, head dangerously in his surgical cloud.

He has come in a car. "Rented it at the airport." And has brought her flowers as well.

He has a slot for the coming year in a network of medicos—a fair start, if a small one. "There's a school of nursing nearby." He rather chokes on that. But he has been impressed by her gumption. There's little left in her house beyond the upstairs bed. No, he had not thought to reconnoiter before arriving.

"That letter of yours. It was like a map."

Please God let it not all wind down, she says to herself when they reach the bed.

It hasn't, bedwise, whatever's to come. "You didn't used to want sex with me on top" she says, on the second round. "Not ever."

"Scotland was cold." He's not smirking, but the bloodrush in her is new. She's not jealous. Only wanting his remoteness to be as steadfast as it once was.

"You mean it?" he says after a while. "About not marrying? It's kind of a rock-ribbed Midwest, where we'd be going. If you agree."

She sees so far ahead of the two of them, down the long tunnel which circumstance can be, that her heart turns in her chest, an organ too versatile. One day—he may well offer the ring. And—depending—she may refuse.

By evening—he arrived at dusk—she is full again of love unspoken. Surely he will never be the enemy. She tells him her news. "Mam has a job in Boston. At a hospital." He has already told her that the best Scots is said to be the purest English of all. Her own accent is pure—American.

"Eamon and Rosalie are divorcing." She's having a thing with Matt, the new owner of a harness track that's to be built nearby. Eamon has a new business interest, in an Ohio garage.

By now she and Hal are starving. How wise it is to have almost nothing in the refrigerator. He invites her out.

When he goes to the upstairs bathroom she hears a squawk. "You put my flowers in the toilet!"

His flowers? That's a snag. Remember it. "There isn't a vase in the house. Sorry."

"You could have put them in the sink."

Unseen by him, she clasps a hand to her mouth in merriment. For not the first time, she misses her Mam. It's even possible she has yet to meet the man she can tell the story of Annie Baloney to. If so, she'll marry him. She hears the toilet flush.

Downstairs, she bathes and dresses. The high-collared sweater is a good fit. She's kept all her own clothes, she's no fool, and has just the right skirt for it. When, still naked, he comes downstairs to her call, he's dazzled. "You've cut your hair. I noticed that, first thing."

"Black brings it out, yes." She smiles, rather too broadly.

He smites his bare chest. "What a nerd I am. What a bloody thumping nerd." Since Scotland his slang has certainly become mixed. And her ear, away from Mam, more delicate.

"They may never let me inside a head again" he groans, slapping his thigh. "Not if I can't notice what's outside it. But you're such an armful."

Then she is bent over with laughter too.

She stands up straight then. Nodding she pulls the silky white tips of the blouse she's wearing underneath the black sweater over its collar, edges the white cuffs also over the black. Skirt and hose are black, and the shoes as well. "That's right, Hal." There's no need for his apology. Not when you're what you want to be. "I'm blond."

He's shaving when she knocks at the upstairs bathroom door, saying "Give me those roses of yours, I think I have something for them." She has tied a silky remnant of white over her outfit, she is still Ailsa. A towel would leave fuzz. She is holding a highlooped basket, of the kind people send to the sick, or even to the dead.

Outside the house she leans against the open front door, the basket dangling. From behind her, the man in her house encircles her waist with his arms. It's night now. All she can see are the lights of certain windows in their familiar pattern, and the shadowy bulk of the warehouse that stores wine. Since she put the house up for sale the people here have become more distant with her, but a Row is what she knows. She is young enough to believe that her elders are mistaken. That what you know is never lost.

What's this urge in her then, to see the future beyond even the immediate one? This rush in her to get happiness over and done with?

"We could leave tonight" she says. "I've little to pack."

"Give us time" he says. "Slow down."

She hangs the basket by its loop on the two nails that once held a sign. "I can't. There are people behind me."

Let passersby wonder, as the flowers wither. Let the lilt in her sound as it may. She is not the bereaved.

THE RAILWAY POLICE

This time yesterday morning, I was sitting in one of the coaches of the Mayflower, the early New York to Boston train, on my way to take part in a panel at the monthly meeting of the Interagency Council of Supervisors, a professional organization to which I belong. Inside me, that tender, inverse psyche we all carry within us was as usual at once violently proud of its outer costume and at the same time making mock of it: silk suit sharp-creased for speechmaking, all underwear appropriate to legcrossing on platform, handbag by X, shoes by Y—all a perfect beige armor stopping just short of the creature-skin that no Florida can tan, inside which the little lady sits, quiet and not always sad, in her altogether, of that tint so much too nacreously fair.

And a hat—I am always extra careful about the hat. A person who wears a wig has to be. In bygone days—think of it, only a year or so ago—a person who had to wear a wig was still special, and buying a hat was for her, one might say, an affair of the double incognito, the purchase of a crown to place upon the crown that no one must know she already wore. Particularly if at the bottom of it all, beneath hat, wig, armor and skin, there was still caged but not coffined, ready to run if not rampant, the laughing tomboy of thirteen, putative cabinboy of fifteen, dockside loafer, bankrobber's mascot and Fagin's modern wonderboy in blue jeans and plimsolls with the tips of his fingers emeried; all shapes and types of tramp-Raffles riding the rods under the scurrying cries of the railway police—confidence makers and takers thumbling their young stowaway noses from soup kitchens to the subbasements of all the Statler-Hiltons, freeloading and riding all the flowery, Bowery subcircuses of the world. All of them wearing caps, none of them grown past twenty, and none quite yet bald. My present profession makes it possible for me to observe quite selflessly that my imagination only took up its orthodox womanhood at the moment when the head which caged it had lost its last trace of hair.

The train was just getting into Providence, Rhode Island, due at 10:52, and on time. I know every curve and tockety of the Shore Line, having done all my later studies in Boston, with training trips from there to New York City, that even richer source for our stock-in-trade. It was wise of me to come East after Cooksley Normal; though the wig I bought on the way, in Chicago's Loop, was not very good, it was better than the wrap-around turbans I had been wearing. And Boston, as everyone knows, is tops in social work—there being, further, no mystery as to why this profession should be mine. Even back in Cooksley, I had no trouble with psychological essences and timbres—after all, we had the same magazines as the rest of the country—and my education merely thrust me deeper back upon my own meanings.

For, very early during my practice days "in the field," as the pretty word for it goes in the profession, I knew that, via my work, the sores and seams of my own romanticism were being kept in sight for me at the very time I needed this—for who can say to what imaginations a bald beauty (I am otherwise comely) might not at any time revert? This way, all the while I toured the underworld I loved, a dainty Dante in her own laurel wreath, I was being kept a lady, or being made into one. None of my supervisors then or now (for all who work with the poor must have comptrollers who help keep our heads clear and well-hatted) has ever had to remind me that my work was sublimating me, though they mayn't have known in quite what terms.

And it is natural, therefore, that I have risen in it, though still well under thirty-nine. For I have never wholly deserted the field for deskwork, as most do as soon as possible, though I deserve no credit for having now and then a fierce need to carry slops and mealtickets to the midnight alleys, or to slog the mean streets in search of the company of those tucked jolly under the viaduct, around the fire made after the cop has made his last round, there to watch how, at dawn, the waterbugs streak like lizards from the Chinese restaurant, and at any hour men stride like catamounts, from plain doors.

There's not much danger; this is the neighborhood of my "caseload," where my hat, with its flowers of charity wired by law, probably affrights them, and I am more than likely to end up for a glass of tea with some old client, my one revolutionary gesture to sit, in all my niceties, on the bedbug couch she warns me away from, "Dun sit, dolling, Om afraid from de boggles, dun sit dere."

And I know very well that this is still the world of the poor who live in houses, not vagabondage, just as I know that the poor, at least in cities, are not maypole dancers, their bread not oaten but paper. But their world is still a netherworld ringing from beneath the rich pavements they walk on just as I do. Even the poor in houses are only one step away from the criminal, for they have so much to hide that they can never do it quite honestly. Clean as they might be, they are still gamy, haunted and ridden by barmecide illusion, and I fancied I had almost a right to their underworld by way of my little specialty; I could walk their underside a little way with them, wearing my wig.

The train ran slowly to a stop; the conductor calling out "Providence!" had already been through the train, opening doors. Fresh gushes of air came from them, uniting with the warm, sunny velvet coming in on me from the broad window, outside which houses, running like sixty the minute before, settled into the dull station-scene brilliant in the morning sun, ultimate stillness. The pause at Providence is approximately two minutes, forty seconds, when the train is running on schedule. I was sitting on the double seat just back of the washrooms, the one on the platform side, facing the door. Waiting to get off, there was the usual crowd, trim salesmen with their noses elongated by money-sniffing (the real money flies the air, of course), aunties in hats-on-a-visit, a ruck of the indefinable, middling personages who do crowd-service, starred with the one sweatered girl who is always going down the aisle, jiggle-breasted, to the Women's. The air, once past the train-smell, came in pure and lively, the fresh vanilla perspiration of spring; it was March twenty-first, one day into spring.

And it was just then that I saw the young man hovering on the step, ready to jump off ahead of them all. He must just have come out of the washroom. I saw him from the inside of the coach, and only the back of him. He was tall, had a good head under a good crop of hair, and was dressed in a suit of which trousers even matched jacket; it needed a second glance to see, doubletake, that, yes, from top to toe, though I couldn't see his shoes, he was one fatal thread away from the tidy civilization of the train. The head had been to the barber, but not the last time, the suit was tired from making do, and as he leaned, head bent, hands slouched in pockets, shoulder taking bearings from the wall the way a zoo animal does, I caught, though I was yards away, the whole posture and lion-soil of him—a vagrant, in unmistakable aquiline.

He must have been readying himself to make a running jump for it. For almost in that same moment, I saw through the window the bright, gold-rimmed bumpkin face and blue uniform of the railway police, who put out arms to receive him, and behind in the coach, the conductor's cap, his pale face blotted in the crowd. They handed him over, uniform to uniform. He must have been in the washroom, ticketless. And if he had only permitted himself a hat perhaps or the cheapest cardboard dispatch case, just one patch of greasepaint to keep him on the right side of the line, he might have made it. Perhaps they telegraphed ahead from New London or wherever he had boarded; though it might seem a lot of trouble for just a ticket, it is by taking just such infinite pains that the upper parallel keeps itself from meeting the lower.

For through the window, I saw him led off, and there was that about him which made me sure the offense was no worse than this; he was walking straight and unalcoholic, not with the tension of the really hunted, with the experienced resignation of one who knew himself to be no more than a matter for the railway police. Head still a little bent, hands out of his pockets now and hanging down, he let himself be led along by this round pattycake of a man, winded too, from whom he could have darted like a whippet from its starter. I hadn't had a look at his shoes, of course, and he may have been too hungry. But I caught the line of his jaw and cheeks, good ones too, but just a hairsbreadth, again just a hairsbreadth too unshaven, and something in me trolled out to him, "Oh la-la, that did it. You might still have made it—if you had shaved."

In retrospect, I have the feeling he knew that as well as I did. Two days more of that beard, and he could have been a student growing one, even with that suit on him perhaps, but not—no never—not ticketless too. It takes keeping up, any posture of what you are not, takes a sense of fitness to the point of fashion, and the vagrant won't bother with that sort of thing, not for that purpose, he's too honest for it, or else he wants to be spotted; maybe it's his very function in life to wander about thus exposed, so that others may find their signals in him. They led him toward the steps of a small, official-looking hut a short distance across the station yard, and just then it happened. One of his coattails flipped up, not jaunty, not especially sad either, it may even have been the wind that did it, not his hand, and I saw a piece of white shirt, fairly clean, and a belt going round a human axis. All I had caught was a two-minute-and-forty-second glimpse of his simple, hopeful domestic arrangements. And that was all I needed. I never even saw him go up the steps.

I took action at once—as is usually said of themselves by persons who have been hearkening for twenty years. Such action, boiled up out of meditation, is often absurd unless it goes straight to the heart of the matter, and I did not do that at once—I was not quite able. To unprepare oneself for such a journey is not easy, particularly when it is one that may occupy the rest of your life. I told myself—timidly, I agree—that my proper embarkation would be from that place where so much of the rest of me was, from all that other paraphernalia by which we extend our pet fantasies of ourselves without ever risking the depots of travel—from home.

Inside the washroom, meanwhile, I removed gloves, stockings and girdle, and thrust them under the sink, into the receptacle for used paper towels—a ridiculously minor performance to be sure, but in the light of the whole, it doesn't matter now. As for baggage, it has always been my grief that I could never travel as executively light as even the ticket-world now can. I had, to be sure, my little modern portfolio of articles that thimbled or stretched or reversed themselves, of paquettes that exploded for one use, then melted away—but I also had my wig-box, the overnight one. Made for me, like the larger ones, by a theatrical supply house, it had just room enough for the wig I made use of to sleep in—ah, the comfort of mind, when I learned to do that!—plus a fresh one for morning, and of course it didn't look like what it was.

Nowadays, markedly within this past, disturbing year, wig-boxes have become all too common; though they still keep mostly to the air-lanes and the parlor cars, I look for them in the coaches and even the buses by the year's end—if I myself am able to risk such vehicles at that time. Meanwhile, peeping into mine, I quickly disposed of the portfolio down the slot where the girdle had gone, then tried the sealed window, in vain. The kit itself would have to be abandoned either here or on the luggage-racks outside. Gazing into it, down at the wooden wig-blocks on which my other two rested, I concluded that the latter's destiny would have to be linked with that of their eighteen sisters, this number being an accident of the calendar, seven for the week, plus certain other considerations. In place of these two, I now left my hat, for the Easter joy of some trainman's wife in Canarsie or Brookline. Then, shouldering the kit, I looked at my image in the mirror.

"No," I finally said to it. "Not down an aisle. No drama." The true vagrant, honor-bright refuser of houses, clothing, income and other disguises, appears as my young man of the coattails had appeared to me, unaware of the comment he makes by existing. I could never be that unsophisticate—or perhaps, only after years of the discipline, by the time I had come to be an old abbess of the byways, worn back into simplicity at last after a misspent youth in the world. My present object must be to conduct myself, though within the framework, with all possible reserve—for there is always the question of sanity raised in re those who give up the things of this world. (And today, I already yearn to do it with—yes, it must be said—with beauty. But yesterday, I hadn't come that far.)

Smiling wryly, I said to myself, "Take it easy. Give yourself a head-start."

It's a thing of mine to make puns like that to myself, which no one else notices, nothing but a compensatory psychological adjustment, quite harmless and quite natural—and one which has helped until to-date to keep me well short of the adjustment that is the most natural of all. But that was yesterday. When I reopened the door of the wash-room, less than fifteen minutes had passed. I was back in my seat, with all plans figured out except for the final contingency ("case closed" it is sometimes called, in the profession) by the time we rolled into the stop for suburban Boston: Route 128.

I used to know the 128 stop very well. All one summer, a man who, as the saying goes, was once very important to me, used to meet me there with a car. Cars free people; in summer particularly, they are the vagabondage of the ticketed world. And no matter what season of the year I pass that station, I breathe in again the hot organdy smell of my own sleeveless dresses, of sour-wine picnics where the wine couldn't wait any more than we could, and of meadow-love. Outdoor love is easiest for those who must beware the midnight-rumpling hand. Inside the waiting room, where I had to sit when he was late or it was rainy, the majestically coifed, redheaded stationmistress used to sit eternally in her little box-office, talking now and then in camaraderie with the round-faced policeman whose detail was 128. As far as I could see, he never did anything but point out the phone booth to people who had missed connections, or alert the crowd on the platform to the warning bell rung for an oncoming engine—as far as I could see then. After that summer was over, I more than once dreamt of the stationmistress with her masses of hair, not a wig but dyed, and not the plain dark red, neither bronze nor carroty, of the color which, until I was twelve, had been mine.

"One-twenty-eight," the conductor called now, jumping off; it's a very short stop. I had no intentions of getting off there, now or ever again, but as always, I leaned to look. Usually I saw the policeman, the same one, and once, in a snowy winter, I had seen the woman shoveling—and seeing them was always like a momentary return to a village where people are so little on the move that one can see clearly how all the life-stories have worked out, including one's own. I didn't see her now, but I saw the policeman, same old pieface in dark blue. They must rear a race of them from the cradle, I thought, nanny-faces all, puzzled, even kindly, with waists too big for wearing holsters. For though this one wore no gold-rims, in every respect there was no doubt otherwise. He was a ringer for the one in Providence. Or else his brother. And suddenly my ungloved hands sought to hide themselves, my nude shins rubbed nervously together, and I shrank away from the window, a warning ringing inside me. "Chickie!" it said. "Watch out for the railroad dicks!"

At first I was disturbed by this menial response, one so much lacking the insouciance I had expected, but then reminded myself that with my clothes still elegant, my purse stuffed, such a halfway state of mind was at least sensitive; I had after all scarcely touched upon, much less completed, my full conversion. The minute I thought of this latter, the fluttering pulse in my throat was silenced, and an enormous but active peace settled on me; only dwell on the crowning event that was coming toward me, and all the smaller stratagems flew to hand. After that everything went swimmingly.

I got off at South Station, filled out a telegraph form "Unavoidably detained," changed the latter to "prevented," and grabbed a cab to Logan Airport, in time to board a shuttle plane which would even get me back to New York before bank-closing. Though incomes in my line are never impressive, my mixed family inheritance did include money, not enough, alas, to have allowed me that comfortable eccentricity which might have put me to rights in the very beginning, but there is no doubt that in a modest way I am a woman of property. From now on, the problem would be how to disencumber myself, down to the bone as it were, without incurring the verdict of either sainthood or insanity. I had no wish to decamp altogether, like those irresponsibles who dissolved themselves in a puddle of clothes left on the beach at Villefranche, or from an ownerless car on the Golden Gate Bridge. Any one of these eventualities would make me a mystery, not, as I faintly hoped, a statement. I regret that there's also no doubt that I suffer from a certain ambition, akin perhaps to that of women just before they got the vote—a kind of suffragette swelling, part yearning and part vengeful, of the chest cavity and maybe even the heart. I am well aware that the true vagrant never even knows the nature of what he cherishes, in his case his right to be out of the organized world. Later on, I hope in my own way to achieve that brahma; I see myself holding up my naked head without knowing that I am doing it. Right now, however, though I deplore it, I want all the civil rights in my category.

And so it's not surprising that the minute I got on the plane I started mulling what else I could take off, substitute gestures to placate that fire in me raging toward the ultimate one. Inside the washroom again, the only disposal unit that modern transportation allows us, I made friends again with my image. I was wearing my platform wig, its clubwoman curls now blown by airport and emotional currents into a bad semblance of one at home marked in my mental roster as Careful Disarray, but verging more on the brown than the blonde. (It is discreetly known at the office that I dye my hair myself, not always accurately.)

I regarded it, but was glad to feel full and strong in me the power to delay—"No, not yet. No travesty."

As for statutory nudity, it had no charms for me at this point, indeed the reverse; exhibitionism was at all costs to be avoided. Teeth were excellent *and* personal, eyes never in need of glasses—the clear green eyes born to lucky people of my complexion.

Just then the stewardess knocked, and I watched my hands seek themselves.

"Quite all right!" I managed to say—this time, God save us, with some proper daring in it, and a minute later I was taking off my rings.

To my left there was a ventilator, whose exhaust slot must somewhere reach the outer air. The shuttles don't fly very high, not nearly so high as the pan-orient jets on which I suppose I started my hunt for brahma in the first place. Crouched there, in my palm the little hoard to which I had added lapel-pin and pearls, I waited until we were well away from water, over a tiny settlement where I might predict, if not see, spire and gardens, a railway station too perhaps; then with a smile, imagining on whom that shower of peculiar manna, sent them down.

Back in my seat again, I had certain canny misgivings, the tiresome ones of a woman with too many heads. How small did a diamond have to be not to burst its facets from such a height, how light a pearl, not to smash its baroque? I had retained my watch, and I had an hour to consider the lost rings of all those who had loved me, plus that most durable of all, the invisible wedding-band I had never let myself receive.

What of love, then, for such a woman, for any—for anybody, what of love?

My mother's mother's snakeband ring with emerald eye and my father's father's onyx seal I had worn joined on one finger, cabalistic bow to that minor hitch in the vortex of heredity which had caused me. Dear supervisors all, should they at the agency ever know the circumstances (and I might in time send them the case-record)—I could hear the descant that would follow, in the ballet of headshakes that always formalizes psychological gossip.

> . . . (Would it have been better if the departed's trauma had come to her through some normal community way such as radiation sickness, instead of having been visited upon her via the single, traumatic shock of birth? . . . What hopes could be held for a girl whose own sibling would one day ask her, eighteen years to her sixteen: "Haven't *you* begun to . . . lose any of it . . . all over, yet?" . . . And who then would add in a whisper, turning away a face already shorn of brow and lash, a head already ennobled to its own bone—"What about . . . *down there*?") . . .

Ah, we had our ribald humors, my brother and I, but that day wasn't one of them, not when I had to answer him—for I was never to be as bad a case as he, and still have, though so faintly auburn, eyelashes—when I had to answer him . . . "No." And on the record, I had a word of advice for them, my friends at the agency. Don't be so quick to asperse birth, the plain fact of our beginnings. And don't believe anything but the facts:

Subject (who is I) *and sibling born to elderly well-to-do emigré parents.* Perhaps we were menopausal babies conceived after danger of such was deemed over, since both my parents, as distant cousins from same ancestral town, were well aware of hereditary traces.

Both deceased during infancy of children, who were brought up under amiable legal guardianship, to best U.S. standards of oranges, lambchops, orthodonture and quarterly anti-pronation shoe-fittings.

From extant pics of parents aetat 35, my father's hairline may have been retouched, my mother's even more susceptible to illusion.

Hereditary condition well documented in European medical annals (though not endemic there) via easier observation in small, genealogically related loci, such as the German, North Sea town where my grandparents still reside.

May or may not be Mendelian recessive, thought by some to be albino-related, no official name. (*Not alopecia areata,* which is temporary.)

Males invariably lose facial as well as scalp-hair, fem. data less procurable though subject recalls, from youthful visit to grandparents, family portraits ranging back to the medieval, in which coif-line was shown almost as far back behind ears as a bridle.

Classically appears at onset of puberty, when natal hair of a characteristically silky dark-red gives way to carroty coarse growth which in turn disappears partially or in toto, usually by time of patient's majority. N.B. from subject: We were classical.

And in fancy I could read, over their shoulders, my evaluation (after group study of further history up to March 21st):

Subject, aided by economic status and first-class appliances, has made excellent progress in resolving toward conventional norms the original handicap of birth. Irredentist impulses not to be taken too seriously. As cosmetic use of wigs gains community-wise, subject's sense of unity with the general population will increase. Subject's quasi-humorous diagnosis of her sublimation to be taken as a real testimonial to our profession, fine objectivity from one of the solidest gals in the office.

And down in the corner of our biannual personality sheet I could even read a handwritten scrawl from my immediate supervisor: *Mildly bizarre thoughts a good sign of nonrigidity. Do I detect a sign that my quiet one may be getting espoused? Hats off!*

With all the abstract sociological kindness going about the world, it's hard to get a true story listened to on the level, even by oneself. What could I say, for instance, of my brother, become that perennial movie star whose trademark is hairlessness (in his case not however like old Von Stroheim, a villain, or a horror man like Peter Lorre, but cast as a straight romantic hero). Rumor has it that he is forbidden by contract to show so much as a single hair, some saying that he complies only by means of terrifying sessions of electrolysis, others that he keeps a young valet-of-the-tweezers ever by his side. When first out in the world, we used to envy one another, I him for his public baldness, he me for my disguise. Now we no longer saw each other, having usefully agreed, like enemies in entente, that we no longer had anything in common. Like many ties of love, ours was too painful to eat dinner with.

And so—I looked at my watch—I was back to love again, only twenty minutes out of Logan. And I had two more rings to dispose of in memory.

On the fourth finger of my right hand, where unmarried women often wear a parental diamond or an engagement ring that hasn't worked out, I had worn, until yesterday, a small blue-white Tiffany in platinum, of the size given virgins by young men on modest budgets, as indeed it had been, by the one all hands would have said I should have married, the medical student, childhood friend and sole remaining witness of all my real changes, who had followed me East—and who had declined to make good his promise of marriage if I aborted the child he had already engendered.

"We could adopt some," I said.

"No," he replied, "I want our own first, if you don't mind. I'm going to become a gynecologist."

And so he has done, fat as a woodchuck too, and full of Christmas cards. But he was thin then, and staunch, and what he said sounded unanswerable. I wanted to answer it, at the time still believing that the apogee of life would be to have one secret witness forever at my side.

"But *I* mind!" I said. "I should mind forever. For *them*." He shrugged, and I caught him looking with distaste at the wig I had just bought—the first one.

"Children can learn to be bald," he said.

I was wounded beyond reason by this coldness.

"Already we differ," I said. "Not mine."

I handed him his ring back, strange gesture across the child I still carried (and stranger miscalculation?) for I understood his intent now—to bring me with it, out into the open.

"Keep the ring at least," he said. "Keep it until you marry. Until you do, girl with your looks and plans might find it useful. You can always tell them I died in a war."

Though I never did, it's true that both colleagues and lovers have sometimes murmured to me that one should not cling to the past, so perhaps his ring had been part agent of what he would never have done himself—helped me to hide the present that clung to *me.*

When I tried again to return the ring, he grasped me, shook me, even repeated his cold remark.

"Ours could learn!" he added, shouting. He stood there, hirsute and flawless, as his cards show him yet, the rufous glints all over the backs of his hands, not a spot of baldness in him anywhere, far as I could see, either of the body or the heart. And he could say that to me. It was a beautiful declaration, and I have never yet had another like it. But I knew at that moment why I was right to refuse him. To be acceptable, such declarations must come to the bald—from the bald.

And so we arrive at the man from 128, if not for long.

In the meantime, I had had my further experiences in the dark, not many, and never with any candidate to whom I could see myself making any such avowal—despite which I sometimes found myself in serious need to repress the more ordinary part of my inheritance: almost any woman's urge to avow. So I gave up such doings, and returned to the midnight safety of my old alleyways, to slouching in cool raincoats at the hot bedsides of their sick, sitting up at the wakes of their hardy sorrows, or kicking up the orange dawn in the circle of such derelicts as were too far gone to wonder at the presence of a lady at that fire. Weekends I spent emotion thriftily in the colorful melancholia of the museums and the Sunday exhibitions, quietly enjoying the arts and gems that were the property of the nation.

For this conduct, the gods duly corrected my position in life as they saw fit, from the rear. I received a salary increase, my largest block of securities held a stock-split, and there fell due a trust fund for which I had done nothing but get older. In one of the galleries I was in the habit of visiting, there was a small picture, not for sale, a Picasso of a certain period of his so in sympathy with my life that when I stood in front of it my flesh crept toward it as if it were my ikon. I went to see it again, the money shining in my head, making my brain all one large emerald. And there I met him, or rather, his rich voice, coming round a plush, impressionist corner. I fell in love with what he was saying before I saw him.

It was one of the tender, warm April afternoons that climb like vines from the most ruined steppes of a metropolis; rays of Central Park were falling all over the city and amoretti flew the wind. Any woman with verve in her veins was carrying her beauty like a cup. From my apartment, modestly high in Tudor City, I had seen that, and I was wearing my mother's tourmalines, which are of a peculiar burnt color, like cream glazed by the cook's salamander, plus a silk shift, sweater and sandals of the same, all designed to cast their tans against a skin that could not tan, and at the last minute I had put on the wig that was my bravest, most costly, favorite, if I could be said to have favorites among them, and unworn since I had last dined with my brother—a wig that was as flat to the face as a wig dares to be, and of a plain dark red. It was a wig that would not suffer a hat, nor would I have asked it to, but had anchored it instead with the best of many long-tried substances, pins not being possible for me. (If I mention these frail beauties, sands of makeshift, it is to remind myself, via all I have abjured, of the sterner exquisite I am to become.)

Anyway, as always happens in these fateful meetings, I got there just in time and properly rigged for it, in time to hear him say to the dealer, in a voice rich enough to buy Picassos, which is what he was there for: "Ah, come on, Knoller, you have me over the barrel, if you'll part with it. Kept thinking of it all the time I was away. Most of all in Bangkok. Monks with shaved heads, widows too, often just the common people. Modern Giacometti, sculpture without curls. I tell you, you've never seen the glory of the unadorned human head before. Of course, set against all that incredible gilt temple-patchwork, maybe any passing human skull is a Buddha. And it may be the Asiatic head only or the African—or that you get accustomed to seeing it in both sexes. I certainly never think of it in Rome."

There was a muffled remark from the dealer, and another rich, amused reply. "No, I guess the Western head can't compete, not even the ones bared by nature." And then, "Well, Knoller? What do you say?"

He was standing, as I knew he must be, in front of my picture.

"Here's your rival," Knoller said to him.

I saw the eyes change, lit as if passed over by the salamander. He smiled at me, a tall, powerfully set man not yet fifty and only partially tonsured by time, lean cheeks with a center vertical like a knifed dimple, the strong nostrils that were said to go with large organs of generation, a mouth with a firm ripple. In the end, it was only the dealer who held out.

An affair begun in that season, with the trees just on the point of flower, seems to keep pace with them, with the apple, the cherry and the peach. There was much that was invisible on both sides. His household, which I saw no point in entering, was being supervised for him by his French mother-in-law: I saw the dead wife's picture, her gamine haircut and tiny phiz, like a stableboy in hornrims, and the two children, all three astride horses and wearing seedy clothes that did no justice to their mounts. They could live the preciously simple life that such money can, the kind that if one can forget what manages it at the top and sustains it from below, can sometimes even have a haystack whiff of the vagrant—and can make love in its own meadows. I was not seduced by its attractions, merely by him. When it rained, we stayed in the carriage-house, a mile from the main drive. I never stayed overnight, being always on the way to Boston, and when he came to the city we met, afternoons only, in the flat of one of his friends.

It was outdoors that I was most daring, though the wig I wore was never again the red one. I got him to tell me, over and over, about the monks in Bangkok, and the widows. His own hairline, receded to well back of the crown and worn in a rough tuft there, I persuaded him to have cropped close by the barber, as many men do. His cranial bump was large, and the effect not very fine, but in certain half-lights, country dusks, I thought I could feel a kinship, surely in my case not perverse. He began even to think of publishing, under the auspices of the museum he served without fee as curator, a monograph on the nude head in ancient entablature (and life, of course); there was even, he said, a question of such as having existed beneath the elaborate Etruscan . . .

"Ah well," he said, breaking off and looking down at me fondly, "there's always some question or other about the Etruscans. And why bother your pretty head—" Like any man, he thought that I was developing a flattering interest in his interests, and I, trembling on the verge of delight, thought that he— God help us, and all pairs of lovers. And, very gently indeed, the gods corrected us, from the rear.

I raised myself on elbow, in the lush grasses on which the first pinched windfalls were lying. "I'll shave my head for you!" I said. "I'll—" Pride shook me for what I could show him, for what I could at last bare to that perceptive eye. "Then you can see what a *Western* head . . . I mean it."

His smile showed no incredulity at the depth of my devotion. Then he enfolded me. There flashed before me a sudden picture of the stripling wife, of those buried tastes which men, and women too, were said to have without knowing, but I blotted it out, blaming my over-educated inner eye. Yet I knew that for both of us it was the moment of the not impossible lover—or the moment just before.

"No," he said afterwards. "I'll be the bald one. That's still a man's job." He reached for me again. "Silly curls. I like them." He rumpled them, paterfamilias.

I gazed up at him from my end-of-summer headpiece, so artfully stained with sun-and-saltwater, and made myself remember, as I had been taught, that even in the love-duets of clods, the roles to be played are said to be endless. And then he asked to marry me. And then I invited him home.

He came down the next week, the first of my vacation, and, if we wished it to be, of our honeymoon. Despite this, I had done no extra shopping, having told myself that all honeymoons were—or should be—a mere matter of unveiling. I had asked him to meet me at a downtown theatre-club where an African singer he had never heard was appearing, and before I left my rooms I sat for a moment in their center, shivering in my decolletage, though it was warm September.

The apartment was no nondescript; I had done better than that. It was the proper guise for a professional woman of some means and culture, created for the pleased surveillance of my colleagues, with here and there a few endearing—and safe—touches of family. Before I left, I locked the wig closet which had been put in off the dressing room, feeling as always, as I did so, that in a way I enclosed a seraglio of my selves.

They are very human-looking: wigblocks. At least, mine were. And I had no intention of shocking my dear love by the sudden grotesque of such a lineup, or of in any way taking out on him whatever of the harsher facts had been dealt me. No, I only meant to break to him, by stages, what I already thought he suspected and was waiting for—as courtiers in the old tales waited, in the dark of the robing room or the bedhangings, for the queen's maid to become the queen.

As I passed a bookshelf, I took up a little Parian bust, of some be-wigged English jurist, picked up not long before in a junkshop, only because, aside from its flowing eighteenth-century curls, it looked for all the world like him. I smoothed its marble profile. By gentle stages, stages even of delight, I should lead us both, I to my avowal, and he—to his Etruscan.

Before I left, I paused to look out of my high window. The night sky stood at perfect cloud. Yet I shivered. Perhaps love makes mad only the completely normal.

In the club, he stood up as I approached his table. I saw his look of puzzlement; I had expected it. "You've changed your hair again!" he said. "No, that's not it, you've had it done the way you were wearing it when we first . . . ah, that was sweet of you. I always thought too, that it was redder that day, but I could never be—"

We sat down against all the clashing, to a slow rhythm of our own. He stared at me closely. A nightclub table is built to just such a small radius across which couples may lean stalk to stalk, like negligently stacked flowers, or like two matches fused at the top.

I turned, as if on the swivel of vanity, so that he might see, even in that dusky jazz-light, all I was. A wig is the more risky the less swirls and curls it has to conceal the hairline; every wig has to have some—unless it would be like those poor nothings, the toupees; this wig had almost none. It was cut almost flat, like a young girl's or a boy's, almost gamine. Some wearers, of course, can pull out a little of the real hair beneath, to blend. I turned again, to an inner wish—but he was looking at my eyes.

"You're always changing it," he said; "if I didn't know better, I'd say you spent half your time at it." I looked out on the scene before us, where almost everyone else was pretending to be private right out in public.

"Why," I said, "I'm in the habit of . . . wearing wigs." For how many weeks I had planned that careful phrase, that gay plural! "Didn't you know?" And when he looked blank—"Years ago, they used to call them . . . 'transformations.' "

He said "Ah, is that it?" and after a moment, "Yes . . . I know that my mother-in-law—but I thought it was only older women—" He was still doting on my eyes, one of his hands, in nightclub manners, with mine a-playing.

And I said, to the same swing-a-ding of it, "Oh not any more, everyone's doing it now."

I grind my teeth now, to think of it, how I put my birthright down there with those others.

Then he said, "Well, I may be sentimental, but I like this one best. And tell me . . . I've an idea . . . I've a suspicion—"

A skin that can't tan can blush the deeper; the hot, expectant dye rose from shoulders, to cheek—to scalp. I awaited him, steadily.

"Now, tell me," he said, "isn't this the *real* one? The original?"

I lowered my face, until that flush should ebb. "It was, once," I managed to say hoarsely.

"And now?" His cheek was almost on mine.

"And now?" I said. "And now—almost. Not quite."

Then the singer, Makeba, came in to sing. "Isn't her head beautiful?" I said. "I wanted you to see it." My wig, pat to my head as it was, felt clumsy. She stretched back her ebony head, that long, almost shaven head which needed no goldleaf behind it, on which there was merely the faintest blur, only a hairsbreadth of difference between it and skull, a head drawn all in one swelling line which completed itself again, into which setting the face receded like a jewel. He agreed to all these points, adding only that length of neck also was a point of beauty—that singular head, like a music box with a bird in it, on that neck poised. And once more, he doubted that ever a Western— And I stretched so that he could see that my neck also was long. And then we rose, to a rhythm of our own, and went home.

"Very good," he said when we were inside. Travel-case in hand, he scrutinized the room as if it were a collection submitted to him for the museum, but I had pruned as close to the personality I wanted here as the most careful grower of dull plants, even among the prints permitting myself only that commonplace Cranach nude, the high oval of whose forehead flows endlessly from her other nudity, back, back into the dark. "—very good, but where's the rest of you?"

I thrilled to the roots of my danger, like a cat in her suit of fur. "What do you mean?"

He put the case down, teetering on his heels, as if he were here for forever. "Come, come," he said, "anybody talks to you for ten minutes knows you draw your imagery from some other world than the one you look like—I got it the first ten minutes I saw you. And it's certainly not this one."

Never before had I been wild enough to dream him into those alleyways I had assumed I must give up for him, seeing him there at best like some large balloon in the shape of a philanthropist, which I might perhaps tug after me, on tour. But now, I stretched my neck for him, delirious with his cleverness.

"Yes, like *that,*" he said "—and then you'll say something with a joke at the back of it, or a pun even, that I can't catch. But there's no joking to this place." He surveyed the room again, scanned the books with a nail. "Ah, I begin to see," he murmured. "For the other 'workers,' eh, as you call them. Your fellow workers. That avocation of yours, that I can never quite believe in."

Yet he was marrying me. My legs trembled toward our pleasure, like some girl of the *trottoir* married by a young roué for her purity—which she has. His hand strayed toward the sugar-cheap marble bust of the English jurist, the ripple of his mouth turning down.

"He looks like you," I said. My voice tremored. "That's why I bought it."

He shrugged, smiled, and said, "Sculpture with curls? Or *beneath* them? D'ya suppose they were his own, powdered? Must say he doesn't look too honest."

Oh, he was keen. Somewhere, a little lady, sitting quiet back there in her altogether, had observed this, adding gaily to herself, "all as it should be, invisibles on both sides." I smiled back at him. "I haven't been to *your* place," I said.

"Ah, nothing there," he answered. He was holding the bust to the mirror, its profile parallel with his own. "Guess I carry my crimes with me," he murmured, mugging at himself like a man sure of only a few hearty blemishes. Then he put the bust down, smoothed his own crown where it was tan-bare, and sighed, in the bluff way men can, when they refer to that—fact. "Uh-oh. Soon."

"Soon!" I echoed greedily—what lechers hope makes! I pushed him toward the bathroom, left towels in his hands, turned on lights for him. "In ten minutes." And I went into the bedroom and closed the door.

My vanity there was pillows. There must have been dozens piled in rows against the headboard, all of the tenderest fabrics for hot-weather nudity, in all of the softest aurora tints—dozens of small pillows all cut to the same replica oval, so that if a head had a fancy to lie there in its own altogether it would seem in any mirror opposite to be lying half in a camouflage of repetitions, or if it sat up, to be rising in the midst of innumerable crescent convexities of itself. Egotism—or beauty—always tends itself most saddeningly in the boudoir. And that was the way I meant to appear, to rise for him, no rubicund Titian rosy-packed in her own curves to the forehead only, but calm crescent of the earliest hour, a Western Aurora.

I embowered myself, taking up a mirror. On my lips I left only the faint vermeil one finds on the lips of bisque dolls, for whom, as they sat bare in the shop, I sometimes felt a sororal—ah now, leave that! But I added more eye shadow, knowing from experience that our so perfect orbs, when left unshaded below that other high oval one, tend to occupy more of its beauty than their fair share. Then I stripped.

He was a gentleman, and gentlemen do not knock. More than that, he was a courtier to the end—or almost. What had he expected of me, other than those innocent capers for which the maribou and the veils might be bought in any bridal salon? We were to marry, and with the respectable zest of the song-of-the-week, he wanted "all of me"—but perhaps not quite so much as he saw. He uttered my name. Again and again he uttered it. Then, in a whisper . . . "You didn't . . . you—" Then he came forward. "But . . . my darling!" he said then, ". . . you shouldn't have done it. Not even for *me.*"

Already I knew my mistake, made from the moment I heard him at Knoller's, from my first wig, from age thirteen and before, flowing endlessly back. Any mystery or hope I had made of him—it had all been in my own head from the beginning. But women are slow to unfreeze from their own legends. So I sat there, the draft cold on me in the hour of my only avowal.

"Don't you see how artificial it is?" he said. "Unless it comes from the culture? Otherwise—it's . . . depravity." He forced himself to look at me, even tenderly. "My dear," he said, "there's a difference between art and life, you know." He sighed. "But women never see it. They always overdo."

And though I held myself upright in silhouette, meanwhile repeating inner aves to Cimabue, Ghirlandaio, Piero della Francesca, he never said a word about the Western world.

Then he carefully turned down the light, and came to bed with me. He was a gentleman, even if one interested only in statutory nudity. And I think now that he may have had his own wistful legend of me that I violated: either that I was not all I should be—meadows!—or most romantical of all, to the rich—that I was poor. Perhaps, and this is hardest to say, I was *his* vagrant.

For in the end—I'll come to that. But then and there, hell had its furies, and I my vengeance. Men know earlier and better than we what the razor can do and what it can't. I waited until we were fully entwined, then I rested the crown of my head—which his hands had avoided—on his lips.

After a moment, he shuddered, but I held on firmly, moving it only to caress. And after another moment—though strong nostrils indicate what they will to the contrary—we were parted. Willy-nilly, a small sob escaped me.

"Oh my God," he said, not in ecstasy, and even through the dark I could see how he was aghast.

Then I rose, locked myself in the wig closet, and stayed there throughout all his protestations—a weak opinion of which we both shared—until, at dawn, he at last left me. Art and life, was it? I had taught him the difference.

Three days later, attired in a new Beehive-with-Double-Guiche, and carrying a spare, I left for Bangkok, telling myself that I had good powers of recuperation, perhaps a hairsbreadth too much humor ever to find my solution in *ars amoris*—and two more weeks of vacation. And who should know better than we of the Agency that when people lack love affairs, or pressing money ones, they turn to a study of the ethical world?

Just before I was leaving, the switchboard rang to ask me to take delivery on a package. "Keep it for me!" I snapped, but the doorman said "No, we can't, Miss. It's come in an armored car."

It was the picture that we had both wanted, from Knoller's. I saw the tremendous justice of this, that I should have what so suited me—and what I hadn't paid for, so dearly. But there wasn't time to open it, so I locked it up with the wigs to keep them company, and didn't read his card until I was well out, on the plane.

"Forgive me," he wrote gracefully, "and forget me. I am a dilettante."

Ah he was clever, clever enough even to speak the truth about himself—though I should have phrased it differently. The half-bald often are. Later on, in the hotel, I meant to send him a cable of acknowledgment, then thought better of it and settled for a postcard on which I wrote obscurely, and may never have sent at all. "I have seen them," it said. "The monks of Bangkok."

They walked the streets in the early morning in their orange tunics, going from house to house with their begging bowls, young boys to old men; a man could shave his head to be a monk at any time, could leave his marriage, his children, his aged, and people would understand his reasons; indeed it was expected of every man that for at least once in his lifetime he would live hairless. And agreed, they were beautiful as they walked the dawn-hours with their concept. And their heads (though merely shaven), when met at any angle—the high twin-domes of the forehead brooding toward the welkin, or that sweet rear haunch above the neck muscles, nakedly working—when met at any hour, these were golden unaided, of themselves. But monks though they were, they were men also, and though some women can study up ethically to be anything, I am not one of them. Now and then, I glimpsed the lean-headed, black-garbed widows, but after all, as yet I hadn't had their successes either. And finally, there were the common people, denuded merely to be sanitary, which I already was.

There remained—if I were to insist on a group solution to both philosophical problems and practical ones—one simple course I had never considered myself temperamentally suited for, which however, via an awkward incident in the hotel swimming pool, was brought again to my attention.

At certain hours the pool, a handsome one surprisingly free-form for the East, was deserted, when it was my pleasure to float on my back there in equally free meditation, reviewing the temple-shaped lamps which bordered it, and other more distant pagodas. Actually, the Thai civilization was in many ways also a heavily hatted one—rooftops, headdressed goddesses, dancers—and I found this mentally very supportive. What at home seemed the inexcusable doubleness of the world here seemed merely inexhaustible, and—oh blessings of travel—not my burden.

At these times, due to my having only a spare wig with me, I wore bathing cap merely, one of those shaggy rubber flowers, silly thing, but with a chin strap that buttoned securely under each ear. It is also germane that on this day, the bathing suit I wore was black. For, as I floated, quite suddenly I was jounced, splashed, dived under, sent upright and grabbed round the waist by a man who said, "Tell by that cap you're from the U.S.—*hi!*"

It was my fleeting impression that he was one of those pink-eyed jockey-types who might be either in the opium trade or a representative of American business; it was my firmer one that he was drunk as blazes on gimlets, not frangipani. I batted him away, but he hung on, saying, "Come on baby, don' wan' drown you, jus' wan' see more of you," and binding both my wrists with one of his hands, he tore off my cap with the other. And there we were, treading water vis-à-vis.

Right then and there in the water, he crossed himself. "Omigod, sorry Sister!" he managed to say before he clutched his own head and turned tail. "Sorry omigod, Sister. It never entered my mind nuns went to bathe."

Dressed and downstairs again, I saw no trace of my attacker, but there was now a party of French nuns on the terrace, their enormous, paper-boat-shaped white coifs in full sail. They were several tables away, but in a sense we took tea together. Is it indeed a beautiful arraignment, I asked myself and them, that one in which the skull is first adorned with itself and then forever hidden? I thought of how it must be done, that holy barbering, in community, in gaiety even—a bride. But almost at once I answered myself, hearkening nearer today than I knew. No, even in community, even in communion, I said to myself, it would be an ugly baldness, not a holy one, that tried to hide its birthright under the coif.

One more incident of my tour might be reported. Under the hotel's porte-cochere, a wide advance of steps led up to the doorway. To the left of these, against the façade of the building itself, a line of pariah dogs always rested. Thousands of them, it was said, roamed the city, since it was forbidden by Buddhist law to destroy them—though the police reduced their numbers on the sly. These particular dogs were smart or discreet; they had sought the better part of that public safety whose gradations—from park bench to lamppost, from the outer doors of churches to the underside of bridges—are known to strays the world over. And just as I went up those steps for the last time, one of the dogs—not the mangiest but with a few bare patches—keeping his head on his paws, the way dogs do, rolled his eyes up at me, unmistakably me, and slowly thumped his tail. Dozens of other travelers were going up and down, and to my certain knowledge he and I had never met before, yet he lifted his coattails to me, as it were, in signal.

That day, of course, I ignored it, and continued up the steps of the Hotel Erewan in Bangkok, with exit visa, passport and other credits necessary to the upper parallel, intent only on packing my bags and my conclusions. Half an hour later I had done both, after the fashion of most vacationers. These people here, I told myself, were foreigners, working out their destinies according to foreign reasons; despite our common plight, neither their religion, their bereavements nor their lice as yet were mine.

So I skipped back home, not unfrolicsomely on the way, unlocked the wigs and recurled them, unpacked a picture and hung it in the wig closet, put away my pillows and one wig forever, gave a brunch for some colleagues, after which I spent the night on the wharves, sharing my Aquascutum with I-don't-know-who, who was harmless—in short I went back to being myselves. And there I had been ever since—until yesterday. And to con it all over in memory had taken only as long as it takes to fly from Logan to La-Guardia. Brahma itself comes more slowly.

When I disembarked, I tried after all to leave the kit behind, stowed in the overhead rack under a blanket, but the second stewardess came from the rear and handed it to me, shaking her head like a coy goddess—"Tchk, tchk!" I agreed with her estimate of me—"Tchk!"—ran down the ramp, passing two women carrying familiar boxes, and caught a cab which deposited me at Rockefeller Center at 2:48.

Standing in the entry to the Morgan Guaranty, there was a woman not carrying one, but wearing one. It was the best of its kind, every hair human, delicately Aryan and singly sewn, but she had been ill-advised on the streaking, which was contradicted by several small tufts of reality she had coaxed out at the sides. I even knew her procurer, who turns such cases over to an assistant. Under my stare, she reddened, then bridled—there's never much finesse to these liars-without-cause. I waited coolly, until I was sure her eye had certified my carefree, blown strands as being dumpily my own, then I murmured, "Next time, get Duvoisin himself," and swept on. Let them cover the earth, these towhead triflers, layercake beauties, fake Marie Antoinettes who will never know the guillotine; they would never catch up with me, who had, as it were, one more head up my sleeve.

For meditation, there is no place so pure as one of the patrons' cells in the safe-deposit vaults of a bank like the Guaranty; the silence whines on diatonically, set to a combination whose tumblers never fall. After transacting my upstairs business in a gay welter of powers of attorney to attorneys, and notary seals each as firm in design as one large drop of blood from a cardinal, I went downstairs to the vaults. The men there greeted me profoundly, like butlers trained to be grandfathers, or vice versa, and I them, in the proper responses—over the years we had trained each other well—and then I took my long box, of the usual raggle-taggle of certificates and costumery (which I meant not even to open), went into my cell, and sat down.

Though the vaults also have a powder room which might be recommended to wandering duchesses—chairs Louis Quinze, soap Roger & Gallet, and as far as I had ever known, never another customer—I had no intention of staging anywhere within these precincts my recognition scene with myself. But in this air, thick with the dead-storage promises of thousands of keys, I ought to be able at least to settle on the punctilio of my new life—was it allowable to carry money with me from the old, and what kind of portfolio? Tramps carried kerchiefs on sticks, or used to, sailors their duffel, and so forth—what would be classed as strictly O.K. and necessary for such a vagabond as I? Some of the strays I knew toted gear which was surprisingly personal, like the beggar who carried a bus conductor's coin-gadget—that was it, let the personal be my law! But for the time being I must give myself a little leeway; it would be a shame if, through the overscrupulous zeal of novice or convert, for want of a fiver or a kerchief, I should end up in looney-bin or pokey, instead of where I should be, afloat upon the marts and purlieus, quietly on view.

I sat there for some time, daintily ticking over my little etiquettes—and goodbyes. Say goodbye to R. and Gallet!—where I was going, and in what guise, I'd be lucky to get past the matron in a Howard Johnson's. Say hello to the life of honest dirt, where hot baths are for kings or Salvationers, and every amenity except air has to be fought for. And say farewell to the romanticism of those who work among the poor with their hats on. Admit that the hardy maintenance of my birthright would entangle me in a thousand ruses and stratagems to which my present one was child's play. Accept the fact that honesty requires the most artful dodging of all.

In the *tara-tara* of that thought, bugled through these halls where everybody else was hiding something, I stood up and almost saluted, hand on curls—but managed to bring my hand down again, empty.

Not yet. One more place to go—and one more little white lie wouldn't hurt me. So, though my curls burnt my fingers, with that in mind I was able to leave the cell, go through the little ceremony of the key, and walk past my grandfathers the way I had walked in—having kept trust with the Guaranty Trust.

As a reward, I suppose, I was allowed to catch the next cab immediately. But the minute I heard myself give my destination—the office of the attorney to whom I had already given so many powers of—I knew my own weakness. How often I had seen it in the profession!—how those who are merciless in self-criticism often feel enough absolved by it to stay right where they are. True, I had business with George, but after that there must be no more offside destinations. Cringing there in the cab, I came to grips with the one power I hadn't delegated away and couldn't, the one little estate of dull memories, cranky habit-grooves and old private nosepickings, that was locked in my brain forever and is the one which keeps most people from revolution—the power of home.

Matter of fact, it was George who helped me on and away, merely by being who and how he was; in the years to come I shall remember him as we do the last person we saw on shore.

In appearance, George is attractively speckled (with gray, of course)—a silver fox in pepper-and-salt suiting. One doesn't shock George, at least verbally. As with most conservative lawyers, the bulk of his files records a steady round of those good little Czerny exercises which practice money. But George's absorbent manner—that of a man who has gone through everything from divorce with mayhem (if only by proxy), to the problems of setting up trusts for the most secret illegitimates or monsters—is guaranteed to set the putatively criminal layman at his ease.

Behind this limber crime-side manner, he conceals a personal family life of the most Euclidean convention. If I could have depended on this alone, I'd long since have told him my secret, thereby acquiring the comfort of a sounding board, and yes, perhaps a little legal flirtation across the already admirable image he has of me. But his vanity—which certainly would have been to reply that such as I weren't at all new to his experience—until yesterday would have offended mine. The need to be unique dies hard with those who already are—and how to get out of *that* corner with sincerity will be my worry from now on.

"Cruise, eh?" said George. "Archeological—you pay to dig? Or once round the Greek isles before the engine explodes? Or a schooner for suckers? I know you."

And how I counted upon it! "Tramp," I said. That's all—I left the rest to him.

"My dear girl." In George's eyes, I can always see how I look to him—a pleasant sensation, even yesterday. "Tramp steamers went out some years ago. They all have tile baths now. Any that would take on passengers." He squinted at me, and I could see myself sitting on the axial line of his binoculars, a small client of charms just right for the afternoon teabreak, but not as tidy as usual. "You're not thinking of doing a Birdsall?"

"What's that, George?"

"She crewed it. Round the Horn, and the crew never knew she wasn't a—until . . . Let's see now, what year was that . . . ?" He leaned back, intent on bringing in Birdsall in the happy, duckshoot way he always brought in all such citations.

"Oh, no, no." I lowered my lashes. "Not in this partic—not in my situation. I just want to—get away from it all for a while. And though there's no reason for us . . . I mean, for people like me to be anonymous, I mean, incognito . . . I mean of course we already *are.* But it'd be kind of fun."

"Ah." He twiddled with satisfaction. "Us."

I said nothing. George does not leer, and I did not blush. But from then on, our business went with dispatch.

"I agree with you," he said, in process of changing my will. "Ernest doesn't need it. Not he." His disapproval of my brother is based on what he believes to be E's exhibitionism. In time, I shall wonder—and perhaps hear, from a distance—what he will think of mine. "But it does seem a shame that a girl like you can't find a better beneficiary than the Seamen's Institute."

"Oh, I could—" I said. "There's a friend—but so rich already."

"Oho," said George. "I mean—oh no. Not in that case." He beamed at me. "Rich enough already, eh. Sure you don't want to change your mind and let me book you on the United States Line. Get you a seat at the Captain's table. And for, er—any companion, of course."

Just then, the secretary brought in the tea-things. George's windows are high, located in a cozy circle of other enormous buildings nestling round their view. There was a freckle of sun still on the harbor, and from within, the sense of lucid well-being that comes to one, toward end of day, in business offices dedicated to some furnishment which has been running quietly and profitably for a long time.

I envisioned myself at the Captain's table, on my head—which I would hold à la marquise, with the creamy arrogance of those models who know themselves to be the impresario of some extraordinary fashion—perhaps the narrowest chaplet of gems, custom-fitted to be worn banded Indian-wise, across the forehead. For, wouldn't I do better to strike a blow for my rights from the topmost purlieus of the upper parallel, instead of grinding away at my own moral behavior like some sidewalk artist, or from even farther below?

On the Shore Line, for instance, on the west side of the tracks somewhere past the outskirts of Harlem on the way to Port Chester, a large sign always caught the eye, as it had mine only that morning: Madame Baldwina's Bridal Salon, so help me God. Though it was probably merely the ornate fancy of a lady named Baldwin, its possibilities had always amused me, a railside salon of the imagination, never to be patronized except in the mystic flash of empathy as I passed it, but its clients all in my category, all, like me, crouched in the ultimate creature-skin. And now I saw myself, a sudden bride from that salon, rocketed out in the name of my patronne upon the clean, savory, hot-bath-and-massage world of fashion promotion: Madame Baldwina model photo'ed at the Fontana di Trevi, at the Colony and on a bicycle in San Luis Obispo, Miss Baldwina at the Opera, at a first-night, at a Fair. At the Captain's table. Or taking tea with her lawyer.

"What's so funny?" said George.

"They run color ads of the fashionables, don't they?" I said. "On the U.S. Line."

Just then, the secretary made one of the squashed noises given forth by the free and equal of the democracy, to remind us that they are.

Celebrities—she'd often seen them lined up at the rail on sailing-days, or coming into port. She'd even seen my brother. And at her picture of him, the small, clean whirlwind of the morning bore me up again, high enough up—or low—to see that if I joined him, in the world of fact-exploitation where he waltzed with his image, I should merely be upholding the single standard of Myself.

"No?" George said. "O.K., have it your way. At least you've cut that dreary job of yours. Why a girl like you . . . I never. Let those women I've seen you with—let them do it—spinsters who wear *Femme.* Why should a girl like you wear a hairshirt for the rest of the world?"

Such references always give me pause. I raised my lashes, short ones tinted but not added to, as I must so often have done everywhere—in hope. "A girl like me, George?"

He smiled at me. "A golden one. I always thought so." George had a very Edwardian father—who often thinks for him. I smiled back at them both.

At the door, he even patted my shoulder. "Give you any trouble," he murmured, "just you run to papa." I stood still as a totem, and let him do the waltzing and weaving. To deceive, as I knew so well, one often need merely stand still and let other people's conventions do the lying. Otherwise, I couldn't have got him to make all these arrangements so blithely—but it was for the last time.

Perhaps he caught an ave atque vale echo; so many of the Edwardians were poets, or Latinists. "Listen," he said, "it's spring, so even a lawyer can say it. Gather your rosebuds, honey. You're one of the few women I'd say it to. Go on and do it; live a little. Just don't lose your head."

Do nuns, on their last novice afternoon, make puns? What could I do but kiss him and hope that this would help him to remember, when he came to judge my state of mind at the time, his own last words to me? And then I said goodbye to him and all the offices of well-being. And then I caught the last cab.

Why is it that when we return home unexpectedly soon, doubling back on the lone prowler of last evening, the stumbler into clothes of the early morning, that we seem to smell the prowler just left, on whom we even seem to be prying? I stood on my own threshold, one of a life already repudiated, and already so nostalgically dear to me for its angel-pains of good or bad, that even to shut the door behind me was an act of dissolve. Then I went round the windows, letting in the last tender shoots of sun and air. The place was to live out its lease in dust covers, and if I hadn't returned by then, my man of so many powers was to use one of them to pack it all off to the warehouse, where, as long as paid for, it might rust for my return under the best possible preservative conditions for sentiment, a little town of life in one room, among so many others of the same. (I had once paid a chance visit to the Manhattan Storage; like a tour of Pompeii, everything sooner or later is grist.) And on the new roads to come, if ever I needed a conundrum to put me to sleep, I could meditate on the odds of my returning to rescue it.

So now, after my morning's hard work at discarding goods, money and other irrelevancies, there was very little else to dispose of, except—the crux. I had kept cut flowers about, but had never had plants, or close friends I must board them with. The air here was only mildly impregnated with the damp, lily-pad affections of some of my co-workers, mostly those whom George had taped so shrewdly, plus a few livelier echoes-in-stereo of the married ones, women of such bursting mental health that they exhausted their families in the expression of it, and had to get away now and then with the girls.

Going down the hall to the bathroom, I had my sharpest moment of—what? The hall is four feet wide, perhaps three times that in length. Nothing hangs there but a few dim lithos. To the right, almost brushing one's arm and looming toward the eyeball as one passes, there is a high lacquer chest, dark and ungainly, put there because it will fit nowhere else. The light is poor. In short, it is a hallway, with no emotion of its own. One goes down it mindlessly, thinking of other things, or of the room at the end of it. Yet when I started down it yesterday I had to stop, whelmed, mourning exactly those unmarked moments. I could have wished for a bundle of them, an old cluster, to take with me. The power of home is in the unmarked moments. My shoulder, my soul, fitted this groove. Is this commonplace? Since I needs must follow the ordinary at a wallflower distance, I have no way of knowing.

Then I went to the wig closet. I knew all about my feelings here, a half-lifetime of them having brought me where I was, so had my answers ready, and experienced no pang. I had come to make my adieux.

The quality of the wig closet is intentness, less ordered than in a laboratory, not as cluttered as a beauty parlor is, but more desperate than in church. Its aims are smaller. Sometimes, when I entered and stood before that long line, I understood, for an ancient, frightened pause, the Old Testament's fleshly fear of idols. There exist wigblocks whose smooth, oval headshapes have been vulgarized with bright cloth covers on which faces are even sewn, simpering masques with patchwork lips and sequined eyelids. Mine are all of the simple, natal wood, their only face that same planed abstraction of one, like the frontal of a casque, which serves them all equally for countenance. All have therefore the same blind, downward look which seems to know the service it performs. They are without obligation to be female. Nevertheless, they are demure, enough so that if one could attach to each block a body molded in its own spirit, I have often thought one might find oneself with a fair replica of the little lady who sits within the skin.

As I faced them, eighteen in all, I remembered the two who had refused to be discarded, and taking them out of their box, set them beside the others. They were none of them in the state I liked them best. Suddenly, I whipped off all their wigs and cast these aside, in a pile. (My sentiment toward the wigs themselves is clear enough; close though we are, I have for them the same feelings I harbor toward women with hair.)

Then they faced me, lyric abstracts of the human head, even almost the poem of it, but too much the appendage of human use ever to be sculpture, and being all alike, one sad step away from art. I suppose that is what most idols are. I stood there for quite a while saying what I thought was goodbye, long enough until I understood what I was really saying. Hello.

Oh larks and gaiety!—for that's what it can be, sometimes, when we finally desert everything we have, in order to greet everything there is. Did you never wonder how it feels to be one of those—the men who walk out of the door one morning natural as life but are never to be seen again, at least not in the proper places? Or perhaps one of those whose unlaid ghosts are still reported—the owners of puddles of clothes left on beaches, of the ownerless car, left for all to see, on a bridge? I often used to wonder how it felt to be one of those—the de-campers. And now I have a notion of how it must be, even for the wife-deserters, the fathers of five who tiptoe out and over a back fence of broken bottles—how it feels for all those who light out and start walking the underside of the pavement, upside down, like a child's drawing of Chinamen on the lower rim of the world.

Glee—that's what it feels like. Half of it, of course, is for the stone rolled away from the neckbone, but the other half is the glee of running. Queer then though, how they'll still give each other little helping flips of the hand, or sit, though silent, in each other's company—for the fire perhaps, but even on a warm day, as if each saw the same, funny, handmade grail in front of him. Or not really. For I never met a manjack among them who didn't believe he was running toward the facts.

Rough champagne, that, and the price is high—but it's the drink we're made for. On the fizz of it, I went round gathering up my portfolio, while the door to the wig closet, a silent choir loft looking down, remained open. I chose toilet articles, at first trying to stick strictly to a philosophy of need, but that's not to be had for the asking; in the modern world, what is need? I would be taught it.

I took a plaid car-blanket of consoling Scotch warmth and color, and a change of inner and outer clothing—unfortunate that the lightest and warmest should be cashmere and other silky telltales—to supplement the sturdy undergarments, slacks and stout shoes I had already donned. (If the vagrant is often dressed too warmly for year-round weather, it's because Aesop is a liar; it's not the ant who knows most about winter.)

To these I added a head-scarf (for colds) and then, thoughtfully, one of my old turbans from Cooksley. Even nudists must be practical, and I would in time have to get my living. Did I mean to beg, steal, or wash dishes?—here again it came to me that circumstances must be my moral instruction. (It's so hard to remember that just because one is running toward the facts doesn't necessarily mean that one has got them—or ever will.) And at the last minute I added a short veil of gauze.

The veil was connected with a slight ambition of mine already burgeoning. For it's entirely possible to be both honest and frivolous, a role that men deny exists, of course, since only women are perfect for it. It seems to me in no way odd that Paris, the goal of so many professions from eaters to lovers, should also be mine. Not that the underside of New York is to be despised; a vagrant who has got even as far as one of its boroughs has come very far. But from books I've read, Bohèmes I've listened to, there appeared to be no place for one of our sort quite like the banks of the Seine, or perhaps the barges. (After that, with the onset of age and maybe wisdom, perhaps Athens.) And though from now on I mightn't look it, I knew myself to be very conventional really, if not at heart, as they say, then perhaps from the bottom, where the conventions are more normally located. So, for Paris in the spring, I carried gauze.

Then I shouldered my strap-bag. An Abercrombie pouch of fine leather and canvas, veteran of picnic weekends of yore, it made me look all too much like the *poule de luxe* of vagabonds, but time would soon darken us both, tanning us not with holiday but with the truths of exposure, like bright pennies in water. Then I turned to go.

And then, it was my heart—which I have, oh I have—that rose in me, bubbled like a drain in which too much had been cast, but stood by for service as hearts do, imperfectly beating. The door to the wig closet was open—what use now, locks?—but I had intended to go straight past it. Had I? Had I forgotten what was hanging there? Have you?

It hung in its own niche, well above the wigs, or did until yesterday—Knoller's picture, Knoller's Picasso. I have sometimes suspected it to be of rather too small a size for the general run of those of his works classified as of that period of his known as the "bone period," but even if it shouldn't really be a Picasso, neither the donor nor I had been bilked. Surely the blue behind the figures is his blue, the shore they sit on his pebble-crazed, wind-eaten shore, the canvas itself only a pause between two claps of wind. They are his figures, the two terrible bones with knobs for heads and an eye between them. Sad clasped, they sit against the blue, and how human is bone! Who, in their bleak sight, would call for hair, or even flesh, to cover it? But in their lower parts they are joined, as if to remember where flesh was quickest and bone may still be, in the parts where love is made. Sad clasped they sit, against the blue. I took off my last wig, and laid it before them.

Though I might stand there until Christendom come again and all the bones did rise, I should never be as free, white and equal as they were. They were art and I was life, with a hey nonny nonny—I won't say for which of us. Meanwhile, though I had already disposed of them by bequest—to Ernest—I found that I didn't want him to have them after all, or not without me. Someday, they and I might present ourselves before him, for such a family reunion as is given to few stars of the cinema. In *Californie,* on my way to Paris, perhaps, on the odd beeline which is the zigzag one must expect of roads that were to be as open as mine. Meanwhile, I would take them along with me for my personal, the very psalm of my life, as sung by somebody else.

I found they wouldn't fit in the pouch as yet, someday perhaps, as needs wore out or were discarded. I wrapped them in a chamois—useful for windows, should I go out washing them—and put the picture in a Harvard book-bag, which it fitted exactly. Then I had a glass of water. Then I ate a chocolate. Then I went to the bathroom, came out again, shouldered both bags, and stood in front of the door. Scarved for the journey, but otherwise rather cold about the ears, my head hung down, a donkey awaiting its Giddy-ap and Gee. I stamped my foot at myself, but the door did not open. And finally, I was able to open it and then shut it behind me, first tossing the keys inside. So I abandoned the roost for the road, the long, sweet domestic life of "What-I-feel" for the sterner shake-a-leg of "What-I-am." It was nothing like my young dreams of going for a cabinboy—though it might turn out to be the most masculine thing I've done yet.

In the elevator, luckily self-service, I was nervy. All of me felt weak and exposed, like an invalid up on his pins again but not without a suspicion that there'd been more to the operation than supposed. I got past the doorman without difficulty.

"Taxi, Miss?" he said, but of course I declined. Ever since a certain event in both our lives he had been particularly respectful; unless my scarf slipped, he would remain so.

"Cheerio, Duggins," I said. "And watch out for more armored cars."

It wasn't until I boarded the subway that I realized those words had been my last address to the first-class-with-loungeseats world I was leaving. I decided they would do.

It was just dusk when I got off in the neighborhood of my case-load, the locale I'd chosen to start out in. Honeymoons might be nothing more than unveiling, but all unveilings were not exactly—well, yes it was cowardly of me. But I couldn't afford to start out on 42nd, a street under constant patrol for all the exhibitionists that were there already; yet in the subway, where the bashed-in people will tolerate anything, I would never be noticed at all. Later on, when I was really in practice, in that happy future when all would be ordinary again—at least for me—I planned to work my way uptown, even to hare off to the better country resorts, at weekends. Right now, I found myself not really conservative, but choosy. Which means timid. I suppose there's no exactly right place to be reborn in, but I've not done so badly. This neighborhood is ruined, but lively. If the same is said of me, I shan't be sorry.

One way to start the ruination was to get rid of all the extra money I had by me, all in packets thin enough to be slipped under a door, but when totaled, rather a sum. The teller had been horrified; banks so disapprove of cash one would think they hadn't got any. It's credit, of course, that makes the planet whirl smartly; cash is for scum. I was scummed to the ears with it. It wasn't that I still kept any special brief for the poor-in-houses as people; I had long since been aware that their mechanisms of kindness or the reverse were at best about the same as anybody else's; nor was I even any longer romantical enough to expect any change in that area in those of the viaduct, though I preferred them. But the difference between rich and poor isn't only cash or credit; it's scope. To my professional knowledge, windfalls were scarce down here. These were my reasons; the facts were, that even in the most decently uncovered heads, the poor can still be a damn headache.

I had a modest forty-five cases in my load—and they were all special, of course; that is, they were the ones I knew. As the evening darkened, and I toiled up one after the other of the tenement stairs as I had done so often before—one couldn't trust the mailboxes, from which even government checks were regularly burgled—I carefully kept myself from any sly satisfactions of charity that I might have dragged with me from Tudor City, but couldn't help being merry. I delivered to dark fanlights only, but had all their habits so closely by me that few return visits were needed. Now and then I stopped at a stall to have a slice of pizza or a knish or an ice, and almost every other one of the old hallways still had toilets—the whole evening was like an old household whose marvelously simple conveniences I was learning.

In my envelopes were bills of small denomination, in sums ranging no higher than $250, the limit I had set in order not to have the matter noised about, or to alarm the receivers, to many of whom good fortune was never anonymous or gratuitous. On most, I had written something not instructional, just enough to show good intention, and that it was for them. And on each, I tried to hit a note median between their fantasies and their needs—"For Rosie's piano"—she would never play it; "For Mannie's funeral"—he had already had it; "For luck" to the gambler; "For the patent leathers"; "For the pimp"—since after all, wasn't this what I was doing for myself?

As I went up the stairs to leave the last envelope—for my old client whose politeness was always to warn me away from her own bedbugs, I felt relaxed and yet a-tingle, greased for the long birth-canal and ready to slide into the light. The fact was that my scarf, a Liberty tie-silk, ill-chosen to stay on a bare skull, must have slipped its knot sometime back—later I found it caught inside the lining of my Aquascutum. But I was by now too tired to notice anything but that the old woman's door was dark, or to recall that her insomnia went without electricity except when visited. Her hearing too, was as sharp as the rats she kept at bay with her broom handle. I had no sooner stepped to the door, hand not yet in pouch, when the door opened. She knew me, almost at once, I think. But she was a resourceful woman. She didn't want to.

"A dybbuk, a dybbuk!" she shouted—which wasn't likely to wake anybody in this house of Italians. Then she shut the door. But she was lonely. A minute later, it opened a crack. "If you are a dybbuk," her voice said, "touch the mezuzah on the door above, it will rest you, then leave yet, hah? If you are the worker from the agency, come in."

Her kindness to dybbuks melted me. I entered. She was ready for me, already moaning and ritually gnashing. "Oy, what an accident. What to happen, Oy."

"Not . . . an accident." Confiding was new to me. "I—we—" I don't know where I meant to begin.

She opened her eyes. "Those Italienisches. A *fight* maybe?"

I opened mine. Could she think they had scalped me? "No—no—"

"So, ah-hah, I thought so. Those crooks," she said. "You go to the priest," she said. She hissed it. "Go to their priest; he'll get it back for you before they sell it, such a beautiful wig."

I wept then, from shock.

"Oy, dolling," she said, rocking me. "All of them you have, so byudifful. Musta cost a fortune. Those crooks."

We were on the couch. I noticed she no longer bothered to warn me about the boggles. It's no trick at all to come down in the world.

That cheered me. I dried my tears. "Does everybody know? That I wear them?"

"I don't know wedder from everybody?" she said sulkily. "Me. My friend Mrs. Levin the beautician, she said it. And maybe we told Mrs. Yutzik in Hester Street, she's an invalid."

"And the Italians," I said. I thought it best to leave it at that.

When I was ready to go, having found the scarf, she scuttled off, telling me to wait, and returned with something wrapped in newspaper. "Put on to go home," she said. "And good riddance to it." She struck her own brow. "Such connections it has, in the mind. Wait till donstairs, hah. To put."

It was a sheitel, the ugly wig worn after marriage and meant to be known as such, shiny red-brown and bumpy as their Friday bread. That reminded me. Down the block, yes, there the baker was already at his ovens, it must be half-past three. I missed having a watch, but the disciplines must begin; later I would be rewarded for its loss by a spryer time-sense, the total loss of one that comes to those without watches. For every so-called loss, I could look forward to other gains.

I went in to buy rolls, and while the baker's back was turned, dropped the sheitel lightly on a tray of the breads which would always tell me, newspaperless though I might be, that it was indeed Friday. I did this in imitation of my friends under the viaduct, who saved as queerly as anybody who was not on the move, but when they threw something away, did so with an indefinable elegance. Then I retraced my steps to the old lady's house—she would have to chance it on the mailbox—and dropped in my last delivery, whose inscription read: "For a couch."

On the way to the viaduct, I looked back at what was already yesterday. Yesterday is a village now, already a place so little on the move that I shall always be able to look back to see how all the life-stories have worked out, including mine. I moved on.

The viaduct is a particularly coveted one, having at its opposite arch a public convenience, far enough away so that there is no smell, even downwind. Fires are not allowed by the city, of course, nor sleeping, but several niches in its fin-de-siècle architecture are excellent for either. The neighborhood, too, still a family one though on the fringe of the peculiarly livid hells of the Bowery, attracts a remarkably high class of loiterer, few winos, no hopheads, no feelies. Old men with Joaquin Miller beards still abound in the world; young ones "on the beat bit," as they like to say, are setting up their new generation of the same (though I sometimes think it a shame to waste all that sincerity on such little experience); then there's usually a scattering of Puerto Ricans who haven't made it to Harlem yet or are making away from there, also now and then a crone or two (princesses-royal of the paper bag and always the least chummy), and here and there a tart. The Seamen's Institute is nearby; though we see none of them here, it lends a churchly presence. Down the alley is the all-night Chinese restaurant. Altogether, in the gradation, not a bad setup for a novice.

As far as I could see, no one was installed there yet, certainly no fire, though that might be due to time of year. Down here, the obscurities of night become doubly soft as one approaches the river, doubly tender, as if hiding only babes in cabbages. The cop's last round was at four, but some of the nicer ones rarely made it—what they don't see don't hurtem. Doesn't. (Hmm—why not?—don't.) Out in front of the arch, some yards distant, there is a public bench, under a lamppost.

I sat down on it, weary, not gay any more, but not sad either, perhaps in just that state of mind when the noumenon stops nagging and not-so-blind young phenomenon gets its chance. Or perhaps it was just that in the bad sections of New York the old lampposts are so beautiful. This one hung its long, graceful urn against a sky dark as the inside of a much larger urn that enclosed both of us. It swung itself a creaking inch or two; get born, sister; get born. The wind that blows my shore is a small one. I wished for the society of my kind—those under many hats in many places, or at home in their most private wigs a-sleeping. I wished for my brother. But my crusade is the smallest also, running to a company of one. So it was just here, that it began.

Without scarf, I could feel how the light shone gladly on the forehead that keeps us from the apes they say—with the help of that even whiter, high naked oval above it—below which my eyes, without their false shadow, must be gleaming beyond their fair green share. I didn't need a mirror to unveil in, or swear a resolve to, but arched my neck like a swan's, shifted my scalp, reserved ear-wiggling for a less sacred moment, but let the breeze play like a sixth sense around them. When the time comes, it's like grace or death, perhaps. When the time comes, it's nothing much. Except that you don't always hear the cop behind you.

It was my first formal confrontation. I spoke first, as one always should to the establishment, and very distinctly. "Good evening, officer."

He gasped; he must have thought me a boy. It was rather a comfort that he didn't gasp more than he did. The New York police have of course seen everything and twice around, including the man who regularly walks lower Fifth Avenue in tam, perfect Glenurquhart kilt—and lace panties—or the beggar who stands in full beard, a costume out of Parsifal and a smile like a sneer from a pulpit, in the West Fifties, on wild-weather Sundays. At the thought that I might be classed with these, I held my heritage the higher, if wanly. What could I say to him, except as it has been said by plumpers-for-the-fact eternally: Officer, it's mine.

He drew nearer; my uptown accent had stayed him, but he came on nevertheless. "Wotyer doing here . . . Miss?" Nearer, he looked puzzled;

perhaps he had caught a resemblance. I decided to declare myself, thinking that this might settle it. One learns.

"Don't you know me, Officer?" Delicately I framed my hands over my brow, just enough to bring out the face.

"Why, *Miss*—" he said. "Why, Miss—" Pity crept over his cheeks with its mild, coronary pink, and I knew I was lost. "Why, it's the lady from the agency. Whatever are you doing here?"

"Oh . . . just . . . taking the air. Lovely, isn't it?" It was no use; he was already backing away from me.

"Work done now, eh? You'll be getting along home, eh. Not a place to hang around this late, even though we—" he gulped—"know you."

"Oh, after a while. It's the first night of spring, you know." That *was* a mistake.

"Mmm," he said. "Live far?"

"Not very far," I said. I was learning, but one last try. "Officer, would you oblige me in something?"

"Why yes, of course, Miss." Eager. "Get you a cab?"

"No. Just take off your hat."

Without the hat, I could see that his hairline was well receded, almost gone. He was a middle-aged man, not bad-featured but heavy-headed, with small ears and a flaccid, white jowl; when that faded red line had finally left him, he was going to look, from the front at least, like a polar bear whose grandmother had come from County Kildare. Yet, if he took off his hat, no one would run him in for it.

"Thank you," I said. "That's all."

"And you're welcome, dear," he said. "Fine evening, indeed now. You enjoy it, love." He crooned it. "Stay right where you are."

When he came back from the call-box, of course I wasn't there. Ruses and stratagems were all coming on as well as could be expected. But I was still an apprentice, on a warm evening. I had left behind my precious Aquascutum.

From the side-window of the Chinese restaurant, where I ordered a pot of tea, I watched the officer come back and go away again. Under the lamppost, in the pool of light where I had first asserted my birthright, the bench was bare. Except for the loss of my raincoat, it seemed almost as if it had never happened. I was as used to this "except-for" brand of kismet as anybody else on the planet. But I found I had no desire to live by my losses only, no matter what graceful interpretations I might make of them. Oh, I had so much to learn, and at this hour, all of it stared at me at once. Is there a preferred style to be honest in? Was it quite the rough-and-ready to do a bunk on a cop by having tea?

The restaurant, empty now, was just that sort of land's-end in which people so often sit at the end of their own wits, or at the beginning of them. The tiled floor, of the pattern of beer parlors in the days of Nellie, the Beautiful Cloak Model, had had scratched on it all the intervening sorrows of grime; the walls had once been painted in landscape, in those peculiar Corot-forests of varnish and gravy-fleck down which one could never wander far. Yet, over even the dingiest of such Sing Wu's, there hangs always a certain paper fantasy, something of fans and kites, and out there in the kitchen, moth-plaints of a language not cognate—not the worst kind to hear in the background when one is taking stock. I wasn't out to be a heroine—I wasn't serious enough for it, I just wanted to be ordinary. But I didn't seem to be Freudian enough for that either, at least not to the police. From his croon I was sure he was a man who knew all about how to be. The ones who do, they're always the enemy. Watch out for good will, sociological and psychological—all those of kind intention who would kill me for my own good, either by keeping me in my place or sending me back to it. Oh, up with the coattails and all that, of course, but it was a long way between signals, and already the second day of spring. And right now, at the hour before dawn, when the blood-sugar level is lowest, I needed to be told that taking something off could be as positive and worthy an act as putting something on—a policy our children aren't bred to. I could make use of a fortune cookie that said it.

When I shouldered my bag again, and put down the money for the tea, the two Chinese who had been chittering in the back came forward. Though the old Chinatown *tongs* that brought them here were said to be dying, recruits like these still arrived regularly in the poorer eating-houses. Two pale boys with coarsely shining hair, lips swollen with youthful serenity, and inquiring nostrils, they had waited upon me together, teaching each other how to learn by serving a single pot of tea in unison. Three weeks ago, perhaps, they had been in Taiwan, and their landscape still walked with them; I could see their bent backs sculptured in the field. There is a kind of innocence that hangs for a long time about people who leave their homeland early. They don't know precisely what events, which people in the new land, must be called strange.

And now once more, as these two ovaled up to me, bowing and curving, I was reminded of how, in Bangkok, Oriental gesture had always seemed to me to be fluently addressed to a point beyond me, its immediate object—as if all but me were chorus to a play whose main roles were being played elsewhere.

Surely my tip, modestly suited to my new status, couldn't have caused all this twittering. "English?" I said into it. "Do you happen to speak any—"

In their seashell language, they deprecated themselves, humbly powerful. Grow grass they could, or set a table of teakwood thoughts in this wilderness, or mend the sky—with a gesture—when it was in danger of falling—but no, they spoke no English.

When I finally understood them, I couldn't speak either. For, finally, one brought me a small wooden salad bowl, cupped my hands round it gently, as if valet to a personage, and even more humbly set my money—the quarter for the tea also—inside it. So, once again, I saw myself in somebody's mirror, and this time I smiled.

As I left, tucking the bowl under an armpit, I pressed my palms together and bowed over them, glad that my travels had educated me enough to say thank you in monk language. In their final flurry of bows, they seemed even to be pointing me on my way—to the viaduct.

When I looked back, they had stopped bowing. One leaned in the doorway, staring out into the neon-thumbed night. The other, head bent, studied the carnation reek of our gutters. And I?—I'm a silly woman—I tripped along mystically, thinking of all the new roles my new head might have in store for me. I thought I saw the pattern of the life it held out to me and all wanderers, a life that was all episodes, through which I was the connecting string. Though these were to fall tangential as snow, it was my fate to unite them. Is *this* ordinary?

And is it customary to stand still on the pathway and give thanks to the general scene that you are in it, uncomfortable as you are? I did that! When the wild jackass coughs by night in the desert, bringing up all the poetry he has chewed by day, that's what it must sound like. For, think of it, I had never before felt the absolute hilarity which comes of knowing that one's equipment is equal to one's intentions! Face to face with the diorama of where I could go—(and would) up to and including captain death's table—my head fairly dizzied itself. I turned it yet once again—this large, superbly bare fact on my shoulders. I wanted to thank the boys back there for being my signal. Then it came to me—that I had been theirs. And that this was the inexhaustible doubleness of the world.

When I got to the viaduct, I found out why they had urged me here. One of the niches was occupied, by I-don't-know-who, rolled up in my raincoat. I sat down next to him, pushed my pouch against the wall for a pillow, and considered him, snug in my coat there, if it rained.

Would he lend his half, in that case?

Does the future of the world depend upon it?

And would I steal it back for my own, when I woke?

Does the future of the world depend upon it?

Along toward dawn, he roused himself, stumbled toward the public convenience, didn't get that far, but in a gentlemanly, sleepwalking way, managed to put a fair distance between us. Behind him, the night went up one lucent step. Head bent, he looked from the rear as if he were praying. I appreciated his courtesy.

So, when he came back, I said in a cheery voice, "I'll lend you back the half you stole, eh?" Bleary-eyed, he nodded, without another look at me, and so we lay down to sleep, back to back, in mutual trust, or a draw. He and I were harmless.

I lay for a while on my elbow. Before me, the ordinary phoenix-fire of day was rising. We are born, we live and we die; crouch and adore. I watched the waterbugs streak like lizards from the Chinese restaurant, the men stride like catamounts, from plain doors. In the inexhaustible doubleness of the world, are there signals everywhere, wild as grass, that unite us? Or must we unite them?

What is imagination? I used to think it was to struggle against the facts like a fly trying to get out of the cosmos.

Come, you narks, cops, feds, dicks, railway police, members of the force everywhere! Run with us! If the world is round, who's running after who?

In the cold of morning, I wrapped a scarf about my ears, but loosely, no deception, and lay down to rest with plenty of leeway until well after sunup, when the first rounds are once again made. Children can learn to be bald. And so to bed. What is imagination? And so to dream the answer, which I knew of course, but could never say. And so—I was born.

The Last Trolley Ride

I

There were once, *said my grandfathers Jim*—this was years ago—two sisters named Emily and Lottie Pardee, nice girls with pleasant enough small faces and ankles too, but they lived at the end of the town, and nobody could keep them in mind. Ever so often, people would suddenly remember this fact, that nobody could keep the Pardee girls in mind, and this would last for a while, but then that would pass out of mind too. Their parents had been the same way; they would be at church and at church suppers like anybody else, and they were invited to weddings too, like everybody else—and afterwards, when people were going over the affair in their minds, they could recall very well that the Pardees had been there. But scarcely anybody ever recalled afterward that they ever got to any of the really important places where things were transacted, like last minute phone calls to come to supper, or small meetings in the vestry or grange, which hadn't been arranged for, or even picnics and pajama-parties, when they were young. And when the parents died, leaving the girls with the neat little house out of town to keep, and, it was said, a tidy little sum to do it with, alas, it was soon clear that they had been left this other inheritance too. For one might have thought that lots of young sparks would be drawn to that cozy fireside—even two at a time, since there were two Pardees—and that with the automobile coming in as strong as it was, there would be a double wedding out there in jigtime. But it just didn't seem as if this would ever happen. There are some people born to live at the end of a town.

So what the sisters did, for they had a sort of quiet spunkiness between them, was to have a bay window cut into the front of the house, and they set up to boiling fritters in it and selling them to eat. The fritters were wonderful; sometimes they came out of the hot fat like a butterfly and sometimes like a blossom, but always they were miles lighter than a doughnut, and gone quicker. It was a queer kind of eating experience and a delightful one, but the kind more or less remembered afterward as a one-time affair, without needing to hunt for it again. People tried to be faithful, sometimes sent their children for a treat or came by themselves for takeouts, but a taste for fritters never seemed to settle itself to a time of day, enough for regularity, and there's no doubt that the best business is regulation business. There was one young man named Jim, he used to come, it began to be said, some said always when Emily had her turn in the window; some said no, it was Lottie—but the truth was he couldn't stand sitting in that lighted window, at the one little zinc table and wire chair. If they'd had two chairs and tables put in, it would have helped, but they hadn't. He never thought to bring a mate with him at first, which would have helped matters too. For although he was a man, and even in those days, even without many automobiles, men could get about easier in love than women, Jim had a trouble not unlike the sisters. He had been born at the other end of the town.

I don't know that this needs much explaining, even now. Though in his case, it wasn't a question of railroad tracks but of barges. On the Erie Canal, there was always a part of barge life that was family and respectable; the wives and men too could go to Sunday church and did, though it couldn't always be the same one, except now and then through the year. That was the difference. For the people of the upstate region—whether they live forty miles from a great lakeside or ten from one of the fingerling small ones—are a landlocked people. And they want it that way, though in those days, without so many cars and planes, you could see this clearer. It troubled them too, maybe, that their state was so various. The people in the towns and farms of that nor'nor'west part of New York State had given their hearts to the chasms and ravines mostly, and there wasn't much left over for water. Winters, on the short, overcast afternoons when the dairy farm ponds were frozen, of course they skated them, and summers, many a canoe was flipped onto the smaller waters, of Honeoye maybe or Canadice or Hemlock. Otherwise, they sat in their tight dark winters, which the women hotted up with calico, and stared out at the numb farmland through air the color of an oyster; nine months of the year there is never much sun in those towns. Or they drove out to look at that hill near Palmyra where Joseph Smith the Mormon had his vision, or past Oneida, where a community had once hammered silver into free love. And when the barge people came to town—even though a family of these might get to their church several times a year, and come around steady as a season year after year, married as close as anybody and maybe as schooled too—the others looked at them with eyes that were the color of oysters, even though maybe they themselves had never seen one.

At least that was the way it must always have seemed to Jim, as a barge child. At times, he even went to school on land with the others, but although he had a last name like some of theirs, and once in a while even kin here and there, it was the once-in-a-while and the general scatter that did it; he might as well have been a gypsy, or one of the Italians from the wineries which had made a little Italy out of the hills around Naples and Hammondsport, who went to the Pope's church. Or else it was the water itself that was an invasion to the others, the farm and townspeople, even though it was the found money that worked their truckland and wetted their apple orchards and humbled itself to carry down from the flour mills at Rochester and the knitting mills at Cohoes, and everywhere else. Summers of course, there was more roister on the canals, and the farmboys meanwhile had their noses hard to the grind; if a runaway farmboy was lost to the barges, he might as well have been lost to the Indians in the days before these were all on reservations—for the amount of hullaballoo that was made. And even when Jim's parents retired to the little wayside house by a bit of water, which was all that was left for him to return to after the war—and where else should he come?—still, for all the changes that had been made in towns and roads and people, there was still a lingering difference between him and them. A town that size always has people who remember its gypsies. And even if not, as Jim would often tell the mate he'd brought back to share the house—war-buddies, the town called them, quite fondly—even polite as the town was to him now, and even if he could see for himself that what with the house-and-lot developments going on everywhere (this was nineteen-twenty) that if he stuck around long enough he'd be an old-timer himself, still *he'd* be the one to remember, even then. Barge people had their own way of remembering, half land, half water.

It was all in the names of places, the difference between them and the town, he'd now and then say to the mate, across the deal table in the kitchen of the little house, after the dinner they'd cooked quite neatly, and just before they got down to talking, night after night, of what kind of business they'd go into after they'd saved enough from the fat, steady but no-account jobs they'd got into but wouldn't stay at—no, not they. Jim's mate had come from the coal mines of Pennsylvania out of Lancashire, England, when he was thirteen, and farmland was to him what the canals were to Jim—though to him, by an even more cut-off memory, it was of what he'd never yet had. He didn't talk much, either of what he had had or he hadn't, but he could sing of it now and then—and he could listen.

"It's all in the names of the places," Jim would say. "There isn't a square foot of New York State that isn't within spitting range of some kind of water—falls, rapids, lake or creek—and within day or two range of the great waters. You wouldn't think that this inland fever would hit some people this way." But it did. It was his contention that, let a New York town stand back only ten miles from a river and it called itself something like Middlesex or Woodsville, or Horseheads or Roseboom, or Painted Post. Nice enough names, but landhungry, in a town way. The canal names were another breed, wider and lazier, lots of them Indian or classical, or marined from elsewhere, or simply practical, like Lockport. "Three canals of the inland waterway, there were at the beginning," Jim would say, in the special, swinging voice he kept for this use, though the voice itself knew that this was nearly nineteen-twenty-one, and the canals were done for. "The Erie, the Champlain and the Oswego. Then, only as far back as nineteen-oh-three—I was already eleven—they even voted to make way for the new big ones, to hold barges up to one-thousand-ton burden. Troy to Waterford, along the Hudson. Kept the old part of the canal, up the Mohawk, to Rome. Rome to Clyde, the canal takes in the Oneida and the Seneca. Rivers, mate. Westward from Clyde, it goes up to the Niagara, at Tonawanda. I was born Mohawk to Rome, just outside of Oriskany."

"Aye," would say his mate, who had never seen big water, not even from the troopship. By the map though, pulled out on the table for his education, he could see well enough that Jim had barely escaped being born outside of a town called Whitesboro one way and a Middleville the other, but he never pointed this out, nor the plain fact that many of the waterway towns had a landlubberly enough sound, and many of the mountain ones a wail of water. To him, the hills around here looked enough like Scotland to be Yorkshire, and he knew well enough what it was those hills—and what they had or hadn't in among them—could do to people. If people here aimed to keep their feet out of water, no matter how much they had of it, it could be these powerful hills alongside, and so wild in the beginning, which had been to blame. Bears and bobcats, even now. But this he never said, either.

And all this was only after-dinner talk, transportation talk really, of the kind men always get involved in, even if it's only how long by bicycle to Maple Avenue. Though, in their case, it was preparatory to whether the joint business would or would not be what had begun to be called a "garage." Nor did the town's semi-distant way with newcomers, or even with its own, much bother them; if the two of them spoke between themselves of such things, it was only a joshing way of admitting to each other that in certain ways they were shy. The town was a nice, pert one, with most of its clapboard in good condition, plus half a dozen mansions made of the small cobblestone that used to roll up on the shores of Ontario, and a lot of silent money in the sock—also not too many grannies with hair on their chins, or other characters left over from before the world got smart. Indeed, Jim and his mate often spoke of it, how it was in the air here that the young people were in control—or soon would be. It was just the town to make your way in, once you knew your way. And its name, if not the most dashing, still had bits of nature in it—Sand Spring.

Shy they both were, though they went everywhere with the returned soldier's bold air of still seeing the world, and Jim's mate blamed his own hanging back on his not being American enough yet. He was away on one of his surveying jobs, the two three times, three it was, Jim walked over to Pardees—which meant two miles to town, one and a half through it and four on the other side round by the lake shore. Oh yes, there was a lake in Sand Spring, but back of it there was a rack of hills, making the town a sort of valley—though like all the valleys in this double country it was only a temporary valley, between the hills holding their breath and the waters holding back. Anyway, it was a lot of walking just to appear casual, but to bicycle all the way just for fritters went against the grain, though it was the ideas of the fritters that got him—set up in a bay window for all to see, four miles out of town!—plus a little bit the idea of the Pardees.

For if those girls had been left none of that family business to go on with, it was no fault of their being women; women had run that sort of business before, just as women had now and then done the same on the canals. Whose fault was it, certainly not those two girls', that there were getting to be no livery stables any more? It was something along this idea he had in mind, as he walked. He'd had women before; he wasn't *that* sort, and except for just now he wasn't even particularly backward with those you could marry. But at the moment, as he told his mate later, he was thinking of how the barges were going down, dropping down, derry-down, into a lock they'd never get out of—and how the livery stables were already almost gone. Those who lived by the wheel, or the clop-clop of a horse, or even water, were always being flung offside, and in the moment that whelmed them there was maybe a kinship between them, or maybe a warning, like those failed families that sometimes get together on a back street. Even for a bargeman, who always has some allowable thinking time, Jim had been a dreamy one—not that the mate was far behind. But these thoughts were not unlikely ones for any man who was thinking of setting up the first auto agency in a town, and nearly the first garage. In any case, this was how it came about that his idea of the Pardees wasn't pushing at the fact that they were young women.

It was three times he went there, no, four. The first and third times he went, there was a crowd of others, or some. On the first time, as he told his mate later, they were just the selection of people you might see lined up outside a mechanical Dairy Cream bar on any roadside today, not important, you understand, but interesting just the same, and always about the same. Only this time, being of the neighborhood, some of them were in the house. But all the rest of it was queerish, or maybe just for those times, or maybe—just for him. She had set herself up in the bay window, you see, stove and all—and although there was nobody sitting just now at the ice-cream-parlor table and chair, she was going at it, wire basket dipping up, and a great bowl for the finished ones and a sweep of the powdered-sugar canister, and then back to the wire basket again—never done. And it was at her doings people were standing to stare. It was Emily. Lottie was back there in the front room, which had been cleared of its rugs and put down with lino, and she was flitting about as much as a roly-poly like her could, serving, serving from a tray and probably eating too, and—it was hoped—taking people's money, though as he came up to the sight of it all, it was more like a lakeside party—that moment of a party when if stopped to be looked at, it is queer.

As he came up to the house, the sun was going down on the lake in front of it in a stew of orange, and behind it there was that grim, green light which always comes from lakeside woods at this hour—on a fuller body of water, one of the great ones, the light would have been blue. Or brown-black, he thought, though he hadn't the idea quite yet how much the actions in the bay window reminded him of the way barge life was always moving, while the land and people stood still.

But what he did fancy to himself in passing was that what she was really doing, up there, was making the minutes into fritters, and when he went inside to taste them, he didn't change his mind. "Quicker'n a minute," one man inside even said, as he poked his child in the stomach. And it was true, just like it is true of some ice-creams even today; these fritters, really a kind of puffball with barely enough outer crust to hold them in life, were gone almost before you could taste them, no matter how many you had—and the child, after a number of them had been popped into him, opened his bewildered red face and began to cry.

Jim went outside again, to look. She was still making them, cooking up the minutes in that same hard and perfect way women will do handwork of the silliest pattern, as if it were important and admirable. Since that sort of handwork bored him stiff, he went away that time, but not without casting a look about for the stables—until he remembered that these would have been in town of course; this house, wintertight as it might be for the climate, would have been their "other house," as people who had gone into town business here sometimes said of the home farm. Or else the Pardees, having lived long enough over the stable while the money was being made, might have bought this house later. Still, it was odd he saw nothing in the small barn, not even a wagon, or even on the back porch, a bike. But as he cast a look back over his shoulder he saw that they had the electric, even way out here, though they had waited until the very last of the real light to turn it on; people were sparer with the cost of it in those days, when it was still new. But now they had snapped it on, and with that, the party look was gone, and the place was only one of those halfway businesses with a porch still to it, and people going away from it to homes that were still all home. Enough fritters had passed by. It was time.

The second occasion he went there, he told his mate, he sat in the window at the table, there being no other customers except a neighbor child and baby brother she was taking care of, this being a choice house to hang around, of a Saturday afternoon. It struck him as a bad sign for business that nobody else was thinking of it as lively enough for their Saturdays, but he said nothing of this, though this time he and the sisters did get to talk. Lottie was the older by four and a half years, and just as clearly the baby; not that she was whiny, just that she hung back waiting to be told whatever, meanwhile nipping from the trays. It might have been thought that she was waiting for a man; some women eat like that when they are. But from what came out later, it would seem that, round and soft as she was, and always waiting to be told, and pretty in the face as a kewpie doll, she was one of those women who aren't made for sex but for sugar, whole igloos of it, plus all the tender emotions—crabmeat patties to curd-cream—of a richly wooing diet; it wasn't her fault if some man mistook the pink deepness at her neckline for something more than a roastbeef flame. Emily was quiet, but in a livelier way, and skinnier, from taking the lead. She had a small face, with two furry black eyebrows she was lucky didn't meet in the middle, and large eyes that were either farsighted or near, but so vague they kept you from seeing how neatly her hands were going. From what the town said when it bothered, he knew she was lucky all round—she was the sort of girl who no sooner does she declare her intentions to go for a nurse, then her parents come down with bargain-rate last illnesses she can learn from, right at home.

So there he was, sitting up in the window, all asses' ears and beer etiquette, not knowing whether he could look into the back kitchen, where the sun was still shining in from that side of the house, it being not yet one o'clock, or whether he ought to stare out at the lake. The two Pardees were enclosed in high aprons that tied at the back and dropped from neck almost to ankle, a kind that must have been bought at bazaars before their time and used to be worn by ladies when they served at such bazaars or went into the kitchen to oversee the maid. Here in the shop, these signaled that the Pardees were at your service, but ladies still. The kitchen, despite its moment of sunshine, was full of that kind of doubletalk; was this an outright shop or just an amateur operation; was this all just a pretty moment of fancywork for two healthy girls who didn't have the nerve or the need to get work in town—or were the Pardees poor? And was this Sand Spring 1920, or Sand Spring 1898?

The sun dazzled a dishcloth, then moved ahead dead center over the roof, casting the pupils of all below into temporary shadow, and the whole sweep of the house, from bay to kitchen, into the nice gloom which came of knowing that in a short while the glare would strike the lake. Everything was live and fresh enough here, nothing dead or eerie or shut-in; not a yard from his nose, on a rack near the special stove which had been set in the window, other dishcloths and towels smelled of the outdoor ozone they'd been dried in—it wasn't that. And if he wanted surety that he and the Pardees were alive and ticking, there, in a big iron pot as big as a cannonball, there were the minutes bubbling—it wasn't that. Lottie was making the dough and Emily for the moment was feeding the sweet scraps to the two children as if they were puppies, though her job was to tend the pot, lifting and lowering the wire strainer, putting in the raw and taking out the finished, then a whisk of sugar and onto a plate, and all in a rhythm that knew beforehand how fast he would swallow; four minutes from now she would be once again at his side. If he ate five dozen of those things, he would still have eaten nothing but an hour.

He watched everything, nevertheless. For the life of him, he couldn't have told later which sister had informed him that the proper word for what he was swallowing was baynays (from the French of a recipe come down from a Canuck in the family) but more commonly called bennies—or which had told him that the stove, a tall affair of many intricate drafts, warming ledges and ovenwells, grandly crowned by helmet-and-spike, and painted aluminum, was called "Bismarck." Like many a couple who lived together, speak up as the sisters might separately, the effect was of unison. And why not, if their experience of living was to be as unison as the Pardees'? Why else was it that if he asked some of the foolish questions in his head—which he wouldn't, being already stretched enough by asking himself—or even if they answered willingly enough, which they couldn't, they would still tell him nothing he and they didn't both already know? For the doubletalk that was in the house wasn't theirs or his; it was the town's—and the fact that they all knew this already was what, past or present, made it a town. Otherwise, as he asked his mate later, why would it be that a man could come back from such a Flanders of a war, plus two years of schooling the war had gifted him with after, and still wouldn't know his way in life any better than the town's way, *once he had plumped for the town*? Out in the world back there, as back as far as Europe, for instance, he had known his way about with women, at least to the point of sleeping with some of them—and even before. Right now, as the mate well knew, back East, not four hundred miles away on the coastline of this same state, the world was full of flappers whose dresses wouldn't reach Sand Spring until Sears, Roebuck chose to send them maybe two years from now—and whose manners would take a lot longer. Or was it that, back there, he and Jim had only passed through? But once Jim himself had got here, no matter what he might do—and he wasn't fool enough to think that a lot *didn't* get done here—the town would still make his conversation for him. By his taste for a freedom outside it and his stubborn wish to be of it, it had neatly returned him almost to the state in which he had left it, a watery young'un, Sunday scholar in its visitors' pews, or at its back-row desks. Coming back to it was like coming to court must have been, in the old days; the gossip here was like a sieve. Yet the current was bouncy enough, returning him up down like a fountain, or a woman, for his help and his chastisement too.

He closed vainly on another bennie fritter. And found that Emily and another dozen were at his side.

This time, though she moved off almost at once, like a good waitress or a thoughtful lady-of-the-house, they held a silently monitored conversation. The town said (in him and for him) that her father, in his eagerness to make ladies of the daughters of a father in the horse trade, had kept her from all the things that even ladies were now doing. And in her and for her (no matter what Jim himself might say to her) the town would pretty well have taken care that she address him in one or other of the characters it held proper to him; whether it would be as a war-buddy, or as a fellow with his gypsy life not yet lived down, he'd soon see. Though surely, some pioneers in conversation broke out of the preordained.

He was to do it, too, though not then and there. By the time he'd swallowed up eight of those things, he'd remembered the vague kinship which had walked him over here. However, the decline and rise of transportation, and people with it, was too wide a subject for the soda-pop chair he was sitting on, so instead he put his fork in fritter number nine. He'd been using a fork all that time, finger freedom not having been offered. Then, at number ten, the sun, just as if it hadn't been inching along all that time, reared over the house in a leap like a horse and struck the lake to white, and splashed all five of them inside there glare-blind. It was over in a second. Outside the bay window, a line of red cannas he hadn't noticed before started up like an audience, all tongues. On number twelve, he spoke. "How you folks get to town from here?" he said.

He got several answers, this time slow enough so he could assign them to their dealers. To his surprise, Lottie spoke up first; he was to learn that she could speak up smartly enough when it was a case of what she couldn't do, though the full extent of that wasn't known even to her, until the end. "Never could get the hang of a bike," she said, looking modestly down at what would someday be piano legs and hams, but right now, though bursting, were still young peony fat; he judged her to be about twenty-four.

Then Emily spoke, in a thoughtful way. "Shanks' mare . . . might be . . . the best." He wasn't sure whether or not this was a statement, but it was the "might be" which got him, moving away his idea of her away from "one of the Pardees" almost to Emily—the idea of her being a woman, squeezing in between. He judged her to be old for her age, about nineteen, one year younger than the century, he being nine years behind her. The century line was still much in people's ways of reckoning when he was a boy; you watch how it'll be as the next one hoves to.

Just then, one of the next-door kids who were still underfoot, the girl one, spoke up, first giving a swipe to her baby brother for dribbling his sweater on the floor. She had one of the fritters between her small thumb and finger, and staring at Jim, she popped it in and ate it, even chewing as she spoke. He watched, fascinated, it being probably the only time human teeth ever got one of those things. So, her words came to him delayed. "Neighbors," she said. "Ne-*eigh*bors take them." She drew down her long little jaw, making a face she must have seen somewhere. "Us."

When he got out of there, after quickly paying his fifty cents for all you could eat, which was the arrangement, he stopped at a bend in the road to look back. There were obligations neighbors paid by right, or even goodness of heart, and still made faces over, which their children could copy. This still didn't mean that the sisters were poor. The town said they weren't. They might just have to be careful—which meant he needn't grow a sympathy the pair hadn't asked for, though as their only customer of the afternoon he felt a certain right at least to judge their enterprise. Why it should be a place where he heard the doubletalk so keenly, he couldn't imagine; though in any town there were bound to be such places, he had always imagined them as more private. The afternoon was bordering on rain now, with the swift changes that came to these hilled waters. The stall in the bay window, dark as if it had given up hope of further trade now that the sun had all but gone underwater, seemed itself full of passing clouds. Of a sudden, as if the sun down under there had turned over, and the lake given up an aproned woman, her arm dripping, there flashed into his mind the simple reason for the stall's presence. Those girls knew what the town's verdict on them was, just as he and every soul around each knew of his own. "Nicer girls you'd never want to talk to—when you're talking to them." Some women wore flashy garters to keep people looking at them, or took lessons in coloratura. Those two had done it homestyle, dime a dozen or fifty cents an hour. It was their bid to stay in the eyes and minds and thoughts of people, not to be winked out.

When he got home, he tried to tell something of this to his mate, who listened willingly enough, and was moreover a man who never really forgot anything he was told, not anything—four and a half months later he would look up from his plate and say, "What's about this Lottie, you once said."

And what about people—aren't the tags and loose ends and final catchings-up enough to break anyone's heart? But at that moment the mate was just in from a trip which had taken in Cazenovia and Skaneateles, bully towns for auto setups or any other, both of them, and he was already wild on tomorrow's trip over to Chenango and Wampsville; if it was left to him there was a real question whether those two wouldn't have a chain of dream garages before they had a real one of them—and a homemade New York State atlas into the bargain. As for the other topic; once they had got the map, they lost it there. Maps take in people like that all the time.

And on the occasion of the third visit, Jim's mate having gone down the Genesee to two towns just outside of Cattaraugus which he was sure to be in love with, their names being Almond and Angelica—see the map for yourself if you don't believe me—Jim again went to the Pardees alone. But this time people, and gossip too, had got there before him. It was a Spanish War Veterans picnic, with the families of course, some of the granddaddies being from the Civil. The Spanish ones mostly weren't even fair into middle age yet, some of them not much more than ten years older than Jim. It wasn't the kind of continuity he was interested in, but it was the kind a man can't avoid, even though his own war is hardly in the Legion clubhouse yet, except on the plaque to the dead.

Before he plunged in, his eye, which these days was seeing business thoughts everywhere, saw the place as a picnic grove with tables and docks and beaches, and even a place for boats-to-hire. Second thought told him it couldn't be done—except by a stranger maybe—for it was not yet the town's way to hire these things out, instead of just leaving them to be called on, or borrowed (though twenty-five years later, that shoreline was all cottaged and concessioned and pounded down like a beachhead; as for the woods in back, the jack-in-the-pulpits had long since taken their sermons elsewhere). He saw that the veterans had very kindly brought their own tables and chairs, and even more generously their own food, including the usual chocolate cake, which no doubt could be chewed. White pitchers stood on many of the tables. Though a few children were straggling untended in and out the side of the house, there was no trade going on from house to picnic; nobody except Bismarck was in the bay.

On his way there, two of the veterans who worked in his factory greeted him. At the door, a woman smearing a child's happy mouth with a hard cloth nodded at him, turning out to be the night librarian where he sometimes went to read. Inside the kitchen, he saw only Lottie, peeping out, not cooking, though there were signs she had been—maybe a batch or two she'd been feeding the children for free. His mind made up at once what had happened to Emily; she had gone to be a nurse. He was neither disappointed nor pleased, recording merely the idea that Lottie was a woman too—and that either sister was more interesting when alone. Together, they were merely a situation. What he might intend to do, he addressed to that—it made no difference to him to which of them, as long as it was only one at a time, this being how his previous experience with women ran. He didn't mind having an experience, in between the maps and the building-sites, even if it risked being a serious one, which in this town it sure would be—maybe it was time. But this day and age, a grown woman ought at least be alone for it. So he smiled at Lottie's neckline, strode over to the table in the window and sat down—lucky he'd had no lunch. After four or five dozen of those things, he wouldn't want any, though from the novelty of it and the rhythm of the girl at his side he might be left with richer appetites, like a love potion in reverse. Had the sisters thought of this too?

"Oh . . . but we didn't—" said Lottie, and he stared at her, speaking there as if she were answering him, fat pullet-hands clasped at a chest with a depth curve in it like the beginning of a two-hearted valentine.

Then steps sounded, and with her long, light stride Emily came in; she must have only been to the bathroom, or in the house somewhere. Though she might have been his first choice if he'd been offered one, he looked at her now with some enmity.

"We weren't going to—" Lottie said, a hand out toward the stove, her eyes on her sister. "Were we."

Emily said nothing right away; she had that power, not always an easy one for a woman to have. It gave him time to wonder if the picnic people had angered the sisters into retreat by their not buying, or was it the opposite entirely, that the sisters were too delicate with acquaintances to push their trade? But more than anything, he wondered not only why he never thought of the town's doubletalk as much as he did here, but why he never understood it better than he did here—though from all sides. It never occurred to him, the lake air being as calm as Hiawatha here, and the quartered-oak floor of the bay jutting out so strong upon it with its cargo of housewifery—that its owners might not know themselves why they did what.

Just then, the two men outside who knew him rapped on the glass. Weatherstripped though it was, it was no proof against their sharp summer voices.

"Which one is it, Jim? Can't have 'em both. Where's your mate?"

They kept up a chorus of this, knocking their tin mugs against the house, until a couple of the women came and got them, not without peering in themselves, though all that handwork women do makes them manage their eyes better.

"See what you're in for, Jim!" one of the men called out, and the other man, with a grinning wave of the hand said something too, but the lake air sopped it away. The white gloom of the afternoons in these parts came and settled, temporarily taking away the spring; always in these parts the winter comes and stands for a moment, in any season. The two girls watched it, a land-ghost they were used to, but Jim thought of canal weather, different always from the very land it traveled, the mornings blue with their own business and boat-notions, even in a freeze, or a fog. As for other ghosts, no matter what the mixture of names was around Sand Spring, none of the three saw anything but what was immediate. White people didn't see Indian ghosts. Nor do many in the modern age see classical ones—though those three would have a chance at it.

Lottie, at the glass, peered after the two men. "They must have been rushing the growler," she said.

Jim stayed mum; in addition to his inborn barge-quiet, he'd learned in France to get along by watching expressions. But Emily had already seen his, having picked up that talent right at home.

"No," he said, as if she'd pulled a string in him, "I don't know what it means. Rushing the growler—what's that?"

"You can see he's never lived over a stable, or near a saloon," said Emily thoughtfully and over his head—as if she and her sister were standing in their shifts, talking him over at bedtime. Again, like last time, he had a sense of messages given and taken between her and him, if only by being withheld. She hadn't much of a neckline. No criticism—but the differentiation was going to have to start somewhere. He had a sneaking wish that one of the sisters could have had a sign on her somewhere, such as having the name of some former girl of his who had worked out, or a string of amber beads like his mother's. To trust entirely to luck in these matters had always seemed to him a bit dirty; it was more gentlemanly to proceed from choice.

"Of course not," said Lottie, equally over his head. "He grew up on a barge."

They often talk like this, very literal, very simple—the sugar-people, the fat ones. From which other people take it that they're as simple inside, and what's worse, they take it so themselves.

Curiously enough, though he was thinking of them both in their shifts, it wasn't Lottie he could see best, for all her marshmallow meat, but the other one. He could see her standing in hers in front of him, or even naked, thin and intense, more emotion to her than there was line, though she would have her points of it, and a little knock-kneed, like women with good legs often are. What he couldn't quite see was whether she would be embarrassed. There was a chance she wouldn't be. But what he could see—as clear ahead of him as that the men outside were still laughing and the sky behind them was a mackerel one—was that he would succeed with one of the sisters here. The question was—which?

Does it seem to you that the climate intervenes less nowadays in conversations? In the old days there was more climate of course, you can be certain of that; has to be, to make them the olden days. But surely the climate came and stood of itself more in conversation than it does now; it expected to be watched—a matter of all kinds of lore from skies to a wet finger held to the wind—and it gave you time. He wetted a finger and held it up so that either girl stood to one side of it. There to the left was Lottie, waiting to be told, a ripe fruit maybe, but bunched very close to the bough. And there on the other side was Emily, in her upper lip that willful, deep trough down which a kiss might well slide against duty. Which way the wind blew was plain as his forefinger between them. In the bay window, blank now, the afternoon, special property of women such as these two could well come to be, took over. Mornings were child's gold and the evening belonged to the married, the courting or the social. Night, where it was not for sleep, was for hawks and harried travelers, and thieves. But in towns like these, whatever their names, the afternoons were the special property of the spinster. He squinted at the two sisters along the finger. They would never get separated until they married. They would never marry until they got separate.

"But your *war*-buddy," said Lottie, "he was brought up in England."

He nodded, though only a woman would say it that way instead of just plain "buddy"; still, it showed interest, and as he told his mate later, she was the first to mention *him.* Otherwise, he could see they had no intention of telling what "rushing the growler" meant (though he could guess) or rather, they meant him to tease it out of them in more of these stretched conversations—and suddenly he had had enough of it; he had passed over that hairline divide which always hovers between what a man can take of female activity, and what—no matter how lively his motives of love or rape are—he can't. He'd had all he could take of this fancywork that placed the heaviest burdens of meaning on the lightest nothings, especially since he saw that Emily, making one of her quiet moves that somehow always drew more notice than Lottie's louder ones, was now at the great gray-helmeted stove, which must have a property that most of its kind didn't, of holding heat without showing it. Or, were there any others of its kind?

Now, when a house, an ordinary one by its neighborhood standards, it could be in Sand Spring *or* Flanders, begins to take on a special significance to a man (whether or not he can bear it), so that mere cakes become butterflies and stoves become eccentric or dear in character—and when that house has woman in it—take warning. For, in spite of all this heavy-light business, whimsy doesn't come natural to women; most of the whimsy in the world comes out of the men. Look back on the books you were brought up on; see if I'm not right. Sure enough it was the sisters who had mentioned the stove was christened Bismarck, but who was to say what family historian or politicker had once named it? And who was it was looking at it now, thinking, as he said later, that it was looking right back at him through the grizzle-gray eyepiece of its armor like an old iron eunuch, not missing a thing or a person that came in the kitchen door?

From inside one of its ovens, Lottie drew out another of those black cannonball pots somebody had provided this household with, the dark ages maybe. This time it was a smaller version, of a size to contain a potion, but on her setting it in front of him it only disclosed more of those damned yellow fluffs—he couldn't get one more down him now if he was blessed for it, or even if he was to be offered one of the women with it, she as nude as the fritter, both of them spitted on the devil's toasting-fork. Outside the window, he saw that the tables were empty, the women and children scattered, most of the men of the picnic being gathered along the shoreline, strolling or in groups of jokers, and he longed for that pair who knew him to come and rescue him, with whatever guffaws. In the foreground, between him and them, on the table nearest to the window, one of their stoneware pitchers reared large, in another and a realer world. There was no barrier like a window. Mentally, he jumped through the glass—or the small Robin Goodfellow soul of him did, and landed neatly on the cold mouth-edge of the pitcher, just before it dove into what wasn't lemonade, from what he could see of those waterside stragglers, but beer. Well—as he said to his mate later—luckily he was able to recall that there were still doors to that house, so he stood up politely enough, though he may have licked at his dry mouth a bit—and made ready to bolt.

It was Lottie who leaned across him—to pick up one of the dainties in the pot. That double valentine she carried in front leaned with her, in fact splitting wide enough to show him, since it wasn't a whore's and her sister was standing right by her, that some kind of mental innocent owned it. It wasn't this that got him.

"Try one," she said, and though he choked a bit, of course he knew that she was addressing the tiny eatable she held pinched between two cushiony fingertips—and wasn't even really offering it either. In fact she was murmuring to it like to a baby.

"Day old, you're different," she said. "Way I like you best." Then her lips parted softly, so that he saw the gleam on their jello-pink insides; then she nipped the poor thing—that's the way he thought of it—between her milk-fine teeth, and it was gone, to what pinker recesses he could only imagine—and certainly did. But just before it went down her, the tip of her tongue came out partway to meet it, nothing gross, delicate as anything, indeed not like a bodily flicker, more intelligent. But it was this that got him.

You are all bound to think of us as a generation that didn't scarcely smell the dark angles of closeness, fleshly closeness, much less speak of them; isn't true of course—how do you think you all got here? Never trust what one century thinks of another, much less one generation. It was only that we didn't speak out so much in a crowd as you do. And you seem to us like a solid row of tongues hanging out day and night for excitement, and only getting dry for it, in all that wind. We see you falsely of course—as falsely forward as you see us backward.

Don't you think I know that and so calculate my vision of us both? And when you are able to correct yours that way, what'll you be? Old?

Anyway, it wasn't too much of a mistake that saw Lottie's tongue as the liveliest part of her, and jumped to her quick show of it as to a sexual flicker more common to other parts, which was where it took him. Not that he knew yet whether or not he'd made a choice.

For leave it to Emily, as was learned later, to take up a moment of surprise, hers or anybody else's, and kick it further up the ladder. What she did, or he thought he saw her do, was to leap past him, through the window. Anyway, she leaned across him, just as Lottie had done, but without stopping—and without the neckline of course—and continued past him, her apron skirts in serene sail, with perhaps a bit of ankle added—a sight of some interest, though not as piercing. A next moment's revision told him that she had merely stepped gracefully through the bay, which opened French-style—but by this time she was already back over the sill, with the white pitcher clasped to her, and a smile. And in all of this, there was no competition with Lottie, though there was certainly something, just what—he couldn't say. She set down the pitcher firm center on the table, reached an arm behind her the way queens sit, without looking, and appeared to pick a glass from the air there—unless anyone wished to note that her tidy little rump backed against a shelf. She poured from the pitcher. He was so dry, he would have drunk chicken's blood. It was beer.

She lifted her chin in time to his long swig of it, then bent her head again, tucking in her smile. "I rushed the growler," she said.

Lottie giggled. "It means to go down to the saloon for beer," she said. "And to bring it back in a pitcher. Or a can."

So there the two of them were again, in unison.

Or maybe not. For Emily, pouring him another, spoke singly into it, so that the glass he took held her question as well. "What's your . . . buddy's name?" she said.

Jim looked into the glass before he drank, and it was a long moment before he answered. He was feeling that tickle of terror which comes from a person seeing ahead of him into life-probabilities which nature should have kept him from seeing, and ordinarily does. As his mate and he agreed much, much later, too late to be of any use, it was like looking at a map of the future—not dead cert, but a tour you could surely take—not knowing whether to learn it hard as you could, or to screw up your eyes and run on the double away from it. For there was Lottie, her eyes bright as candy in a curved jar. And sitting at the small table he had just deserted, leaning those heavy eyebrows on her knuckles, that girl who every time he saw her he thought should have been blackhaired, not brown. And here he was, and his mate, bumbling all over the map of New York by day, but—by this other map—not far. Any of them could count up the possibilities; perhaps these two already had. He was struck with the terror of it, and the charm. Two and two—but *which?*—makes four.

"My . . . mate?" he said. The word buddy, for the comic strips, the sob-sisters of the Stars and Stripes even, and for the town of course—never crossed the two men's lips. "My mate's name?" He smiled to himself, a true bachelor's smile, for from the odd-timeness of jobs and even meditation, he and his mate spent more time alone than the dinners they had together, though when these came about, the talk and the silences matched well enough; this was what it meant, having a mate. He let the smile broaden to include anybody in the room. "We're twin-names," he said. "I thought you knew."

On the sill where she had stepped over, a feather rested, blown in from nesting maybe though it was early for that, a clean feather silk-smooth at the top, not separated anywhere, with a fluff toward the pen-tip of it, from some middle-sized bird, nothing fancy, but whose tail nobody had yet put salt on. He smiled at it too. The sisters knew of the names, his and the mate's; there wasn't a chance that they didn't; in a Sand Spring, the structure of the gossip at least let one see what were impossibilities too.

Gently he reached down and picked up the feather. He wasn't a picker-up of pins or a sufferer from any of the nerve twitches that came in about ten years later, but to a boy grown up on a deck, the soil that was so wild and itinerant under the feet of shore boys was always precious, as well as any stray pebble and shot from it. Whereas to a boy from the coal caverns, as his mate always remarked, a clean deck to walk on would have been like silver, and the towns the mate fell in love with, one after the other, were always clean. The two of them were opposites then, not unlike a pair of sisters. And this was enough of parallels, at least for now.

He had no hat on, ever, so just before he bolted, he put the feather behind his ear. "Maybe that's why we came to be buddies," he said from outside, leaning back into the bay again. "My mate's name is Jim."

II

Oral description cannot touch that spring—and not because it is gone—or that there will be others just like. Washlines left out on its evenings had a mystery, and even to the well-sighted, an arbor in a garden sank back in the twilight like an Italian arch. Projects were touched by it, or people were moved to them. Even the plans for a Ford agency were affected, the way a plain street, with plain maples and horse-chestnuts, is one morning littered with the wildest yellows and greens. And when the householder has swept these away, then down come the whites. It was a time of clearness and short, lovable mysteries, when a man may well be afflicted with a keenness of sight for things he has always known aren't there.

The mate had found his town. At least—after days and days of his circuit-riding under those wind-glassy skies, toward horizons which were one moment riotous and the next second as neat and sharp as a pruned hedge—when he burst in on the dinner-chops with a statement to that effect, it was clear that the time had come; he had *had* to find it, just as much as if a giant traffic-hand had come down in the road before him, holding up a sign that said STOP THEN GO. As he said to Jim, if they weren't to let themselves be chosen, they must choose. In this town that had found him, there was a house to which was already attached the means for just such a business, agency and garage, as they wanted, also a half-acre of frontage for expansion, also—unimportantly of course—an owner named Skinner. Skinner didn't particularly want to sell; in fact, said the mate, the idea had not yet occurred to the man, but they were going to get that setup from him—in an honest way of course—if they had to hire three wolves to blow him out of there.

"Three pigs, it was," said Jim. "That story is the other way round. I mean—one wolf. Not even two." But he had to laugh. The two of them looked at each other, grinning. They weren't looking in any reflecting mirror. Jim couldn't help knowing he was handsome, a tall, rolling-gaited man with a fresh complexion, whose pink cheeks annoyed him with their youth. The mate was shorter, though not as short as he looked, with a chiropractor's neck and arms, or a pick-axer's, and not bad-featured in a pugnacious way, but swart enough to keep him always at the razor, and not above a sneak of talcum on the jowls. Like many from the mines, he had a fine voice, the speaking one too—and he couldn't help knowing from the women, beginning with his own mother, that he had a smile. And where Jim's head was close-shaven enough for a phrenologist, so that in some lights his blond hair seemed white, the mate's black crop shot forward in a forelock which made him look as if he was being pulled along by it—even to himself. Looking back at them both, they were a nice pair, part of the grinning being that they knew it. Slice either of them, and you'd get only honesty, tempered with need but not yet burnt by it.

"Pigs is pigs," said the mate, adding that Skinner's house, and certain others in the neighborhood, had been built by Swedes, a Swede carpenter, and scrubbed by his faithful fry ever since—or almost.

"What's its name," said Jim. "This great town."

"Names, names," said the mate, but he was smiling. "It's on the main road, of course, but it's just a section. I don't think it's on the map, really." Then he leaned back and laughed so hard he had to slap himself. He jabbed a fork at Jim. "Going northwest, ask for directions, they say 'It's just after you get to the Palewater Reservoir, mister.' How's that for you? But if you ask going southwest to it, they tell you 'It's just about after you leave the Champion Woods Pulp Company.' How's that?"

"No name," said Jim. "Where in the love of God is this place? What's it near?"

They got out the map, which spread itself out in a resigned way. The mate's finger trembled, skipping over the Adirondacks, going due west as if it were a dowser's, then due south. When it found the spot, it could barely hover over, jouncing with excitement. Jim looked at him, inquiring, then down at the map.

There for sure was Palewater, in one direction. And there was Champion Woods, in another. Between them, on the main road, there was a minim of space which when it stretched to human scale must be quite comfortable, though Jim's spirits sank a bit at the idea of its being on the road well enough but without a town to it—of course they had to have the road. But he'd been thinking of some deep green well of a town, up to which the lively motors would come to drink, man-made and hearty, but then somehow fade, fade away again, leaving the place natural.

"Look harder," said the mate. He moved his finger away. There are four directions to a map, after all, and Jim had looked in only two of them. He looked crossways in a third direction, then, following it down, in a fourth.

"By God!" said Jim. "By *God*, Jim!"

A few miles in the fourth direction, there was Oriskany—where he'd been born.

They spent the balance of the night talking equities and amortizations and other money talk which a session with the local banker had taught them quite well, but that night there wasn't anything professional about it except their solemn, joined manner; it was as if they had entered upon an agreed magic dialogue which would keep old man Skinner from selling before morning. Most selling and buying, once it gets past sensible need and projects into the future, is nothing but this kind of personification and magic, with maybe some group madness thrown in. And most bankers even, and businessmen—but that's another story and no time for it, except to point out that Skinner—who promptly became Skinflint in the partners' talk, and must have aged twenty years overnight in the bargain—was actually himself only one grade less innocent than a chickenfarming type, and only about forty-three. Since the next day was Sunday, they drove over to see him. Cars were already well in of course, though still called autos, and had been in for years, and taxis and buses too; don't think the dates are wrong here; we are simply still in the period when they hadn't taken over yet. The mate and Jim had no Stutz Bearcat; they had a Ford. It got them there just before supper, a quarter of five o'clock.

Skinner must have thought they had dropped from heaven, even though they had telephoned ahead. He was the mouse-haired, hysterical type who should have married a big woman to boss him, and maybe with psychology to help him along with his woes he would have, but these were the olden days, and instead he'd married his wife. She was just bright enough to drop children like rabbits, and pink-eyed ones too, just like herself, but she was also the legatee of this house we two were after.

We. But there—it's been understood all along, hasn't it, who that pair was?

Well, to go on, there was the house—and the barn (for it was a farmhouse, and the barn was the greater part of it)—the barn of stone-and-mortar, ledged for posterity and for a sunlight it hadn't quite been able to get that far north, and a seventeen-ninety over the door. The house itself was later, but good too, clapboard, center entrance, double chimneys and a fanlight; that Swedish carpenter had passed through Vermont. There were no Adam mantels but what use would the partners make even of five fireplaces with such a good draw?—and the house was good seasoned wood all through, made to stand, and no plumbing or heating yet, which would keep the price down, and of course, there in front, already let into what had once been the second parlor, was the grocery store and store window—which was how the Skinners skinned along. This would be the partner's office. As for the barn, it already housed a Model T Ford lost in it like an omen, to show how many more of its kind that barn could take on. Outside, there was already one gas pump, and over the acreage behind all, a hill for the sun to rise out of, and across the post road built by the first settlers, a woods for it to go down into. Oh, it was a fine setup that had caught the mate's eye, or would be, once the Skinner litter had been cleaned off of everywhere, the pair said to themselves; there's no litter worse than a bad farmer's, and Skinner, among other things, had been ploughing up the acreage for something. Even the store was half-hearted, with signs the family had been at their own groceries, and tawdry ones too. The barn took Jim's eye at once; it was beautiful.

The trouble was, the place had no need or real reason to be at all, any more; none of it did, not barn nor house nor the land. But how were Jim, who didn't know about land yet, or the mate, who'd never yet had any, to know this—that such a property, in such a place, can pass from hand to hand and still, like an amulet, keep its first stubborn luck attached to it? Even the Skinner litter would be a deception, prompting an industrious buyer to think he was the man to make the change. The trouble with these houses that last is that they were built for nothing but *once*—and for the post road. They last and last, but they won't ever pervert to anything else, not to summer places, because of the road, not to business ones, because of no town. But people are always trying, in their stalls and stores and eateries, and of course anyplace having such a sunup and sundown has a good deal to do with it. So it has come about that these houses on roads without towns are the badlands of America in a small way, just as those great glory holes at the center of the continent—the canyons and deserts—are its badlands in a grand way, land where nothing more than carnival or show, or a surprise of the spirit, can ever be arranged. But these other smaller places—being so random but still everywhere in the lymph and life of the countryside and the cityside too—there's nothing to be done but to spit and to stamp on them, and to start all over again in these new developments, as is being done now. As for the partners, one look at Skinner with that fine hill and all its works behind him, and they were convinced they had come just in time.

A price was quickly agreed upon by all tycoons present, said sum first being tempered the partners' way—by reason of their willingness to take over all mortgage arrears as soon as they had the money to do it, and then tempered Skinner's way—by reason of his willingness to wait. Imagination was therefore left free on both sides, to rejoice in its bargain. The partners, for instance, were welcome to visit their property-to-be at any time, and in the next months tirelessly did so. Skinner, in taking them the rounds of their estate, often pointed out to them improvements they would make, when he was in a large mood, or repairs he hadn't been up to, if he was in a restrained one—to both of which they agreed, like the indulgent landlords they were. Indeed, imagination was rampant on all sides that spring; even the children gathered at the fenceline when the partners left, to stare sullenly at the new owners, and behind them, sometimes the wife too. Skinner enjoyed it most of any, stepping with the lordly pace of a man whose property is wanted, and as came out later, making no more mortgage payments. The property itself needed to do nothing, being everybody's dream.

The new owners themselves worried a little, as they felt the advancing lures of property, heavy and light. As they would leave it, at a sundown, the mate often shook his head over it, looking back. "That woman's no housekeeper," he might say, as he had said that first evening, or something like. Jim, blinking equally in the golden outpour which hid somewhere behind it his watery birthplace, always summed it up his way, never varying. "Well," he always said, as he too had that first evening. "Well, that lets out Sand Spring."

During those months also, the trips to Oriskany—as they had taken to calling these, though they never went near the namesake town itself—seemed to take the place of other close relationships, or rather, to free them for still another kind. The mate, though still traveling regularly on his job, no longer found new land-and-home treasures, or was dulled or sated to them, now that he was owned. He found himself thinking of women again, or at least of kindly waitresses along the way, many of whom were extra kind in this magnolia weather, and it was no trouble at all to persuade Jim to ankle along with him in that sort of teamwork. The two of them found that the States were no different from Europe in these matters, only, in a queer way, more cynical. And don't be surprised that these matters are mentioned here. For, just because we seem to be constructing an idyll here—and maybe we are—doesn't mean that a man doesn't remember the more humdrum pleasures of such a time, as well. What is an idyll, but that part of a man's life which he will remember with clarity for all of it, so that all his years his tongue can go on touching it, as on a live nerve?

As for the Pardees, these other matters, that is, other women, even helped Jim remember them, whereas along the line of the sisters' usual destiny they might have been forgotten—though how so-called low women often help out the high ladies might not be appreciated by either side. But so it was—and so it sometimes occurred that he went to the Pardees for a pretended fourth time—the whole route there: two miles to the town, one and a half through it, and four round by the lake: all of it—but only in his mind. Meanwhile, in Sand Spring itself, people now and then tried to josh him about the sisters as the two veterans had; a love affair in such a place is often half audience. But as summer came on, it happened as might be expected; people forgot. Jim, on the other hand, though he didn't get out there, found himself mentioning them now and again; clearly he thought of the sisters as staying the way they always were, suspended, if not actually waiting. And if this had no direct value to the sisters themselves, nevertheless, somewhere along the stations of life they had gone up a bit. In one way or another, for somebody, they had not passed out of mind.

—

And now—the mate. We haven't talked much of him or seen his side, though we will. Perhaps we had better do it now; that way we will at least know more about him than he did himself. As the intenser emotions go, the mate certainly wasn't a late starter, but he wasn't hard about them either; he was sudden. To judge him correctly, as he went at a woman with his bull forelock, this ought to be said. Jim was a more practical man; he let himself dream of love. But the mate was romantic, he wanted a wife. That is, now that a house and lot had come his way, or almost, he wanted children to staff it, and that's one way to do it. He was always on the hunt for reality. Of course, he thought of all this as practical. But if you're going to be hunting reality instead of submitting to it, it's best to be sure you're hunting all of it. What the mate actually wanted was to find himself at the prime of life a self-made man, and everything tidy. In Lancashire, as a blackish boy called "our Jim," he'd seen this kind of life or thought he had, as far above him as the bit of blue sky to be climbed toward from the bottom of the mine. In France he thought he'd glimpsed it too, pointing it out to Jim in farm after farm of the kilometered farmland, every last tended inch of it cantilevering slowly toward heaven—until laid waste. In America, he said, once a boy had arrived here, it was no longer necessary to look upward, only to wait to be of an age to work and to root as prescribed. For this country, now that it had untangled itself from its own notions of Hiawatha, was already up in that fine blue, with almost everybody here. He'd pointed *them* out to Jim also—the tidy possibles all around them—a whole hemisphere of the self-made. Jim, floating his own watery pastures, had nodded, unable to communicate more than a tinge of his transportational feelings, of all the crowds of barges and liveries going down, derry-down, one after the other, ever since the first ape got down off the first limb of time.

"Down?" said the mate, his eyes staring ahead even of his hair. "Not in our time. What else can you expect of course, if you get mixed up with horses? Or sail." He knew barges didn't sail in that sense of course, though it was a question whether he knew that earlier in their history he would have had a point about the horses which had pulled them; he was speaking generally, or so he supposed. "Not in our time," he repeated. "Not the way the wheel is going now."

They were just finishing off half a lemon meringue pie bought at the local Sand Spring bakery, and it was awful stuff; back there so early in the century it wasn't all good homestyle cooking, though at that period only a bachelor might know it. With his fork, he scraped absently at the hard pie-shell left on his plate, a sign of how bad it was, that even this lightning-careless eater had balked.

"Ought to be another bakery here," he muttered; this was early in their housekeeping together; after that, for dessert they ate fruit. *"Down?"* he said again, at the same time digging the flat of his fork so hard into the crust that the tines clanked on the plate and the gray, floured bits flew. He was always a violent-moving man, everywhere except in his work which was so delicate; well, you know him, you know. Then, as if he knew this, catching himself about to slap Jim on the shoulder, he carefully rested his hand there instead. "Not this kind of wheel, not in a hundred years, Jim. Why—" He smiled slowly enough, his eyes blind on that horned hair of his forever probing forward. "And the first hundred years is the hardest. "Why—" And then he had to slap Jim after all, his hand coming down even harder than first intended, so that even brawny Jim had to cry, "Whoa."

But the mate's cry outshouted him. "Wheels?" he cried. "Why, son-of-a-gun; they'll be *our* ladder!"

So this was the mate, who was at the time, as you know, a surveyor. Already he had measured half of New York State with the aid of his old Gunter chain, and day after day was increasing his score; how should he know that this land-knowledge of his, pendulum-tied to the ground though it was, was still not necessarily of the earth earthy? So, this was the man who, when the most important kiss of his life, the wedding-kiss, still tasted deeper of fritter than mouth, didn't think one thing more about it. And this was the man who, standing in a parlor not the minister's and with sponsors not really kin to the bride, but with enough of the proper feather-hats tremoring and already so willingly remembering, and the bride like a rose in her rose satin since it wasn't a formal wedding, the pointed bodice of her as small at the waist as anything in Sears—this was the man who immediately after that kiss could shout out (with what the hats and even some of the watch chains could only take for heartiness since otherwise what else would they make of it?)—this man could shout out, *"I can see my* GRANDCHILDREN *now!"*

But let's wait a bit on a wedding which—and you might guess why, if you didn't already know it—concerned more than the mate. Let us get back to that time, past spring, on into the hottest summer, and after countless trips, sailing trips one could just as soon call them, to Oriskany—when the mate looked up from his stewed peaches to say, "What's about this Lottie, you once said."

He saw that Jim began to tremble. "Why, *Jim*," he said. Around the house they always named each other quite naturally, not having any trouble knowing who was who. When out of the mate's presence, Jim always called him "my mate"—not having to identify either the mate or himself to others being one of the virtues of Sand Spring. Whereas out of Jim's company, the mate, as if to emphasize that Jim belonged in the town more than Jim himself dared imagine, or as if referring to his friend's two years of higher education, or perhaps merely to qualities of character or reflection which gave him precedence, always called him by name—Jim. On the rarest occasions, as in the case of bankers but not waitresses, the mate would mumble out his own last name, then Jim's very much more clearly. There too, as in all their later walks of life, though he might tease Jim for his style of reflection (the while his own style of impulse never gave him time to ask for advice much less take it) the mate always gave Jim a tender, courtly distinction—the way one might treat a man wiser than oneself, even stronger, whose head, though ready and hard enough for any fight which came at him, was, nevertheless, compared to the speaker's, short on horn.

"Why, Jim—" said the mate slowly, "I wouldn't want to cross you up in any—" Nor would he. On their nights out together he didn't ever. He didn't have enough vanity for it—though more vanity would have changed his life, if not saved it; nobody gets saved. It wasn't that he didn't see people; he saw all his targets well enough, from old Skinflint, to the land he wanted the way a woman wants velvet, to the women too. As he once told Jim, he saw them all sky-blue upward, that was the trouble, as if he was still down there looking up to where they were all crowded waiting for him up there in the clear, hard azure of that hole. What he never saw, not at the time, was the sight of himself going at them. He does now though; he's been seen to start out, then stop himself, many a time. And it helps him of course to know, as Jim knew way earlier, that though some nip and tuck is worse than others, nobody gets saved.

For right then, what shook Jim was another one of those glances at the future, which is all that philosophy ever is, isn't it? "What's about this Lottie," the mate had said. Jim coughed, to clear his voice. "I said 'Lottie and Emily,' didn't I?" he asked. "Surely I said 'Emily' too?"

The mate regarded him. Jim was never a target to him; maybe that's why the mate sometimes looked at him as if safety was there.

Jim saw that too—as the mate could always be sure of—but just now Jim himself was wondering. Had there been anything special in the way he'd said it, months ago? Or had it been in the way the mate had heard it—in which case, had it been with a hearkening toward something in Jim's manner or something strictly private to the mate? "Surely I said 'Emily' too," Jim said. "Didn't you hear it?"

Still the mate didn't quite answer. After a pause, he said, "Are we ever going out there, sometime?"

Whether they would or not, wasn't what had given Jim the shivers.

It was—that if they did, things had already been settled, or else were being, now. It was—that right now, if the choice hadn't been settled on already, in secret archives somewhere—the choice was being made.

"Sometime," he managed to say, even nodding.

The mate nodded slowly back at him. "It was Lottie *I* heard," he said.

—

And this is the way things were in that part of the state when the last summer came for its interurban, overhead-track trolley cars. Here several explanations are in order, all of them swimming in the full, sad pleasure which is to be had in the description of any event single enough for its influence to be seen, yet faithful to an old cycle—and gone. We can let the cycle be for the nonce, having already said enough of barges and stables. But there still has to be explained how the main street of a town the size of Sand Spring, a street scarcely big enough for its own traffic light, came to be the terminus of a passenger carrier line which—though it never reached its plotted end a hundred miles away in the town of Batavia—did go along, neat as a parlor car on a leash, for twenty-nine of them, only to end up against a hillside in a gentle meadow as wide as a small lake, in among the rushes brimming the sides of an even smaller stream called the Little Otselica. To explain this will be an easy pleasure, follies of this sort being so familiar to everyone, and so acceptable when committed by the worldly—as this one was. Lastly, we have to speak in detail—some of it loving, but still so that you can see it and maybe even smell it—about the mechanism of that fine old sparkler and grinder, an electric traction trolley car. This won't be any harder, however, than you will someday find it to talk abour your old Thundereagle, or Hawkspit, or whatever it is you call those ruby-throated sports cars.

A Folly, says my dictionary, is a costly structure considered to have shown the builder to have been foolish. Add to this, that to my mind a folly is never really very national in outlook; men have been known to build castles-on-the-Rhine up the Hudson, and along the Colorado a Petit Trianon. Follies like these don't say much about the spirit of a country. Or much that's profound. But to my mind, a real, home-grown folly can be very local; I would know one of the upstate New

York variety anywere. On land, that is; what to say about the ones on wheels is still in question. But in any case—whether it's a castle standing dark against the vegetable green of an impossible mountain, or the friendliest tramline trying to sputter between mile after mile of people's herbaceous borders—what such a Folly shows is the spirit of the owner, just before that breaks through into humanity, or dies back into it. And humanity meanwhile being what it is, the kind of folly which delights *it* most is the hopeless expenditure of a man very well known not to have gotten his money the soft way, the whole history of his happenstance meanwhile being common knowledge round about home. On all scores, Adelbert Riefel's folly was of such a kind.

The Riefel house, running to pillars in the front, strange Amsterdam-style peaks in the servants' quarters behind, and two lions couchant before—and as such merely one of countless minor monuments to the last quarter of the last century—is still to be seen, and still appears to belong to a town larger than Sand Spring. Built on a fine central plot at the beginning of its owner's prime, always in heyday use in its carriage days, and later cut up into first-class apartments which never went unrented, it took care of him at the end of his prime, or what in some men would be past it, so that, except for what it harbored in its basement, the house itself was never a folly at all. Adelbert himself was the son of a scholarly Swedenborgian farmer—which belief we were taught in those days was part religion, part a sort of science—though that might be contested now. Adelbert, as far as anyone could see in the beginning, took over only the science part; like many another son of scholarly religionists, he went after money. First off, he went after a wife with it; he was a thinskinned redhead with a profile which must have taken on quite a nimbus at the courting hour, and indeed stood him well otherwise, all his life. Her money, it was said, was his stake. And the business he went for was fresh and decent enough: garden seed and related products, arboretums to hog-chows to fertilizers, but the rumor was that he was not benevolent. He was said to have taken advantage of all the financial panics of the eighteen-seventies except the last one, foreclosures sprouting an empire in his pockets. Mrs. Riefel sweetened the scent of their money by acquiring—at first not in the home house but in a conservatory in a rented one on New York's Fifth Avenue—one of the largest collections in the east of cattleyas, which she told the home garden club later was a *fancy* word for orchids. Then, at about the time of the last panic, though the Riefels were still unquestionably solid rich if no longer fancy, they came home to stay. People always wondered why, in Sand Spring this kind of change not being considered reason enough. Maybe the people Riefel'd grown used to taking advantage of out there had become his enemies—or his friends. He was still a young man, not even forty, younger than his wife. Maybe Swedenborg had bit him in the brain after all. Anyway, he came home.

Although Sand Spring social life wasn't of any level for them to lord over, give the Riefels credit, they now and then visited the cousins they had in town, and now and then had them formally back. According to them, he was as polite as all get out with them and with everybody, with the staff that served the house (a cook and a man from the "east," by which the cousins meant eastern New York of course) and with the rest of the neighborhood—he was even polite with his wife. According to these cousins, to whose social advantage it was of course to keep up the legend, anyone could see that formality was ingrained in Adelbert now. He had a library, so-called but also with books in it, in which he spent some time. His shirt collars sat out above his jackets in a way that none of those townsmen could match, even those who bought the best Rochester had to offer, and his cuffs were long. He was used to sitting in on committees and, it was suspected, champagne suppers, and though he didn't take much of anything himself, kept a small cellar for occasional visitors from the East and sometimes farther, though compared to western New York's groaning board his company dinners to anybody were very plain—the kind it took this sort of formality to be able to give.

Oh there were all sorts of details which would have been overlooked by anybody not as intelligently interested as the cousins—or the town. If he had the habit of light women, these were certainly not in the neighborhood, nor of course would they be; he would have mistresses, it was argued, whom he met in a hot, plush love-nest somewhere, though certain returned emigrés from the city (after all Sand Spring was less than four hundred miles away from it) said no, not that way, that it might very well be a much more rarefied business; in fact it might be what in smart circles was called not a love affair, but just "an affair." Certainly he went regularly to New York, though the manner of his goings and comings anywhere, if by nature distant with the town, was never furtive; now and then anybody could see him and often did, though even if the observer was only a foot of railway platform apart from him, and courteously spoken to as well, it still seemed to be from afar. He was at that time of his return a partially bald but still good-looking gentleman, who, if it was possible to compare him with his coevals about town (which it wasn't), already looked older than they did and yet younger; this latter characteristic was to emerge more and more. What we were looking at, I think, was a natural-born aristocracy, which the money had only added to—by keeping him in a certain state of organizational and philosophical health.

You've seen the type, we all have, and I've no doubt that the story of Adelbert Riefel, especially in those little details if not the big ones, has its place and specialty in the social rises of America at large, but we haven't got time for more of it than is strictly necessary, which some of it is. For remember the Riefel basement. In it there was already growing that engrossing folly whose later development, though it still didn't take up all of his time was to suck up almost all of his money, and would be of some concern to you also. For truly, in the furtive wheel-chain of life-events, those that can be picked out for sure as single and separate are very valuable. And it is a surety that without the folly that grew from Adelbert Riefel's basement, to become, as follies may for a time, a kind of practical enchantment—you grandchildren here and your daddies before you—all those unto the second and third generation that stem from Jim Eck and Jim Morgan, heretofore known as Jim and his mate, and in general to be known so hereafter—might not have been born. I'd go further, I'd say the odds are, in spite of occasional spurts of possibility (like that just now recounted mention of the Pardees) that you all would *not* have been born. And I ought to know.

Now—to the Folly itself. Your generation, I don't suppose it cares anything much yet for models or modelcraft that are not in the way of science or business—I mean model trains, boats, planes, collectors' soldiers, even model toy warfare. You're all for the hot-rod, or the stock-car race, or even the Saturday afternoon parachute jump at the county fair—for the moment, you're *in* it, as you like to say, for *real.* Chances are you don't know anything more about that other world than the Lionel trains I once got for all of you, all of them now in attics, or maybe one or two balsa-and-rubberband airplane kits you and some crony bought at a dime-store and put together when you were thirteen. And I don't suppose your sisters know any more about it than their old doll houses and tea-sets, or care—though there are always some women who go on to those other little pretties almost at once, to tiny furniture replicas of Williamsburg kept in a cabinet, or toy gardens with Dutch bulbs in them the size of nailheads—or even in their own lifesize houses, in not such an easy-to-see, boiled-down way, though in the end maybe nastier. Many childless couples have this fondness for the wee also—wee dogs, wee talk—and the Riefels were childless, but what fastened on Adelbert was not for coyness or charm, and came over him alone. It is a passion which can come over a grown man—maybe one who's never had much of anything, or maybe a millionaire in his maturity—when either of them cries or sighs to himself "What lack I now?" This is the way it begins, often—but often there's more to it, much more. You can't see it yet. Wait.

I understood it better, him *and* it, when, a middle-aged man myself and down to New York on a business trip, I happened to go shopping for toy trains for all of you children—grandchildren by marriage, and grandchildren by right. It was after-war time again, nineteen-forty-six, just after V-J Day—Victory-Japan, in case you never heard of it—and countless wheels we could all see had been turning like mad for years, as well as the silent ones also, which we could hear quite as well. But the little toy ones for the moment had stopped. That big toy store on the Plaza said that if the metal allowances were permitted they could still have what I wanted by Christmas—this was only August—but I wouldn't be there then, and they had nothing to show, to order on. After they understood that the castles and drawbridges, anything with soldiers foot or mounted, didn't attract me these days no matter how medieval—"We understand perfectly," said the salesman, "we can scarcely wait for the *domestic* stuff, I mean the peacetime, ourselves"—

they gave me a list of hobbyist shops where I might find secondhand plenty of what I had in mind. I chose a shop on Duane Street called the Train Center—trains, a simple standard set of childhood ones, being all I had in mind. This shop was out of business, I found, but I found another on Park Row, and another on Church. I had an afternoon to kill, and I killed it, and meantime old Riefel, whom I'd seen that summer of nineteen-twenty, and whom I had things to thank for, once more came alive.

You space-eater, you of the hot-rod—ever stand in one of those concentrated essence places called a hobby mart? Ever stand in a motoring headquarters for planes, boats, cars, railroads, and miles of track and roads for all of it, and miles of air too—which isn't more than fifteen foot square? Only to find out that people don't only buy them, they make them, with dinky models and construction kits and a host of suppliers and factors to this world—or they have them made for them, nowadays everything from TT trains to HO trains and roadways, to Frogkits and Minic Ships? From there I wandered into a shop that stocked ship-model supplies, blueprints and fittings, woods and veneers, then on to a shop that made only "experimental" models, by God, then to one which only did repairs. I saw them all—and, out of sentiment let's say, I've even now and then kept up with them, though not to buy. You of the Thunderbird, ever hear of model-car racing? Slot-racing? With equipment radio-controlled? But it was already all there in essence back then, the world still hasn't digressed that much, and it was then I understood what you've got no cause to yet, and what Jim and his mate didn't have any cause to understand either, the afternoon that Adelbert Riefel let them see his basement plan.

It's that after a certain age, and only after, there's a certain pleasure in seeing the world once again in miniature. Call these things hobbies if you wish, or if they get larger, follies, but they're not of childhood, nor of those akin to senility, and are never the devotions of youth. As for seeing the world in small but perfect, perfectly tidy, or having an urge to make it so, that's as it may be; this is the passion the partners thought they were witnessing that day. But I'm inclined to think otherwise. I think of it as a passion to see a world in small all right, but an enchanting and difficult one, a world with all its power lights always blinking on and off again, always in need of experimentation or repair. A world in small, all right—but for *real.* And I think of it as a reflective passion. Some of us, as you have good cause to know, take it out in talk. That's the commonest way. But Riefel had done it this other more solitary way, and perhaps even here had done it uniquely, for in shop after shop I saw nothing like he had, and maybe there never was. The urge to be unique in these affairs persists; maybe you remember what I came home with that year, the French-gauge electric train that no transformer could ever make really run? But Riefel's fault, and no doubt his reflections too of course, ran deeper. And—so did his folly. For in the end, he tried to see his world both in the small and in the large.

He must have had his small system custom-made, perhaps even in Europe, the cars and the whole thing, though that afternoon he didn't tell us this—the partners that is—saying only that he'd drawn the entire design and blueprints himself, taking the whole of one year to do it—the year he and his wife came back to Sand Spring. The execution of the plans had taken two years more. Maybe this explained the trips to New York, or maybe not—for when the mate made his acquaintance forty-odd years later (on a train connection out of Albany), he was still going there. Mrs. Riefel had long since died; her orchids had withered, replaced by housekeeper's fern; the house had been cut into flats. In one way of looking at it, he was only an old man of eighty-odd living on the funds of a once-grand house and on only one floor of it: did I say he retained just the basement floor? But in another aspect he was marvelous, sharp as ever but quietly so, none of that eighty-year chirp in him; in a ghostly way he was still even redheaded—and going to New York. But perhaps, yes—though we couldn't know for sure of course at our age—perhaps he wasn't quite so distant any more. Although it was the mate he'd first met up with, he appeared to know about Jim; here was the town again, at its function.

"I understand you two are mechanical in bent," he said, shooting one of those cuffs. The cufflink in it, as the mate described and Jim saw later, was as modern as anything you might wear, but in those days was still very advanced—an abstract design. "Perhaps you'd like to take a look one of these days at my little system," he added. He always referred to it that way, to differentiate it from the big one. "Of course I can't quite keep it up in the style to which it was accustomed, can't get the parts for it. But it's still worth a look."

Worth a look! We knew (the town again) that this was precisely what very few people did get; the cousins, in addition to knowing all the other nuances of his history, had continued to keep the town well informed. It all began, they said, back in his financial days, the peak of them, when he floated some debentures for such systems, or whatever it is that men like him floated. While men like Harriman and Frick had been doing it with the railroads, our Swedenborgian had sectioned out this little specialty of his own. Perhaps he'd even been the czar of it. Whether or not this had been true, the toy system we saw that afternoon was in commemoration of—or reflection on—a czar.

Though this was what impressed me most, and you may record still does—once inside, we had to stare first (though he certainly didn't make us) at the living-half of the basement. For though the entry door had been very natty in a way entirely new to us, we hadn't been prepared, even by gossip, for all the tricks of books and low shelves and high-hung pictures, and colors, and white spaces and black nudes, and—culture, I suppose it was—we now saw. I don't have to prepare any one of you; get married even here, you'll have it. It was merely certain parts of Paris and New York at the time, that we were staring at. Or nineteen-sixty-six, in Sand Spring. Only, this time we didn't feel any flicker of the future to make us tremble. Before it might have had a chance to, he opened the door to the other half of his establishment, and there we were, in his system or staring down at it, at his vast little world.

Did I say it was a trolley system? It was, of course, though it wasn't the one in *this* room which had ruined him. Though his story was all in trolleys (or as the bond issues said, tramways), the one we were looking at wasn't the one which had solidified him down from really gossamer rich, years before. That other system which *had* bankrupted him or nearly, over the period of fifteen years during which it had been built, brought up dead against a hill, but nevertheless run, and during a subsequent period of five in which he had paid back local investors who wouldn't have paid him in similar circumstances but whom he chose to call his creditors—religion again!—well, the two young men standing there didn't need to have that trolley system described to them, by cousins or anyone else. They had ridden it many a time, sometimes when it carried them near one of the few places it was near, or now and then, on a warm spell like this one, for the fun of it, with a girl. For Riefel, after his miniature was completed, had done what a fool always does, or a hero (he was Jim's and the mate's for a while): he had exaggerated. Intending to glorify man and country, but forgetting what small potatoes both were in that neighborhood, he had imposed his vision not just on a basement room, but on a region. The state hadn't helped, nor the public much either, but he had done it, whether for Mrs. Riefel to smile at him over dinner for, after a hard day in the conservatory, or for him to show off to someone else (the prospectuses and finally the pictures maybe) on hot Sundays—did I say he always went there Sundays, summers and winters too?—in New York. Anyway, with his own money, he had gone and completed to the third stage an idea which had graduated from the stock exchange to a hobby, and should have stayed there. He had gone on to build his transport system not only for real, but to human scale.

The two young men gloated down on this other one; they shook their heads and shuffled, open-mouthed. The way they hungered (until it was seen that their interest was mechanical not reflectional) it might have been thought that they were old. Riefel smiled, watching not his system, but them. Unlike most owners of machinery, he seemed not to want particularly to be asked questions on it itself, but Jim and the mate were at liberty to examine it, which they did for a long time. When Riefel finally sat down, his cufflinks glittered and shook; this might have been all that was said between the three except that it was clear to the pair from the first that they had touched him in some way; they could only think it because they were a pair, for afterwards he sometimes called one of them Damon, the other Pythias, though never especially caring which name went with which. And it was plain that he wanted to give them something—not the system itself of course, which the whole town knew was willed to the Smithsonian—but something he must have known wouldn't be apparent to them for a long time. Well, he gave it, eventually—as most of us elders do. Meanwhile, that evening and others, the pair looked.

And now, if I describe a trolley transport system through their eyes, so that you can see it and maybe even smell it, it won't make any difference, will it, that we are describing that one, complete in that room, instead of the huge, lumbering one that used to be on the road going from town, outside? The two systems were meant to be exactly alike, and except for the fact that natural wear-and-tear was a lot easier to repair on the large one than on the smaller—ha, wouldn't think that at first, would you?—and except for one other difference, they were. But when all transport of this particular brand is gone into eternity, which should be any day now, what difference will it make to the sound and shape and smell of what I tell you, that the smaller one of Riefel's systems ran the full projected hundred miles (scale so many inches to the mile) all the way to Batavia, while the other ran only twenty-nine miles, scale a mile to a mile of course, to the Little Otselica, then jammed up against a hill? Won't you still have all the information you need for that last trolley ride we're coming to?

What the two young men saw first was the artificial landscape of course, the stations and car barns, tunnels and bridges and aqueducts that any child's railroad set, any rich child's might have. But, where even then these would have been crude plaster-of-Paris glaring with smeared oil-color, and the roadside trees made of that fuzzed green permanence which is the exact opposite of chlorophyll, Riefel's landscape which he had painted himself was most vague and delicate for such a construction, running to pale hillside curves and winks of mirror-water; the green, when bent to be looked at, wasn't one color but dotted, and the trees themselves, which from a distance appeared to flourish, almost to wave, were not trees. In this way, it was the cars and their tracks which were made to stand out, those long cars, some with a maroon stripe from stem to stern beneath their windows, some with an Indian earth-brown one, but all the cars of the original gamboge paint worn now to the true trolley-yellow, and above all of them, the electric cables in one long pattern extended, like a black stitch learned by a master crocheter, and beneath the cars, in ess-shapes or flashing stretches, the tiny curves of pure steel. That way, the whole machinery of cars, tracks and cables, whether resting in silence, or in full, rocking motion with switches sparking and the incessant clang of the trolley-bell, appeared to be situated in or moving through the misty-moisty of early morning or dusk or even dreamland—but the cars themselves and their immediate paraphernalia stood out with the utter and clear concreteness of the real world. Only in one important matter Riefel hadn't done what was attempted by his other effort, the *Batavia–Sand Spring Interurban,* as the larger system was known. Here in the miniature one, there had been no attempt at passengers of any kind.

Here, the only passengers were the giant eye and arm of the owner (who needed to be organist, machinist, conductor, trafficman and Jupiter himself, all in one) and the equally giant, transported eyes of the audience. When the two young men had got through looking on, down and in, and even riding, which was the effect intended, Mr. Riefel allowed them to insert their great forefingers into the cars, to flip back and forth the caned seats, which reversed for the return journey just as in any system, and to touch and even take apart the dummy airbrake, handbrake and controller-box, which in each car were proper replicas down to their minutest inner parts—and even workable, had there only been provided hands of a size to guide. And here he stopped to give them a long lecture on the history of the "tram" or street-railway, British, American and Continental, from Liverpool, Edinburgh, the Potteries and Brixton, Vienna, Paris, Budapest, Nice, to New York and Washington, steam, cable and electric, step-rail and grooved rail, open conduit and overhead conductor—until he had brought them, a-clang and along from the old horse cars with the straight stairway, into the very presence of the single-deck, eight-wheeled, two-motored, center vestibule or transverse-seated, steel-tired, trolley car which any American of those years, in his rightful riding mind though surely not knowing as much as this about it (but even if he woke up to find himself seated in one in his pajamas), would certainly recognize.

The lecture, delivered by an expert lover, was the best the young men had ever heard on this subject, indeed the only one. Unfortunately, the times being always in every generation what they are, there is little need for us to quote here, other than to touch upon, for purposes of that later ride, some loving hints, tips and confidences on the subject of trolley riding, which we might never get anywhere else.

He talked for instance of the tiny rheostats inside the controller-box, of the shift from "series" to "shunt" which helped give the characteristic hitch to the grinding-along movement of these cars.

"The old cast-iron chilled wheels," he said. "You should have heard those."

He made them notice that, this being a country system, the roadbed wasn't paved, as required in cities, but laid only with a sett edging along each rail, the remainder of the surface being completed with tarred macadam, as could be done in country districts.

"This was also one of the economies we could put in on the Sand Spring–Batavia," he said, with a nod which, though neat, was the first old man's gesture they had noted in him.

Already they had noted for themselves that over and above the wheel-sounds, there was a constant play and obligato composed of the intermittent gush of the airbrake, the ting of the bell, the hard pull-up of the handbrake which at various points was required by rule to be tested, and wherever, by means of a movable switch, a car was deflected from one road to another—a zazzle of sparks. With a fine tongs, they themselves could turn clockwise the motorman's controller, though not grasp its wooden handle.

Finally Riefel, after advising them on the relative costs of conduit and overhead construction (the last being cheaper) ended with a little homily on design, pointing out that in the miniature system, as in the Sand Spring Interurban, the two overhead conductors were supported by ears from bracket arms carried on poles on one side of the road only, rather than by span wires strung across the roadway from poles on each side.

Now, all this time, both young men had been wanting to say something more than Oh and Ah, something to show their special comprehension, the way one wants to do when a man shows you the mechanical love of his heart. Accordingly, the mate seized this moment. He nodded. "That way the cables are much less of an eyesore."

From Riefel's eye on *him*—not cataracted wide, noble and frozen, the way an old duffer's eye should be, but still moving young and shifty—the pair knew at once that such words as eyesore were not remotely applicable to the system ever, not if poles had been strewn like matchsticks—or maple trees and telegraph poles—along the roadway here, or outside. But aristocracy has better reproofs, or folly has, both leaning heavily on superior information.

"Put it this way, gentlemen," said Riefel. "Dispensing with poles altogether is possible, and can improve the appearance of a *street. If*—all you *have* is a street." He touched a finger to the controls, lightly, but did not set them going.

"Where permission can be obtained," said Riefel, "span wires are sometimes strung from rosettes attached to the walls of houses on either side—of a *street*."

He paused, while footsteps were heard at the ashcans outside the rear wall of his estate, and a few seconds later, through the high small grilles that windowed the basement, the housekeeper's shoes went by. Already the visitors could see how uncalled for the mate's comment had been, even silly. Houses on the path of the system here, as on the Sand Spring–Batavia, were only occasional. They could see that this was not a village street but countryside, at times even open country, wild and imperial.

"But this is an *Interurban* system, gentlemen," their host continued. "Village-board ratifications, individual permissions? The object is to avoid all that, in favor of cheap, unoccupied land. The object, gentlemen, is *distance*."

He said all this in a twenty-by-forty basement room, but it didn't sound crazy, no more than it would once have done in a paneled room bank-high somewhere—or no more than other systems have, at other times. "That method," he continued. "The method of the rosettes?" He pursed his mouth as if they had mentioned these, not he, and as if, behind those words he was meanwhile ticking over whole manuals of methods he wouldn't bother their patience with. "This method has been largely adopted in *Germany*."

Given the times, the emphasis was perfect. They saw what a salesman he was, final proof being that, watching his manicured fingertip, they hungered for him to set the system all to going again, all the dream-miles of it, bells and switches, sparks and clang—but he didn't. Hungry they remained.

When they got out of there, they spoke of this, of what a salesman he was, and of what lessons he could teach them for use in their own business, though lessons of just what remained back too far in their minds to be fastened on precisely, or just on the tips of their tongues. But curiously enough, the fact that they saw the folly too—could even ride out on it to Otselica, sitting in real seats—made no damn difference. As prospectors themselves, the sight of a folly like this could even make them tender, over another man's noble mistakes.

"Felt like a stockholder myself," said the mate. "A possible one." From his tone, it was an interesting feeling. "Open my mouth, I thought, and one of those debentures will float right in. Ho-*lee,* Jim. To own that sort of thing, not only land, but a whole—system."

"And did you notice, Jim" said Jim slyly, "he always referred to it as the *Sand Spring*–Batavia? Never, not once as people do, as the *Batavia*–Sand Spring."

After that, the two managed to go back fairly often, more often than not with some tribute token from their nimble fingers, maybe wire replacements, or hard-to-get parts for the motor-generator or static transformers; once Jim made a tiny battery with his own hands, and once the mate dealt with one of the bogies—that's a swiveling truck, you hot-rods—from the main body of one of the cars itself. They got used to the housekeeper coming in there, down to the basement, with a pitcher of grapejuice or lemonade, the pitcher being one of those huge, zinc-lined, silver Reed and Barton coolers which good houses in that part of the state and westward used to be sown with, and they got used to the sight of that dandified cufflink pouring it, neither of them missing the good whisky he must have known they never drank anyway. Beer, on the other hand, wouldn't have been proper to the relationship; from him, who never drank it, to them, it would have been almost an insult; these social distinctions, or menial ones, run very fine. Or used to. Meanwhile, if Adelbert Riefel had any champagne memories, these didn't appear to bother him, or else were spared for other environs; as for his two visitors, whatever the effect upon them of civilization—as I believe it is called—they were unaware of it. When the three of them bent over a section of track which was out of alignment, or examined an insulator, or touched up a chipped platform-finish with a bit of japanning, none of the party of three ever spoke of anything but what was immediate; nothing hots up the present better, does it, than a bit of mechanism to repair?

So, as that spring wore into summer and was finally lost there, and the basement system flourished—looking sprucer and running better, its owner said, than in the last thirty years of his tinkering—it came as almost a surprise to the two partners when, as August came forward, town chatter recalled to them that the terminal moment was drawing close, ever closer, for the Batavia–Sand Spring. For the Interurban, however one might choose to put the rest of its name, was dying, not at the usual rate, which had seemed to keep pace with general mortality, but speeded up now, as a transportational disease sometimes does, so that everyone can see its end coming. In this case, state bonds issued to underwrite the cost of a highway along that very roadbed had found no want of subscribers; at midnight on the thirty-first of August, the Interurban cars must stop forever, officially dead.

There are always some, however, who will make a celebration of anything, and indeed they may be wise. Not every turn of the wheel can be as clear as this one, at least to a certain section of the populace, at a certain time. Not every system dies, clean and elderly, in a field. Who celebrated the last phaeton, chariot, *growler*—yes, we'll come to that; who, for that matter, in that neighborhood and eastwards, the last ridden-for-need, non-racing horse? In this case, a full centennial not being in order, the event would take the simplest form and a very chaste one compared to some which have been heard of—in the shape of a last trolley ride—to the end, ride a cockhorse and back again—of the system itself. Whatever junketings and picnics always cluster around such affairs began at once to do so, but the men of the committee in charge, seeking for more dignity, suddenly found it. And in America, this kind of dignity means history, no matter of what kind. Mr. Riefel, follyist but founder too, must be invited, if not to preside over the fête, then to be present and honored in the character which thirty years had given him, as a "past pioneer." It was a question whether he knew of his own transformation, unconnected with the company as he had been since it had lost him his fortune; but in any case, such an invitation, to a man of his distances, was difficult to broach. The cousins, dead as his wife's orchids, could no longer advise. The housekeeper wasn't up to it. His tenants couldn't say they knew him well enough to ask him—who in the town did know him, more than a nod and a greet? But, as usual, Sand Spring had been watching. So, it was entirely natural, just as it was for the two Pardees to go on being forgotten in so many connections, for the two Jims to be remembered in this one. "Unless," said one of the committeemen, with a backward chug of memory which was for this town in no way remarkable, "unless—and of course it's no use to us—wasn't there once somebody in New York?"

If so, the two young men, as they walked toward the Riefel house one evening, bearing the town's invitation, handwritten by one of the librarians—knew nothing about it. Still, they were troubled to be carrying such an elegy with them, for so they considered it, on a night when they felt themselves so essentially alive.

The mate, whose hands were always cleaner than Jim's factory job allowed his to be, had the letter in a fist, but put it in a pocket as they approached the portico of the house. In the black-green dark, the big place with its several apartments all lighted looked solid enough, if not festival, and the porte-cochere still possible to carriages. Were they taking advantage of their friend, to bring such a request out of the blue, not an *up* blue, but fairly a down one, the mate wondered? Or, Jim wondered, was it an act of friendship to do it at all? And as was so often their custom, they wondered these things aloud. The Riefel lions, gloomy as usual, gave no hint. The basement door, ivory black and with a thin gold knocker, snooted them, but this was usual. There remained for Riefel himself to help them with what advice could be given—and it was Riefel who gave it. Their problem was merely to think over what it was he gave them—for forty years after, if necessary.

When he let them in they saw that he had his smoking-jacket on, as always when he had been working on the system, plus the foulard neckerchief which he wore when taking "infusions" for his "catarrh." If things went as usual, he would apologize politely for the latter, the only apology he was ever heard to make. Shortly he did so, and as per custom, took them into the other room where, stripping his cuffs, he prepared to entertain them with a brief display of one or other of the elaborately worked-out schedules in the system's repertoire. This was the moment, ordinarily, when either of the pair would bring out whatever they invariably had for him. "Look here, this lightbulb I found, think it's small enough?" Jim might say, hauling out a pocketflash bulb that might just screw into a streetlight, or the mate would bring out a battery, the size of four sugar loaves, that he had made himself. Today they brought nothing, and he didn't wait for it.

Next, usually had come a moment when he offered them a choice of the schedule to be run off; you understand that in a run of a hundred miles, or even twenty-nine of them, and in thirty years, there could be a good many variations, mock breakdowns, accidents, full and partial runs, which could be evolved, a favorite run of the two partners being: *Let's see you run as far as Pell's bridge in sixteen minutes* (one minute of ours being five of the system's), *run into trouble* (the least being to have some foreign object strike the vertical gate of the lifeguard, the worst being to have a "passenger" struck by the axle-boxes of the rear bogie truck, when leaving the car), *then change cars and return.* Riefel didn't wait for a choice here either, but without preamble gave them the full hour program which they had seen only once before—that first time—in which all the powers of system, landscape and the hand at the helm of all of it were to the fullest vaudeville displayed. It ought to have brought down the house, as it had then, but this time they all sat silent. Then Riefel did something he'd never done before—made a criticism. "One thing I've never been able to add to it," he said.

"What's that, Bert?" the mate said quickly—no *mister* or pulled forelock for him, for which Riefel, who always winced with pleasure at this style of address, may well have picked him up in the beginning.

And: "Maybe *we*—" said Jim.

But Riefel shook his head, tapping his fingertips to a rhythm, making and unmaking a finger cage. "Oh—I suppose I could burn some oil, make some sort of blower. But it's really not tenable. Nor should it be."

"What's that, Mr. Riefel," asked Jim. "What *is* it?"

He was turning his beautiful cuffs down again, and linking them. "Just the true trolley-smell," he said. "Just—the smell." He quirked at them, to show he shared their amusement, which however hadn't yet appeared. "Just as well," he added, linking the second cuff. "A line has to be drawn somewhere. Just as well." What with the unintentional rhyme, it sounded, curiously enough, like an elegy. Then he stood up.

"Boys," he said, though often he called them "gentlemen"—"You might as well hand over what you have for me." He even held out his hand toward the mate's pocket. It was the town again, though they never knew via which part of it. He had known about the letter all the time.

He read it in their presence, no excuses and no comment, only in his narrowed lips and raised nostril a glimpse of how once, when he had wanted to be, he could have been rude. It may even have been that he wanted them to see this, to see him too, in full vaudeville. But they hadn't the experience for it, to enlarge on any further suggestions or displays he might have given them—what did that pair know of tickertapes and board rooms? So, in the end he had to tell them his answer, straight out. "No, boys," he said. "No. But I'll give you an answer to take back with you."

He went to a typewriter which must always have been there but they had never before noted, under one of the nudes they so often had. To the town-committee's letter to him—handwritten in the best Spencerian for courtesy, he rattled off a reply at sixty words a minute—for modernity? Who knew, after all, what was this man's cultivation? He slipped the sheet into an envelope which he left unsealed, and handed it over, back to the mate. "Read it if you like," he said indifferently. Then he smiled, with that nimbus which might still have caught him a million, if not a woman, even then. "But not here."

They understood then that they were dismissed; though the pair acted so often in unison, each was still as sensitive a young man as any to be found acting on his own anywhere.

Jim spoke up this time, the mate after all having had the letter to present. "Then, Mr. Riefel—" he said—it was curious how this "Mr. Riefel" sounded more intimate than the mate's "Bert"—"Then you're not—"

"Going?" said Riefel. He glanced down at the letter he had just answered. "A last trolley ride?" he said. "And a medal?" He looked down again, as if to check what hadn't been important enough to remember precisely, or else didn't cater to his brand of recall. "For a past pioneer?" At a jerk of his head, quickly gentled though he didn't smile again, the ascot fell back from his throat. He didn't look ruined any more than he looked eighty. The ruin, if anywhere, was in the minds that looked at him; it can be wondered if for lots of follyists it isn't the same.

"Oh no, gentlemen," he said. "That isn't for *me*."

He was telling us what the world is, for a man of risks—not that we heard him.

"No," he said, gentler with us than we had ever heard him. "No, you two go. It's for you." He gave us a searching look; it could even be said he bowed to what he found. "Yes, you two go," he repeated. "It's for you."

Then the pair went out of there, never to see him again or thank him, or curse him, for what it took two weeks—and forty years after that—to understand.

Outside, the two walked along with Riefel's reply. Should they read it, they asked each other; did he mean them to? From street lamp to street lamp they pondered, in separate silence, and aloud. In their ears that alternating voice echoed, offering them advice they couldn't see, calling them gentlemen, then boys.

"What did he mean!" The mate's voice was angry. "About the trolley doings. That it was for *us*."

Jim was silent. "I dreamed," he said then. He turned excitedly. "I just remembered. That he shot himself. Tomorrow morning."

They both saw him according to their joint experience, his chin at that certain ghastly angle, blood all over the olive-green foulard—which was a color quite suitable to combat—alone on a foreign field all his own.

"No," said the mate judiciously. "That's *your* dream."

They walked on. The mate reared up his forelock. "It's a cinch he doesn't see us the way the town does. Or only. Reason I always liked going there." There was an implication that they wouldn't go, again.

Jim thought it over a few paces. "He sees us," said Jim.

Finally, one of them—it doesn't matter which—opened the note and read it to the other. It contained absolutely nothing the librarian couldn't have read out in the children's reading-room—nothing beyond a formal thanks and a formal refusal, saying that he would always have an interest in transportation, but expected not to be in town for the ceremonies.

"He just wanted to get us out of there," said the mate disgustedly. But a few steps onward, he stopped again. " 'No, gentlemen,' " he said, in a falsetto that certainly wasn't Riefel's. " 'No, that isn't for me. It's for you.' " He turned to his companion. "You suppose he meant we shouldn't go for the town; we should get out of here?" He paused. "Or—Oriskany." They had spoken to Riefel of it. The mate considered. Then he shrugged, drawing himself up with a pomp that was a little growing on him; after all, there has to be some answer to the terrors of the world. "I suppose he only meant—we were young."

"And simple," said Jim. He looked down at the note. "We did the wrong thing. That the town asked us to do it isn't any excuse."

"They only wanted to honor him."

"For what? For being—passé?"

That was a word much in the newspapers, those days.

"For being self-made, that's what."

Jim already knew the mate's aspirations, of course; his own were harder to explain, though he had tried. He wasn't sure he was a man for risks, though he might be one for responsibilities. What worried him uniquely was the thought of so many men returned from the war with twenty-twenty vision, but still, if they weren't careful, going to live it out in the dark, not knowing which of the two choices was happening to them. What he wanted—almost as good as a religion it would be, mate—was just to understand what happened to him, as he went along. Was that so enormous?

He tramped on awhile. "Maybe they don't know why either," he said. "Why they asked him."

"Who?"

"The town."

The mate trudged along, hands in pockets. "Passé, eh? Then why should those hijinks be for *us?*" He gave an angry laugh; how mystery always angered him! "What's he preaching?"

The pair mulled the rest of the way home without talking, like two apprentices leaving the house of a master who had never quite seen fit to declare openly the nature of the subject under study.

At their door, the mate gave a snort, then a swagger. "Sunday week, that junket is—You for going?"

"Why not?" said Jim. "Nobody's going to shoot himself over it in the morning."

Going up the stairs, the mate yawned and stretched. "Transportation interests, huh. Maybe we ought to sell him a car."

But a few days later, they learned what these interests had been. Riefel had sold the house, as the good income property it was, for a crackerjack sum (the town's phrase) only to reinvest it promptly in some crackpot scheme (its phrase also) for motor coaches to go down the very highway which was to supersede the Batavia–Sand Spring. The housekeeper was retiring on her annuity, only waiting for the new owners to take formal possession—and for the Smithsonian. As for the basement, except for the art work and the books, which Mr. Riefel had taken with him where he was going, the rest of the stuff there was left to her also. Apparently he had already everything else necessary where he was going—in New York.

"Sonufa gun," said Jim. "So *that's* what he was saying!"

"What—buses?" said the mate. "That was his interest, huh?" He wasn't stupid, only not reflective—or unable to wait to be. And Jim, to give him credit, always understood this, just as the mate gave Jim credit for being such a thinking chap, if slow.

"O.K., buses, New York City, what does it matter. Can't you see what he was saying to us?" Jim had to walk twice around the table, he was so excited.

"What?" said the mate, much used to these dialogues, which he thoroughly enjoyed. "What's the revelation?"

"I'll tell you what he was saying." Jim whipped a napkin from the table, folded it around his own neck, ascot-style, and raised his chin, Riefel-style. *"See my dust,"* he said. "That's what he was saying." Then he pulled the napkin off again, and sat down to his meal.

The mate made no reply for a bit, as often when he was stumped, or slowed. *See my dust.* It was a transportational interest all right; it could be the supreme one.

The two of them could see it underwriting—or overriding—all others, a little searing tail-light disappearing round the bend.

"Going away *permanently,*" said the mate after a while. Such had been the message to the housekeeper. "At eighty." He shook his head, the prime of life not being connected in his mind, with age. "Old *men*—" he said.

That's a chorus for you. For *you,* hot-rods.

Old men, old men, old men. And young.

And so there we have it all now—the war, the town, the Pardees, Oriskany, and Riefel—and the two Jims. And all entirely natural.

We need only a ride on the Batavia line, to make it all clear.

III

People came who wanted picnics. The August day at the start was one of those gray, limp ones which make bunting look weak, but the powerful trees of the region would have done this anyhow. Even at the edge of town, at the siding where the four long, striped cars waited, the trees were as thick as if only they held the year up; once past it, and the green billowing would go on for miles. Nobody minded that it wasn't a day when colors flew; a couple of the mothers were heard to say tranquilly that the children would be the quieter, for not having to match their doings to a broad sun.

"Local adage?" whispered the mate, digging Jim with his elbow. Usually, he never went at the town for any of its doings—as was sometimes Jim's privilege. For months at a time, the mate's very speech would be as Sand Springish as if he had been born there; in matters like these, his control, then and later, was scarcely to be believed. Today he looked marvelous, with life, if not top good looks. He had as much as said so to the mirror himself, while shaving with a razor stropped to a murder-edge and singing over and over a little catch that Jim had never heard him on before. Talcum was delicate on his jowl, and he had on the tweed jacket he'd got in London on their way home and had stored since, but the bow tie he sometimes wore for the waitresses was supplanted by a proper four-in-hand tie. Jim, though not as rakishly clean, looked all right alongside; he was never a dresser. He was a worrier though, or some would call his bent by that name, and now he didn't answer, scanning the crowd, his hands squirming a bit in their pockets. Bunting had its own way of theatering up a crowd, as if the parts to be played were already evident; within its framing ribands and below its fluttering pennants, grannies jostled what used to be called sparking couples and drugstore cowboys; family circles were storming the cars to set up two seats facing one another, then tongue-lashing the juniors for slapping back the seats too roughly; everybody looked distinctly himself as long as he stayed away from the trees; the trees could do nothing just now but wait. A group of black-cloth notables clung together, speeches in hand; the ceremonial part of this jaunt would take place at Otselica, or so everybody supposed.

"All sorts here," said Jim, his eyes roving; then his hands came out of their pockets, having found what they were looking for. "I know what it is," he said, smacking his thighs. "We forgot lunch." They hadn't forgotten to bring it; they hadn't made it. Domestic as they could be inside the house, outside it, like bachelors, they forgot.

"There'll be hawkers surely," said the mate comfortably. "Or the Women's Auxiliary, with a bang-up supper. Can't be bothered ourselves with aught of that, today." Jim had never heard him speak like this, British but not his own Lancashire, more like one of their comics. The mate's forelock went up, as he surveyed crowd, trees, women, men and children—the world. The small exclamation he made then might have been in his own woolly, boyhood dialect.

"What is it?" said Jim. For a moment he had half an idea that it was Riefel, here after all for his honoring. A charge of disappointment—as of a hero dropped—went over him. The mate saw it, and understood it too, and shook his head. "No, Jim. Going toward the rear car." He lowered his voice. "Am I right? Look there."

He was right of course, about the women if not the hawkers. A buzzing line of them, burdened with salad bowls, pitchers and the like, were climbing one after the other into the rear car, surely setting up a commissary there. But this wasn't what made the mate's hand clamp Jim's nape in a vise, forcing him to stare only one way. Tag at the end of the line, a procession of three straggled after. The two girls in front might have been any young pair, sisters or not, one thin and striding, one full-blown—but the thin one had a large wire strainer on top of her bundles, and the rosy one held in her arms a cannonball pot. The sun glinted through the trees now on this strange armor, as the pair came shyly but steadily forward. A boy with a handcart pushed after them. The potbellied iron affair in the cart might have been the sisters' catapult, trundled along to storm a town's ramparts. It was too small to be Bismarck, but it was a stove.

The mate came around from behind Jim and stood in front of him, watching, and continued so all the time the stove was being hauled up onto the platform of the car, though the girls had long since disappeared inside. His hands crept to his tie and he spoke thickly to the tip of it. "We'll eat, luv," he said. "Ohh, we'll eat."

By the time the ten o'clock departure hour had stretched on, in the way of outings, to eleven, the mate had managed everything, Jim following behind. Inside the commissary car, a few tame husbands and boys at their mothers' apron strings were helping make things fast for the journey, and the mate, quickly attaching himself and Jim, in short order found himself at the head of the crew. The day's plans were for a box-lunch on the way or there, an evening supper at Otselica, for which the women had brought everything from Sterno heaters to wrapped ice, and a moonlit journey home; it was the full-moon part of the month. There would be swimming, of the mild, foot-or-two-deep water which mothers love, if the dryish Little Otselica would cooperate, and opinions were that after such a moist summer it would. For, just as it sometimes happens with a certain dinner-party, a regatta, or any other form of social endeavor which may or may not revolve around some science of human motion, every portent for this day on the Batavia Line—even the gradual gilding of the sun through the trees as the cars waited there—foreshadowed success.

The rear car had been singled out because, unlike the ordinary ones whose seats were arranged toast-rack style from stem to stern, it had an open middle section where two pew-style slatted wooden seats faced one another, leaving a space between where the picnic goods could be piled; Riefel had a car like it in his system at home. Front and back of the center, the seats were like the trolley-style anywhere, made of that old yellow cane which wore forever—or would have—and with a metal handle at the aisle-side top corner of each, so that the seat might be reversed for the return ride. In the last seat, forward of the platform where the stove stood in readiness for unloading again, the Pardee girls were sitting. Both of them had a high color, whether from pleasure at the committee's having remembered to invite them, or over their own business initiative in getting themselves here, who could say? Jim, for the life of him, couldn't walk straight over; he didn't even want to begin all that doubletalk again, but in front of him the mate was working steadily toward that end of the car, and might have made it first if a sweet, Quakerish old lady-hen with a round eye, tight skin and china teeth—I can see her yet—hadn't stopped him for talk and then proclaimed—"Why these poor boys have no lunch along!" In the general banter—"Now just who were you counting on?"—Jim found himself facing the girls. He'd only got as far as a nod when the mate came up the rear, close behind him. Jim turned—yes, that's how it was, Jim turned—and the mate, coming abreast of him, stopped short, and gave the two girls the once-over. He meant to treat them as ladies, then and later, but a little of the waitressy warmth came through. Lottie had her plump little hand in the box-lunch; perhaps that was why she raised her eyes full wide, while Emily, for all her spirit, lowered hers. The mate's eyes were on Emily, no doubt of it.

"You're not . . . Lottie?" he said.

She shook her head, smiling slightly, but her eyes on Jim now, as if to inquire what story he'd been handing his friend.

"Why no . . . she's Emily." Lottie had just swallowed, and now she laughed comfortably. *"I'm . . .* " A few crumbs clung to her small, freshwater-pearl teeth. And it was Lottie, the behindhand one, who moved over easily and made room between her and her sister for the two men. The two men looked at each other; for the space of a breath perhaps they gave each other the once-over. Then Jim, the behindhand one, slipped in front of the mate and sat down beside Emily, and the mate slipped in docilely after, next to Lottie—after all, he was only wanting a wife. Her dress wasn't lowcut, but that bust of hers made any dress seem so, and the mate, being the shorter man, would have the closer view of it. On his other side, Jim was floundering in that worst of doubletalk, when a woman isn't saying anything at all. He had a feeling that whatever he said would set the tone for everything ahead of him—maybe they all did; the feeling itself was acknowledgment that a moment of choice had passed forever by. When his remark came it was another of those nothings. "You got to town," he said.

At first, the picnic in itself wasn't too much for personality over and above what a hundred years of lemon tea, and chocolate cake for the ants to eat, has trodden into memory's communal ground. Even eating in a trolley car—or auto, or aeroplane; just *plane,* you boys say—doesn't much change the reflections common to eaters of the hard-boiled egg. But here, once everybody relaxed into the riding, which happens in any vehicle, then they had the novelty of an outing in one in which they had ridden unthinking on daily errand and jaunt; it was the way it would be if the New York subway should stop forever, and the populace have a day of picnic there. There were stops for comfort along the way, with much hopping on and off of children and one almost-left-behind nursing mother who ran out to flag the lead car just in time; at each stop everybody remarked how well the committee had done its work, in even going ahead yesterday to Otselica, to set up facilities there. Everybody also reminded everybody else that the route was now being observed for the last, the very last, time, since when traversed again, it would be dark.

So far, there hadn't been any wonders of the world, only the two bordering townlets where they had stopped off, separated by a country road; for most, this was as far out on the Batavia line as any had ever been. But as soon as they had left behind these two hamlets, the leafage and the gradual wildness began; soon they were running along handily through a lovely vale, between arching trees which now and then met and tangled high above. It was a tingling pleasure to feel lost this way, probing a limited unknown, with the car grinding and swaying along its high wire, between one's legs that secret teasing of the motion, and all around one the caravan's sense of good provisions hard by one, and homely friends. There were no houses here to hold the span wires between them as in Germany; this was unoccupied land. The little boys aboard made a game of counting the poles.

The air grew cooler, delicious with vines, and those who had brought sweaters were wondering whether they should be the first to fuss themselves into them, when—the lead car stopped, with a lurch that sent people and packages against one another, but nothing broken, just one little boy down in the aisle. The news came relayed back, after an ominous quiet of precisely two and a half minutes; there was a jam in the overhead wires due to overgrowth not having been pruned—nothing was wrong with the current however, all would duly be well. And in a few minutes, with a crackle from above, and a sizzle of the sparks the children complained were so hard to see in the daytime, they were off—a picnic scare, a picnic adventure, precisely to scale.

This happened untold times before the morning was over. It was impossible not to feel better acquainted all-round, characters emerging ever stronger, naming themselves from the settled corners of the car: the lady and children in seat Left Two, the couple up ahead with the big basket, the little Quaker hen forever nodding, the motorman up ahead, whom all were shy of speaking to, because he was to lose his job. The sagest heads of all nodded over the line's demise; clearly it had been the costly upkeep which had done it; no, said others, not with patronage it wouldn't have; it was because the line didn't go anywhere. "Twenty-nine miles to nowhere!" somebody said. "Unfinished, if it had been *finished*—" said another. Whose fault was that? Nobody was heard to mention Riefel by name in any connection, but several spoke of the buses to come, most with contempt; where cars as handsome as the one they were on had failed because people simply wouldn't, didn't, how would buses—and on a roadbed as wild and unpopulated as this? They were drawing along now, for once uninterruptedly, through the last few miles before the terminus; some wag had put up a sign which said "Shin Hollow," and a little farther on "Great Bear Mountain," which was in fact the name of the hill. Now the car swayed and ground on through darkest woodland; the committee had had a man on the tracks clearing for a week before the excursion—buses *here?* Nobody could visualize it. Then the motorman spoke up, nasally proud; indeed he had been promised a job with the new buses, which however were going another route, and everybody was relieved for him yet irritated, since if he had been listening why couldn't he have volunteered this information earlier? Conversation on this point all but stopped; appetites had started. A few voices persisted, halfhearted, on the subject of progress; consider how their own town had grown; since when had so many people in it barely known each other's names, as some here? Since the *war.*

The children meanwhile, hearing all this above their heads, looked wise without knowing it; something new was going to be added to the life ahead of them; they were on the voyage they had all along known they were, the original voyage, *out.* Box-lunches opened everywhere, decided on quicker than sweaters, and with food, the talk swung round again to character; there were those two boys down in back to be kidded, the ones without lunch. But they're provided for—"Watch it, you boys." Livery stable, a voice remembered. Boys? They're men, those two boys. "Veterans," whispered someone, and character sank again before this most remembering word. "It's the last time," mothers said to children who already had the look of those who had been kissed by governors of the state, and would grow up to shake the hand of some President. Remember it. It'll be different, it'll be dark—going back.

The Little Otselica. The creek and the hill. At about two o'clock in the afternoon they reached it, that perfected moment on trolleybed, roadbed or airstrip—the *stop.* There, broadside of the road, was the big bear of a hill which had provided the bygone stockholders an excuse to desert and curtail (though in Riefel's home system it was tunneled through), against Riefel's professional counsel that a transportation system cannot curtail, none of them can, being wars against nature; like wars, they must grow or fail. But now, the central carbarn, from whose peaked weathercock a flag had been lifted, and all the other outbuildings, all built of good stone, trellised and guttered in that homelike style in which small provincial railroad stations and their ilk used to be, stood out against the hillside like a village whose inhabitants, piped away by some pied spell and now released, were thronging back. The committee went first, in their black garb rather like a funeral it was true, but right behind them the women came marveling, gingering up everybody's spirits, including their own, with their polkadots and kangaroo-pockets full of children; the spirit of picnics, and cemetery visits, is always feminine. Certainly there was reason to marvel; from comfort stations to water fountains, to stalls, tables and even a dais in the "main hall" of the carbarn, the whole effect was that of a village built for one day. Even the creek had come up to snatch, with a three-and-a-half-foot depth of water, just enough for a child's scream to convince its mother it was drowning. Only the stationmaster's dried garden, lacking a resident these two years past, could not be revived. In the office behind it, the committeemen retired at once to huddle over their speeches, thus at once creating a government and a populace—everybody else could go free.

The two buddies and the two sisters could now devote themselves seriously, in a circle on the grass, to the eating which had begun, at Lottie's insistent offers, in the car, and now advanced from mere sandwiches to a spread that required damask napkins and got them; where other women reached the heights via cold chickenlegs, the Pardees' hamper, an affair which ran to real cutlery and continuous magic disclosure, opened on a capon still warm in its juices, and a creamy oyster pie. Thanks to Lottie's provenance—for though she quoted no recipes, gave no sign other than the loving way she patted the cloth like bedlinen and cradled the food in its napery, surely the feast was her doing—there was enough for everyone, except perhaps Lottie herself. But on this one afternoon perhaps she didn't mind; what she clearly asked of any hour was to be able to nibble it away in company under the perfect excuse of such an occasion; if the two bachelors had had any early squeamishness about "accepting" it was eased, in watching oysters go down Lottie's throat as if to their duty, and that posy mouth redden, as if with rouge. She was a dainty eater always, and also—if the flow of food and the prospect was constant—could acquire a kind of conversation. Articles were often read by her, as she ate alone sometimes, at home; did they chance to know that some cows in Japan were kept in stalls, fed beer, even massaged, to make the most succulent beef in the world? She didn't know but that she'd almost be willing to be a cow, in Japan.

"Wouldn't mind eating you," said the mate, lowering his eyes, but if Lottie heard him, as she dabbed after a crumb lost just where his glance was, his gruffness was so solemn that it couldn't be rude. The mate, who in the car had once or twice studied Emily, perhaps to make certain whether or not those dark brows did meet or could, never glanced at her now.

And what of Emily, stuffing herself like the rest, who looked anywhere she liked—at the day, the crowd, the mate and Jim almost impartially, though perhaps not much at Lottie—occasionally raising a lazy, drugged arm from where she was lying full-length on the grass in a dress that matched it, and who now, her brows knitting once and then smooth again, leaped to her feet in one movement, as if clasping a trestle let down from the sky, and said in that caroling voice of hers—"I shall swim!"? Disappearing, she returned in the same heavy blue bathing dress, sleeved and bloomered, darkening to black in the water, that others already in were wearing, but she carried no boudoir-cap of the kind that were here and there ruffling the Otselica, nor the canvas shoes which laced most ankles—her feet were bare. She swam face down, with a boy's stroke, her piled hair sailing the water. Jim and the mate, having brought no suits, watched her from the shore. Though the stream was only a few yards wide, when she rose, billowing in that blue-black drapery, and started for shore, she seemed to be walking toward them from a distance, and when she called out something they didn't catch it; even when Emily spoke normally, it was always the silence Emily spoke from which one heard. A few feet away from them she stopped, the water draining down her legs, and tossed her head at them. If they could have eaten her, the taste would have been like venison.

And so all that day, as in the night to come, events dispensed themselves in the mists of natural action. In front of the hill, as twilight came on, the rounded carbarn, grouped with its flat-roofed outbuildings, glimmered like a natural farm. But then, when it came time for supper, and with the others the four entered the huge "hall" which only the committee's helpers had glimpsed, the two men stood back, in rank silence. Stalls had been set up all along the great length of the pounded dirt floor, and among these they caught sight of the girls' stove—but that wasn't why. Instinctively, both men looked up, expecting to see a few chinks of sky, but here in this place the overarching girders were securely roofed. And unlike that other place where the two had met, there were rails here, domestic to the ground, of the same kind that in the center of town made a bicycle skid on its way down the avenue. If the trolley cars themselves hadn't been removed from here, any resemblance might never—the mate spoke first.

"Is the hangar, our Jim, isna it?" he said. "Is the hangar, for fair."

One could smell the oily rags; for certain there was that smell here; the crowd's hubba-bubba dwindled to the sound of men—mechanics, pilots, ground-crews. There was missing only the latticed sky, dirty or shining like a mussel-shell, beneath which he and the mate had worked their rags and told each other of barges and blue glare at the top of mine-holes; all that was missing was the down-whanging whine that sent them for the ditch and the brave, incoming putt-putt that stood them up to squint—planes didn't sound like artillery shells in those days. As if all the shell shock had been waiting there, Jim's ears filled with these now.

They all saw how white he was, the mate said later.

Emily spoke quick, reaching out her hand. She was back in her sailordress with its middy-tie, her hair damp-dry. "Come along, Jim, and help me." She took his limp hand in hers. "Come along and help."

He went along, but as it came out to the mate in bits later, for some hours it was to Jim as if the war had come down and in upon him like a plane itself—"like a plane landing through the roof onto the dining-room table, mate"—it was the war-thrust, at last becoming real to him, through no longer being so. Which was the realer then, was it daily life, for all except the dead on plaques? Could it be? Nobody in the hubba-bubba here in the hall, even the lamed or the bereaved, was thinking of the war in the overmastering way it ought to be thought of—held like a major wound in the mind. For some hours, he must have tried. Of all the remaining hours, through the din of supper, until he found himself with the others being loaded into cars for the ride back—he remembers nothing else.

"But it would take a Christ to do it," he told the mate later, and they both recall that they even solemnly discussed whether this was a reason for them to take harder to religion or give it up altogether. For you must understand that many of these bits being pieced together for you here and now, came out during a lifetime of friendship, and relationship too; half the time even you young fry don't stop to think which of the two Jims' grandchildren you really are. What if the main and most of what happened that day didn't come out in words between those two until a cold winter's day forty years later, when one said to the other, "Want to drive along and look at something; got something to show you, Jim," and two old men sat talking together, nonstop except to ease themselves once or twice, against a hill? The trip back, the ride back; that's when things really happen, even in memory. Though—even if nothing so secret had ever come out in such plain words before—all those forty years, both of them knew.

"Emily sat you down in a chair next to the fritter-stall," the mate said—that much later. "She managed you. You were cashier. Can't believe you don't remember, even *now?* And I was the barker, why I yelled myself purple, we must have sold more of those things that evening than the girls had sold in a year. Funny how, though I'm not much any more for even the best bread and cake—always begging your and Emily's pardon, and knowing what you've done with them—I can taste those crazy little snippets now."

"Recipe's lost," said Jim. "She always said."

"Sure is," said the mate.

And after a while and some further conversation, the two old men got up, brushed the loam from their trousers, got in the mate's Cadillac, and drove off.

But back to that day much earlier, when, after the commissary car had been reloaded, the two men and two girls left all that gear to the old hens who preferred to stay with it in the rear car, and made for the front one. As they climbed into the best seat of all, the last ones of each row, next to the back platform—where they could sit two by two and across the aisle from each other, the mate clapped Jim's shoulder hard.

"She bowl you over?" he whispered. "Or was it the heat?"

(Have I said it was getting sultrier and sultrier?)

Jim didn't answer, except with his shoulder, which took the blow unmoving.

"He's all right," said the mate out loud to all and sundry. "We knew you were O.K., Jim. Once you started making change."

And so he was O.K., for forty years, but still, those forty years later, going back in the Cadillac, and still being of the sort he is, and not too much shakier, he asked the old mate, "—and do *you* remember what you came up close over my shoulder and said to me while I was making change? Now I *remember.* About Lottie?"

"Yes, I remember it," answered the old mate, his voice final. And neither of them said another word about it, all the rest of the way home. Some things even memory is too late for, once they come out all of a piece. But we both remember it now. The crowd was full of faces; the body-heat in the carbarn, and the storm coloring the air sullen, made them appear mazy and on fire all at the same time. Behind in the stall the girls were busy but not forgotten, the one sister who was heard loudest in her silences and the other who was only something to see, but so much of it. The mate's hand was hard on the shoulder, the shoulder steady. "She's as solid a woman as anybody would want to stand by him. She's a dream."

"You mean—*her* . . ." said Jim.

"You know who I mean," said the mate.

Then, at least in that part of the world and its wars, it was time for the last trolley ride.

Lottie even said it out loud, in the tone of one who reads articles. "It's the last of the old Batavia. We must remember it."

"Remember what old Bert said?" said the mate—who was now sitting next to her—to Jim. "He never could get it, the true trolley smell."

Think he never notices—that's what people often think of the mate. And then, months after, or forty years on—out with it. Anyway, it was the last anybody there spoke of Riefel.

And now to the night. Will you be shocked at the story from now on, and if so, *which part of it*? That's what I'm wondering. But even if we held hands in a circle, a séance, and tried, your generation could never tell us; you're not shockable yet, you think; you wouldn't know. And now to that night.

All the time they had been loading, that sulphur-green quiet before a summer storm had been building, so that children cried out, peevish against the invisible weight in their breasts. The night grew glassier. Outside the waiting line of cars—a whole arkful, racked up tidy with their bundles—the moon was high over the hilltop, struggling with a barrage of clouds. *A ring around it last night*—clustered up in all the front seats, as old women do, the hens were telling over the almanac of their bones. The head motorman, their cossetted pet whom they had fed and nagged and now looked up to trustfully, up in front with his back to them, now suddenly got down again, and was anxiously observed in consultation with the other two drivers. Meanwhile, in the car at first so welcomedly anonymous to the two men and the two girls, character once more began willy-nilly to surface to the faces and to peer from unexpected corners: veterans, librarians, other stallkeepers met tonight. In answer, their own town faces surfaced, and they sat with their eyes lowered: the two buddies, and the two Pardees. Nobody spoke. In the yellow gloom of the trolley car, it was the familiar moment, the one before take-off, before—lurch and away!—the gathering clop-clop of the post chaise. The motorman climbed back in, and waited. Then thunder was heard, bringing the hills in closer, as it does in these parts. Then they were all lively at the windows, pulling them down as the storm broke, and the spell with it, or so it at first seemed. Inside the sealed car, while the rain swept white over the windows, the chatter softened almost to dove-talk, the tender, fraternal talk of the safe. Then it was over, and—they had started! Who had noticed it, the spark and the start, except maybe a child? What a success even the storm had been! It was a real cloudburst, the hens said.

Then they were swaying through the trees again. For the party in the rear, the spell had just begun.

The trees were a dark aisle of plumes now, as if the train of four trolley cars was running a gauntlet which never closed in. The trees held the night up for them, out to them, and there was only twenty-nine miles of it—unbearable not to crush it around someone and to one's breast. A waitress would not have been safe here. How locked and stoppered all their mouths were, in the moonlight that leafed their faces, through open windows that poured their first ride together back at them, cool summer balm. There was a zest in the air no sweater could slake, only arms. If the silence went on like this, or back into chatter, this ride would be their last anywhere; all felt sure of it but could do nothing. Only twenty-nine, eight, seven—back to autumn, to Oriskany—and out of mind. At what mile of it the current in the overhead wire went out—and stayed that way for two hours by hen-watches—I wouldn't be able to say. But I shall be able to describe it to the inch, to the nerve, as a man's tongue does, touching it. If you laugh at it, I'll smile with you; if you shock at the wrong moment of this account, I'll slap your faces.

Well . . . a few motormen's lamps were lit, of course, one glassed-in red oil-glow to a car, just the right light for the old to nod by, or the mothers to cradle their lot with a *put your head down,* but nothing to what the moon did for all the other restless ones. Two by two or in bunches, all the young folk, except for two pair of them, slipped to the back of the platform, then down. All had to pass the two men and two girls sitting in the seats chosen as the most anonymous, the best. As the others went by they would see the mate and Lottie stiffly figured in the lurid light, her bust, his forelock. Across from them, the other sister and the buddy sat rigid too, but like those garden statues which have the beginning of a stone smile. And after a while, if any hen was watching, she could have seen only the one pair, in the red light still unclasped. Opposite them, that other pair had gone.

Just outside the car, the trees flung themselves in dark fountains, like Versailles. Then came a meadow, shimmering like parkland and as vast, then more trees. Through the window, and a round break in the trees like the bright end of a kaleidoscope, the mate watched that other couple disappear until they were gone. Though their story might take years to be made into words, as he sat there beside Lottie he knew it already, and forever.

Out there, where it looked so mysterious—"Oh it was," said Jim forty years later, "and I don't mind telling you of it; indeed don't we almost *have* to, now?"—out there, Jim walked along beside Emily, slow through the wet grasses and in rhythm too, though they had not yet touched even hands. A paragraph from one of Riefel's manuals, he said, kept blotting in and out across his sight—"For simplicity of operation the overhead system is best . . . supply of power is not interfered with by heavy rains or snow . . . duplicate conductors are used and repairs rapidly executed." He hadn't known until now that he learned things so profoundly, and wondered that she couldn't hear these words *duplicate, execute* attached like a hissing refrain to his steps. Then he thought of what the motorman here had called out: "Take two hours at the outside to fix things, two and a half at the outside; things are that wet!"—and exulting life over miniatures, he laughed aloud on that black air—and was heard.

It was silver air that the mate saw, though he could no longer see them.

But under the trees, the air was surely black, in a patent-leather night with a gloss whose source could no longer be seen, and the ground was dry. Jim saw his own coat, miraculous on the ground, and couldn't remember laying it there. Then it was the moment that the locusts stopped, and in that buzzing silence, he thought he remembered everything else.

He could see the barge-canal, the lock bearded with green at the waterline, then the pocked brick and the flower-stuck crannies of the sides—if the barge was coming up in the lock—or the waving weeds on the lock's broad lip, even under the crossbeam of the gate, if the barge was sinking down. He could see the linkage, like an overhead wire or an underwater length of line, between trolleys and barges, though what it meant he couldn't say, or why it was a woman, the frittering women, who made him see it; she and this were fathoms deep. The war names came on now as never before and tumbled through his kisses, from Verdun to Chateau-Thierry, all the great plaque-names he had never been at, down at the bottom of the faintest script of those he had—and all telling him what up to now he had avoided: that it was his lot, his common lot to have to choose between terror and charm in all the moments of life past and to come—either to remember blood and death, to rise on their crests toward acts of atonement and change he knew he was not capable of—or to sink, sink, in the arms of the daily, under the daily charm. He remembered the washlines of that spring, and their mystery; what was the message of daily life, of a profundity that never stopped?

As he wrestled there, the town came and stood at his side, almost as if it needed to have people break out and away from its conversations—even lived by it. By how much or how often a man himself broke out of it, was that how his life was made?

And all the time, there was Emily hot as roses under him, learned in all that Europe hadn't taught him, or virginally born to it. She made him feel as if she was on the barge—a figurehead of those lost certainties—and he was on the land. The doubletalk that belonged to life was inside her. He reached it. She played him up and down like a ball on a fountain, and all the time, he saw the seriousness of her eyes.

When they came back to where the four cars were still lined up on the track, with the electric lights on again inside, they managed to attach themselves to a noisy young group just coming out of the woods from another direction, their trumped-up catcalls and banter fake even to themselves. "Why—" he whispered to Emily, doing it for the intimacy—"the woods are full of us." Looking back, he whispered to her, "Anyway, we've left the town there." He was bold enough to say so, if somewhat darkly, to the mate, not a week later, when certain preparations were already in order. Whatever Emily thought, they had stepped back into the car just then, and she had turned majestic, her cotton dress somehow straight as tin again; that he had slipped beneath it surely no one would believe. Nothing showed on him he felt sure, not even to his friend. When things go so right, a man's flesh—and I suppose a woman's—feels calm and even, doesn't it? Only the mind, mindless to its roots, is drenched.

The interior of their car, left in the pall of one red lamp, had changed. Now that the current was back on, it was bathed in yellow light reflected from all that varnished wood and cane, portaled by the in-pressing dark. In other ways too, it was like a picture. The mate and Lottie were the center of it. They hadn't changed their seat, instead seemed to have grown there, with big hamper and box beside them, or was it that the balance of the car—old wives and young, widows and a few men either old or woman-humbled—had turned to or gathered round them? The mate glanced up once as the others trooped in; he was talking. All were listening to him. Lottie's eyes were gleaming, and her fresh mouth too; though candy was circulating from a big goldpaper box beside her, no one would know she ever ate the stuff, except for the heap of candypapers in her lap, between her demurely draped knees. The mate had been telling them what people ate and drank in the county of Lancashire where he was a boy, such talk being a way to the hearts of many, as well to one. He had been discoursing for some time.

"They'll offer you tea, luv," he was saying—to everybody, or to one. "And they'll offer you what they call 'ornaments' with it. 'Ornaments, luv?' they'll say." His voice was charming, self-charming. "And what'll they mean by this?" He roared it.

Just then, Emily and Jim sat down in the seat across the aisle, and they and the others who were trickling in, immediately they were seated, turned round to watch him.

"What'll they mean?" he asked in a smaller voice, like an actor. He flicked one glance at the pair in the opposite seat, then did not look at them again. "Why—" he said, in the big voice "—why, they'll mean whisky, or rum!" He turned to Lottie. Sitting down next one another, their eyes were just even, he being short legged but long waisted, her waist being where one could not quite tell. "That's what they'll say, luv," he said to her, and for her only. " 'Will you have ornaments?' "

But if nobody therefore looked at Jim or Emily, or seemed to search for other miscreants, this didn't mean nobody knew, or wasn't going to gossip about such walks in the woods, later. If they let it go for now, this was because another morsel had been handed them, more tangible, and—wrapped in candypaper as it was—more palatable. This way the town could claim itself audience only to what happened in ways which were seemly. This way, the proprieties were kept—and the mate and Lottie were assisted by them. And no one at that time, not even Jim and Emily, took their need of such assistance as a sign. For in the sight of all, as is said in the marriage service—in the golden, interior light of half-past ten of an August voyage, in that arkful of people, idly waiting among the crumbs and the children sleeping like pigeons, waiting to ride home again—as well as to endorse, countenance and recall by date any and all contracts or other engagements entered upon during said voyage—in the sight of all, Lottie and the mate were holding hands.

As the motormen signaled one to the other, and the train of cars was off again, this time to ride silkily all the way home, the mate stretched an arm straight across the back of their seat, but the hand dangling on her shoulder, and began singing. He had a light baritone voice, sweet enough to be a tenor's had he been Irish, and he was singing the catch he'd begun the morning with.

"Four *arms,* two necks, one *wreathing,*" he sang, "Four lips, two hearts, one *breathing;* fa *la*-a-*ah,* fa la-a-ah, fa la la la la *la*!"

Through all the bypasses of the night, the whippoorwill starts, and once a stop and an owl-call, as we went banging through the countryside, he sang it. "Four lips that mul-ti-*ply,* all in-ter-change-*a*-bly!" and after a while some in the car answered him: "Fa *la*-ah-a, fa la-ah-a, fa la la la la *la*!" There was the special smell; combined with the clinging odor of fritters, it made a perfume they knew they were never going to smell again. The lights were out again now, but only for the babies' sakes; the motorman's searchlight, cast on the tracks, seemed the other end of a glowworm—a trolley car is long. Deep in its well somewhere, a voice called out, "This is the life!" and another answered, "This *is* life," and a third one said, "Oh, razzmatazz," and none was identified—who speaks in his own voice? But everybody knew what was meant; we were just as smart in those days—in our Greek-revival farmhouses, which we didn't even know bore the name—and before, back to the days of Greeks a-riding the Aegean, in what was probably called the last trireme. People have that kind of dull knowledge built in the bones by time; it's only poetry and uncomfortable when they mention it. Or song. So they rode on, and at last came the solemn forever, the stop. It was the last time, the last in life or eternity, and each leaned back in his seat with the pleasure of one who had survived even that. People make these solemn ceremonies for themselves of course, just the way they have to cast back and cast back over an event of love, to help remember they've had it.

Short of weddings not one's own, somebody said—or funerals ditto, somebody added—all were agreed it was a perfect experience. And so, Jim and the mate named Jim and the sisters Pardee had their audience, captive to them as they were captive to it, and this was the way, with a fa and a la, two and two made four.

—

Weddings are supposed to be all the same, it being the long, long road winding away from them that counts. We ought to describe these two nevertheless, leaving you, the fruit of them, to judge.

Lottie, as the elder, was to be married first—"Did you know she was older, Jim?" asked the mate, and when Jim nodded slowly, the mate came back with: "Oh, not that it matters, I've still got the edge on her; it's only that sometimes, it's hard to believe." He was leaning in his old place for talk, in the dining-room archway of the little house they shared, and he looked less burly than usual; the worries of approaching matrimony had scored dark circles under his eyes.

"Emily does—look older," said Jim carefully. During these intervening weeks, though confidences had come to a standstill for the moment, in a queer way this had further ripened the friendship; since the old, dangerous nights in French territory, they hadn't been so tender and sparing of each other's feelings and needs.

"Ah—it's not looks." The mate spoke judiciously also, now that each was speaking of his partner's choice. "That's a wonderful girl you've got there."

"There's no one like her," said Jim with a deep laugh he couldn't help; he was stunned by her, enthralled. He and she were meeting daily in all the places that were open to rural lovers, building themselves the kind of private legend that never hurts a marriage; he had climbed out of her window; they had slept naked in leaves. Often he had climbed in his own window at dawn. Lottie might have kept herself from knowing what her sister surely didn't speak of, but the mate couldn't help knowing of it.

"Ah, that's where I differ." All this ah-ing was part of the mate's new manner, as practical master of his own romance. "Lottie's—like everyone else. And I shan't mind that, you see. It'll be a help." He waggled his forelock, where once he might have clapped Jim's shoulder. "But *she's* just right for *you,* you old dreamer. Whatever you do." This was the first casual reference to another decision—to split their business destiny—since the decision had been made. "So we're both satisfied."

It was the uneasiest conversation they had ever had between them, but still the mate lingered.

"Goes a bit heavy on the eats," he said. There was no doubt of course as to of which sister he spoke. He looked over at Jim—gawking there by the mantelpiece as if he was pinned to it. "But that's good for the milk then, Jim, isn't it?"

"The milk?" It took Jim a blush to understand. "I suppose," he said then, imitating the mate's heavy manner. "Seems to be I have heard that. Yes, I suppose. And beer too, they have to drink, don't they." Mercifully the phone rang—as it did a lot these days—interrupting this exchange on nursing mothers. From the way the mate answered, it was Lottie, and Jim signaled quickly, as usual, for the mate to take the car. A car was still conspicuous; he and Emily went shanks' mare. Lottie and the mate went much to restaurants. So, here too, as the mate said, everybody was satisfied.

Later though, to Emily, Jim spoke of his own doubts, though delicately, not mentioning the milk. For you must understand that though he and she might not be every conventionally plighted couple of those days, socially, just the same, they were living through a state of being which is almost unknown now. In those days, the "engagement period" was as much a part of the common experience, and with actions and emotions proper to it, as is today the state of being divorced. It was the time when the male, being usually the less innocent, had to act it the more, while the woman formally took over the future of their days. Was he being less responsible than the mate? "Children—" he said. "Of course, we'll have them. But I have to tell you something." He hesitated. "I—never really think of them much. To tell the truth, I never think of them at all." Was he unnatural?

Truly there must have been few like her, for she only laughed, as he told the mate later. "It's because we daren't," she said. But a few more days later, speaking of her sister and the mate—which Jim didn't mention to the mate, though Lottie may have—she said, "I don't want to think about *them;* that's who I don't want to think of. I've told Lottie that!" Jim was left to wonder why, and to chalk it up to engagements. When he asked her, she said only again "I'd rather not think about them at all."

Despite which, the wedding was a double one. All the considerations which throng at such times had forced it. Counting in Oriskany, there were three houses to be disposed of, and two jobs. Here money came into it, with a bouncing surprise. The Pardees were indeed fairly poor now, but by the cleverly twisted will of a father not inclined to trust too long in horses or women, as soon as his daughters married men acceptable to the will's trusteeship—and who would doubt that Jim and the mate would be—each girl would be ten thousand dollars rich. It was a will which mightn't have held water if tried in court elsewhere—even as drawn by Sand Spring's most prominent lawyer, whose partner was a trustee—but recall that in those small days, the town was the court. After that disclosure, came the effects, each to each, of that much money. Oriskany, the mate's choice just as the idea of a garage had been, clearly fell to the mate; with Lottie's dowry he could buy it on his own—and begin. Jim liked the Pardee house well enough, the more so for its being on water; he and Emily would take it, with fair compensation to the other two of course, and think awhile whether to sell, or stay and somehow make use of the land. The mate, because of the needs of his house, would have to give up his surveyor's job; for the same reason, Jim would keep his factory one. The mate would need the car. All four would work together beforehand to put both houses in order, tidy for destiny—and dynasty. Jim's house, the house of the two men's bachelordom, would be sold.

When the news of all this came out, the two men found that they had in all ways disposed of themselves just as the town had estimated and favored they would—and that the town was now ready to make them part of the town. People of the type who always offer themselves to such processes soon did so, the lawyer's wife insisting on the use of her salon for the two weddings—both providentially without family to crowd it—while a few miles away, the rector where Jim as a barge child had attended his longest spell of Sunday school, now held out his church. Both offers were accepted, for two-thirty in the afternoon and four-thirty respectively; if it was to be a round-robin affair, hadn't it been so from the beginning?

The night before the wedding, the mate took the car and went off by himself. Just before he left, he stood in the archway of the dining room, looking at Jim, who was at the table, picking over old correspondence he wasn't planning to take with him. The mate stared, until Jim looked up, inquiring. At this, the mate shook himself all over, as if out of sleep. "No," he said. "You wouldn't want to." Then he went out. Jim must have been asleep when the mate came in, and slept on so late the next morning that the mate, up bright and early nevertheless, had to wake him—or else perhaps the mate never went to bed at all.

On one of the rare, glorious afternoons then, which October in that region sometimes trails on into early November, the four participants assembled, attended by divers hats and feathers and waistcoats; among them, who should be there but the Skinners from Oriskany, the two veterans from Jim's factory and the mate's boss and apprentices, the banker, though without his wife who was too grand for it, and the librarian?—when one gets down to it, relations can always be found, on pre-winter Sunday afternoons, even eager to be. Their names and faces are darkness now, though the watch chains glow, the feathers still wave. Of the four principals, Emily was to be Lottie's bridesmaid, then Lottie, as the first bride, would serve as her matron of honor; each of the two grooms, serving as each other's best man, guarded in a pocket his friend's marriage-ring. There were no other attendants. Neither bride was to be formally dressed. The lawyer was to officiate at the first wedding in his own parlor; he was also a judge. Since it was a civil ceremony, no one gave the bride away, but the lawyer's wife came forward from the kitchen where she had been helping the maid with what was still called the "collation," on the way doffing her apron and putting on a hat and a pair of gloves. And now we are privileged to set aside the bare facts of forty years ago, and stare.

Lottie's dress, it can now be seen, was one step too pink, as if she had tried to go beyond the candy-pink which was always so becoming to her, and had stretched too far, toward blood. It was hot in the lawyer's high-ceilinged room with fireplace and furnace grate both running, and as the plump do, she sweated. The sweat was dainty enough, smelling of Sunday and fresh cotton knickers, but as the marriage service wore on between the four standing so close, the dark crescents under the bride's arms were the serum-pink of separated blood, and the smell of the new satin made a man think of rutting. She remained dainty yet, with her thoughts falling back into dells of sweetness, and the mate beside, shoulders bulging and neck throttled by his collar, was the dancing bear. But at the end, it was the bear, with that great cry of *Grandchildren!*, who spoke.

Then it was "clop-clop and away" to the rectory, or to whatever sound by a lawyer's Packard is made. If, on the way, anyone murmured, "Wouldn't if he'd said he could see his *children* be enough?" then there is an advantage to double weddings, in that a lot about them is strange.

Meanwhile, what an artist memory is, at leaving out what is unimportantly important—the sound those wheels made—and bringing forward instead the sound of shanks' mare on gravel, as the rector leads us up the path and his wife doffs her apron and joins us! Emily, whose dress is unstained and as stiff as white icing, has chosen to be married in the church. The brief slice of afternoon between parlor and church is brilliant Finger Lakes weather, harvest weather, with the vines shorn but the grapes and pumpkins still gold and purple at every farmstall on the hills, and the cold November of Great Lakes weather still to come. It is the time when hills and water are in perfect balance here, that only time of the year. Inside the church, which has been warmed also, the four figures exchange places. The bride has a hat on, and this is only the chapel side of the church, but the Episcopal service falls in drapery behind her, folding back and back, like a wedding-train. A matron of honor in pink gives her away, or does what matrons do, very serviceably. This is a double-ring ceremony, but the mate and matron drop neither. Around these four, as the rector drones, the chapel gives its own responses. To the left, a high memorial window gave out the text And They Were Not Divided, in sun-dusty gothic citron and blue, but this meant death, and the four pairs of eyes turned casually away. Far back in the kind of history which got itself embossed in memorial windows, a pair were not divided even in death—but this had nothing to do with the couples here, at least now. Can you remember it, the time when death had nothing to do with you?—if *remember* can be called the proper word.

To the right of the two couples who were joined as if in a knot by the rector, there was another window as high and wide, but so shielded by a hanging of church velour dustily roped back near the floor, that what it shielded they never saw, maybe only the sun and the air, the light and the damp. Above the rector's head as it bent to them, but yards away behind it and lit with one votary lamp, the solid wall was incised with names whose worn gilding could not be read at that distance, though gold leaf was fresh on a text above. Throughout the ceremony, until the marriage-kiss, Jim's eyes kept returning to it. After the first congratulations were over, he went up to the wall, as he said "to see what war it was." The mate joined him there, and the rest of the party, already clustered at the church door, respectfully averted their attention from the two buddies, who were perhaps enjoying a last stray minute of bachelordom.

Together, the two men looked up at the text above the names. *Take what ye have,* it said, *and hold fast till I come.*

"Poor chaps," said the mate. " 'Take what ye have.' Well, *I'll* take it—now."

Jim nodded, staring at the text above. "I can wait," he answered it. "I'm not a soldier any more."

And it seemed to each of them that he spoke in his own voice.

The rector, coming up behind them, said, "It's the Civil War, the Civil. No part of this state had more Union dead than we did around here, did you know that? And hereabouts, this is the oldest church."

The two men nodded politely, and each took this moment to slip his ten dollars into the rector's hand.

As the party made ready to drive away from the church, few in it neglected to tell the young pairs that they had left their youth there. As the cars drew up again at the lawyer's door for the wedding-feast, some kinder soul, gazing up at the cold blue over the rooftop, where a short sunset was nipping westward, murmured, "Applejack weather, now."

"And I'll drink you under the table in it!" said the mate, leaping out first, and almost bashing in the front door before it was opened to him.

Behind him, Lottie looked up at Jim and Emily as if, though married later than she, they were somehow her mentors still. "Will he really drink a lot of it?" she whispered. The mate heard her, and turned round. "I do a lot of everything," he said, leaving no echo to wonder what his bride did know of her Jim, except Emily's silently tucked smile, over what she knew of hers.

Do you know how applejack from that part of upstate New York—not from the wine-hills but from the apple orchards—is made, or used to be; how the full brew of all that's in it is frozen away from what won't freeze, leaving nothing at the core of the ice but the apple brandy, nothing but almost pure alcohol? At the wedding-feast, some of the younger people circulated a vintage bottle of it—last year's. In addition, two bottles of Great Western champagne were supplied by the lawyer's wife. In spite of this, the mate, when requested to sing, stood hard as a rock, though he would warble none of his home songs or any of those which made his voice sound tenor, and concluded with those ballads of the late war in which everyone, musician or not, could join him. "It's a long, long way to Tippera*ree*," they sang, "it's a long way, to go." And "How long, oolong," they sang, "you gonna be gone?" The songs all spoke in some such way, whether speaking of absences or windups. "There's a long, long trail a-wi-yunding," the mate sang, "into the *land* of, my dreams," and the others answered him, "Where the *ni*-ightin-*gale* is *sing*ing and a *white,* moon, beams."

So then, they all drove away in the cars that everyone either owned or had borrowed, and for a while after, all the houses of guest and host and principals were lighted up, then dark again—from the Pardees' house on one side of Sand Spring, to the house in Oriskany, on the other. Only the little house waiting to be sold, the one where the two Jims had been, remained altogether dark. And it was a long, long time until morning.

For more than a week of nights and days, those honeymoon nights and days when it is allowable for no phone to ring or horn to toot in the driveway, it was a long time until morning, until the one when, at four o'clock of a cold hour, the door out at Pardees' house was pounded dead awake, and the two there, running down in their night-clothes, opened up to the sound of a car slipping away, and Lottie, fully clothed somehow or other, a shawl falling away from her, face dented and bloody, neck and arms bitten and scratched, as if she had met an animal in the woods, but the bloody marks dried brown, as if she had finally conquered it—fell through the door.

IV

So, that's the windup, or the beginning of it, for those four, who seem to me too young ever to become grandparents to a generation like yours. You, standing here, only just old enough to be off to war or marriage, seem to me far older than they, and I shouldn't be surprised if you felt it; your youth comes out in other ways. As for the forty years more of the story, you know all of it except for these few private parts of it now half exposed—plus whatever two old men can finally tell you. All the rest of it, you grew up with, and scarcely consider a story at all. It's no news to you that the two Jims, though related to some of you only through their wives, are called "Grandfather" by all of you, so close are they to both you and each other, though one still calls the other "mate." Nor is it any skin off your noses that although Jim and Emily had a fine parade of four children which surprisingly didn't begin until several years after the marriage, and the mate had only one solitary cub, conceived when we all knew—nevertheless, four out of the six grandchildren stem from the mate. This is the way, in daily life, matters even themselves.

That way, all the money the mate has made (not real tycoon wealth but the considerable estate, in company shares and accrued income, of a man who, during the Second World War, went from a small job in the

Remington Arms Company to the directorship of small-arms contracts for its nearest rival) can be divided without strain, particularly since any farm he touches even in the most gentlemanly way, usually turns against him, into money too. Even then, big spender as he is on others, in the gifts that come up in him now and then like terrible belches, of generosity of course—like the sloop he gave Jim, who didn't any more want one than the barge it was supposed to take the place of, or the coat Emily could only wear once a year on the New York City vacation, for who can wear mink in Sand Spring?—even then their brother-in-law, as he is still known to the town, is hard put to it to spend his money, maybe because his own home expenses are so small. For I suppose it never occurs to you—or has one of the women in the family told you, no doubt very romantically?—why your richer grandfather lives on in the small house that his friend brought him home from the wars to, in the twenties, the house which was once scheduled to be sold?

Meanwhile, if Jim and Emily's two grandchildren, with their parents, aunts and uncles before them, can only look forward to the glass-shelved mahogany bookcases and modestly solid silver of a first-class Sand Spring Dutch Colonial built circa 1935, then it doesn't matter anyway, since the second generation are all associated in a family business which no one would presume now to call matriarchal, and this generation in turn has only two to whom to hand it down. For anyone in town who assumes, as many do, that the mate has money in the Aswami Baking Company—put there at some time or other, either when it began, or in one of the crises which small businesses have, or when it was finally incorporated—is wrong. Emily and Jim could never have let him put a cent in it. After that night they couldn't be in debt to him, and there must be no more partnership. In this way, Jim expresses silently his lifelong pity for his friend, to whom he expresses aloud only his equally and lifelong sincere admiration. And Emily, in her woman's way or merely in Emily's, was left free to expiate to herself or approve—whoever knew which with Emily?—what she would *not* do, that night or ever, for her sister, and indeed considered herself to have done for the mate. In this way, the three could remain as close as you have always known them to be. For no matter what tales you may have heard or not bothered to hear, only now is it becoming clearer, now that two old men have talked, how the four of them became three.

Forty years ago or four hundred, to take in a woman bloody and beat from her husband, must be the same. They would bind her and bathe her, and once it was plain that no doctor was needed, perhaps when she had been fed and was asleep, then those two, still in their nightclothes and maybe with the tender muckiness of their own love still upon them, would sit down. The facts which later became common knowledge to the four of them (and only them) were these. Lottie's wounds had only been surface ones; what with the dents and puffs and a few streaks of blood that could well be spared, it was only what another pair might have done in a night's fierce cleaving—but made strange by the shawl and the hour, and that she had come at all. To say nothing of who had brought her. The mate had brought her, though under whose duress she did not say. For though restless at first—yes, that is the word—once she was tidy and had her tea in front of her, she appeared so calm and settled, so much in her right mind or like her usual self, that though this was odd for the circumstances, they scarcely knew what to ask. He "came after" her, she told them, then she smiled at them as if they should surely understand this, kissed them each on a cheek and went, with her light, bouncing tread that never showed her weight, into her old room. But what did she expect them to do?

When they phoned the mate, at first there was no answer, though they had given him time to reach home. He couldn't answer at first, he told them later; he couldn't bear to, because of the way they knew him, and he them. If he'd been a stranger, he said, he could have had it out with them—their bewilderment, or Jim's—and his rage. He himself, he said, was never bewildered. "From the first hour," he said, "I knew what I was up against." Then he too said no more. But that was later, when they saw him. Over the phone, when at last they reached him, he said only, "No, I won't come after her," but it must have been chance that he used those words, surely meaning only that he chose not to come and get her, at least not just now.

"Are you—all right yourself, mate?" said Jim. What a thing to have to ask!

"No sight for the marketplace," said the mate; then he couldn't go on; he made the queerest sound that said he couldn't, and hung up.

While Lottie went on sleeping, the other two conferred.

"It can't be—could it be—" said Jim, "that she just didn't *know* about it—?" He said afterward that here, even as late as this, an edge of humor hovered—what a riot if it was merely that, then just give the pair time and all would be well, or as with the half the world not as lucky as some, at least smoothed over.

"No, of course not!" said Emily. "We kept horses."

"Well, what the devil—then—?" he said, slow to anger as always. And why he should have been angry at *Emily,* he wondered after. "He's a man, that's all. I know the mate. A bit quick, maybe. And maybe one for the wom—never mind. But he's no brute. I'd swear it." He looked at her square. "And I can."

If she flinched at that, he said he couldn't tell it. She spoke softly, "I can't say what men are, the way you can, or what women are. But I daresay you're right." It was a long speech, for Emily. "And I know Lottie," she said.

"Then—if you knew what—why didn't you—? Why didn't you say something?" How absurd!—he could see that himself—and that they two should be quarreling about it. He never would again, he said after. For she stopped him cold, even if she didn't mean to.

"I'm only a girl," she said.

And she was too—not twenty yet. People like Emily—he said to the mate later—when they do speak, how they go to the heart of it!

"And why wouldn't she," the mate answered, "for that's how *you* are, Jim."

Anyway, when they saw him, that was maybe the worst shock of all. Lottie was gone by that time, taken by Jim down to Troy, to that woman friend she stayed with until Lottie found herself pregnant, some old maid friend. It couldn't be said that Lottie had been deeply wounded that her sister wouldn't keep her on and allow her to take up her old life there; she had been a little hurt of course, but mostly—

surprised. But they didn't speak of her for a moment, now that they saw him.

"The eye I did myself," he said. "On the bedpost." Then there was the blue dent on his temple, which you all know, which never did go away. The scratches were nothing, he said. But one or two had festered; the human nail will do that. Emily went at once to get a basin, though it was two weeks since that night, and more.

"Thank you, Jim," said the mate, while she was out of the room. "And let's not speak of it again, of what or why, unless we have to." He managed a smile. "Maybe someday, when we're old." He put the familiar hand on Jim's shoulder. "There's just something I want to ask Emily."

When she returned, he asked her it, in the middle of her sponging his face. She had put a towel round his neck and was treating his cuts as firmly as any trainer. The iodine made him squint his good eye. His voice wasn't much, not for him.

"When was it, Emily?" he said. "That you decided."

"Decided what?" she said, but they all knew, just as the mate must have known at once that it would have been Emily's force which had refused her sister; Jim on his own could never have done it.

"When I saw her walk into her room," said Emily slowly. "When I saw her walk like that, back into her old room."

The mate nodded, holding his face up to the washcloth, his eyes closed against the water; then he opened them so that she might look into them; he and she were a pair, both of them quick to seize people and size them, not long bewildered. Then he jumped up and went to the mirror.

"About my sister," she said to his back. "There's nothing to Lottie ... except—what one sees."

"And if she were my sister," he said without turning, "I'd have seen it."

His voice was bitter. For we're so trained up to believe, Christian and infidel both, that *all* people are like icebergs, the greater part of them *beneath.* Why must we forget or deny that there are these others, too?

"Why ... Emily—" said Jim. "Why—Jim." He rarely called the mate by their common name. "She's right, do you see? And—if we could—remember it. Wouldn't—could that make it easier?"

The mate turned from the mirror, slowly, fingertips still to the stickingplaster he'd been dabbed with. "For *whom?*"

Emily only looked at them both with her level glance. The mate came up to her, his head cocked the way one has to with an eye puffed closed. "Maybe I'm like that too," he said. "Nothing to me, except what you see."

"Not if you can say it," said Emily, and Jim with a nod agreed.

All three were silent for some minutes. Then the two men both shook their heads, like dogs out of water, away from this kind of talk. "Well—I'm off," said the mate. Instead, he rested the palms of his hands stiff-armed on the table and stared down into its center. "Got to admit it though, I'm dashed. I'm a bit—dashed."

Maybe that's why he's had to be the opposite, ever since.

"I'm making her an allowance, of course," he said. "But I don't plan to go down there after her."

"But otherwise—" said Jim.

"Otherwise . . . I'll have to sell Oriskany. It's her money bought it." He looked at them as squarely as his eye allowed him. "Maybe I'll sell it to you."

He did always have a business head, even at odd times. Of course they both smiled at the idea, Emily the more.

"But if she'll come back—" said Jim, poor Jim, always seeking to make his kind of peace, or to find out what that was.

"Something may come of it." The mate spoke lightly. Then he screwed his face the way a person does when he intends to look mean. "Something . . . may . . . come of it all. We'll wait and see."

Something did of course, the child. And though in these days, a woman mightn't have come back to have it, Lottie did—maybe a Lottie always would. Later he said that he would have divorced her otherwise, but that's blarney; the mate would never divorce the mother of his child, and that's how it's worked out, hasn't it?—in the mate's own way. For, during the months before the child came, it was a sight to see, how he cossetted her, bringing her up breakfast before he went off to the job he'd decided to hold on to, going against the doctor, to push her to eat. And to look at Lottie, though she didn't appear to give much thought to the baby itself that was coming, or even to her having it, everything was smooth as cream. It was repellent, maybe, to see a man use what he knew of his wife to get what he wanted out of her—which was dynasty—and maybe the mate himself knew it was, beneath that blind, horn-forward stare which always came on him when he was after something. And he got him, by God—the lone boy who was dynasty and is dead now, but not before he in turn fathered four of his own; can it be fifteen years now, and the war *after* the second world one in its turn an old one? And the mate has him still—however way many of us are conceived; here we are—or were. And here you are, the fruit of us, burdened with the tale.

Once the baby was born and coddled out of its two-month frailty, everyone knew that things were going badly out at Oriskany. It dragged on so for a few months more, then ended, though there was no more violence, at least as far as was let be seen. Then Lottie left again, this time very quietly, by what private arrangements were never publicly known. That she had made some agreement was taken for granted since, though she made no more forays on her sister, indeed not even a letter so far as was known, she wasn't the sort to manage alone. Then indeed the town could reflect back on how the mate had always been the doting parent and the mother the negligent or perhaps confounded one—and could take the mate to its bosom. For Lottie had left behind the child.

So—the mate never got his garage, or Jim either—though that too remains to be explained. Oriskany was sold—it's funny now to think of the mate having to sell a place to get money—and the money presumably reverted, from a distance, to "the mother," as the town has since persistently referred to her, always in hushed tone. The mate moved nearer Jim, so that Emily could tend his child, which was subsequently brought up during the day with her others, joining its father at night. And that's why such a rich grandfather lives in such a small house; half of reality has these kindergarten reasons for it—this being part of the general undertow and sneakwork of the world. Surely it's also why, when we can see a trolley ride clear, we cling to it.

If Lottie got the best or the worst of things, the town never precisely knew, nor could they tell whether Jim and Emily knew either. At first she was heard of quite simply and normally, as working in a bakery down in Troy. The bakery was in character, and not only in hers—you watch. Later they heard she was working in a similar capacity in the town of North Adams, Massachusetts—and the migration of people, by foot or wheel or hunger, is always interesting—for there is no other town in the state of Massachusetts which more resembles a New York State town called Troy. Why a woman whom surely the mate supported, and who had had ten thousand dollars of her own in the bargain, should need to work in such places, only those who saw her could say. Bulletins got vaguer as times got leaner, and if it was heard that she had invested her money in oil stock and lost it, others had done the same. There was shock when some vacationer reported seeing her in a place called Squaw Village, not what it might sound but one of those tourist places on the Molly Stark trail, with a big country store and Indian tepee setups; the shock was that she had let her hair grow down in a braid, dyed black surely, to add to her squaw-weight, and was on charade in the gifts-and-goodies shop, billed as the mother of an Indian family, in a troup of hired braves and papooses selling everything from carnival glass to saltwater taffy. "Surrounded by *children*!" the shocked vacationer said. By which it could be seen that our town, like many in the region, had in some ways maintained its own character.

Then, in the forties somewhere, it heard for sure—or at least from her—that she was rich again or very comfortable; the oil stock—think of it, oil stock bought by a Lottie!—had panned out after all. It was in Florida that some folks met her; by this time we upstate farmers, and business people too, were wintering in Florida ourselves, and not busing it down there either, flying there, just like the birds. She was very dressy now—the women of the party said—in a way that hid her bulk, and like a well-heeled widow with her bracelets and gold charms. She lived in one of the warm coastal towns where the older boat-crowd sat a lot on deck or by the water, her distinction being, and maybe her respectability too, that she didn't drink—diabetes had lost her a toe. "Didn't *drink*," the women said. "Dressed like Rochester, sure, but there's that bazoom to make you think of Miami," some of the men said. Others said, "Oil stock, nuts, anybody knows what he's worth now, and he's never divorced her, that's all." The wildest tale of all, which should encourage us all as to the civic imagination, was that the mate himself had been seen down there, in that hotel like a French château, coming out of a suite behind her or her image, in the wee hours of the morn. A lovely conclusion, only not possible. True enough, that he's often seen down there at that place or others, and that he goes to some trouble to see that the middle-aged tarts he chooses will look to strangers as if they could be his wives. Seeing him at a table, bending his fine head of white hair very courtly over some nice, fullblown woman with not much makeup and good manners, who'd think otherwise—unless the real wife was known to the observer from before? It may be that he was showing the lady out of his suite all right, and treating her like one—whoever she was. But it wasn't Lottie. To dream of Lottie as her husband's whore or anyone else's is to—well no, it's neither to laugh nor to cry. It's to wonder how a woman who hadn't it much in her to stir the emotions, could hold a man down, and for a lifetime too, and by emotions he never had it in him to have. If to be that is to be a whore, then, poor thing, she was one. But there are those who say she never could have been one conventionally, not even with him. How do they know? Because, though it's said she used to see the boy now and then—for his own good, as maybe Emily insisted—she never came back to Sand Spring, not once. If she'd been a whore somewhere, rich or not, she could have come back to town—and been respectable.

Now Emily, though for her there is no key. For, all her life, unlike the other three, each of whom wanted something in a way which overpowered or colored them—Emily was concerned with the workings of daily living only, and so her mystery, like its, is only hinted at here and there in the shadows and gildings of that ordinary living, and is as hard to see. When the mate, one solemn day, carried his baby into her house to be cared for forever, although she had none of her own even begun yet, she received the infant handily, yet not greedily, in no doubt that her own babies would come along, when called. Though it was a sad day, to the two men watching she left no doubt either that in any day where such a child was, there were still tweaks of joy. The three things she said might have come one by one out of a casket of the sort women keep by them. To the mate, whose face, except for the blue dent, was now healed to an even hardness, she said lightly, "Don't fret, don't fret"—whereas to the baby cradled in her arms she said almost formally, "It can't be helped." Shouldn't it have been the other way round? Or did she hope to make the little man see as early as possible a view of the world—her sex's—in which, if he grew up like the rest of his, he would never believe? Or was it simply that she was one of those who from birth know the position of the generations and can act by it, needing no other compass or calendar.

But in the third thing (which was Lottie's epitaph no matter how much might be said of her later) surely there was also a hesitance in the way Emily spoke, as if some of the verdict—in the way character is apportioned among families, or among women—must surely cling to herself.

The three were sitting in the bay window, out at Pardees'. Coffee was on the table, tea for the mate. In the nearer depths of the house, the baby had been put down; its next bottle was ready on the stove. The stove was Bismarck. On the lake in front of the house it was late August again, one of its lizard-gray days, scaly with mist, from which autumn bursts like a pumpkin, a fruit. All three couldn't help but be thinking how far, from Bismarck to baby, they had come. Outside, on the railless water, the fogline now and then parted a few feet above it in porcelain flushes of vision to which each pair of eyes would put a personal shape. Over her own, Emily's brows almost met, but it was she who first broke the long pause, though silently, flinging her baby-tired arms wide. She could do that—it was one of the things that made her seem tall, yet contrarily could bring her fingertips in again to hold an eyelash; she had stretched her legs wide and closed them again, and in the nutcracker between them brought herself a man. She looked at him now, at Jim watching the water, loving his vagueness, never scolding, perhaps tending it—for both their ends. But today was the mate's day; anything about Lottie belonged to him.

"Jim—" she said. The two men always knew which Jim she meant. She spread her hands—like a sister's—then clasped them. "The sugar-people. That's the way they are."

Each nodded at her, needing no further explanation. Jim, her husband, smiled. It wasn't his day, life hadn't marked him outwardly yet, as it had the mate, but until his inner arguments settled themselves, until he could point to the mark on himself perhaps, his clever girl would always have a word for what the risks were, and the responsibilities. He, meanwhile, was waiting. And there was no shame in it.

It could have been only a few minutes later when she got up, walked over to the great stove, cold as armor these many months in favor of the smaller summer one, and put her hand on it. "I've been thinking," she said. Her clear eyes shone with a forward-backward light. "There's not a decent baking company in town."

The genius of it was that from the first she had said "company." A mere bakery, even if its owners keep in the basement a staff of two floured German madmen—do you know bakers?—is still only a shop. Nevertheless, that's the way they began of course, but with that other word always leavening the conversation and at last rising from it, written neater than Nebuchadnezzar's—on the wall. The name "Aswami" came from a secondhand truck which glimmered at them from a car-lot when they were on holiday up near the Canadian border—"The Aswami Baking Company"—the name of its past owner and locale conveniently obliterated, but an Indian version after all. In the early years, toward her thirties, Emily, selling at the shop's counter—did she ever think of her sister?—or downstairs, scarf-headed, checking over the staff in the large basement of the second establishment, or at Jim's side at an evening party, looked ever younger, almost a child-wife—you'll remember there was almost a decade between them. As for the parties, the two of them, if by choice not in the forefront, were always on the list now, having long since moved to the middle of town and got over their trouble.

In later years, in the business office of the factory they built on a razed property—yes, in Oriskany—as Jim grew more portly, Emily, though no plumper herself, kept matronly pace with him somehow. The children, when they came, were never vulgarly underfoot in the shop, a distaste for this being part of what her livery-stable heritage had taught her, so that by the time the company had been achieved, the children, now parents themselves, could laughingly tell their own, home from prep and boarding schools with perhaps a schoolmate, that *they* had never even had as many cakes and cookies as children normally did, when young. All of *them* called their parents Jim and Emily, oddly modern for them, unless one suspected that in this way the mate's child wouldn't have been shunted away from "Mother" to "Aunt Emily." For which reason—far back in those brown dark days of childhood which precede the light-blazed ones on which young men's planes go down (their last letters to dear Emily arriving later)—it had been done. As for the baking products on which this small, decent empire has been built, these have kept pace with modernity too; the company has one of the best bread to doughnut lines in the upstate area, all properly packed with no more than 10 per cent preservatives—and there isn't a fritter in the lot. But what with automobiles and trucking, and the trackless wastes between towns and appetites, always needing to be covered, it has done very well.

Dear Emily—as much more than old letters still say. If we don't count that young man, the father of some of you (and how does one count death out of one's generation, when it is not among the natural and daily?), then Emily was the first of us to die. She is the first to fall, of that young constellation, and never will there be a better reason for you all to gather here. As might be expected of such a woman, she went from one of the commoner diseases, which was gotten to, as the doctors like to say, in time. When Jim took the mate with him to help order the stone, and they stood in the stonecutter's office, studying that grim manual of texts and design cuts, looking out the window at his samples, it was the mate who suddenly slammed the book closed and said "What do I do in my *business,* when I buy anything! Let's go to an *expert*!" So they hopped in that other car of his, the Bentley he'd got from England—the two men when they go out together always use his cars—and drove to the church.

Time being what it is, the rector was now a young seminarian. And no worse for it, said the mate, to whom it was smart business for the old to deal with the young—who as he said would have everything at their fingertips. Since it was Jim's wife who had died, the young minister deferred to him, and couldn't have been kinder or taken longer to help search out what Jim thought suitable for a wife like that, and a stone.

Neither of the two old men walked over to look at old Civil War names, wars being too new again, but if Jim's search took the long, trembling time it did, this was because he remembered what he had once said in this place.

" 'I can wait,' " he said to the mate. "Do you remember?" And it seemed to him that now, now if ever must be the time to express all that he had been gathering for a lifetime and had never expressed properly, about our place in the world here and his modest place also; now if ever was the time to say it all. But though dozens of texts were brought forth, there was none that satisfied him. It came time for evensong, but the mate didn't press him. The young man, though nobody had come for the service, was going round quietly, turning on lights and so forth, being his own sexton. And suddenly he was stopped in his sweeping. "What's behind that curtain?" the mate said. "I wondered, at the time."

That young man almost fell over his broom, he was so eager; he had seen the Bentley. It must have been hard on him to accept a church so hopelessly faded in congregation as that one, and as you may have noted at today's dedication, though he very kindly returned for it, he has since been called elsewhere. But he had everything at his fingertips that day. "There were to have been two," he said, pointing to the high memorial window opposite the curtained one. "But something happened." Then he pulled back the curtain. The day was one of the short, winter ones, no anniversary of an autumn one and no sunset, but between the darkness outside and the light within, the blank pane perhaps showed up best. So that is how come, two years later almost to the day, which the stained-glass people told us was optimum—Emily's window. The mate wanted to pay for it, but of course that couldn't be, even though he was the one to persuade Jim to have it.

"She wouldn't have wanted such a thing," said Jim.

"In some ways, Jim," said the other old man, "I—other people—knew her better than you did!"

Then the young man put his hand between them. It was the nearest they had ever come to an out-and-out difference of opinion, not to say quarrel.

"She was a *common* woman, a *homely one,*" said Jim. "Words change, but when I was a boy, that's what the mourners used to say at barge funerals, of any woman who had the human touch to her, and had brought with her all the home comforts, during a lifetime that wasn't never nothing but daily." He looked ashamed then, either at his grammar or his eloquence, but with him who can tell? "She was an ordinary woman," he said. "She was a nonpareil."

"I know what you mean, Jim," said the mate. "Even without going to one of your dictionaries. I know what you mean." How he could remember! "You mean—she was like everyone else."

So, between them, that was her epitaph—though when it came to the window, they finally left it to the rector, after all. He chose "Many Waters"; I suppose you know it. Of course you do, with the window, how could you not? "Many waters cannot quench love, neither can the floods"—and so forth. Maybe the mate did help suggest it because of all the water in it, knowing Jim's tastes or thinking he still did—remember that sloop! And it is a beautiful verse.

"So it is, mate," said Jim. "So it is, Jim." Calling the mate by name was meant to repair the sharp words. "But you know something?" He stared through the blank pane at the dark land outside it. "This is a mixed region, around here. I see it more and more."

Later, when he saw first the window itself, back at the glassmakers' of course, not at the unveiling, he both nodded his head and shook it, even though the figure rising from the water in all its blood-reds and milky whites was an angel, not Emily. "Funny thing," he said. "I always see her . . . *from* the water. *On* the land."

And now Jim. He was fond of saying that if there was something he wanted to know about himself he could always go to the mate for it. The mate, if he was there to hear him, always remarked, "Same here. Only, *he* won't tell." For forty years or more their lives had been twined together, but in such a way that if one showed himself ready to drown, the other didn't go down with him but held him; they weren't twins, unless twins can be of totally different temperament. The mate had his Floridas, and did or didn't speak of them. In the early years, the three sometimes had had to speak among them of Lottie, though never of the mate's long undivorcement itself; during the years when Emily did get a letter or two, these were spoken of, but curiously, only in twosome, either of the men to Emily or to each other, but never in threesome; after Emily's death, the other sister was not spoken of at all. In money matters, the town had at various periods thought it remarkable that the pair never minded who was the richer, but the friends themselves knew that too much teetering had gone on in that direction, ever for them to feel constraint. During the stunned years when the mate clung to his job like a man who has forgotten what his hands are holding, then it was Jim, the ever solider townsman, who lent him money for unspecified needs, and it was only during the Second War—at a time when the limits of a small business, if these don't soar, are likely to be fixed—that the mate began to stumble forward, to climb as if he knew there was a top, and finally to claw to it. Until then, Jim, with his strong figure, hair faded and thinned but not balded, and his busy little cockerel of a wife beside him, had looked the younger of the two; now it was the mate, with the powder-white hair which had once been raven, and the kind of tycoon charm which can demonstrate in a handshake that it has known what it is to be shy. Jim, by now, had a particular kind of townsman's face, relaxed but puzzled in repose, the quality which in a younger man is called willing-to-learn. But—as you may have noticed—we haven't yet got solely and wholly to Jim.

For the curious thing about Jim was that one always got to him best through others, which may be why he persisted in claiming that he never quite knew himself. He wasn't an enigma, any more than any of us, but he had thought it his duty to face the world's enigma and study it—or he had always meant to; this meant that if he could wait, others must watch. Why was it otherwise that though he and Emily stood all their lives in handfast, Jim, as against the mate, seemed the more divided? He never minded being in business with a wife, even such a competent one, and never consented to lose dignity for it—though a town will try. The town could do nothing with him or to him, while he studied it. He had his hobbies then, not too cranky ones for a self-styled reflective; about the time he married, for instance, he seemed to give up books at large—or the timid taste which had been tending that way—only to replace them with a collection of dictionaries which, all along unknown to himself, may have been what he had been going to the libraries for. For a while it would seem as if he never read these either, for it was at this period that he took to collecting the names of towns on matchboxes, merely for the way they pleased or teased the something within him which he couldn't explain otherwise; when he drove the highways on a trip to Yellowstone for instance, passing through a state he would chant some such refrain to the children: South Bend, Plymouth, Mishawaka, Peru. But that was only when the children were small, and he could think he was teaching them America. After one particular Christmas, he and the mate tried to tinker over a hobby together; do you ever remember your parents telling you of a year when both Jim and the mate came back from separate trips to New York City—with toy trains? But it didn't last long, and here they did share a likeness; if, like most, as they got older, they wanted only the more to see the world and to grasp it, then this wasn't their style of miniature.

Curiously enough, as their teeter-totter went now up, now down, it was the mate who had begun to educate himself with books—real books. He would do it on his own terms of course, when and if he felt he could get to them, and in his own character—which he so well knew. In just the same way, before a certain trip abroad, he had gone to a language school and demanded they teach him French in ten minutes—which they did, if poorly, and to a dancing school where, in somewhere double the time, he did well. Why he had been moved to do this for a trip with Jim on which they never got to do either of those things, did stay a mystery to him, until Jim told him.

"Why do you suppose I ever suggested that trip?" the mate asked, long after it was over.

"For old time memory's sake," Jim replied.

By that time, like most people, they were pretty good at memory, and each was able to swallow Jim's lie—for what they had gone for was to help shake from them the real death of youth, of the mate's son—not to remember their own. And from that trip Jim did bring back a huge terrestrial globe, lighted from within and girdled with half-life size figures clasping it, the gods of antiquity, holding it up with their spread arms and thighs. He found it in a stationer's in the Strand and had it sent home in sections for his collection: sometime back, he had gone on from his towns, and from America too, to globes. But when brought home, though it glowed as magnificently in the home as in the shop, instead of adding to his collection it ended it, for here the thing was, great with history and glass jewels too—did I say it was sixteenth-century and Venetian?—and even in Sand Spring it was only a globe. That ended all his collections except—as he said to the mate, spinning the globe for him, interpreting its yellowed mapskin in by its own inner light, at dusk of a cold Sunday—except for one. From now on, he said, he would collect only the intangible, where a man had more chance.

"Will you look at that expression of his!" said Emily, watching him. "Worse than the children!" How she always watched, and the mate too—and how they knew him! For himself, he could decide best who and what he was, he always said, in the way *she* spoke to him. For, though often she said to him exactly what she had said to the mate and the mate's baby, on the day when they all had first to face up to things—over the years she had reversed these in tone. When she said, "Don't fret, don't fret now," it was as if to a wise child who knows that beforehand, but when she said, "It can't be helped, can it," she spoke as if to a strong man who bore with the world. As for the children, Jim always said they loved him too much, that likely if he had done more in the world, they wouldn't have. He often said it. So here, maybe if only to help complete the circle within which a family is always judging itself, he was for once heard to participate in his own measurement.

And here we all are now: the four of us—two old men accountably present, and two women accountably absent—plus a listener or two now dogging their footsteps, from the crowd of them once upon a time at their knees. Between a last ride and a first memorial, the distance never changes, though opinions vary on the length of it, some memories going by wheel, others by wing. But all of us are here now, and ready to go back.

V

The day the two old men went back was a day uncolored by water or breeze, tempered only with its meaning to them. As one gets older, this happens to days generally, but on that particular one the friends were driving back upstate from the glassmakers' studio in New Jersey, where they had gone for that private viewing, and now, no matter the weather they passed, the window's high, fragile rainbow overhung the highway in front of them. There is one stretch of the New York State Thruway that nine times out of ten is leaden with Catskill storm-weather, and this they did finally comment on—that neither had ever seen it in sunshine. Then the miles and the signposts took over again, and the silence—and always up ahead of them over the car's hood, above the spot where small figureheads were once attached at the radiator caps, that high transparency at the prow.

"Glass," said Jim. "I'll never understand how it's made. From *sand*."

The mate didn't answer at once. He was driving the Cadillac, in which he always kept the air-conditioner going, and the air they breathed was as pure and excellent as an engine accessory could make it, but voices were hollow. On Jim's side, a sign said NEXT EXIT and gave the number of miles.

"Want to stop?" asked the mate. They had been driving for some time.

"No, not unless you do," Jim answered, and the mate nodded. One of the latter-day satisfactions of their friendship, and no longer the lightest, was that physically they had kept pace with each other, neither's digestion or bladder being weaker than the other's.

"This exit we're coming to," said the mate. "We go off it, we could go on over to Skaneateles, have one of those big dinners at Krebs, and still get home."

"Krebs," said Jim. "Haven't heard that name in maybe—must be twenty-five years."

"Neither have I, come to think of it; maybe it isn't there." They drove on, and in a short time, too short if they met a cop, went by that exit.

"On the other hand," said the mate. "On the other hand, I've had to do a lot of driving around in our part of the state recently. Looking for a factory site. Cheap unoccupied land is getting harder and harder to find." He laughed. "I told the company directors—'I got a couple of farms you can have, at a price. I'll never live on 'em.' " By now the corporation drawl he adopted for business had become almost natural to him, and he could say a thing like that about farms without blinking. But he could surprise himself still, and Jim too. "Anyway, struck something when I was going around—came upon something I want to show you. You game?"

"Sure, why not. Just say how far, if I should phone. That housekeeper will wait dinner otherwise."

The mate moved his head to look at him, turning on him the bachelor stare of a man who ate in restaurants, and had argued housekeepers and other points too, with Jim.

"Guy behind you wants to pass," said Jim, but it wasn't the mate's driving that bothered him; the mate always had one eye on the road.

"Let her cook it," said the mate, "we'll get there. Though how you can want to tie yourself down like that—" He increased the speed which momentarily he had let slacken. "No, it's not far. Given a decent road—" He gave a short laugh. "Well, if it had one, I wouldn't have gone there and found it. Even so, in this thing, can't be more than an hour from home. Just that you have to go round it."

Where, to two natives of the district, could anything unknown to them be so close? But Jim didn't ask it, as the signposts traveled by. The mate drove on silently, until the definitive one, where they left the highway. Then he spoke, when it was no longer needed.

"It's on the way to Batavia," he said.

When they got there, they sat in the still car for a moment, then with one accord each opened the door on his side, stepped out, and turning on his heel, regarded it—sky, tumbled-in roofs, mossy underbrush to treetop glory—all. The windshield of the Cadillac was extra-wide, but there was too much ruin and growth here ever to be encompassed by it. Was cheap land for progress always so beautiful? They numbered it with their eyes—here outbuildings whose flat tops had melted into moss, there a great curved hangar of swallows' nests, on whose leaning timbers only fantasy tipped a weathercock, pointing not crazily, into the wood. All the facilities were here. And here was the hill, all the inhabitants of that village-for-a-day—except these two—long since piped back into it. It stood there like the massive bulk of their lives. Only those others were gone—and the steel rails.

The Little Otselica was running. One of the men—it didn't matter which—leaned down to it as if to stroke it for choosing to, then when his knee cracked, stood up shamefaced.

"Must have had a wetter season than we thought," said the other, but it didn't matter who, or if both saw the impress of a bather, her piled hair floating the water. The time had now come for memory to be the same.

Each of them found a stony stump to sit on, or a porous stone.

"Going to put your factory here?" said the one.

The other shook his head. With a wrist flick he waved aside the hill, annihilated it. "No problem there. But still the same trouble. Place still doesn't *go* anywhere."

But this was only the preamble. In the uneasy stillness, the nose of the Cadillac, parked in grasses, reared alert. And after a while, one of the men began at the beginning.

" 'Rushing the growler,' " he said. "Know what a 'growler' was? Came across it only the other day."

"No. Never even heard the word, except from you."

"Must have used them when they wanted to get there in a hurry. Eighteen-sixty-five, the dictionary said. Funny how it leaped right out at me. It's a horse-drawn cab."

The other tinkled his car keys against the stone. "It's all transport," he said, and drew a flask of brandy out of a hip pocket.

They had a tipple.

"Applejack weather," said the one holding the flask, staring behind the trees, where should be a sunset. Though there wasn't, the other nodded agreement; he too could smell the air of youth here, that pure autumn alcohol.

They had another.

The one got up from his seat, rubbed his backside and took off his coat to spread it on the ground.

"Damp," said his companion.

"Got me a sweater on." This was plain enough, but he looked at the coat on the ground a long while, before he finally sat on it, hugging his knees. "Tell me something," he said then. "Surely now it's all right for me to ask—and you to tell it." He looked down at ground between his legs. "It was her, wasn't it, you really wanted, Emily." He looked up at the other, asking it maybe only for her memorial.

But the other couldn't give it. "No," he said. Whether this was true or not, nobody would ever get anything else out of him. "I knew from the first . . . that it—" He finished the swallow left in the flask, and tossed it on the ground. "But it was Lottie I heard."

Then he shifted on his stone and looked down at his companion. "Anyway, I always thought— You and she. When you went off into the woods like that."

The other glanced up at his friend, then away. Did his friend really want to listen, to what he almost yearned to tell him? "I don't mind telling you it," he said at last, scoring the grass at the coat's edge with a forefinger. "Don't we almost have to tell it, now?"

He told it, putting in as well as he could of what had passed through his mind then, or had been huddled over through the years later—all he wanted to understand and had waited for. Was this its moment?

When he had finished, the other wasn't staring at the trees any more, but at him. " 'I can wait,' you said," he said. "I always wondered why you said it. When you already had it."

And maybe that was part of her memorial. But the man on the ground, on the coat, sat wondering how friendship, even with the help of wars and time and family, could ever have knitted him to this other so different one.

And the man on the stone swung the car-keys in the arc of a surveyor's instrument, thinking the same.

"And the time *she* came," the one on the coat finally said. "To our door. We always wondered, of course. What really happened between you." He paused. "You don't have to tell it. Not even now."

The man on the stone got up then and walked away, stretching his arms, presenting his back. "No, I want to. Somebody should know. And maybe, even if I got marked early by it—maybe that was something."

"Sure is," said the man on the ground, staring at his own greed to know, to be marked out—against which even happiness, or even its memorial, were not quite enough.

The other came back to his stone and sat on it again. He leaned forward confidentially, as over a business deal, but it was a time before he spoke. "It wasn't so much that she wouldn't do it. Couldn't. For love—or for sex either. Though I made her. Or even that she had to . . . to eat . . . even *during*. I caught her with a candy in her mouth—the first time." He paused, easing his collar, "I think I even knew how it would be, before I ever touched her. The night before the wedding, I knew. Even though, up to the wedding, I'd never done any more than put my tongue in her mouth. She liked that. But there was never any—we always went to restaurants. But I knew, that night. The minute you touch another woman, you know. But the night before—what can you do?" He fell silent.

The other nodded quietly, until something else occurred to him. "But—it *wasn't* that?"

His friend leaned his white forelock on his hand. "It can make you want it that way, that kind of—a man can form a taste for it. Or some could say he had it all along. A man doesn't always know his own tastes in that direction. Though I thought I did." He rubbed his face between his palms, and thus cleansed, clasped them again. "It was because I found out—how she *would* do it." He cleared his throat. "For a treat," he said. "For food."

The words echoed, though there were other sounds all around and over them, the soft, meaningful sounds of man-deserted country, that cracking of twigs with which the woods take over, the callings of birds.

"That day she came to you," he continued. "That day, I'd locked her in. Starved her. She could afford to. At nighttime, I unlocked her. And that—was that."

"She told us that she started to walk over by herself," said the other, "and that after a while she heard a car behind her, and it was you. Never another word why. That's all she said, ever."

The other man stood up again, hands gripped in his pockets. His rich voice, a singer's voice, was small. "I unlocked her. And she *came* to me. She offered it." A red went up his throat, to his cheeks, to the blue dent at his temple line. "I threw her out," he said in his natural voice. "I couldn't stand it. It was like training up a dog. That was it. It was like training up a dog."

Up the hill, on the crest of it, the very tips of the trees were barely but persistently moving, exchanging the continuous secret of green. He gave it a look, then walked over to his friend sitting on the ground there, and put the old hand on the shoulder, as always, as if the figure on the ground was the one to be consoled. He always had to do it that way, always. "There was nothing else to her . . . except what one could see," he said, as he sat down on his stone again. "Nor maybe, I sometimes think it . . . to me."

"All of us," said his friend, getting up from the ground. "Nor to all of us." He picked up his coat, stiffly put it on, and sat down on his own stone. He was silent on his own part for a while.

"Lots of these get-togethers, people ask a widower to," he said then. "Somebody will always bring out a picture of her to show me. Nine times out of ten it'll be one of the ones taken that day. Either from somebody's Brownie, or that long official one with all of us at the windows, or lined up at the start. And when they hear I never got one, they say, "Jim, don't you want one? Here, I can spare it. Here, take this." And maybe they can spare it, maybe nothing came of that day for them. *But, so can I spare it.* And I always tell 'em so. 'I have my own picture right handy,' I always say. 'And what's more, my picture has a back to it, and a smell. I can see the *inside* of the car, and Jim and Emily; that's me and Emily, bending over the cookpot.' And they say, looking sorry for me among one another, 'Oh no, Jim, the cookpot was never inside there; that was back in the hall.' But I say no, that's the way I remember it—or prefer to. 'I remember it all,' I say, 'better than a movie even, better than a Brownie by far.' And then maybe because I feel sorry for them too and they only mean to be nice, I always give them a little laugh. Or maybe because I can't stand for the town to think me a fool. 'Oh,' I say, 'I never have any trouble at all now, keeping those Pardee girls in mind.' "

He fell silent from where he sat now, it was an easy reach to put his hand on his friend's knee. The two old men stayed that way. From the hillside, with what human cargo locked away inside for all anybody knew, from the treetops, deserted in all their glory but not knowing it, from the Little Otselica, no sound came. And then they heard it.

What are these whippoorwill starts in the night, in the bypasses of the night—or is it day? Is this Sand Spring nineteen-twenty, or Sand Spring eighteen-ninety-eight?

It is the ride, banging through the countryside. I can see the long car, the lone car riding its dazzle of rail, and all our heads popping out of the chowder, all our heads at the windows at one time or another, riding the wine-dark night. There are stations, there are stops, and once an owl-call. Then—the solemn forever. Fa-la. Fal-la-la. La, *La.*

The two men listened to it fade. It wasn't dark going back now; it was marvelously clear.

Then the two men got up, with one accord, and looked about them. Had this clearing been kept for them? Was the quiet scene before them awful or serene: Or was it only cheap land for progress, beautiful and stubborn? Each felt he ought to say something about it, but came back to his own life—and halted before speech, even here. One of the two had been marked very early by outer events, but the other even earlier by inner ones. One had left his place of birth but had never doubted his place in the world—and had found it; one had come back to the place where he belonged and had lived his life there—full of doubts. Warriors, returned from wars, and hearing such annals as this afternoon's, could no doubt fall upon one another's shoulders, lean in one another's arms, and heave there; even in modern times, it has been known.

Each for a fact hesitated. But as at every point in their lives when this might have come about—they had been friends too long. Each looked at his friend, his friend standing there in his defenseless prime, and saw how each had come to have the other's facets as well as his own, and why so many of the human race were rightly named—Jim. And this was enough.

Then each walked the other back to the car.

And there, not surprisingly, what with the motor running for the heater to warm them, above which good and faithful sound the voice could slur or sharpen into the practical—it became easy to talk again.

"Housekeepers!" snorted the mate, not moving to go yet. "Jim—will you listen a minute?"

And Jim listened willingly now.

"I know you won't come back to live with me. And though I know I asked you, one time, I don't know now that I really want us to."

"Oh—?" said Jim, who couldn't keep back a disappointed look, as if now, he'd been about to say yes.

"Because I've got a better idea." The mate warmed the small of his back against the seat, but at the same time thrust forward his forelock, so that all the tendons of chin and neck tightened; maybe he was used to doing this in front of women. The effect wasn't bad. Then he looked Jim over—whom bereavement had thinned, taking away his potbelly. The mate nodded, satisfied. "We're going round the world," he said.

Over Jim's howl of laughter, he talked only the faster, retiring them from business, property and family obligations in a dozen sentences. "The day after the dedication," he said. "The unveiling. That's as good a time as any to tell them. We can leave the day after. The day after, we can start out."

"But I've *seen* the world," Jim murmured. "At least a good part of it. Right here. And you've *been* round it. You flash that card the airlines gave you, often enough."

"Oh, we'll *stop* places," said the mate. "Six months at a time, if we feel like. But you have to give people at home a solid explanation they can hand to others. 'Going around the world, those two,' they can say then, and everybody understands it. Have to do that, when you're leaving *permanently*."

Then Jim sat up as if he'd been struck, saying "*Ah*." After a while, he said slowly "But we're not eighty yet. Nowhere near it. I wasn't born till ninety-three." But he couldn't keep a little smile from playing round his mouth.

It was the mate's turn to murmur. "People do it younger these days. This is modern times."

They were both smiling like idiots now, talking out of the sides of their mouths, like old lags. The mate opened the window, and bellowed to the whole audience, of which there wasn't a cow or human—"What are we waiting for!" And Jim answered, "Nothing, just start the car!" but when the mate had done that, his passenger broke into another laughing fit, from which he cried out, "*What* a folly, Jim! They'll never have seen a folly like this one!"

Who was meant by "they" was not spoken of unnecessarily, but you may need to know for later, to keep it by you. It was the "they" to which all such follies are addressed. So, that afternoon theirs was decided upon—or forty years before.

At first, though the car started up all right, the wheels wouldn't catch, having sunk, during the men's meditation, deep into grassy mud. But the two of them were a sturdy pair yet, canny with machines too, still with the strength to push and shove, and the sense where to wedge a stone under a rear tire—and at last they were free of the treacherous mud of cheap land, had shaken the dust of the old Batavia road from their spokes, and were rolling again on the highway. The pure, long hood of the Cadillac pointed like a prow, freed of rainbows, and they saw the weather once more.

Old men, old men. And young.

—

And so—*said my grandfathers*—we're going round the world.

We won't ask you to forgive us old men for taking up your time and trouble. The last thing you want to do is forgive us—and we know why. It's because we're what you're going to be. How could you forgive us for that? But we had to tell you. We made our miniature, and we had to show it.

So you're going to another war, said my grandfather, and you there are going to fly a plane in it. The girls among you can only listen of course, but maybe they can go along for the ride. They're civilians.

So, listen for *us,* said my grandfather, while we go around the world. Such odes as we make for the dead, any of us, are really for the confederation of the living—for all those who cannot even remember their own spilt blood, once it has dried; all their lives, men returned from the wars have plunged for charm. We are buddies all.

They speak in their sitting room voices, first one, then the other—our grandfathers—but already as if a clap of thunder has helped them disappear over the horizon.

Who speaks in his own voice, asks my grandfather? And my grandfather answers for him, to him and us. Not we. Not you.

It's all transport, said my grandfathers. In the first things are the last things; this is the roll of the wheel. Wheel and sail, horse and wing, we are going round—fa la la—the world.

How long is it by bicycle to Maple Avenue? See my dust.

See my dust. See my dust. See my dust.

Even from the air, said my grandfathers, faded and gone now.

Even from the air—you won't learn more.

A Note on the Type

The principal text of this Modern Library edition
was set in a digitized version of Janson,
a typeface that dates from about 1690 and was cut by Nicholas Kis,
a Hungarian working in Amsterdam. The original matrices have
survived and are held by the Stempel foundry in Germany.
Hermann Zapf redesigned some of the weights and sizes for Stempel,
basing his revisions on the original design.